THE WAR WIDOWS

The war's over, but the battle's just begun...

Nothing ever happens in sleepy Grimbleton, until two strangers – both claiming to be the fiancée of a dead soldier – arrive in town. Susan, who has escaped from Burma, and volatile Ana, pining for her Greek island, find themselves united in grief at the loss of Freddie Winstanley – the father of both their children. Freddie's sister Lily takes them under her wing, and the circle of friends expands to include Italian Maria and uppercrust Diana. Supported by this new-found sisterhood, Lily dares to dream of spreading her wings, but as each woman's courage is tested, can they find happiness after the heartache of war?

THE WAR WIDOWS

THE
WAR WIDOWS

by

Leah Fleming

Magna Large Print Books
Long Preston, North Yorkshire,
BD23 4ND, England.

British Library Cataloguing in Publication Data.

Fleming, Leah
    The war widows.

    A catalogue record of this book is
    available from the British Library

    ISBN   978-0-7505-3008-8

First published in Great Britain in 2008 by Avon
a division of HarperCollins Publishers

Copyright © Leah Fleming 2008

Cover illustration © Rod Ashford

Leah Fleming asserts the moral right to be identified as the author of
this work

Published in Large Print 2009 by arrangement with
HarperCollins Publishers

         ·int of Library Magna Books Ltd.

Printed and bound in Great Britain by
T.J. (International) Ltd., Cornwall, PL28 8RW

Acknowledgments

A chance encounter in a swimming pool in north-west Crete sparked off this story. Thank you Helena Charlton (wherever you are now) for sharing some of your history and giving me the idea. Thank you Manolis, Sofia and Marialena – the Tsompanakis family – for your wonderful hospitality and friendship.

Once again I've borrowed some of the landscapes from my home town, Bolton, but none of its people. I have used the premises of the Sabini ice cream parlour as I recall it as a child but my Santini family and their history is a figment of my imagination and their ice cream sodas could never have tasted as good as the ones I slurped through a straw all those years ago.

I am indebted to the following books for information:

A Detail on the Burma Front by Winifred Beaumont (BBC Books)
Wings of an Angel by Colin Barrett (Vanguard Books)
A Burmese Legacy by Su Arnold (Coronet Books 1996)
Chindhe Women (The Women's Auxiliary Service Burma) by Sally and Lucy Jaffe

Crete: 1941 Eyewitnessed (Efstathiadis Group)
Crete: The Battle of the Resistance by Anthony Beevor (Penguin Books 1991)

Once again many thanks to Maxine Hitchcock, Sammia Rafique and the team at Avon for all their enthusiasm and help.

For Jan, Madeleine, Menna, Lyneth, April,
Kathryn and all the Lichfield Register friends,
past and present.

'We have eaten bread and salt together,
sorrows and joys shared...'

Prologue

August 1947

Her big day was here at last, after all those years of daydreaming how it would be. The bride opened one eye and peered over her bedroom. It felt as if she'd been courting sleep all night and not a wink in her direction. But what sort of girl slept like a top on the eve of her wedding anyway? Except hers was the wakefulness of the wary, not the excitement of a nervous bride.

'Bless the Bride' was the popular song that went round and round in her head like a needle stuck on a gramophone record.

Her eyes skimmed across the room to where the outfit was hanging on the back of the door; not the white slub satin, cut on the bias, with beaded sweetheart neck the family would expect, nor the fancy rig-out that Princess Elizabeth would be wearing to parade down the aisle of Westminster Abbey in November. The linen two-piece suit was sensible, fit for the simplicity of Zion Chapel and all the dos thereafter. It would get a lifetime of wear and probably be cut down into cushion covers or a kiddy's party dress one day. This was 1947, after all, and there were few coupons to lavish on new clothing when there was a home to furnish.

It was just that she didn't feel like a new bride – or a shop-soiled one either – and pink was not really her normal shade, but it would brighten up a grey Division Street for the few minutes it was on show.

Her ensemble was a modest Grimbleton version of the New Look that was all the rage in Paris, with its tight-fitted jacket and full skirt to her calf.

A year ago, she would never have imagined herself wearing anything so daring.

A year ago, she hadn't even known the women who'd sewn it up, embroidered the lapels and sorted her matching gloves, hat and shoes with such loving care.

A year ago, they would've been just strangers' faces in a crowded street.

A year ago, she would have chosen Glacier Mint white or caramel cream, not rose pink. What a colour to put on Lily May Winstanley!

She sank back down onto the bed with a deep sigh, burying her head under the eiderdown, not ready to face the morning. Who would she be at the end of this momentous day?

One thing was for certain. She owed everything to the bunch of dolly mixtures chance had thrown her way last November. Their arrival had turned her world upside down. Where would she be now without her Olive Oil sisters? What must she do next? How had it all begun?

1

Business as Usual

November 1946
It was a normal Monday washday rush at 22 Division Street, Grimbleton. First there was a mound of coloureds and whites to be sorted out, young Neville Winstanley's silk blouses and knitted jumpers separated for hand washing, a pail of his soaking pants to be scrubbed, last week's overalls from the market stall and Levi's boiler suit left until last.

Polly Isherwood, the daily help, came in early to watch the setting-up of the new Acme Electric Agitator enthroned in the outside shed. Esme Winstanley came down in her tweed dressing gown to inspect the whole procedure. She still couldn't believe a machine could do a week's washing without shredding seams or blowing up the whole building.

'If that thing tears all our smalls, don't come asking me for coupons, Lil,' she snapped at her daughter, never at her best first thing. 'It's the slippery slope to idleness in the home, relying on machines to do your dirty work. I don't trust those paddles. Whose big idea was this? Someone'd better stand over it, just in case.'

'I'd have thought you of all women would be glad to see the back of all that slavery in the

15

scullery, pounding dolly tubs and winding up the mangle. What's wrong with a bit of help in the home?' Lily argued back.

Mother was always preaching how women were the backbone of this country and had kept the Home Front going in two world wars. She had marched the streets in her Suffragette colours in her youth, on fire with indignation at not getting the Vote. Middle age was softening her militant ideas.

There was no time for anyone to be standing around like a statue with three generations in one house. The Winstanleys were lucky enough to be the first in the street to own this labour-saving device and Lily, for one, thought it was a god-send.

'I've no time to stand and watch over it,' she said. 'Polly'll be around for the morning. She'll keep her eye on it with the handwritten instruction sheet stuck on the wall, and she can slip a few of her own things in the washer.'

'All that electric it's using up – what if the power goes off and all our week's wash is trapped in the drum? Your father would turn in his grave...' Esme snorted back, wanting the last word on the matter.

'Don't start all that again. Dad was all for progress. He'd be pleased no one has to rise before dawn to heat the copper boiler. We're living in the modern age now. I don't know why you're getting so worked up. Business is doing nicely; we've never missed an electric bill yet.'

'When you're a married woman with a home of your own you'll worry about bills and lights left

16

on. We've spoiled the lot of you, giving you driving lessons, a van and a fancy education. Now you've all got ideas above your station.'

There was no arguing with Esme when she had got her Monday mood fired up.

'Oh, Mother! I'm duly grateful so let me get on with my breakfast or I'll be late for work! There's many round here who'd give their false teeth for an Acme.'

'Lily, that's very cruel. You know I can't stand for long without my hip giving me jip.'

'All the more reason to let Polly get on with her job then. That's what we pay her for.'

'I suppose so, but it doesn't feel right to be standing around like Lady Muck, giving orders. It's the thin end of the wedge. Vacuums, irons ... it'll be refrigerators next. It wasn't like this in my day,' Esme sighed.

'Lil's right for once. We're the envy of the street for having a washing machine,' said Lily's sister-in-law, Ivy, from the doorway, carrying yet another armful of her little son's clothing.

She was wearing her glamorous pink quilted dressing gown, which puffed out like a satin eiderdown. The effect was spoiled by a line of steel waving clips in her hair, making her look like one of Flash Gordon's robots.

'While I remember, Lil,' she added. 'Remind my husband to fetch some butterscotch sweets back from the Market Hall. Callard and Bowser's, the best, not that cheap stuff from the corner shop, and a quarter of dolly mixtures for the little laddie. No use me asking Levi, he'll only forget.'

'Neville'll choke on them,' sniffed Esme, who

17

disapproved of all the sweet bribery dished out to her grandson.

'Never! He can pick them over while he's on the potty. It helps him concentrate.'

'You spoil that bairn. All my children were clean and dry by the time they could walk, none of this pandering to whims and fancies. I've seen that little monkey sitting until his bottom has a rim round it and then you dress him up like a doll and off he goes in a corner to relieve himself. He needs a smacked bottom, not dolly mixtures.'

'I know,' Ivy simpered, 'but we do things differently now. Oh, and, Lil, grab me something from the lending library while you're passing. Something lighter than the last rubbish you brought me. What would I be doing with *War and Peace?* We've seen enough of war in this house.'

'What did your last slave die of?' Lily muttered under her breath. What was the point? Since Levi's return from the war, she'd slipped down the pecking order at number 22. Still single and the daughter of the house, she was at everyone's beck and call.

'Lily'll open the shop this morning and do a stocktake so Levi can have a lie-in. She won't have time to be doing your errands, young lady,' replied Esme, coming to her daughter's rescue for once. 'He made a right racket last night tripping on the steps, and I *never* thought to hear such language on my stair carpet.'

At last, some welcome support, but it was shortlived.

'But while you're there, can you try and get me the latest Nevil Shute novel or another *Forsyte*

18

Saga? But not the first two – I've read them. I'd go myself but it's the Women's Bright Hour committee, followed by a speaker from Crompton's Biscuits this afternoon. I'll be giving the vote of thanks, of course, seeing how Crompton's is a family business, so to speak. How's Levi, still in the land of Nod?'

'Sleeping it off, so Lil'll have to take the bus this morning,' Ivy replied. 'He'll be needing the van. They made a bit of a night of it at the Legion, an Armistice night lock-in. Beats me how they get the booze, with all the rationing, but parading is thirsty work. You know how it is when the lads get together. Well, no, you wouldn't, Lily. Walter never made it to the Forces, did he?'

Why did the woman always have to rub in the fact that her fiancé, Walter, failed his medical?

'He'll need a stomach liner for his breakfast, then,' Esme added.

Bang went all their bacon rashers for the week again. Levi's nights out at the Legion were getting to be a habit, leaving his sister to open up and set the stall in order. Not that she minded back when the war was on. She was proud to be holding the fort while the men were away, but now he was back he was happy to play at being the manager while she did all the work. It wasn't fair.

Esme had seen the pout, the flash of steel in Lily's grey eyes. 'Now don't begrudge your brother a bit of extra, Lily. We're lucky to have our boys in one piece when there are so many families still in mourning. Being a prisoner of war took it out of him. He was nothing but skin and bone when he came home. You had it easy, my girl.'

19

But that was two years ago. It was Freddie who was still out in the Middle East doing his duty. There'd not been a letter this week. Perhaps that meant he was being shipped home for Christmas, as they'd promised. She couldn't wait to see him again.

Levi had milked his hero's return for all it was worth, though his limp and scraggy bones were long gone. Time to make a fuss of her little brother, who had been on active service since 1940.

Freddie wouldn't recognise his big brother. He was not the lad who marched away all those years ago; the ace outside half who once had a trial for Grimbleton's professional football club, the lynx who could shin up and down an apple tree faster than any of the boys in the street, who used to have a spring in his step when he swung the girls around the Palais de Danse in a quick step. Levi had gone to seed.

If it wasn't for the Winstanley wavy hair and grey eyes, Levi wouldn't pass for a Winstanley. Now those eyes were dull like damp slate, and he stooped and had grown a paunch, the only one in the family to grow fat on austerity rations. He never looked them in the eye when he was talking and was always turning up late.

Marriage to Ivy Southall had done him no favours. Of all the girls in Grimbleton he could have had his pick – the cream of the grammar school prefects, the tennis club and Zion Chapel – but he'd landed himself with a painted doll who whined like an air-raid siren and put on an accent so thick you could spread it on toast.

She'd spun a sticky web of false glamour around herself and he'd flown into her trap, wedded and bedded within a year.

That was mean, Lily thought, as she was biting her toast and Marmite on the run. You're just jealous because after all these years you and Walt have not got round to naming the day.

It was only right that Levi, who was the eldest, was married first. He'd been to war and back. He deserved to be settled down with his family in the upstairs best bedroom, but she'd done her bit too. It just wasn't the same as wearing a uniform and doing proper war work, though. Someone had to keep the family business – Winstanley Health and Herbs – in the pink, help Mother with the stall and keep the Home Front loose, limber and productive. No one worked fast when they were constipated.

All those dreams of leaving Grimbleton to join the WAAF or the WRNS and travelling abroad were sacrificed. It was only fair to hold the fort. Freddie had been all over the world: the Far East, the Mediterranean serving with the Military Police, and Levi served in the army on the Continent, in France and Belgium, until he was captured. The furthest Lily had been was the Lake District and Rhyl. There was no time to gallivant when there was a war on.

Stop this. It was too bright a morning to be nit-picking. Time to gather her sandwiches and flask and run for the next bus into town.

It was a new day, a new week. 'Every dawn is a new beginning,' said the Reverend Atkinson from his pulpit in Zion Chapel. She was lucky to have a life to live. The poor names etched on the war memorial had nothing. 'For your tomorrow, we gave our today.' How could she forget that?

With a bit of luck Levi would show up at lunchtime and she could nip to the library and to the fent shop to look for some off-cuts for the Brownies' costumes. The Christmas review would be upon them before long, rehearsals and costume-sewing bees, choir practice. No wonder there weren't enough hours in the week for all her jobs. No wonder Walter complained he never got to see her alone. Bless him. With a bit of luck he'd be on duty at his uncle's stall and they could have a sip of Bovril together and plan their wedding day.

Lily stood at the bus stop looking up at the bright blue sky. It looked set fair for the day. There was still a tinge of bonfire smoke in the air. The leaves had turned crisp and golden. The world was lighting up again after years of darkness. There was hope in the air. The parson was right: a new day was a new beginning. No more moaning.

The Winstanleys had survived the worst Hitler could throw at them. They were all in good enough health and in little Neville there was a new generation to follow on. God's in his heaven, all's right with the world, she thought, smiling, and jumped on the bus.

It took a native to admire the finer points of her home town, Lily mused, peering out at the rows of terraced houses that grew smaller and smaller as they drew closer to the edge of Grimbleton town centre, rows and rows of neat red-brick terraces, with whitened doorsteps and cotton net valances at the windows.

The mill workers had long gone to their shift, and the schoolchildren had yet to throng the pavements, but the bus was full of familiar faces all muffled up against the frost and chill. A bus full of grey gabardines and brown coats, sombre hats and gloves holding wicker baskets, printed headscarves hiding iron curlers and pin curls. Not a glamour puss amongst them in pompadour kiss curls and high heels; a drab world of duns and greys, a tired world, weary after so much turmoil and uncertainty, trying to get back on its feet.

But this is my home town, Lily sighed, all I've ever known.

The route into town got darker as they passed Magellan's Foundry, with its chimney belching smoke, the sparks flickering from the half-open door of the engineering works, the smell of tannery where piles of cow hides lay in the sun, and the bomb sites still gaping with half-built walls and rubble that grew purple with rosebay willowherb in the summertime.

Then came Horton's garage, which had taken a direct hit. No one had survived. It still saddened her to pass that spot. Wherever she looked there were the telltale signs of black-sooted buildings, empty half-boarded-up houses in need of repair. It would take years to freshen up the town.

Yet only half a mile into its heart were majestic civic offices, the town hall, with its Palladian portico, a bustle of shops and streets, and down the side street the magnificent entrance to the

Market Hall.

It still gave her a thrill to walk through the doors, to see the huge iron-vaulted glass roof high above her head, the smell of brewing tea, meat paste and fresh baking mingled with cardboard boxes, cheese rind, starched linen and newly mopped tiles.

The market was quiet on a Monday morning. Everyone was spent up after the weekend. Only the usual customers wanting a tonic or to use the weighing scales would grace the stall before noon. Plenty of time for Lily to dust over the stock, sort out the warehouse order, and chat over the football results with passers-by.

She drew back the canvas curtains and sniffed the familiar smells of dandelion and burdock, liquorice roots, cough linctus, linseed, herbal smells mingled with embrocation oils: a heady brew that filled her with nostalgia.

Winstanley Health and Herbs was more than just an alternative chemist's shop, it was a piece of Grimbleton history. Lily's grandfather, Travis Winstanley, was one of the first stallholders, a founder member of the Market Traders' Association. No one could accuse him of being a quack selling remedies from the back of a wagon. He had studied the science, kept himself up to date and advertised his cures far and wide in the district. He had patented his own 'Fog and Smog Syrup' to clear chests of soot and grime. In summer the family made up elderflower skin cream and, in autumn, elderberry cordial, roaming the highways and countryside for produce.

Travis's son, Redvers, took over the business in

24

due course and trained up his children to respect their calling. Thank goodness people got piles and warts, stomach upsets, skin rashes and embarrassing itches as regular as the four seasons. Dad knew more about the internal workings of Grimbleton bowels than any quack in the district. No one wanted to shell out for a doctor's bottle, though there was talk of a free health service that might affect them one day. So far so good, though.

But despite their father's efforts, Levi was always half-hearted about the business and Freddie had no interest whatsoever. The one thing that united all of the family, young and old, male and female, was an undying passion for football and devotion to Grimbleton Town United in particular. 'The Grasshoppers' were now making slow progress through the ranks towards the First Division. It was Lily's father who suggested the team use an osteopath to sort out any bad backs. He even found them Terry Duffy, who got some tired legs up and running in the Cup tie against Bolton Wanderers that nearly went to a replay at Burnden Park, alas to no avail.

Then Dr Baker kicked up a fuss and said Terry was taking his trade away and got him kicked out. Redvers threatened to resign from the Board but it was an empty threat. When the Grasshoppers were doing well the whole town was on fire; when they slumped it was as if a blanket of cloud hovered above the mill chimneys. A win was the best tonic for all. Lily supposed it was because football and romance ran side by side in her family.

Esme had been a player in her younger days, turning out for the Crompton's Biscuits ladies' team. They had played a friendly on the town pitch and that's when Redvers and Esme eyed each other up across the turf and the dynasty was founded.

Even Lily and Walt had met standing side by side to watch one of the special friendly matches laid on during the war. It turned out they both worked in the Market Hall, he at the far end in his uncle's stationery stall. Small world indeed, and now when they could match shifts, they went together to see their team of local lads.

Sometimes when she drew back the stall curtains Lily half expected to see her dad smiling, pristine in his white coat, waiting to help his customers, his thick wavy hair slicked back, his moustache waxed and with that twinkle in his blue eyes that charmed the ladies.

How she had missed him over the years since a sudden stroke took him from them! Mother had taken to ailments and fits of misery since he had gone. She blamed his early death on the Great War and his time in the trenches. He was one of the few of the Grimbleton Pals Brigade to make it home in one piece.

'It weakened him, took the stuffing out of him. Not that he would ever say a word about it, mind,' she sighed. No one talked about the Great War much. She was glad he hadn't known both his sons went into another war so quickly after the last.

He had his own theory how to keep world peace. 'If only we could play life fair by the foot-

26

ball rules,' he would say. 'There'd be no more war. We'd just get on that pitch and give each other hell until full time. Sort it out clean and proper.'

Not that he practised what he preached, for standing next to him at a match was a revelation. He would yell and rant and cuss and swear. 'Get them off, the pair of sissies! Hang up yer boots, lad, yer shot was a twopenny bus ride from the goal!'

If only the Zion minister could have heard his trusty steward letting rip at the goalie, Lily smiled.

Theirs was a special bond built on his delight in having a girl in the house. 'This one's the sharpest blade in the knife box.' He would point to her with pride. 'Not the fanciest to look at but she does it right first time, my Lily of Laguna. If you want owt doing, she's your gal!'

He would be proud that, like the famous Windmill Theatre Revues, they never closed for the entire duration of the war. Together with Esme, Lily had kept the stall going against the odds when all the rules and restrictions came into force. Many herbal stores were forced to close but they decided to open half the stall as a temperance bar, serving juices, hot cordials and a good line of medicinal sweets and herbal homemade cough candy, dispensing what little stock they could.

It was a tough time, fire-watching in the evening, keeping the Brownie pack alive with badge work and salvage drives, but nothing to what her brothers had to go through in Burma and on the Continent.

She was looking at her wristwatch, surprised that it was mid-morning already, when a welcome figure tapped her shoulder.

'Time for our cuppa?' Walter towered over her in his brown dust coat, pointing to the café opposite. She could sit down and keep her eye on the stall at the same time.

'You bet,' she smiled, pecking him on the cheek. 'Where were you yesterday at the Armistice parade? I missed you at the cenotaph.'

'I was there with Mam but you know it gets her all upset. We went home early.' You couldn't fault a man who was kind to his mother, but Lily had been hoping to invite him back for tea.

'Hey, you missed a cracking match on Saturday, two nil to the Grasshoppers. They're on a roll this season.'

'Yes, I've been hearing reports all morning,' she sighed. 'I had to stand in for Levi again.'

'I saw him in the directors' box with all the toffs, lucky beggar.'

'I just wish he'd give me a Saturday off, once in a blue moon. When did you and I last get to watch a match together?'

'It was the best game this season.'

'So everyone keeps saying, so shut up,' she snapped.

'The lads were on form, Wagstaff dribbling the ball down the outside right, passing to Walshie and he spins it straight in the net, brilliant!'

'Walter Platt, don't torment me.' She tugged his sleeve but he was oblivious.

'The second goal came just before half-time. I reckoned we finished them off there and then.'

She missed the crowds gathering, the noise and cheering, a chance to let off steam. Redvers had taken them all as a treat and left them at home as a punishment. There were chips in newspaper on the way home, which no one was to tell Esme about, for it was too common for a Winstanley to eat in the street.

'When we're married we'll bring all our kiddies to see the game,' Lily sighed, imagining a five-a-side of gleaming faces.

'Oh, no, love, it's not a place to bring youngsters with all that swearing and rough talk, and there's germs to think about.'

'It never did us any harm,' she replied, surprised by his attitude.

'Mother says it's all that standing as did my back in. I grew too tall for my bones.'

'I thought the doctor said you had a bit of a curved spine...'

'It's the same thing,' he replied.

'No, it's not. It means you're born with a bend in your back,' she continued.

'Oh, you do like to go into things, Lil. All I know is, it never bothered me until I was out of short trousers, when my legs just sprouted like rhubarb. I bent over one day and couldn't get up. Never bin right since. You've no idea what it's like to live with backache.'

'I'm sorry, it must be a pain,' she said, seeing the grimace on his face.

'So you should be. You're going to have to nurse it when we're wed, with one of your liniment oils.'

'Shall I give you a rub down later?' she winked.

'Lily Winstanley, none of that sauce from a respectable woman! Mother can see to it, thank you very much. By the way, could she have a few more liver pills? Her stomach's playing up again.'

'Has she thought of trying a lighter diet? She does like her pastry and her chips,' Lily offered, knowing that Elsie Platt was a little beer barrel on legs.

'A widow's got to have a little comfort in life. We've no money spare for fancy diets,' he said, staring across at her stall. 'It's all right for your family.'

Money was always a sensitive topic between them. His wage was small but steady, and her family had two wages and a war pension and shares from Esme's connection with Crompton's Biscuits. Better not to go down that route again.

'It must be hard,' was all she could say. 'Did you go and see that house for rent in Forsyth Lane, the old cottage by itself? It'll need doing up. But it's worth a second glimpse, don't you think?'

'Oh, no, love, Mam says they're built over wells, and damp, and it's a bus ride away from Bowker's Row. It's much too far for her to travel.'

'You didn't even look, then?' Lily felt the flush in her cheeks. When would he do anything off his own bat? 'That's a pity because I thought it was ideal for us, half in the country but on a bus route. It was you who wanted to have fresh air and a nice view.'

'Perhaps we should try for something bigger and bring her with us? She gets mithered when I'm not there.'

And I shall go mad if Elsie Platt is on the other side of the wall listening to our sweet talking, Lily thought, but swallowed her words back just in time. 'It says in my *Woman's Own* that a young married couple should be alone for a while to set up their home.'

'What about your Levi and his wife? They live with you.'

'That's different...'

'No it's not.'

'It's just that Waverley House has five bed-rooms. They have their privacy and a baby.'

'So, we'll be having babies and Mother can look after them for us so you can do all your gallivanting.'

'I'm not gallivanting, just serving my commu-nity. I'd hardly call choir practice and Brownies gadding about!'

'There you go on your high horse over nothing. It was just a suggestion,' he barked.

'I'd like us to start off together on our own,' she repeated, sipping her Bovril and noticing his shirt collar was frayed at the edge and needed turning round.

'Then we'll have to keep on looking until we find something that suits us both.' His voice was hard and his lips were pursed up just like Elsie's whenever they arrived back late.

Lily looked at her watch. There was still no sign of Levi. 'I'd better get back. Are you coming for your tea tonight? We can look in the *Gazette* to see if there're any more flats to rent, then borrow the van and go and view them together.'

'If you can give us a lift back home first and get

31

my mam's washing. Now you've got that new-fangled machine, she was wondering if you'd lend us a hand and throw a few things in for us.'

Anything to oblige, Lily mused. Word travelled fast and Elsie was not one to miss a trick. Would she expect the washing to come back ironed as well?

Oh, don't be mean, she sighed. Walt's mother was widowed young in the Great War, her son is the sun, moon and stars to her. The thought of him leaving her clutches is painful and threatening. Be grateful you can help them out.

They were just about to part company when Sam Parker from the upstairs office suddenly appeared round the corner, waving to Lily. 'There you are... I've just had a phone call from Levi. Can you shut the stall and come home?'

A flush of panic rushed through Lily's body. 'What's happened?'

'I don't know, he didn't say, but he said you were to get back to Waverley at once.'

Her mind was racing with possibilities. Had Mother been taken ill? Had the washing machine blown up and left them homeless, or was it a pleasant surprise? Was it the one surprise they were all waiting for? Freddie was back at last! That was it. He had docked and turned up without telling them, sprung a big surprise on everybody. That was just like her young brother, giving them no time to make preparations. They ought to have bunting fluttering over the street, and flags flying and lots of balloons if there were any in the shops.

'Freddie's come home. Oh, Walt! He's sprung one on us, the devil. Mother'll be beside herself.

What wonderful news! I'll call out Santini's for a taxi.'

'That's a bit extravagant,' he said. 'Fred won't be going anywhere fast.'

'I haven't got the van and I haven't seen my brother for six years. I'm not missing a precious second of him.'

Ten minutes later she was riding through the town with a grin from ear to ear. Just wait until she saw that cheeky monkey. She'd be giving him an ear-bashing.

Suddenly the whole town looked brighter. They rose up the cobbled street to the top end where the Winstanley residence stood foursquare on its own.

It was at the point where the grime turned to greenery, the country met the town and houses were spreading out with gardens backing on to fields. Waverley House had four bay windows edged with cream bricks, a smart tiled porch and steps leading to a small path with gaps where the wrought-iron railings had stood before they went for salvage.

She paid the driver and turned to face her home. Only then did she notice that all the curtains were drawn tight.

2

The Telegram

Esme Winstanley watched the colour drain out of her daughter's face when she saw the telegram in her lap.

'No! No! Not our Freddie... The war's over. I don't believe it. They've made a mistake.' Lily collapsed in a heap, sobbing, and Neville stared up at her, not old enough to understand that their world had just fallen apart.

'I thought he'd come home to surprise us... I was so sure... I never thought it was bad news. The war's over...' she repeated.

'Not in Palestine, it's not. That's why he was sent over there to quell the terrorists. You know what happened when they blew up the King David Hotel in Jerusalem. Things have got worse since then,' said Levi, not looking at her.

'Have they got the right name? It could be all a mistake. They get things wrong, don't they, Levi? Look how they thought Arthur Mangall was dead and he turned up as right as ninepence.' Lily turned to her brother for comfort but he just stood there stunned, silent, shuffling while Ivy fussed over them, trying to be the ministering angel, putting a cup of tea in Lily's hand.

'I've put you some extra sugar in it,' she smiled.

'I hate sugar,' Lily brushed it aside. 'He never

said it was dangerous, or am I the last to find out?'

'You don't tell your nearest and dearest you're living on a minefield that could blow up any minute. I'm sure there's a number to ring for more news and there might be something on the six o'clock Home Service.' Levi turned to his mother for support but she could only shake her head. The news had not yet sunk in.

'They don't tell you anything on the news. We found that out in the war,' Lil snapped. Her face was ashen. 'It's not fair.'

Whoever said life was fair? thought Esme, but she bit her tongue. The girl was not up to listening to home truths and she hadn't the energy to move from the chair and reach over to her. It was as if someone had kicked all the stuffing out of her.

'Another cup of tea, Mother?' whispered Ivy, hovering like a wasp about to strike.

Esme shook her head, wiping her glasses on her apron, trying to suck the last ounce of information from the telegram itself.

A patrol of 3 vehicles moving west along the Tel Aviv-Wilhelma was mined going over a small wadi. The charges were detonated to catch the rear vehicle of the convoy that caught fire. There were 3 stretcher cases, one of which was Sergeant Winstanley who sustained serious injuries. He died of his wounds in the 12th British General Hospital.

Not much to go on but enough to flood her imagination with dreadful pictures. She peered

35

around the sitting room for comfort, but all the familiar objects were drained of colour: the patterned Axminster carpet square faded by the sunlight in patches, the holes burned by Redvers and his cronies smoking cigarettes; the grease stain that 1001 wouldn't shift; the one when Freddie sneaked engine parts in to repair and didn't put down newspaper.

How she'd shrieked at him! 'Take that dirty thing out of my best room!' He was always getting into mischief. But never to see her handsome son again... Now she could look Polly Isherwood in the face, a mother who had lost both her sons on the Atlantic convoys. There were no words for what she must have gone through.

Never to hear him shouting through the door, 'What's for tea? I'm starving!' Not to see his size elevens dirtying her sofa covers as he lounged over the armrests, listening to the wind-up gramophone, driving them mad with his jazz records. Never to ruffle her hand through his curls and clip his ear in jest. He knew just how to wind her up into an elastic ball.

She turned her face to the fireside but it was only lunchtime and no fire was lit. Rations were strict and they needed to save supplies for the winter. She glanced at the ghosts smiling from the row of silver frames lining the top of the pianoforte: baby Travis, her first-born in his broderie anglaise christening gown, who never made it to his first birthday; Levi and Lily sitting on the piano stool in sailor collars, trying not to wriggle and squirm.

Lily had a face on her like a wet weekend and

Redvers said that portrait had gone all through the war in his breast pocket waiting to scare off any Hun who dared get too close. She was always the serious one of the three, too tall and lanky for a girl, with her donkey-brown hair, straight as a die which was a dickens to tie in rags to make ringlets. It was the boys who got the looks in their family.

She stared at Freddie's picture in a tortoiseshell frame. Her son would smile forever, as young as the day they waved him off from the station; their precious Victory child born after the Great War, now sacrificed in biblical lands.

You shouldn't have favourites, she scolded herself, but he had stolen her heart the moment he'd snuggled into her breast.

None of this, Constance Esme. Bestir yourself! There's a lot to do. They must think about a burial service, speak to the minister, inform the newspaper of their sad loss. Happen it was better to be busy after a loss. Less time to think.

Curtains closed on to the street meant only one thing, and soon the neighbours would come knocking. She must make sure they got her name right for the obituary notice. She hated her first name and had dumped it as soon as she left school in favour of Esme. Constance had always felt like a tight corset, while Esme was a softer free-flowing garment like the white gown she wore on the Votes for Women marches, before marriage and the Great War put paid to all that gadding about. A lifetime ago.

She stared at her wedding portrait. She was so pinched and laced up tight there was a look of agony and apprehension on her face. She needn't have bothered, for Redvers Winstanley had been a thoughtful husband and a good lover.

Freddie had had those same blue eyes and thick lashes, wasted on a lad, but Lily had got her own pale face and brows, and identical scowl when under threat.

There in her son was Redvers' cheeky grin, which had wooed her across a football pitch. There'd been such an uproar about her wearing a short divided skirt in public but Richard Crompton's daughter was not one to be put off in those days by a bit of derring-do. Pity Lily, with her long legs, hadn't got her own get-up-and-go...

Both her lads had that mop of curls. A wide grin and curls were a fatal combination with the ladies, she reckoned. Even little Neville was going to sprout a fine crop of dark curls.

It was a pity poor Lil's fiancé, with his jug ears, had nothing to recommend him but height. They were both stay-at-home birds, not fly-by-nights. Perhaps they were well suited; neither would set the world on fire. He would run her ragged with that mother of his, and she would be like a lost sock in the Acme, going round and round after them. From where Esme was sitting he looked a lazy lummock, but she could be wrong.

Redvers took life at thirty miles an hour round the bend, lived fast and died early. His loss was such a blow and left a gap no other man would fill in her life, but to lose a child went against nature; to lose two was more than she could bear.

She could see Lil and Levi were too stunned to take it all in. Ivy would do her best for her

38

husband. That one knew where her bread was buttered. Sometimes Esme caught her eyeing up her china cabinet as if she was making an inventory of all her best pieces.

Ivy was a jumped-up factory girl who was put in Crompton's office to help out and began to call herself a secretary. She had collared Levi almost off the troopship home. Now she did nothing but moan and groan how hard it was to rear a baby on starvation rations. The doctor said her insides were all mangled up and she must have no more babies. Neville was to be an only child.

What a sissy they made out of him, in his silk romper suits and smocked blouses! His hair was still in ringlets and needed a good cut, and Levi never put his foot down enough. It would all end in tears.

I don't know what's happened to this new world, Esme sighed. In her day the Almighty just dished out kids and that was that. He then took a fair few of them back again one way or another. She would have words with Him about that. With family planning they could pick and choose the size of their families but the country was crying out for more babies now. Everything was topsy-turvy.

Lily was right. It wasn't fair to go through all that bombing and shortages, worry and uncertainty, sacrifice and service. What a relief it had been when it was all over – and now this...

Crompton's Biscuits had turned production into special orders. She had helped in their nursery and on the market stall, joined the WVS and

Welfare Clinic. 'Family First' was the Winstanley motto.

The town had pulled together like a family: rich and poor, old and young, in one valiant effort against the enemy. Now the threat was over it was as if everyone was scuttling back into their burrows. Neighbours were becoming strangers again, scurrying away behind their net curtains, and the pews of Zion Chapel were emptying fast now the threat was over.

You shouldn't deal with the Almighty like that, picking and choosing your moment when to worship or mow the lawn. It was a matter of trust. She didn't understand what He was playing at, robbing her of half her family, ripping her heart with such pain, but He must have a grand plan, like those Turkish carpets the Reverend was on about last week.

Every carpet had a deliberate flaw in the pattern somewhere to prove that men were mortal and no match for Allah. Well, now it seemed as if the Almighty would have to explain Himself in due course. She wanted to shout in His face, 'What do you think you're playing at, taking my children? Have we been that wicked that we need bringing down a peg or two?'

No, she prayed. Forgive me. You gave us Your only son to show us the way... Help me bear this pain.

Solace would not be coming from the usual treats: a glass of Wincarnis Tonic Wine, the latest Mazo de la Roche novel by her bedside, afternoon tea with the old Suffrage Society members in the Kardomah Coffee House. This was a time when a family closed in on itself and drew strength from memories of happier times. She wanted her children wrapped tightly around her for company. Family First...

In the days that followed there was a constant stream of visitors to their door and it was Lily's job to sit them down and give them tea, explain that they knew little more than what had appeared in the local paper. Freddie was buried in some far-off military cemetery with full honours. There were letters from his commanding officers and the padre, from his friends in the Military Police, cards of sympathy from neighbours and school friends.

Even the Grasshoppers sent a deputation to ask about the funeral: Barry Wagstaff and Pete Walsh stepped into the parlour, caps in hand, and sat while Lily rehashed the same story over and over again, trying not to cry.

'If there's anything we can do, Lily, you've only to ask. Freddie was always one of our gang,' smiled Barry.

'Just get promotion in the league, that would make him proud.' It seemed a silly thing to say but she wasn't thinking straight or sleeping. Dr Unsworth, their local doctor, brought Esme a sleeping draught, which made her groggy, but Lily had refused pills. Someone had to keep alert when there were so many details to arrange. Levi had drowned his sorrows once too often and now had a bad cold, so Ivy was fussing over him.

Walter kept Lily company when he could but all their plans to talk weddings seemed out of

41

order now. It was 'Family First' time.

'The Winstanleys've always been good to the club. We'd like to send a wreath from the lads,' offered Peter Walsh, the star centre forward and on stand-by for the England Reserves.

It was strange to see the boys with scabby knees, who had kicked balls between pullovers in the playground, now smartly dressed in navy blazers and grey flannels, full-time professionals earning five pounds a week.

Lily always had a soft spot for Barry when they were kids. He had once rescued her from a fierce dog on the walk home from school. He had lost his right back friend, Stewart Higgins, on D-Day. The team was still struggling to get back some form and grow some good players from the youth sides.

Pete was a surprise find amongst the boys, who had come into form just at the right time. He looked very dashing, not a bit like the skinny mallinky long legs who used to tear round on his go-cart with Freddie hanging on for dear life.

Suddenly the days were racing on from that terrible Monday morning. Enid Greenalgh, ever the faithful friend to the family, stepped in to open the stall while Lily saw to the answering of letters and trying to coax Esme to eat.

There was still a pile of unopened mail on the mahogany hallstand waiting for attention, but Lily had neither the time nor the energy to see to everything.

Reverend Atkinson suggested a memorial service. 'It will give you all a chance to say goodbye,' he advised. 'Freddie should be honoured in his

42

own town and his friends given a chance to attend.'

'Whatever you say,' Lily replied, only half listening. She was too angry to pray. Then practicalities began to distract her flittering brain. How would they provide tea for hordes of guests? Where would they get the extra rations? Who should do the readings? What hymns would be suitable for a fallen soldier? Would Mother hold up under the strain? Would Levi stay sober enough to be of use?

Ivy produced a list of guests to invite, people Lily had never heard of from the Green Lane end of the street, the posher part of their district. Ivy took the hump when it was ignored in favour of chapel friends and Freddie's pals.

Then Lily found herself awash with tears, fingering the letters he'd sent, full of jokes and rudeness.

What's fresh in the street, Sis? How's the Acid Drop [his pet name for Ivy, whom he had never met but summed up accurately]? *When are you and Walt going to name the day? If there's not a date on the calendar when I get back, I'll be buying you two a ladder and bus tickets to Gretna Green. How's the old canvas on two tent poles? Have you straightened out that bad back of his yet?*

In Burma there were lovely ladies to do that sort of thing most effectively. Believe me, once he's had a massage he'll be able to go five rounds with Joe Louis.

He brought the fizz into the family when Redvers died. He carried on with the same practical jokes, silly songs and roving eye. The house was always

43

full when Freddie was home. Now there was a sadness and silence that hung over them like a grey pall of fog, separating each from the other in their grief.

Neville was playing up, sensing the atmosphere, screaming and having tantrums at the slightest thing. Freddie would have been Walter's best man, even though the speech he would have given would not have been for the minister's ears. Lily had always been the shadow to his sun, stealing warmth from his glow. Now it was dark, grim and oh, so cold, and winter hadn't even arrived.

Later that evening they all passed the cards and letters around the fireside, trying to work up some enthusiasm for planning the memorial service. No one was in the mood to make any decisions. Ivy was sulking, Levi was trying to catch the nine o'clock news for a bulletin on the situation in Palestine. There had been no mention of the explosion so far.

It was time to make another foray into the unopened mail that had progressed from the hallstand to the back of the mantelpiece. A London postmark took Lily's eye. They had no relations down south so it must be from one of Freddie's comrades' mothers who had heard the news and wanted to send her own condolences.

She opened it quickly, read it, read it again and passed it round.

Dear Family Winstanley,

It gives me pleasure to introduce myself to you as the intended fiancée of your son, Frederick.

He told me to write to you if ever I came to England and inform you of my immediate arrival in your town.

The kindness of your loving son is manifold. We met at Church Parade in Rangoon where I was of assistance in the canteen of the Women's Voluntary Service, Burma. Distance has separated us many years, but not affection. I have carried your address with me for just such an occasion. I look forward to meeting you.

Yours sincerely,

Susan L. Brown

(Certified teacher, Rangoon College)

'What do you make of this?' Lily asked. 'Do any of you know a Miss Brown?'

Esme peered over her glasses at the thin blue tissuey paper. 'I don't understand. The woman says she's "his intended fiancée". What does this mean?'

'Either she is or she isn't,' Levi quipped, not taking much notice.

'Sounds as if she's just arrived on a troopship from Burma. She's been teaching in Rangoon,' Lily added.

'She must be a missionary then,' offered Ivy. 'He's a dark horse, your Freddie. Not a word about a fiancée, was there?'

'No, but that doesn't mean there wasn't one... It's nearly a couple of years since he left the Far East.'

'Perhaps he was going to spring her on us when he came home. "Mother, meet the girlfriend. By the way, she's soon to be my wife."' Levi mim-

45

icked his brother's voice. 'Trust our Freddie to keep a pretty girl up his sleeve. He never could resist a beauty but a missionary's not exactly his style.'

'She says they met in the church in Rangoon, wherever that is.' Ivy turned the page over. 'She's in some centre awaiting instructions and will send us a telegram when she can come north... Funny she hasn't gone home to be with her family.'

'They'll be serving out in Burma. Well, fancy, Freddie...' For one dizzy second Lily was talking as if he was still alive, as if the joyful reunion was soon to happen. This poor girl knew nothing of his fate. What on earth would they say?

'We can't just let her go on thinking he's coming back. Better write and tell her,' Ivy advised.

'That'd be too cruel. No, we must tell her properly. It will be such a shock. She might want to be at his memorial. Why didn't he tell us about her?'

'Don't ask me! I'm only the brother – how would I know what went on in his mind? You're the one who he wrote to, Lil. He was your blue-eyed boy,' Levi sniggered.

'Levi! That's enough. All will be revealed in the fullness of time,' Esme sighed, and turned her face to the fire. 'It's out of our hands now.'

They didn't have long to wait. The telegram announcing Susan L. Brown's arrival at Ringway Aerodrome was in the post the very next morning. Someone was going to have to break the bad news, and quick.

3

An Unexpected Legacy

'Someone's got to fetch that poor girl from the aerodrome,' ordered Esme, still clutching the telegram as if it was going to bite her. 'I think I'm going to have another of my turns. My head is spinning.'

'Someone's got to open up the market stall, I'm late already, Mother,' shouted Levi as he waltzed through the door. 'Count me out.'

'Don't look at me,' said Ivy. 'I've got to take Neville to the clinic. Lil can do it. It's her morning off.'

Lily was making a list of arrangements for the funeral tea. 'I was hoping you'd all come to give me support.'

'Take Walter with you then,' snapped her sister-in-law.

'You know the seat in the van gets to his bad back.'

'That's not our fault, Lil. If he got off his backside a bit more...' sniffed Esme, reaching for the aspirin bottle.

'Don't start that again. Leave him alone. He can't help it.' There was no getting out of this taxi service now.

'What you see in that lad–'

'I'm not listening.' Esme could be so cussed

47

when one of her heads struck without warning, but with this terrible blow none of them was on top of the job.

'I'll go on one condition – that *you* tell this girl... I'm not. Poor lass'll be wondering why he's not there to meet her.'

'You'd better not wear black then,' suggested Ivy, looking her up and down with dismay.

'I've never worn black, not even for Dad, and I don't intend to now. I've no coupons left,' Lily replied, knowing her suit was looking shabby.

'I bet you've squandered them on that Brownie show again. You'll never get a trousseau together at this rate. I had to beg, borrow and steal to get mine.'

'No one's thinking about weddings,' said Esme, putting another spoke in that wheel.

'Who said anything about *trousseaus?* Walt and me just want a simple do, no fuss,' Lily snapped.

'Just as well, for the Platts will be too tight to fork out much when it comes,' Esme continued, wiping her glasses on her apron.

'I'm not listening. You don't know him like I do,' Lily replied, making for the door and out of the gloomy atmosphere. Why couldn't they all pull together in their sorrow, not keep picking at each other?

'Fetch us a cup of tea before you disappear,' Esme yelled from her chair.

'Ivy can do it. I'm off! Mustn't be late.' Lily was out the front door and down the steps, not waiting for reply.

'Come on, Gertie, old girl, don't you let me

down,' she urged the van to start, rocking back and forth. 'I'm coaxing you gently so no explosions.' She didn't want passers-by scurrying in all directions for cover. Time was getting on, and she prayed there was enough petrol in the tank to get to Ringway Aerodrome. Levi had a habit of running the van on empty.

Thank goodness the war was over and road signs were back up again or she'd be in trouble. Still ten miles to go and no petrol coupons left for emergencies. It was a good job there was an inborn magnet in her nose that knew when she was heading in the right direction. This was no drive for the faint-hearted. Why did she always land the worst jobs?

Driving would give her time to sort out her thoughts, to catch her breath, to mourn her brother. She still couldn't take it in. It seemed like only yesterday that he was born and she'd seen him in the Moses basket. He was her own toy, better than any dolly; she was always the one to push him, pick him up, carrying him to school, kicking and screaming, when he wanted to run home. Miss Sharples had called her into the infants' room when he'd wet himself and refused to sit in the chair.

She smiled, thinking of the time she'd shoved her exercise book down his backside when he was outside the Head's door waiting for a caning. He'd bunked off to play football in the park. One scrape after another but she was always there to cover for him.

That precious vow of silence, one for all and all for one, was their secret code. No telling Mother

49

and Dad when Levi and Freddie met girls in the park instead of going to Sunday School. She always managed to sneak three stickers for their attendance card so no one was any the wiser.

Football was always there somewhere in the mischief. It was forbidden to play on a Sunday but that never stopped their practice matches with Pete and Clive down the field by the dell. Everyone assumed Lil Winstanley was a Goody Two-Shoes, the white hen who never laid away, but she knew that if ever she had needed a favour, they'd be quick to honour the bargain. The trouble was it was too late now. There was no one on her side, not even Mother.

In normal times, being at the wheel was fun but being the only available driver today was a thankless task. How did you break such terrible news to a total stranger who was coming halfway across the world full of hope and expectation? Who was going to tell this poor bride-to-be that she was already a widow?

She hoped she looked the part. No one could accuse her of being a fancy bandbox but she did try to be neat and tidy. This was no ordinary errand. These were not ordinary times.

The bucket seat was low down, bagging her skirt, and the bit of rust by the door had kept snagging her lisle stockings the last time she was out in the van. How many times was Levi asked to get it seen to?

There was a pile of other mail addressed to Freddie waiting at home, letters from foreign parts that none of the family had the heart to open yet. It was years since they had waved off the youngest son. Lily could hardly recall his gruff voice except when she read his cheery letters.

Tears were rolling down her nose again. It was hard to drive. Now she must tell lies to a total stranger. No wonder Polly Isherwood looked so pinched. She carried her grief with pride but it was etched into the lines on her face.

How did people survive such loss? Walter lost his own dad in the Great War and his mother clung to him like a limpet. There are always those who're worse off than you, she sighed. But now war was over and the streets were full of demob suits, it was so painful.

At least Gertie, usually slow to warm up, was purring gently while Lily was daydreaming. Where were the peppermint chews in her handbag? Dash it! She swerved, missing the turning to the left.

'Where on earth's the aerodrome, Dolly Daydream?' she muttered. Talking to herself helped to pass the time, but she needed to concentrate.

The Winstanley family was a right box of liquorice allsorts. Mother was a sherbet lemon – sharp on the outside but soft and fizzy inside, after a glass or two of Wincarnis in the evening, and took a bit of softening up. Dad had been a bar of Fry's Chocolate Cream. Ivy was definitely an acid drop and Levi was a brazil nut cracknel, sweet one minute and tough the next. Walt was her favourite, a Cadbury's Chocolate Caramel with the squidgy centre.

As for her own attributes, a Fox's Glacier Mint, plain, serviceable, good in an emergency, would just about sum her up.

51

Sweets were something special now, being so carefully rationed. Neville got everyone's ration in his ever-open mouth. He liked dolly mixtures... Sweets, food ... no time to think of such stuff now.

Rationing was worse than in the war these days. Levi had hollow legs to fill but he somehow managed to scrounge a few extras from the U.T.C. – 'Under The Counter' – brigade. Not easy when there was always Ivy's sweet tooth to satisfy. Her big brother needed to have his comforts when he was married to such an ambitious woman. Ivy was always making big plans for them.

They were living rent free in Division Street so the couple could save for a new house across town, one day. Ivy had her son, her husband and a dream of living on the south side, close to the golf club. She knew where she was heading.

If only life was that simple, Lily mused. It was two steps forward up the slippery slope to the pinnacle and one step backwards most of the time.

Esme blamed Ivy's scheming on going to the pictures. 'It might cheer you up for a few minutes but it gives simple girls like Ivy big ideas, American dreams,' she explained.

It wasn't as if Lily didn't have dreams of her own: dreams of travelling abroad, a baby in a Silver Cross pram, dreams of the Grasshoppers winning the Cup at Wembley, of going to watch them in London to cheer on Freddie's old gang. Even the dream of a cottage full of babies with Walter seemed far off now. There was always one crisis or another.

Someone on the wireless said what the world

52

needed were babies to keep the numbers up. Dolores Pickles at number eight had yet another bump on show – was it the ninth or the tenth? – and all the reward she would get for being faithful to her Church was a tin of biscuits. Ten kiddies and she'd get a tin of biscuits for her suffering. The Pope himself would be hard pressed to find a tin of biscuits anywhere in Grimbleton, and Mother should know. Lily's grandfather was one of the big noises in Crompton's Biscuits. How did the old slogan go?

Put your taste buds to the test
Crompton's Biscuits are the best.

'Just concentrate! Where am I now?' She peered out into the gloom. 'Getting nowhere fast. Come on, Gertie, we were volunteered for this mission whether we liked it or not so keep on top of the job for once.'

She felt like a lost sock in the Acme agitator washing machine of life, like the juggler's dinner plates. Spinning around from one job to another, that's me, she sighed. No wonder there was never any time for daydreaming except when alone in the van. That was the time to think things through. There was no justice in this world. Two world wars and what was there to show for all the suffering but exhaustion, drabness and telegrams like this one landing in their lap? There were thousands of families like them still mourning the loss of loved ones, unsure of the future, trying to hold everyone together in harmony.

At last! The barbed wires of the perimeter fence

came in view. Ringway Aerodrome was in sight and it was not too late. Lily's hands were trembling as she plonked on her brown felt hat with the pointed brim and fingered her gloves. The moment of truth was nigh.

In the pictures, airports were scenes of adventure, romance and the promise of far-off places. How she longed to be boarding an Air France Dakota for Le Bourget and Paris, or even a trip out over the runway would be fun. Arrivals and departures were exciting, but not this time. This was going to be a nightmare and the sooner it was over the better.

4

The Leftover Brides

The plane landed with a judder onto the wet tarmac and Ana Papadaki looked out of the window with relief and dismay, her insides fluttering as if a flock of doves were on the wing. This was Manchester, her new home. Soon she would be meeting a new family. She hoped they could read the broken English of her letter well enough to be waiting for her today.

The classes in the transit camp in London were very basic. Speaking was no problem. It was writing that was a strain but she was determined to make herself understood.

Dina, her baby, started to whine and she gave

her the strap of her leather handbag to chew on. She was still cutting teeth but her little mouth opened into a howl of protest. There was a dampish patch from her nappy seeping into Ana's flimsy skirt.

Ana lifted up her child, jiggling her at the window to distract them both from the unexpected delay. There was nothing to see but Nissen huts, brick buildings, grey skies and concrete. She could be anywhere in war-torn Europe. This was not how it was supposed to be.

Such excitement had soared within her when she'd stepped aboard the plane. At last! This was the last lap on their journey towards a new life, a fresh start away from the horrors of the past years.

Dina brought worries as well as hope into her life, but stepping off the plane into the autumn chill, Ana felt as if a damp cloth was slapping her face. So *this* was Manchester.

The passengers clucked like chickens when the plane landed, jittery women with babies puking on their shoulders, all dying for a pee. Her first thought was, would the soldier's family recognise her in the crowd? Would *he* be there to meet them?

She could hardly recall his face. It felt so long since their tender farewell at Piraeus eighteen months ago.

First there was a rush for the toilet. Dina was tugging at her hair. Ana was glad of the Red Cross clothing parcel with its little siren suit and pixie hood: warm clothing for a baby in this dampness.

Her own thin dress felt like underwear, and the oriental mother opposite had only a silky summer dress covering her tiny frame with an ill-fitting suit jacket; probably her very best outfit. How shabby she felt in a headscarf alongside other passengers in fur coats and fancy hats.

Ana held on to the woman's little toddler in the queue so that the Eastern beauty could relieve herself. Together they had watched all the other mothers jumping into the arms of their sweethearts, one by one, lots of hugs and kisses and children thrown into the air with glee.

Perhaps his family were delayed or the bus was late. Perhaps she had given them the wrong date or the wrong address. She was grasping the well-thumbed envelope for comfort. This was her ticket to a new life, this proof of their correspondence, and the address was the one link with her lover. He must have filled in the forms to sponsor her and their child or she wouldn't have got this far.

There was a draught on her bare legs, and she wrapped her jacket tightly around her skinny body. Five years of labour and hunger had taken its toll on her frame. She still hadn't recovered from the camp years of starvation. How she managed to fall for a baby so quickly she would never know; a woman brought back to life by the kindness of one Tommy soldier who wooed and won her in a dance hall in Athens.

He was not like some of the other Tommies, who could only shuffle across the floor, but moved with grace, gathering her up in his arms like a fair Rudolph Valentino. He treated her

56

nursing uniform with respect. She was not some easy whore ready for a quick fumble in return for a bar of soap. He was tender and understanding when she recoiled from his lovemaking at first. There were so many bad memories to expunge of her time in the labour camp.

Now she looked so shabby in her faded frock and felt hat covering her dark copper hair. 'My ginger Greek with freckles,' he called her, surprised that not all Grecian women were black-haired and doe-eyed. Her hair was straggling across her cheeks and she could feel tears welling up.

She was not just any Greek woman; she was from Crete, the home of the gods, the most ancient of all the islands, and the most beautiful, in her eyes. It was an island torn apart by war, where the women were descended from Minoan gods, pale and golden, and the men fierce fighters for independence, a proud race. So proud of their women, that someone like her could never return to its shore.

Dina was struggling out of her arms, staring at the other little girl, who was muffled in the same Red Cross cast-offs. The oriental mother smiled and reached for her own child.

What a pity her little one was so plump-faced and plain – pug-nosed, Ana observed. It felt mean to be making a comparison but anyone could see Dina was prettier.

There were just the two of them left now, sitting in the draughty arrivals hall of Ringway Aerodrome like abandoned luggage, watching every movement in the doorway, every coming and going to no avail.

Suddenly Ana shivered and her heart went thump, thump. No one was coming. She would be sent back home, abandoned. Did they not know she could never go back home: an unmarried woman with a child, dishonouring the family name for ever? It was better they thought her dead.

A strict code of honour had been broken. On Crete women like herself were shadows, fit only to live in caves, out of sight. It would kill her mother to bear such disgrace. If there was anything of her village left since the Germans invaded Crete in 1941... But why think on those things? What was done then was done in the name of duty. What she did in Athens was done for love and gratitude. He would not let her down. It tore her heart to be an exile but that life was over. To open such memories was like unlocking her battered case left behind in Canea, her hope chest, smelling of camphor, stuffed with postcards, embroidered linen, lace work, damp and discoloured with age, her frayed dowry never to be redeemed: all those long-faded hopes and dreams like butterflies that have lost their wings.

War washed away all that past life and the age-old customs that went with it. Her only duty now was to survive for her child's sake. This was the start of a new life together.

But dreams betrayed her each night when the island came alive: a wine-dark sea shimmering at sunset, the green mountains of the Apokoronas, snow-capped, stretching high in the distance, and the soft breezes off the shore stroking her cheeks. She could smell the scents of home: wild thyme, lemons, and watermelons like footballs. She tasted honey and sand on her lips. In the shade of the vines the zizzies screeched.

Suddenly the scene would change to smoke and darkness, the stench of burning rubber and cordite, on that first morning of invasion.

Ana was too busy in the makeshift hospital to watch more parachutes descending into the olive groves around the city of Canea. The daily bombardment crushed the harbour buildings, trapping whole families, men and boys digging them out with their bare hands. Everyone lay in wait for the one doctor while she and the other nurses wiped blood and tried to clean bandages. Her apron was filthy, her copper hair spilling out of her headscarf, but there was no time for neatness.

'More white devils' umbrellas from the sky,' shouted a terrified woman. Their beloved island was being attacked again. Around her were British Tommies prostrate with mortal wounds. The bombs had done their worst and they were soft targets. This was no time for politics. It was enough to know Stelios, her brother, was out there shooting anything that moved. Their stone house had a cool cellar; she hoped Mother, Eleni and Aliki were hiding. How many times had this town suffered the aggressor?

'Look, Ana ... it's like shooting birds out of the sky ... pot shots,' someone laughed. Parachutes descending like coloured balloons onto the shore, the groves, rooftops. Guns blasting out from Malaxa's hilltop battery.

For months they'd been waiting, feeling the

tension as British troops built defences – tired men evacuated from the mainland, ill equipped, with sallow-cheeked pale faces, who were wondering just why they were there. Her father was fighting with the Fifth Cretan Brigade far away in Northern Greece. With all their crack troops far from home, now the city was left to boys and old men, who must defend their honour or die in the effort. Freedom or Death! This was their slogan.

All morning they brought in wounded men. There were tales of Germans butchered on the roofs even as they fell, but this was the Red Cross and they must accept any wounded, whatever the uniform.

'That'll teach them,' sighed Dr Mandakis, grim-faced as he covered the sheet over yet another enemy soldier, hacked to pieces by the fury of the mob.

Now the wounded were piled alongside each other, enemy, defender, stranger and known faces from the city streets. The medical staff worked by lamplight, stitching, sewing flesh together, mopping brows of amputees, giving sips of precious water to the dying.

I shall recall this day for the rest of my life, thought Ana, seeing sights no decent woman should have to witness, and still they came...

There were rumours, rumours of street-to-street fighting, children carrying scythes and axes going out to meet the foe and showing them no mercy.

If they win, we shall pay for this, Ana sighed, with a chill in her heart. There are too many of them.

Her back ached with weariness. It was looking

more like a butcher's shop than a makeshift hospital. Someone had made a Red Cross flag out of sheets and daubed it with blood to hang over the roof. Perhaps when the bombers returned it might save them.

The young nurses took it in turn to relieve themselves, sip lemon water, bite on the hard dacos bread, anything to stop the hunger.

At dusk, Ana found herself by the temporary mortuary, no longer sickened by the stench of blood and death. It was not a place to linger but it was cool and quiet. She sat down, too tired even to pray. How could things happen on such a beautiful May morning, when all the roses and flowers were still in bloom?

Then she heard a strange moan. Her heart jolted: a groan was coming from under the sheet, then another groan. Someone was alive under that sheet, waiting to be buried alive in a shroud. She thought she was dreaming. Tiredness must be taking its toll. She walked silently towards the sound, stepping over a line of stiff bodies on the floor. There it was again, and she pulled back the sheet.

Under it was a soldier in olive-green fatigues, fair-haired, his blue eyes flecked with navy blue, staring at her in terror.

'Hilfe ... hilfe.' His eyes cried out to her. Here was the enemy at first hand, a boy no more than her age, lying terrified, at her mercy, mistaken for dead. She saw the deep bruises on his battered cheeks.

In that moment, Ana knew she could silence him for ever, call for one of the guards to finish him off. But she was transfixed, unable to think. The world stood still. She was a Red Cross nurse, dedicated to taking no sides. But he was the enemy, this bronzed, handsome boy. His eyes were pleading for life. This man had a mother and family far from home. He was serving his country, doing his duty, but on her island.

'*Oh no!*' she panicked, pulling the sheet off him. There was a side door where the carts came to collect the bodies. It was dark.

He staggered to his feet, dazed, wobbling.

'*Go!*' She pointed to the door.

'*Danke, Fräulein... Mein Name ist Otto... Wie heissen Sie?*' He towered above her. This boy wanted to know her name.

'*Oxi* ... no name,' she croaked in broken English, having no German. 'Go!' she ordered, opening the door into the dark narrow street. The boy staggered out into the alley, defenceless but alive, soon swallowed up into the night.

Ana slammed the door, pulled away the sheet and dragged the bodies to fill his gap, appalled at what she had just done. *I have betrayed my country, God help me!* She crossed herself. No one must ever know of this treachery or her family would be dishonoured for ever.

Feeling sick, exhausted and defiant at her action, she struggled to justify what she had just done. Surely the boy would be felled before he left the winding alleys of the Venetian port? He was an easy target, even for a child. Ana shuddered. Her duty lay with the living, not the dead.

'Ana! Ana! Where are you? Have you been asleep?'

Perhaps it was a dream, just a nightmare, and tomorrow she'd find it had been all a figment of her imagination.

But when the sun rose like a ball in the east, nothing had changed. She had met the enemy and his name was Otto. His face haunted her dreams. For that one act of mercy, she'd been punished over and over, but now there was no time to dwell on such horrors.

The two women sat together on the bench, moving closer as if to gain courage from one another. The daughters on their knees reached out to one another. A tall woman walked past them, staring. Someone brought them a cup of tea and they sipped it politely. Ana did not know what to say to introduce herself to the oriental girl, even though her English was better than most.

'You wait also for soldier boy to come?' she asked, looking again at the clock on the wall. 'It is late.'

'Mr Stan will not forget. I wrote many times,' smiled the young woman, sipping the tea, her back straight. Her voice was clipped but the English was good.

'My man is at camp, maybe come. Maybe he send someone,' Ana nodded. 'Where you stay, in Manchester?'

'No, it is a town called Grimbleton. I will live with his family when he is a soldier. I sent a telegram. He will come soon... This is not tea.' She grimaced, trying to swallow the terrible taste, and Ana laughed. She would never get used to this dishwater either.

'We go Grimbleton also,' Ana nodded, wishing this drink was hot strong Greek coffee with *glyka* – lots of sugar – but she had not tasted real grains for years. 'My man has a house there for us to stay, my fiancé.' She paused. She wanted to be thought respectable, even to a stranger.

'We shall see each other in the village then?' answered the other mother.

Ana nodded at the tiny woman, who was sitting so pert, her glossy, black hair in a neat bun at the nape of her neck. Her face was heart-shaped. With those wide eyes and dusky skin, she looked delicate, like a china doll. 'Where you come from?' Ana asked.

'London ... it has been a long way, a long story to tell,' the other woman replied, her eyes lowered as if she did not want to be reminded of her past. 'And you?'

'I come from Athens ... Greece.' Ana did not want to give her true identity. 'It is a long story how I come to Manchester with my Dina.' They smiled politely and fell silent.

'Your child has hair like gold,' sighed the oriental girl. 'My soldier has hair like a sunset too. It is not a colour we see often in hair. Somewhere I have a picture. Would you like to see my intended?' She was rummaging through her straw holdall but stopped suddenly to inspect a man as he hurried over to the desk looking in their direction.

He was tall and lanky, dressed in a black suit with hair flattened down into a centre parting, on his face a thin moustache. The officer looked at them both, gathered up his papers and strode across towards them.

'No one's come for you yet? Are you sure you're in the right place? This is Manchester. You can't stay here much longer.'

Ana looked at her neighbour and promptly put her cup down. 'I go nowhere. I wait here. They will come.' She had been in too many displaced persons' camps not to know how to get attention. Making a fuss had saved her life, got her food, got her and Dina safe passage. She would open her blouse. That soon got them going. She was a proud daughter of Crete but she knew how to fight. But first she must give him the facts. 'I have letter. This is right town. I not move. I have baby to feed,' she pleaded.

One thing she had learned about the English was they didn't like a fuss: no loud voices, tears or wailings. They liked fair play but done quietly, no digging in of heels.

'I also have a letter,' chirped in her neighbour. 'We will wait.'

'Please yourselves, but if no one's come to collect you soon...' the official sniffed.

'They will come,' they said as one, more in hope than certainty.

By the time Lily made her late entrance through the foyer of Ringway Aerodrome there was no one waiting for her; only an escort officer giving two foreign girls an ultimatum.

'I'm sorry, ladies, but yer time's up. I did warn you. If no one comes to collect you, it must be reported and you'll be sent back to your own country.' He looked at his list and at his watch,

65

brushing his hand over his Brylcreemed hair, clearing his throat.

They were the only people left, sitting with toddlers on their knees in the draughty arrivals hall, looking forlorn as they scoured every coming and going, to no avail.

Suddenly the oriental girl stood up and flung herself on the floor on her knees in a bow of total submission, her black eyes peeking from beneath a battered straw hat while the child, in brown leggings and pixie bonnet beside her, watched open-mouthed as in halting but perfect English her plea was made.

'Honourable sir ... this is a big mistake. I have my letter here. I send a telegram. He will come for me,' she pleaded. 'We do not want to go back out east.'

This is terrible, Lily thought. That poor lass must be desperate to be humbling herself before a stranger like that. She could hardly watch. Poor refugees coming all this way by sea and air to a strange country that demanded papers, checks, medicals and questions, and no one to greet them. It was a disgrace.

And just who was the other reject in the printed head-scarf? She looked like one of those displaced wanderers of war you saw on the Pathé News: a war bride or perhaps the bona fide fiancée of a British citizen. The two girls seemed such forlorn figures, abandoned by heartless Tommies who had, no doubt, promised them the earth. They looked so helpless Lily just couldn't sit by and do nothing.

Her heart went out to them but where was

Susan Brown? Did she think she too had been abandoned in the cold, clutching her bags in a panic, Freddie's letters burning a hole in her pocket? What must she think of his family?

Lily watched the golden-skinned child cowering into her mother's blouse for comfort until the mother pulled her away and the child's mouth opened into a huge howl of protest. There was a tincture of dirty nappy she recognised only too well.

The muffled toddler was lifted up. What a welcome to Manchester! To be left behind with no one to greet them was a dreadful fate.

Passengers from the next flight were already hurrying through the hall, looking out expectantly as they were met by waiting relatives. Was Susan Brown among them? She would be searching for Freddie in the crowd, not a stranger. She must have wandered off somewhere, but where in this rabbit warren of buildings?

Perhaps the girl was in the toilet trying to spruce herself up after such a long journey, putting on warmer clothes? If only Lily knew what she looked like. Better to ask again at the desk, but the plight of these two Orphan Annies and their babies moved her to offer some help.

It was those summer dresses with ill-fitting suit jackets – probably their very best outfits – that moved her to pity. Their offspring at least were well padded in siren suits with pixie hoods, wide-eyed with terror. She would have to do something. She was a Brown Owl and Guiders knew their duty.

Perhaps there was some hiccup at Immigration

and Susan Brown was delayed somewhere. Freddie must have filled in the sponsorship forms or his girlfriend wouldn't have got this far.

The second mother looked thin and shabby in her faded frock with a striped headscarf covering her dark copper hair. Wisps were straggling across her cheeks and there were tears welling in her eyes as she helped the oriental mother from the floor. Suddenly they both started to rock back and forwards, keening and hollering so everyone stopped to stare and the children howled in sympathy.

No one was coming for them. It was a terrible sight, tugging at Lily's heartstrings. Something must be done.

'What is going on?' she asked the official.

'These lasses'll have to go back. They are the third lot of abandoned refugees I've had to sort out today. More paperwork and more tears. If only our chaps wouldn't promise these girls the earth, but that's soldiers for you. Where that Greek comes from she'll be in trouble. Women like her end up put out of the family for bringing shame.' He was pointing at the headscarf, shaking his head.

'Can we get them a cup of tea?' Lily asked, feeling even more sorry for the two rejects, who were now huddled on the bench together as if to gain courage one from the other. It would give her something to do and a chance to search for Miss Brown, but with no photograph to guide her, Lily was beginning to panic. What if the girl set off for Grimbleton on her own in the dark? There was no direct bus route without going into

68

the centre of Manchester first. Anything could happen...

A woman in an overall brought some chipped cups of tea on a tray and Lily handed them out to both strangers with a smile.

'Your soldier boys will come,' she said in her brightest voice. It was late. Perhaps Miss Brown was on the next plane from London.

'Mister Stan will not forget. I wrote many times,' smiled the oriental young woman, shaking her head at the teacup. 'No more tea, thank you.'

'My soldier is at camp. He come. He send brother,' said the other.

'Where are you from?' Lily asked, hoping to take their minds off their predicament.

'London,' answered the tiny woman.

The two of them were like peg and prop. One was tall and statuesque, the other tiny like a bird.

'And you?' Lily turned to the girl in the headscarf.

'I come from Athens ... Greece.'

They all smiled politely and fell silent, lined up like a set of jugs against the wall until the official Lily had spoken to at the information desk hurried over. He was beaming with relief, looking at each of them and clutching his papers.

'Winstanley... Any of you for Winstanley?' he mouthed slowly.

At last, thought Lily, her enquiries were bearing fruit.

At the sound of the name the two women rose as one. 'Yes,' they replied in unison, standing expectantly and then immediately stared at each other with suspicion.

Lily sat down with shock.

'This is Miss Winstanley, she's come to collect one of you,' said the officer, but they both also sat down promptly and shook their heads.

'There must be some mistake. I've come for Miss Susan Brown from Burma,' said Lily.

The man was pointing to the oriental girl, who was back on the floor, prostrate again, her head buried in her palms.

'Honourable sir, I do not know this lady... She is not my Mister Stan,' she sobbed, pulling her child into her chest away from them.

The other girl grabbed her hand. 'Get up, Miss Susan. Your Mister Stan has sent for you. Lucky, lucky you.' She turned to Lily. 'I wait for Sergeant Winstanley. She wait for a Mister Stan.'

Lily felt her knees shaking. There couldn't be two Winstanleys anticipated, could there?

'Not to worry,' she whispered. 'If your name is Susan Brown, then it's me come to collect you. I'm Lily Winstanley, Freddie's sister. I'm sorry I was late.' Stretching out her hand as if to gather up Susan in one fell swoop, there was no hiding her relief. 'Freddie said you were bonny but I was expecting ... never mind...' There was no hiding her surprise.

'Freddie, you know my Freddie, Miss Lily?' said the Greek lass, jumping up excitedly. 'I have his address: twenty-two Division Street, Grimbleton.' A piece of paper was shoved under Lily's nose. Arms were flung round her. 'He is coming for me too?'

'Hang on,' Lily gasped, stepping back quickly. 'Not so fast... It's her I've come for: Susan Brown

70

from Burma, Freddie's intended. I don't know anything about you. Show us that address again,' she said, peering at it intently and then at them both.

'But that is my address too,' cried Susan, peering at the lettering. 'My Stan lives at twenty-two Division Street, Grimbleton. It is written on my heart.'

The other girl folded her arms. 'But I am Anastasia Papadaki. Sergeant Freddie Winstanley is *my* man and Konstandina is his child. I name her after his mother, Konstantia. It is the custom, yes?'

'No, No! I am Susan Liat Brown. Mr Winstanley is *my* intended,' screamed Susan. 'And this is his child, Joy Liat. He is my man. I have his address. You, lady, are a big liar! I have a photo... See!' Susan produced a tattered sepia photograph. 'It was taken in Rangoon before he left on a ship, when I was a teacher. See ... we are in a concert party.' Her smile was triumphant.

Lily peered at it with dismay. There was no doubting that was Freddie grinning at the camera, dressed in a Pierrot costume.

'Give me here. On the bones of Agios Vasilios... *Ne! Ne!* Yes! That is Freddie, *my* Freddie. We meet in Athens when I was nurse,' said the Greek, refusing to give way. 'She is liar. Susan is dead!'

'How am I dead if I am here with little Joy?' Susan shouted back, clinging to the toddler. 'She is his little Joy.'

There was a deafening silence as they both stared at each other. Lily's heart was thumping a drumbeat. It would take the judgement of

71

Solomon to sort out this mess.

'Oh heck,' she said, scratching her head. What have you been up to Freddie? she sighed.

They were all looking to her for guidance. 'What do we do now?'

'These women go nowhere,' ordered the officer, already pink in the face. 'Not until the man in question comes to collect them in person. He can't have two wives in this country, whatever he's been up to. So one of you is going to be disappointed, I'm afraid. Sergeant Winstanley must choose his bride.'

'That might prove difficult, sir. Can I have a word in private?' Lily whispered to the officer.

He pointed to a corner out of earshot, both looking over at the mothers, who were each wishing that the other would disappear into thin air. How on earth was this mess going to be sorted out?

Miss Brown was standing frozen like a statue, tears rolling down her face. Anastasia was standing with her arms folded. And there were the two kiddies to consider: were they both really Freddie's little girls? The two of them then came storming across, led by the Greek, who was all fired up.

'Come on, missy... I no trust them. They hide words from us. We have daughters. Maybe there are two Freddie Winstanleys. One for each of us.' Miss Ana was taking charge. 'You and me is going to sort this out.'

The officer stood in their path. 'There's been a development,' he said softly. 'I'm sorry but under the circumstances, you must both go with Miss

Winstanley and sort this out amongst yourselves, the two of you and the family. His mother is waiting to meet you. Good luck!'

He looked relieved to be shovelling this awkward problem on to the stunned woman in the tweed suit. And Lily was too shocked to do anything other than gather up their luggage and propel them towards the door like a taxi driver.

It was raining hard as they trooped towards the black van with no time for Lily to put on her mackintosh so it would hide the black armband sewn onto her sleeve. The mothers would be far too upset to note its significance or the fact that they were getting soaked.

Somehow cases and bodies and children were crammed into the back of Gertie. The gloomy ride back to Grimbleton was a blur of steamy windows accompanied by the ammonia smell of wet nappies and the sniffing of tears in the back. Gertie coughed and spluttered in protest at the extra weight but trundled them northwards. If only she was driving the bigger Rover saloon but it was still in the garage, standing on bricks, out of action for the duration.

What on earth must these two poor lasses be thinking? Lily felt her hands shaking at the wheel. Perhaps it was lucky that the windows were steamed up so they missed the worst of the soot and the grime, the gaping bomb sites around Manchester, the dark satanic mills.

Lily's heart was thudding as the streets of Grimbleton came into view.

What on earth was she going to do with two of them? What would the family say to two women with the same address? How did they explain away two little girls, not the size of tuppence halfpenny? What would the neighbours think, and Walt too?

This would be the biggest bombshell to hit Division Street since the air raid in '41. I'd like to give that brother of mine a piece of my mind. He's gone too far this time, she thought.

Then she remembered he was dead and these two didn't know. None of them would ever see him again.

The baby, Dina, was whimpering, tugging her back to reality. Freddie may have passed away but he'd sure as hell left quite a legacy behind.

5

The Day War Broke Out Again

Susan peered at the back of the driver's head, at the roll of brown hair anchored with pins and at the felt hat. What was she doing in this clanking van? Had they been kidnapped? Why was she crushed in the back with strangers and the smell of stale bottoms? This was not how England should be, surely?

It should be a beautiful carriage and horses like the picture on the tin of chocolates that Stan brought as a gift to Auntie Betty, her guardian. There was a pretty house with a golden grass roof. Roses tumbling from the walls and a blue,

blue sky. She had read many school books with castles and great stone palaces in them, wide parks with tall trees, but nothing like this.

Outside it was all grey and sooty, no moonlight on this wet afternoon. Gaslamps flickered like troubled spirits. For all she was brought up as a Christian girl, she believed her grandmother when it came to honouring the *nyats*, those guardian spirits of house and home. She whispered, *'Kador, kador,'* so as not to incite their anger. It was bad enough to be sharing this van with the imposter who claimed Mister Stan was the father of her child. The liar! He would not be so quick to take another woman after their tender embrace.

After all the preparations to get to British soil, home of her late father, Ronnie Brown, the hoarding of rations and planning, the obtaining of permits and passports, nothing was as she had dreamed. It was true British soldiers liked Burmese girls but never got round to marrying them, but she thought Mister Stan was different.

'If anything happens and you need my help, beautiful flower, just write to this address,' he promised when his leave was cancelled quickly. She had carried his words close to her heart in her tunic pocket when other Tommies asked her for a date. Was it all the lies of a cheating man?

She clutched 'Precious Teddy', the teddy Auntie Betty had given to Joy for comfort. It smelled of home, of spice and pickle, cigarettes and the ship. Something was wrong. But she had not walked hundreds of miles out of Burma, fleeing the Japanese through the jungle, to be

75

stopped now.

Burmese ladies might look like delicate orchids but their will was made of iron. Sometimes in her dreams, she was back in those hills on the trek north from Rangoon in the summer of 1942. Fear stalked them all the way. There was one valley where the sun hovered over the ridge of hills above them, and when it slid away the hills seemed to crouch down and whisper, 'You'll never get out of here alive.' They called it the valley of death and many succumbed to dysentery and bite infections. They were town people, not used to rough terrain. She was younger and more nimble. She walked with the children, cajoling them to keep going, singing songs to cheer them. 'It's a Long Way to Tipperary' was their favourite.

One night they were attacked by bandits who torched their camps and stripped them of their bundles, cigarettes and rings, and separated the girls from the men. The women clung together, fearing the worst of fates. They would be sold into slavery but not before the men had sampled the goods, she was warned.

How wonderful are the ways of God's angels when rescue came that very night from a patrol of young Japanese warriors who saw the flames. They killed the bandits and gave the Burmese rice, sharing their rations.

Su could never understand how the enemy could be kind one minute and vicious the next. An officer took her aside and asked if she was British.

'No! No! Burmese,' she protested. 'I am ayah to these children,' she lied. 'I'm taking them to safety. War is not a place for children!' He nodded and let her go.

Under cover of darkness, they were allowed to slip away unharmed. How strange that it was the enemy who showed mercy.

Wrapped only in her long skirt, she had trekked for hundreds of miles with rope tied around the soles of her sandals for shoes. She had lived while others died of sores, starvation and exhaustion. Their bodies were consumed by the creatures of the jungle. Of the hundreds who set off on that epic trek, only the young and the tough survived to reach the Assam border.

Here there was respite, food and medicine, and she found kindness among the nurses. It was they who persuaded her to turn round and walk back to join the Women's Auxiliary Service of Burma, helping the wounded men off ships and giving them char and wads, smiles and dances.

Mister Stan was her reward for all her duty, waiting at the station to guide them, parading in the church, dancing and singing. He was a good man and Ana was a big liar!

When they got to his house and they saw she was a real lady who could drink tea from a china cup with her little finger held just so, everything would be 'tickety-boo'. She had brought real tea in her case, not the floor sweepings she had drunk so far. The truth would come out and the Greek girl would be sent packing. They would see she – Susan – was a true lady with proper manners.

'Manners maketh the man', she had been taught. She knew her Shakespeare. She held herself straight with neat ankles and slim waist. She wore an English dress with almond oil on her hair. Her skin was not dark like an Indian's. She was true Anglo-Burmese, with skin the colour of warm ivory. When she walked down a street heads turned. Once they saw her they would know she was true fiancée of Mister Stan. The big liar would be found out!

Gertie glided to the kerbside without breaking wind and drawing attention to their arrival.

Lily peered out into the gloom and took a deep breath. 'This is it. Come inside, ladies,' she smiled, trying to look in control.

The two women didn't budge, transfixed with terror, shaking their heads at her request. Their girls were fast asleep. There was no coaxing the two of them out of the back. If only there were interpreters, liaison officers, on hand to negotiate this tricky situation. They would know how to defuse the time bomb waiting to go off.

At least there was no reception party waiting on the doorstep. It was dark and the curtains were drawn. What if Mother had been standing stern-faced with a bolstered bosom and breath like dragon smoke belching into the night air, and Ivy hovering to inspect the 'missionary'? To Lily's relief, the coast was clear.

'Come inside, it's cold out here.' She offered her hand but they shrunk back in unison. Admittedly, Waverley House was not looking its best in the dusk and mizzle, with its blackened brick fascia and windows bulging from the sides like frog's eyes. The shadows on the pavement, lit by gaslamps, flickered like her failing courage. There was nothing to do but leave them in the van and run up the steps to open the vestibule door.

The mosaic tiled floor smelled of Jeyes Fluid. Everything was spick and span. Polly had been busy, a fire blazing in the hearth and twinkling brass ornaments flashing. All was in readiness for the new arrival to inspect. Lily crept towards the parlour, hoping to find Esme alone. Better to isolate her, explain the little local difficulty before she jumped to the usual conclusion that it was all Lily's fault.

Ivy was standing in the bay window pointing to the van outside, all dolled up in her best skirt with box pleats and John West salmon twinset, her hair fixed in cardboard waves. You could be seasick on those crests. How did she have time to titivate her hair when it was as much as Lily could do to roll hers up like a hosepipe round her head?

'At last! We nearly sent out a search party for you.' Ivy paused for breath. 'Well, where is this mysterious ladyfriend then? I hope you drove her up Green Lane to show her the better end of the street. No one wants to see rows and rows of terraces and factory doors, and it's a good job we had a cold meat platter waiting or tea would be ruined. I've had to feed Neville and now he's all messed up.'

Lily hovered by the door, clutching her driving gloves, flushed with anxiety.

Levi was quick to seize the moment. 'What's up with you? You look as if you've lost a bob and found a tanner. She not turn up then? I thought so, and all that wasted petrol,' he moaned, glancing up from his *Evening News*. 'I knew you'd be hopeless...'

There was no response to his jibe.

'What is it? The cat got your tongue?' snapped Esme. 'I can see summat is up with you.'

Hang on, why did they always expect her to pull the rabbit out of a hat, make a tanner do a bob, dance a fire dance? Good old Doormat Lil, the oily rag that did all the dirty work. Well, now they were going to get such a jumping jack up their backsides and no mistake!

'There's been an unexpected development.' That got their attention. 'It's just ... there's two of them in the van so I thought I'd better come in and check with you first,' she blurted out quickly, shuffling from one foot to the other like a child waiting to be told off for scuffing her best shoes playing football.

Ivy was pushing her out of the way, making for the door. 'Two of who? Don't stand there like one of them girls in Lewis's Arcade. Show me!'

'Wait!' Lily whispered. 'There's two ladies, two, er ... Mrs Winstanleys, or so they say, and they won't come in.'

'Don't be daft, Lil. You dozy brush, you've brought the wrong lasses! No wonder they won't come in. I'm going to see for myself,' snapped Ivy, storming down the path.

'They both had our address, Mother. What was I to do? The airport wanted shot of them once I told them about Freddie. I said we'd sort them out but then there's the kiddies... We have to do right by them.'

'Kiddies!' Esme was on red alert now.

Ivy shot back through the hall like a bullet out of a gun, speechless, her mouth opening and shutting like a goldfish gasping for air. 'Levi! You'd better get out there. Call the police! There's two foreigners with screaming kids in our van. We can't have them in here. What will the neighbours think? And one of them's ... Chinese,' she mouthed in a whisper. 'I'm taking Neville upstairs. We don't want any part of this. Wait till I get my hands on that brother of yours,' she screamed, storming up the Axminster stairs two at a time.

Esme, winded by the news, sat down in a heap. Ivy had no tea strainer between her brain and her mouth, Lily sighed. Freddie couldn't help them now. She stood in the hall, not knowing which way to turn. 'At least they do speak English of sorts, one better than the other,' she offered. 'Poor souls had no idea about each other. Both sat there waiting for the same soldier to pick them up. You could cut the ice in the back of the van. What was I to do? I couldn't leave them, not with little kiddies in the middle of winter.'

'Levi, come up here. We're keeping out of this mess!' shouted Ivy from the top of the landing.

'You'd better calm your wife down.' Esme took a deep breath and rose again, her chest heaving under the gold link chain she wore when expecting company. 'I suppose I'll have to deal with this mess myself.'

'Perhaps I should get Walter over to help us,' Lily offered, feeling in need of some support.

81

'Whatever for? He'd be neither use nor ornament, Lil. Leave him be.'

There was nothing to do but follow Mother down those steps, throwing prayers to the Almighty, hoping for once that she would find the right words to calm the frightened passengers and not have them running through the dark streets in fear of her fury, Lily thought. Better to push in front and get the first word in herself.

'This is Freddie's mother, Mrs Winstanley. She wants to speak to you,' Lily mouthed as if to a child. 'We have tea for you inside and milk for the little ones, yes?'

The two girls looked at each other and then at the grey-haired matron who hovered over them, gold chains clanking above a smart grey two-piece jersey suit.

At least her face softened at the sight of these waifs and strays taking the sting out of her bite momentarily.

'Come in, ladies. We must talk to you and outside is not the place. There's obviously been some terrible mistake.' Esme pointed the way, looking up and down the street to see if there was an audience.

Were the curtains twitching across at number nineteen? Doris Pickvance, the local 'News of the World' was going to get an eyeful if she spotted the little procession of refugees, babies and baggage squeezing out of the black van. It would be all down Division Street by chucking-out time at the Coach and Horses that the Winstanleys were opening a hostel for displaced persons.

Slowly the girls edged themselves out of the

back, crumpled and forlorn, unravelling their clinging toddlers. Lily picked up a fallen doll as they made their way up the steps.

'Where is my Stan? Why is he not here to greet me? I wrote him many letters. What is wrong?' Susan was clutching her struggling child, who was draped over her shoulder, her eyes on stalks as faces peered down the stairwell.

'Come inside and sit down,' said Esme in a soft voice, moved by the plight of these orphans of the night.

They sat down shyly, not looking at each other.

'Lil will get you a drink.'

'No, thank you,' replied the Burmese woman, sitting upright like a ramrod. 'Please, where is Stan? I wrote and he said I should write to you. No one came to the ship to meet me.'

'You are Miss Brown still, or did my son make you his bride before he left?' Mother was looking down at her ringless finger. Lily didn't know where to look so she bowed her head.

'It was our wish to marry but the Army, it said there was no rush to "marry foreign". I told them straight, no beating bushes, Mister Stan made promises and he gave me a gift.' She unlaced her shoe and fiddled in the toe, bringing out a pair of solid gold earrings studded with bright rubies. 'I kept them safe with our precious baby.'

'That's as may be, Miss Brown.' Esme glanced briefly at the jewels, trying to look unimpressed by the size and depth of their colour. Then it was the other girl's turn for a grilling.

'We don't even know your name ... Miss...? We had no letter from my son to say you were

83

coming.' There was the sharp edge back again.

The Greek girl shuffled in her bag for papers. 'I am Anastasia Papadaki,' she said. 'Freddie gave this address to write him. It is lucky I arrive the same day as this woman.' Her eyes were flashing like steel daggers at Susan.

'Are you engaged to my son? Have you got a ring in your shoe?'

Anastasia shook her head. 'He was good soldier. I have terrible time but I help Tommy soldiers get out of Kriti island. We meet in Athens at the end of war. He bring me food. He give me your name to come to England. I come to find him and show him Konstandina. See...' She whipped off the little pixie hood to reveal a head full of sandy-red curls. There was no mistaking those curls or the sea-blue eyes and long lashes. She was the image of Freddie.

'How do I know you're telling us the truth?' said Esme, standing firm. 'Neither of you has any proof.' She was weighing them up while Lily passed round the silver tray of biscuits laid in a cartwheel of pink wafers and bourbon creams, the last of their rations for the month, hidden in an old tin from Ivy and Neville. Suddenly the toddler was alert, curious, stretching out fingers to snatch a treat, but Susan shook her bowed head.

'Just look at that child, Mother. She's the spit of Freddie,' Lily hissed. 'I think we should tell them the truth and get the others down.' Lily drew in a deep breath and swallowed. 'There is no easy way to say this–' she ventured, looking at the two women.

'No, this is my duty as head of this family. I'll do it,' Esme interrupted. She drew herself up and turned to them both. 'I'm afraid my son, Freddie's, had an accident. He is ... was in Palestine on duty. There was an explosion. I am so sorry but he did not survive. He will never be coming home now.'

There was silence as the words sunk in.

Anastasia crossed herself and Susan shook her head. 'I saw the black scarf on your arm. I think something bad is going to happen. Black is for sorrow and sorrow is etched on Daw Winstanley's face.' The Burmese girl spoke softly, bowing her head.

'What we do now?' sobbed Anastasia.

'Make a cup of sweet tea, Lil,' ordered Esme.

'Poor Mister Stan. Poor Susan Liat with no Stan to welcome me. No home, no village, no grass roof house and roses by the door, no sitting in the cool of the evening while Stan smokes his pipe. Do you know how many gold bracelets Auntie Betty sold to buy our ticket? The journey was so long and the war so terrible. I walked through the jungle from the Japanese. Many died. Mister Stan says he loves me and will send for me one day. What do we do now, Daw Winstanley? I am not going back.'

Susan sat there weeping, and Joy touched her tears with her podgy fingers, unaware all their plans were in ruins.

Then Levi slithered into the room like a snake coiling his way round the furniture, followed by Ivy with her pinched cheeks and puckered lips, smelling of setting lotion and pre-war perfume.

They were curious enough now not to want to miss out on the story unfolding. Ivy sniffed a quick glance at the two women as if they were a bad smell.

'Whatever they have to say, Mother, better be said in front of both of us,' she snapped, pointing at them.

Lily sometimes wondered about Levi and Ivy's marriage and what private disappointments had so quickly soured the two of them.

'We won't speak ill of the dead. Freddie is not here to defend himself. It's what we do with them now that's my greatest concern,' said Esme.

'I am sorry to bring trouble to your door,' Susan sniffed through her tears. 'I was not brought up to be a nuisance. My father, Ronnie Brown, was a British soldier. He died of sickness and when my mother remarried I went to live with her sister, Auntie Betty. I know English ways. I went to a Christian school. I have my teaching certificate from Rangoon College in my trunk. I have sold everything I have to be with my intended. Now I don't know what to do. Do not turn us from your door.'

Lily shook her head. 'You're both tired and shocked. There's a bed upstairs prepared for one of you but we can find a camp bed for the other. We'll not turn strangers in distress from our door, will we, Mother?' Suddenly it became important to stand up for these strangers. 'You were friends of my brother and you must stay until you sort yourselves out.' That got the hand grenades flying overhead.

'Mother! There's hardly room for four extras!

86

What about ration books and bedding? Neville'll be upset,' whined Ivy, lips tight like purse strings.

But Esme was standing firm. 'Lil's got a point. Neville should have been out of a cot months ago. He can kip down on a mattress in your room. He's too big for the pram in the hall. Our guests will have to share the boys' old room in the attic and the kiddies can top and tail in the cot for a night or two.'

'But, Mother, it's not right to encourage immorality. They may be lying to us, for all we know.' Ivy was clinging to her argument and her territory, but Lily knew that the first salvo had reached its target when Esme came to her defence.

'Just look at that kiddie, the one with the long name ... Concertina. Anyone can see who her father is. It tears my heart to see those kiss curls. And as for the other lady, school teachers in my experience don't lie. What's done is done. We won't turn them from this door, not at this time of day and after such bad news. It's hardly Christian, is it?'

The girls flashed her a look of gratitude but Ivy wanted the last word as usual.

'Levi, tell your mother it's not decent. It's not fair on Neville, having heathens in the house,' she said. There was not an ounce of sympathy in her voice. At least Levi had the decency to stare up at the ceiling, saying nothing.

'Come on now, if our Freddie led them up the garden path then it's our responsibility for the moment not to make matters worse,' Lily replied in their defence.

'Judas!' Ivy spat in her direction.

'Come on, ladies, Lil will show you to the top floor. You can freshen up before we have some supper. There's enough hot water for the kiddies to have a bath with Neville. They smell as if they need changing,' Esme replied.

'Mother!' yelled Ivy up the stairs. 'Neville must go first. I don't hold with girls and boys together. You never know what ideas they might get. Our Lily is right out of order.'

Lily followed behind, reluctant to leave them alone.

How terrible to have to share a room with someone who's shared a bed with your fiancé. How would she feel if Walter produced another girlfriend out of the blue? What disappointment and grief were bottled up inside these two lasses and no one to understand them now? Each one wishing, perhaps, that the other was dead instead of Freddie. How could she leave them in this state?

Su climbed the stairs with a heavy heart, up three flights and turns to a large attic room with windows in the roof. Levi brought up the cot piece by piece, huffing and puffing, eyeing them both as they unpacked their cases.

'Here we go, ladies, one cot and some spare nappies from the airing cupboard. There's warm milk in the kitchen when you are ready.'

'Joy needs no nappies. She's a clean girl now,' Su said.

'My child is still at the breast,' said Ana.

Levi blushed and fled downstairs.

Alone for the first time since they both stood up together in the aerodrome, they turned their backs on each other, trying not to cry. Su wondered how she could share a room with someone who had shared a bed with her Stan. The disappointment and grief was hanging over her back like some heavy blanket. If only they had married in secret. If only he had stayed in Burma and set up home with her, but no, he got aboard a ship and forgot all about her.

For Joy Liat, no Daddy with a pipe and medals. All her dreams were crumbling to dust.

'I do not understand. Stan is my man, not yours,' Su said, pulling out one of her precious heavy silk *longyis*, a sarong of dark blue embroidered material, brought as a token of her heritage. Now it would serve as a curtain to hide her modesty. She would make a screen of it.

'He say you dead, his foreign girl in Far East. No letters come from you.'

'How could I write when he did not write to me? ... This screen will help us sleep,' she said to Ana, who nodded. Su could see she too had been crying.

There was a knock on the door and Lily hovered in the doorway, drowned in a baggy man's cardigan. 'If you would like, I can bath your little ones. I'd love to have a play with them. Neville is done now. The water is still warm. You must be so tired. It is such dreadful news. We still can't believe it. Mother is taking it badly. None of us has seen Freddie for six years, and now this. We've so much to ask you about him ... but now is not the time.'

She smiled as if she meant every word, such a bright smile and kind grey eyes in such a pale face, not a bit like Stan at all, Su thought. The little ones seemed to sense she loved children and did not protest when she lifted them.

Su stood on the landing, listening to them splashing and laughing as Lily sang with a rich voice, 'Mairzy doats and dozy doats and liddle lamzy divey...'

Stan had a rich voice too. They had played in a concert party together. She fell onto the bed exhausted, curling up into a ball, dreaming of the veranda at home and Auntie Betty fixing jasmine around her coiled hair. She shivered. This England – it was so chilly and dark.

When she woke, Lily had given Joy a cup of warm milk and tucked her in one end of the cot. Ana had opened her blouse to her child and Su saw her magnificent white breasts. She herself was like a child in that department. Anglo-Burmese did not have breasts like melons. Perhaps Freddie was disappointed by her tiny frame and that was why he abandoned her?

It was time to change into her one remaining clean blouse and go down to supper.

They sat in the chilly dining room with a paraffin heater belching out fumes, choking the air with its acrid smell. The wind was rattling at the windowpanes.

'Wind from the north means snow,' said Levi, making polite conversation. 'I don't suppose you two have ever seen snow.'

'I was a guest of the Germans for many years. I have seen terrible snow,' snapped Ana. 'And you?' She turned to Su.

'Just on a Christmas card,' she answered.

'Oh, you have Christmas in your country then?' sniffed Ivy, picking at her tinned salmon for bones.

Su put down her fork. The fish was tasteless and she could barely swallow for anger at this bitter pickle. 'My father was a British soldier. We have Christmas carols and a tree and "Away in a Manger" and Jesus in His cradle. I am baptised Church of England, like my father. I'm not a heathen,' she answered with cold politeness. That would shut up the snake woman.

Ivy turned her venom to Ana instead. 'What religion are you then? Catholic?'

'No understand,' she said, and refused to say another word.

'We are going to hold a service in church in Freddie's memory,' said Esme. 'You are welcome to attend but I don't know how I'm going to explain you both. One, yes, but two of you...?'

'Number one wife and Number two wife,' chuckled Levi until someone kicked him under the table and he howled. 'What was that in aid of?'

'That is not funny,' snapped Ivy with her mouth full. 'We could say one of them was his widow but the other one...' She was looking at them with disapproval.

'Pity there isn't another one of us to go round,' sneered Levi, fingering his moustache, licking his lips and giving Su the onceover.

'Don't be silly. This is serious. People will want to know who these foreigners are. They should stay at home,' said Ivy.

'Levi has a point,' said Lily. 'You don't suppose if we said that one of them was his widow, we could then say the other was one of his comrade's friends, come to pay last respects?'

'One look at those ginger curls and they would soon guess the score,' Esme chipped in.

'Stop this. This is no time for careless talk... Shame on you! You talk as if we weren't here. I have come a long way. I am very disappointed. Now I don't know what to think, and I have no home to go to either.' Su found herself so angry she was spitting out the words.

'Steady on, lass, we meant no harm,' said Lily, reaching out to tap her hand. 'What if we were to claim one of you as Freddie's widow and the other the widow of his ... cousin, say?' she offered.

'What cousin?' snapped Ivy. 'Levi has no cousin.'

'Who's to know but us? A cousin from down south who was killed in the war. That would explain two Mrs Winstanleys at the funeral and their offspring, and no questions asked,' she added. 'I don't know why I'm concocting all this but it's better than the truth.'

There was a hush as everyone digested Lily's plan.

'I don't like the idea. They should not be coming to chapel,' said Ivy.

'Have a heart,' said Lily. 'They've every right, and their kiddies too.'

'Lily's right. For the sake of those little blighters upstairs we can bend the truth so no one gets hurt.'

'It's a downright lie. They haven't got a wedding ring between them,' Ivy insisted.

'Hah!' laughed the honourable Esme. 'They'd not be the first women in Grimbleton to go down to Woolworths to buy a brass ring and hope nobody asked for their marriage lines. It's for appearance's sake we're doing this. No one need know but us. Then we can all hold our heads up high. What do you think, ladies?' she asked.

There was a pebble in Su's throat, choking any response. Opposite sat her rival, who said nothing, only half understanding the conversation.

'Ana, we are going to draw lots and choose who is to be number one wife Winstanley – wife of Freddie – and who is number two wife of...' Su paused to think of a suitable name, 'of Cedric.' She bowed her head.

'Who is Cedric when he's at home?' asked Levi, puzzled.

'I met Cedric on the trek to India, a very nice American boy. He gave us a tin of cocoa from rations. It saved our lives. I like the name Cedric.'

'Then you can be his wife,' Ivy answered with her sour lemon smile.

'Oh, no! I will be number one wife. I have a British passport and photograph of my intended. Joy Liat is his older daughter so I am number one.' She was thinking on her feet, but then Ana burst into big sobs and blew her nose on her napkin.

'These continentals are so emotional,' said Ivy. 'She'll be weeping and wailing in church, making an exhibition of herself. Let them draw lots for who comes and who stays, I say.'

'There's no need to get upset. We will leave it to chance. Come on, son, fetch me my hat and some scrap paper. This is the fairest way,' said Esme as she passed a clean hankie to Ana.

I am dreaming all of this, thought Su: the wind blowing outside the window rattling the panes, rain lashing down on the glass like tears, the flames of the heater and the flickering gaslamps on the walls, the black scarf over the family portrait of my beloved on the mantelpiece. Perhaps I will wake up and it will all be a bad dream. The girl next to me will have disappeared and I will wake in the bunk of the troopship, and my lover will be waiting at the dockside.

This was hardly the way to sort out such a pack of lies and half-truths but it was the best they could manage for the moment, thought Lily. Everyone was punch-drunk with shock and exhaustion, and resistance was low. Better to sort it out now and get their stories straight from the start.

'There you go, girl, dip your hand in the hat. You go first.' Levi was shoving the hat into Susan's face. She picked out a folded slip of paper but did not open it. Then Ana picked out the other, opened it and smiled.

Lily saw the words, 'Mrs Winstanley, Mrs Freddie Winstanley, number one widow.' She sighed and Levi winked at her. It was a fix.

Susan rose from the table without a word and made for the stairs. Ana rose too but Lily held her back.

'Let her have a few moments to herself. It has

been a long day for all of us.' She turned to Esme. 'Perhaps it's for the best if Miss Papawhotsit claims to be his proper wife. Susan has a British passport. Anastasia has nothing going for her but the fact that any dumb cluck can see that Concertina's a Winstanley.'

The Greek girl sat down promptly.

'Tell us about Freddie in Athens. How did you meet? Was he well? Tell a grieving mother about her son. How did he look?' Esme pleaded.

'I knew him very short time. He is kind man. We go many dances and I teach him Creta dancing. He told me to come...' Then she burst into tears again.

Lily did her best to comfort her but half her mind was upstairs in the cold bedroom with the weeping Susan, the frozen girl who looked so lost. How could anyone not feel pity for them both?

She tiptoed upstairs, peering into the cot to see the sleeping half-sisters, top and tail, looking like little angels. Her heart was relieved to see that Susan was fast asleep. By her bedside was the tattered snapshot of Freddie in a Pierrot costume with a golden halo of curls sticking out of his cap, the snapshot the girl had carried halfway across the world. Lily didn't know whether she wanted to cry or wring her brother's neck for bringing this trouble to their door.

In that faraway world, he'd given them both comfort and loving. These girls knew lives she could hardly imagine, had journeyed into dark places just to bring their kiddies to safety and find Freddie again. It made her own world seem

95

so small. No wonder Susan found everything so grey here. Their Grimbleton world was colourless and predictable but at least it was safe and would shelter these storm-tossed wanderers for a while...

Freddie would want her to give them protection but how to explain them away? Not even Walt knew the full truth yet. And his mother had a mouth on her the size of Morecambe Bay.

Still, the Almighty in His wisdom had dumped them here for a reason. It was up to Him to sort this lot out, and soon. All she knew was that tomorrow would begin the Winstanley family's life of lies.

6

Farewell to Freddie

'Where've you been? I thought you'd run away with the coal man,' whispered Walter as he pecked Lily on the cheek. 'And what's all this about Freddie's wife and kiddy? I never knew he were wed.'

The jungle drums were at work already. Lily sighed as she struggled to bring in the washing from the line in the backyard of his house in Bowker's Row. It was starting to rain and his mother was dozing in the leather armchair, blissfully unaware. There would be just time to iron Walt a clean shirt and unpack the shopping she had brought before they must set off for the memorial service.

'We've not seen much of you these last weeks,' yawned Elsie Platt, rubbing her striped brown slippers with holes cut out to accommodate her bunions. Her bulk was wired tightly, like an overstuffed mattress, into a black funeral outfit. A winter coat lay over the back of the chair with a fur tippet and black felt hat. Elsie loved a good funeral tea and a chance to give Waverley House the onceover.

'Levi says it's the talk of the Coach and Horses about the foreign girls who turned up at your place. Why am I the last to know anything?' Walter sniffed, standing over her while she plugged the iron into the lamp-shade.

'What's wrong with the shirt he's wearing, Lil? It was clean on yesterday,' Elsie snapped.

It was hard to explain that a clean shirt and cuffs were important when the whole family was on show. Sometimes after a day on the stall and a night in Yates Wine Lodge, Walt was not as Lifebuoy fresh as he ought to be, poor lamb. She blamed Elsie, whose idea of housework was just to keep the smells down in the two up, two down terraced house. That inbred Lancashire pride in being spick and span with bright white nets, donkey-stoned steps and starched washing had somehow passed her by.

The Platts' weekly wash was a steeping of smalls in the sink and hung out overnight, where it gathered sooty smuts, unless Lily took them back home herself. It wasn't as if Walt's mother had anyone else to look after, but it took all sorts,

97

Lily supposed.

The Winstanleys would only pick holes in Walt's appearance if he turned up shabby. They all needed to put on a united front on this sad occasion. She wanted no more sly digs about his appearance.

'What's all this about your Freddie? What's the sly beggar been up to? I hear there's nappies on your washing line?' Elsie sniggered.

'You'd think folk had nothing better to do than to count washing. It's a long story and we've not time to be gossiping when there's a service to be going to. I've brought the van to give you both a lift.'

'His back won't stand it in the rear of that, dear. You'd better take me and return for him later,' said Elsie, rising to don her outdoor finery. 'Will there be a collection? It'll have to be a widow's mite from me. You know how we are placed.'

'I expect so, but don't worry about it. You'll have to make do as best you can with one trip, though. It's not far and I'm running out of time.'

Did they think she was a taxi service and a laundry maid? There were a hundred jobs on her list and no time to get dressed properly. They were lucky that guilt at neglecting Walt had made her come early to sort them out. He was hopeless without her chivvying him up. That was one of the things she loved about him. He *needed* her.

When they arrived at Waverley House there was another fuss going on.

'They're not going dressed like that?' Ivy stared at these new upstarts. She was bedecked in a dark suit with a fox fur draped over her shoulders. 'Here, I found some mittens for them to cover their fingers. It's chilly outside. I hope there's a good turnout. We don't want these two showing us up, do we?'

This was not a fashion parade or a celebration, thought Lily with only five minutes to tear off her old clothes and put on her winter best frock and tired coat. There was no time even to powder her nose. Usually Ivy would have nothing to do with Ana and Susan, sniffing down her nose every time they came in a room, and the offer of a pair of knitted gloves each was only so they could hide their ringless fingers from view.

The family assembled outside the house for the short walk to Zion Chapel, ambling slowly, flanking the two strangers on all sides to keep them out of view. There was a goodly crowd gathered by the church steps, waiting for the family to process in.

It was left to Lily to kit out Ana and Susan for church with warm coats and hats, stockings and suitable underwear for the chilly climate. They had no coupons for anything new.

Susan was so tiny she fitted into Lily's old school gaberdine mac with a lined hood. Ana was wrapped in Grandma Crompton's old fur coat, which hardly fitted across her swollen bust. But winter was coming early this year. They would not look out of place all muffled up.

Lily held little Joy's hand as she struggled on the slippery pavement in her pixie hood and warm gaiters. Word was out about the strangers at Waverley House pushing a pram. It did cross her mind that half the crowd might be gathered today just to ogle. Esme covered her black hat with net veiling to hide her grief and her confusion. She was very quiet, too quiet, and Lily wondered how they would get through the service without someone breaking down. There was nothing to do but brazen it out.

'You've heard about our big surprise then?' Lily smiled up at neighbours, trying to look casual, hoping they wouldn't notice how her voice was quaking.

'It's all round the Coach and Horses that young Freddie left his mark in Burma,' whispered Doris Pickvance.

'Then they were wrong as usual!' Lily whispered back.

Bar-stool gossip could be so crude. Lily's heart began to thud. What if everyone thought Su was Freddie's wife? How could they pass Anastasia off as his bride instead? Perhaps they should change them round again. All this lying was hard work, so many pitfalls and tracks to cover over. Perhaps it was better to tell the plain truth.

All eyes were on the two strangers as they were led down a side aisle into a series of boxed cupboard pews. The mourners were put at the front in full view, waiting in silence until Reverend Atkinson, wearing his black gown, stood before the assembled family to welcome them and began the special service with the hymn 'I vow to thee my country'.

Lily felt herself choking up. The tune brought back memories of schooldays. Why did she suddenly think of Pamela Pickvance and the ice slide?

It wasn't that Pam was always horrid to her, it was just that she couldn't rely on her as a friend. One minute she was all over her like a rash and then she ran off and ganged up with girls in the playground, pulling faces and calling her names.

Pam across the road was in the top class and 'bonny', which was a polite way of saying 'fat', round as a barrel with a nip on her like pincers. Her brother was even bigger and when the two of them stopped her on the way home to snatch her bus money, it made for a long walk on a wet night.

Funny how she would hand it over without a fight until Freddie started in the infants' and she had to drag him along into the infants' playground. Pam and Alf would wait until she had shoved him in the yard, then pounce. If she'd spent her pennies, they pulled off her ribbons and that meant bother at home. Mother thought she was careless and made her pay for some more. There was no point in telling tales when they lived across the road. She just put up with it hoping their bullying would go away.

Then came the bad snow and a chance to make an ice slide on the pavement, sliding down until it shone like glass. Pam and Alf started shoving her off, making her legs go sideways out onto the road. That was scary and she cried in front of them.

Freddie was watching, open-mouthed, seeing his sister sobbing, and suddenly he rushed at Pam and knocked her over. He pulled her by her pigtails until she screamed and when her big brother came to the rescue, he kicked him in the shins.

The scrap that followed was like Goliath beating the hell out of David until he had a busted lip and a bloody nose and his new winter coat was torn.

'You lay off my sister or I'll shove you down!' Freddie snorted.

'You and whose army?' sneered Alf Pickvance.

'I'll get my big brother on you and he's got boxing gloves and we'll come and get you.'

'Oh, yes,' snivelled Pam, a hole in her lisle stockings. 'I'm telling on you!'

Doris was round next morning complaining that her darling Pam had been set upon by Winstanley ruffians, and what was Esme going to do about it?

Esme rose to her full height with an icy smile. 'What happens in the street between children is not our affair. My children don't fight unless provoked... Thank you and good day!' She slammed the door in Doris's face and turned her fury on her own.

Lily was sent to her room. Freddie got his bottom paddled, but neither broke their vow of silence, their *omertà*: All for one and one for all.

Funny thing was, Pam was as nice as pie after that, and Alf gave them a wide berth. It was then that Lily realised that having two brothers had its advantages. There was nothing she wouldn't do for them then.

Lily buried her nose in her handkerchief. She could still see Freddie as a little lad, not a grown man. In six years all she had of him were a bunch of letters full of jokes and pleasantries, she sighed. They knew nothing of his real life, his war, his lovers, nothing about the real Freddie. He was a stranger.

Both her brothers were strangers and that was what war had done to this family: torn them apart. In truth she'd lost Freddie years ago.

This can't be a real church, thought Ana as she stared around the bare walls as they were escorted down a side aisle into a series of boxed cupboard pews. The mourners sat in silence until a man in a suit and teacher's gown stood before the Winstanley family and began the service.

To her a church was the very soul of a place, set high on a hill or in the market square, painted white, shining in the sunlight, not tucked up in some grimy street like a factory, she mused. Where was the rainbow of colours: ochre, crimson, azure wall paintings? Where were the bells, candlelight and smell of incense?

The walls of Zion Chapel were painted white, the woodwork was dark oak polished to a mirror finish. There were no flowers, no silken robes and vestments, shimmering purples and crimson velvets, embroidered with silver and gold threads, no wall hangings and frescoes, nothing on which to rest her sad eyes for comfort. Where were the scenes from the Gospels, painted between the windows and the walls, by monks centuries ago, some depicting the miracles wrought by St Andreas, Archbishop of Crete? Did Grimbleton not have its own patron saint to adorn with jewels and gold leaf?

She looked up to the wooden rafters holding the ceiling. Where was the risen Christ in glory arching over the cupola in mosaic tiles glistening gold and silver and sapphire in the heavens?

There was nowhere to light a sacred candle of intercession for Freddie. She could not hate him for his weakness. He was a man and men had needs. He brought her back to life after years of darkness. He was her candle of light and she wept that their time together had been so short.

There were no jewelled icons to pray before, hanging with silver tamata, those precious votive offerings, flowers, silver templates with eyes and legs and bodies, offered for a cure. There was no cure for death, only the resurrection in the fullness of time.

She did not understand this English plainness. How could anyone find comfort in such stark surroundings? It felt an insult to all that was holy in her heart. Freddie would not rest in peace until she had found a proper church and lit candles and all the rituals were performed.

She was weeping not for her loss now but for herself and memories of the little white chapel of St Dionysius, the patron saint of her village, weeping for the comfort of familiar faces processing to the great Easter ceremonies and Christmas festival, weeping an exile's tears. There was no going back now.

There was such a silence, no weeping and wailing of death songs, no mother and black-clad widows keening. The sounds of grief could purge away suffering. Her family had kneeled prostrate over her sister's grave, wailing in agony, only to rise and prepare a meal for the living family as if that beautiful girl was not in the graveyard.

Eleni was the first of many deaths in their village, the year the Germans came from the sky, floating down into their olive groves. But no, she could not think of all that again.

They were singing hymns now, ones she could not understand, and there were words, so many words. There was no ceremony in this memorial. There was no body to wash with wine and rosewater, no linen to bind up, no body to bury. How could you lay to rest a man who was not there?

She twisted the brass ring around her wedding finger. It was loose. What would a real priest make of these lies? Susan Brown was sitting in front, prim with her straw hat bound with black ribbon, her luscious coil of hair constrained in a hairnet. She was used to English worship. She was wearing her gold earrings, showing them off for all to see.

Ana sensed there were curious eyes in the congregation, wondering just who these strangers were. There would be more stories to make up when they went back home for the funeral tea and guests sidled up to her with polite questions about her connection to the family.

I will never get used to this chilly air, she sighed, the dampness of the rooms, the smells of soot and smoke and burning rubber, or people with faces like doughy white bread rolls. You made your bed, now you must lie on it, she thought. There is no other way, *sigara, sigara* ... take it easy.

However many layers she borrowed from Lily she could not keep warm. It was as if a mist of forgetfulness and lethargy clouded all her resolve and energy, sapping her hope away. Only Dina gave her a reason to rise each morning to do all the chores her mother-in-law insisted they divide between them. They must earn their board and lodgings until they had achieved their independence from the Winstanleys.

They had been taken down to the town hall, a soot-black building like a Greek temple, where she had to sit in a long queue for hours with Dina, waiting to register as a refugee with child. It was all papers to sign in a language she couldn't read very well, but Lily tried to explain why she must do this.

It felt wrong to be sitting in her best clothes, not in black widow's weeds. Black and grey were the colours of this drab town. What on earth was she doing here?

There were other queues she must stand in to register for identity papers, rations, welfare. She was a refugee with no status. Susan had a passport. Susan had gold bracelets stuffed in her bag to buy extras for her child. Despite their ruse, Susan was still thought to be a regular wife who was just a visiting relative here under sufferance.

Ana's only relief was to borrow the bucket pram and walk up Green Lane to the top shops where the family was registered for groceries. Here she could pretend to be an ordinary housewife with her baby, not a lonely exile trapped by winter in an alien land.

Freddie, I hate you, she sighed, shaking her

head. But how can I hate the man who brought me back to life?

The man with the smiling face and freckled nose who waltzed into her dreams. How could she forget the brush of khaki on her cheek and the smell of eau-de-Cologne. 'Moonlight Serenade', dancing under the stars, strolling through the village square.

You told me about the other woman, how she never wrote and you feared she might be dead, thought Ana. You were sad and I was sad, for I had lost my home and my sister. You filled the hunger in my belly with food from the NAAFI and wine from cellars that loosened our limbs. You filled the hunger for love with your caresses and promises. I heard what I wanted to hear. Were all your words lies as we lay among the stars?

I cannot hate you. You were a gift from God, a candle in the darkness to guide my path. May you rest in peace.

Susan sat in a trance listening to the hymn, such a familiar hymn but in such a strange place. Memories came flooding back, of the high-vaulted roof, the fan whirring, the heat of the old church. She was so cold she could hardly think for the chattering of her teeth.

I am a prisoner now, she decided, a prisoner in a cold dark dungeon with no escape, only lies and sleeping next to the enemy: the girl who stole my sweetheart; the big liar with dark eyes and big bosoms.

Her spirits sank so low she wanted to fade away

107

but Joy bounced on her knee, unaware that she was fatherless and nameless. Joy was the one true precious trophy.

So many babies took sick and died on the trek north, bundles passed down and buried at the border on Burmese soil, little graves in the track. Her child was round and rosy and full of life, a special gift. Big Ana's baby was plain and too thin and cried. Joy was the true number one daughter.

She would be strong for her, fight for her and make her a true Winstanley. She recalled the night Joy was made. Her cheeks flushed and for a second she felt the heat of the tropical night.

It was a night of a thousand stars. They had danced and she had worn her best silk skirt with a blouse the colour of orchid pink. They had walked back slowly to the veranda where Auntie Betty would be waiting, Susan's heart aching, for it was Freddie's last night of leave.

'You go and forget your Susan,' she whined.

'Never, it will be just like the song, *"We'll Meet Again"*.'

'Have you told your mother about me?'

'I've told my friends... Don't look so sad.'

'Why will they not let us marry?' she pleaded.

'It's rules, army rules. We'll be together soon though, and now you've got those earrings...'

'They're beautiful. I love you so much. Come close. I'll let down my hair so you can see how long it grows.' She swished a coil across his nose. 'It smells of fragrant oil?'

'Come here and let me kiss you one more time,' he sighed, pulling her close.

'Now I will give you a special gift in return. I

am not a bar girl or quick-and-easy girl. I give my loving so you will remember me.' She flung herself in his arms and led him down the path to the little wadi, burying her face in his shoulder while he covered her eyelids with, kisses. She felt his lashes like butterfly wings on her cheek.

'You think Susan is wicked to love you? Am I bad?' She unwrapped her skirt and they lay on it, making love under the shrubs to the music of the night.

She breathed in his kisses; he smelled of the barracks' tobacco, a soldier's scent. He kissed her tiny breasts and fingered them lovingly, whispering her name like a cool fan. She melted under him, opening up to him with such joy and eagerness. As he entered there was pain and wonder. Then it was over and she longed for something more.

In the dim light it was hard to see where she ended and he began but the lemony dawn light rose in the sky all too soon. Their limbs were coiled around each other. She could hear his heart beating. They had become as one.

'You're so beautiful. How can I leave you now?'

'You will write?'

'I will write but if danger comes I might not be able to. When the war is over but there are still pockets of resistance in the hills. Stay with Auntie Betty and I will come for you.'

'Promise?' she pleaded.

'Promise. Here's my address in England just in case.'

But you didn't come. You left me for her... You forgot your Susan.

One day soon she and Walt would stand before the congregation for their wedding ceremony, Lily mused. Here was where Freddie sucked gobstoppers under the pew and kicked the back panels, squirming until the clock got round to twelve, when Polly would be dishing out the Sunday roast. Here was where they brought Dad before his burial.

The church was full of memories – celebrations and sadness. It was right they should see off their brother with due honour. What a turnout! Looking up at the congregation spilling out into the balcony above, she felt comforted by the sea of familiar faces. There was all the Grimbleton football team staring down at her. What an honour that they should come and pay tribute to an old school pal. What a show for her kid brother! Tears bubbled to the surface – tears of sadness, not only for herself but for those happy childhood memories, the longing to live happier times again, knowing she'd never see him or Dad again. Then there were the two young girls who sat like statues, lost in their own thoughts, salty tears of disappointment running down their faces. No going back for any of them now. A Brown Owl knew her duty and responsibility. How could she think of abandoning them in a strange country?

Don't you worry, Freddie, I'll be their champion, come what may, she vowed. I shan't let you down whatever the cost, she thought, twisting Walter's engagement ring round her wedding finger for comfort. It had been chosen from a tray of second-hand rings: a tiny hoop of sapphire chippings, modest but so precious, the best of the bunch within his budget and post-war shortages. Walter insisted she chose it herself and he'd pay on the drip. Now it was loose. With all the worry of the past week there was no time to eat. She hoped they'd done Freddie proud.

He'd never been religious but she knew he would have liked the hymns they'd chosen.

Susan was sitting in the front and she was obviously used to English worship. The ruby and gold earrings shimmered in a shaft of light from the side window. Ana sat hunched over, not understanding much, trying to be invisible, clutching her restless baby. What a contrast these strangers were: a copper knob with her golden-haired girl, and the little dark one with her plump toddler whose fingers were into everything.

The organist attempted Freddie's regimental march and they shuffled out, trying to look dignified, spilling out into the street like a flow of black lava. The sky was threatening more fog and ice. The pavements were piled high with dirty leaves from front gardens, the cart horses left pools of frozen dung staining the cobbles brown and yellow. There was no disguising the ugliness of this damp afternoon but hands must be shaken and condolences received before they made for Waverley House and the funeral tea.

Everyone had chipped in to make food for the guests. Crompton's Biscuits even provided traditional spice biscuits. The Chapel Ladies' Bright Hour were organising sandwiches, rolls and tray bakes for the usual suspects, who liked to have a nosy round and scoff anything going. Not that

Lily begrudged giving hospitality, but she sensed most of them were here because of the new arrivals.

Ivy was showing off little Neville in his velvet trousers and knitted jumper. The other toddlers were whipped out of sight for their nap and Esme was giving orders from her seat in the parlour: 'Concertina needs a nappy change...' She had that pained look etched into her jaw when her corsets were digging in too tightly but her eyes were dull with grief and shock.

Ana whipped up the child with a scowl. 'We say in Greece, husband's mother is cross all wife must bear,' Ana whispered to Susan. 'My Dina is not called Concertina.'

Lily pretended she had not heard as Walt made a beeline for Susan.

'Well, I never! This is the new Mrs Winstanley then? He beat us to the altar, Lil,' he winked as Susan lifted her finger so everyone could see.

'No, this is Cousin Cedric's widow from London,' Lily announced loudly.

'I never knew you had a cousin,' Walt continued. 'So that one over there's the bride,' he said, pointing his sausage roll at Ana. 'Blimey! I never thought Fred'd settle down with a copper knob, a ginger biscuit. Who'd a thowt it!' He burst out laughing but Lily wasn't amused. He plonked himself down in the softest chair by the fireside and got out his cigarettes. That would be him settled for the afternoon now.

Ivy was on the warpath, passing tongue sandwiches along a line of guests with that pained expression of hers, no doubt wishing she was a thousand miles away. Susan stood in the shadows looking awkward. This long-lost relative, dressed in her one decent silk blouse and thin skirt, was wearing Lily's borrowed cardigan, which smelled of mothballs. Ivy edged herself round the sides of the room as no one was bothering to talk to her. Esme was receiving condolences from the neighbours. Better then to make those girls useful clearing up plates to take to Polly in the kitchen. They were banging down the cups and saucers onto trays until Esme caught their eye.

'That's my best china you're cracking,' she muttered, turning to Lily. 'If you want any left over for your cabinet one day, I suggest you leave Polly to clear away. Take them upstairs, and what's all this I hear about you and Walt naming the big day?'

'That's the first I've heard of it,' she replied, puzzled. The two of them had scarcely passed two words on the subject for weeks. What was he playing at?

'I'm glad to hear it. A funeral is enough for my nerves, and with that lot upstairs to sort out... Is it hot in here?' Esme was fanning herself like fury. 'There's no brass to fork out on weddings yet. I'm not made of money, Lil. We need you here now.'

'I know, I know. I expect he was just trying to cheer you up,' she sighed. It was good that Walt was showing some initiative but he should have asked her first before blabbing about dates. Weddings were the last thing on her mind at the moment.

'The thought of you hitched up with that lazy loon over there gives me no cause for celebration,' Esme added.

'Oh, give it a rest! It's been a long day,' Lily snapped back, making for the stairs.

'Lily Winstanley, that's no way to talk to your mother!'

'Oh, shut up, all of you,' Lily muttered under her breath. There was only so much of her family she could stomach in one day.

Esme was trying to pin a smile on her face and look in control, but Lily's words were out of character. Giving cheek back like that! All this 'Family First' was exhausting, keeping up appearances and fending off awkward questions. Trust neighbours to smell something fishy going on, but she'd not give them the satisfaction. It was like being in the goal mouth, trying to parry off an attack. It needed everyone knowing their right position on the pitch, no gaps in the defence to let in a winning shot or an own goal.

She'd been touched to see so many of Freddie's old pals. She'd welcome any one of them on board their team, but not Walter, all fingers and thumbs. Lily had scored an own goal in choosing him. Why didn't she fancy one of the young Grasshoppers?

Esme kicked off her court shoes with relief and loosened her back suspenders. She'd put on a bit of weight since this outfit was made, a bit of middle-age spread, and it didn't suit her. Then she saw Pete Walsh heading in her direction, wobbling his tea cup, the Royal Doulton bone china looking in peril on its saucer.

'I'm glad I caught you, Mrs Winstanley,' smiled the tall young man with hands like boxing gloves. 'The lads and I want to thank you for the spread. You've done Freddie proud...' He hesitated. 'But I wonder if I could have a word as I'm a bit flummoxed.'

She ushered him into the bay window recess.

'You know that Susan? Well, someone said she was his cousin's wife from London, only when Freddie wrote to me from Burma, he *did* mention a Susan.' He paused, searching her face. 'It's not her, is it?'

Straight in the net like a cannon ball: one nil! She glanced to see if there were any onlookers.

'So you know about her then?' she whispered.

'He told me about her but not about the kiddy.' Pete looked her straight in the eye.

'What else did he tell you?'

He had the courtesy to blush, 'Just lads' talk and stuff...'

'I can guess,' she smiled. 'You've put me in an awkward position, young man.'

'My lips are sealed, Mrs Winstanley.'

'Who else knows the score?'

'Not a soul. I thought I'd better check it out first,' he said, showing a set of impressive straight teeth.

'I'd rather keep this in the family, Peter. Not a word to our Lil. She's enough on her plate.'

'Silent as the grave, I promise. Scout's honour,' he smiled, and he sidled away as Levi approached.

'You two were in a holy huddle. What did he want? I hope you asked him for tickets for the

Cup tie.'

'Just giving his condolences. He's a grand chap.'

'The boys were saying how good the foreigners' English was.' He winked and tapped his nose. 'Don't look like that. I gave them the party line. I told them they'd both had good sleeping dictionaries.'

'What's that supposed to mean, son?'

Levi chuckled. 'Well, let's put it this way, Mam, the closer you get to someone the quicker you learn. There was this German girl I knew who was fluent in Cockney when she got a Tommy boyfriend.'

'I don't want to know about consorting with the enemy.'

'What enemy?' asked Lily, suddenly at her shoulder.

'Never you mind. Just go and rattle some cups and show the guests the door. I'm whacked.'

'We did Freddie proud today, all of us,' said Lily.

'I wish he'd done the same to us, and that's the truth of it,' Esme sighed, feeling old and worn out. What a web of lies we weave... Perhaps she should tell Lil that Pete Walsh was in the know, perhaps not. They would just have to play the game as it unfolded now.

Ana couldn't wait for the last guest to leave. Susan went upstairs with the girls, who were covered in chocolate. Someone had brought them a treat. Lily's man was sitting in a chair chain-smoking, being waited on hand and foot on account of his bad back. Women were made for men, her mother once said, but this one was a greedy pig. He ate a plateful of biscuits at one go. The room was a fug of cigarette smoke. Ana finished her duties and went upstairs with relief.

She found Susan undressing Dina, who was bouncing with delight naked, and making a joyful din. It was the last straw.

'What you do with my baby?' she snapped.

'I'm getting them both ready for a bath. I will save you the trouble,' Su replied, putting up her fingers to peg her nose in disgust.

'She my baby ... I do that,' Ana insisted.

'Yes, but she is dirty and her bottom is red, you see?' Su answered.

'You fuss. She can wait, I am tired,' said Ana, furious. 'Leave her alone!'

'Sorry, Ana, I was trying to help you,' Su said, putting down the child, but Dina held up her arms and reached out for her, making matters worse.

'Don't. I no need help from you. She can wait,' she snapped, but Susan for once snapped back at her.

'Everything waits for you ... you are a lazy mother. You never wash under your arms, you smell and your baby smells. You stink this room out. I don't like to live with your smells.'

Ana sniffed her armpits. There was a stain under her blouse but she smelled of milk and woman. What was wrong about that? The blouse needed a wash but so what?

'I am clean. I washed yesterday. It is too cold to wash all over when the ice freezes the water. You

117

fuss,' she said, seeing with satisfaction the look on Su's face. 'You have plenty money for soap and new clothes.'

'That is none of your business. I am a British citizen. I know how to do things proper,' Su argued, brushing down her skirt and fiddling with her bracelet.

'Look at you. You all gold bangles and earrings. I have nothing.'

'That is not my fault. You make everyone sorry for you ... poor Ma Ana ... in a labour camp, a prisoner of war. How do we even know you speak the truth? You stole my Freddie. You told him lies too? I have had a bad time too. Why do you quarrel with me when I am trying to help you?' she shouted back at her. 'I have done nothing to you.'

'He think you dead. I not steal him, he was ripe for picking,' Ana argued, gathering the dirty clothes up in a huff of indignation. 'All these silk curtains you are hanging up – you shove your silk skirts in my face every day. You think you are number one wife. I have nothing and now you take my baby as well,' she sobbed.

'I try to help you but you do not like anything I do. You are one sorry lady, always moaning like the wind through the trees. It is cold and dark. It is cruel weather. I cannot help the weather in England. If you want sun go back to Greece. If you stay then pull up your socks and get on with job,' said Susan, folding her arms determinedly.

Lily was standing in the doorway listening, her eyes wide. 'What is going on?'

'What is all this pulling up of socks, Lily? I no

wear socks. It is too cold. I have only one pair of stockings and if I pull them they tear. Then I have nothing on my legs. I have no clothing coupons,' Ana sobbed.

Susan shook her head and smiled. 'It is a typical English saying. It means you grit your teeth and smile when you are hurting inside. No one wants to see your hurts. The British want you to get on with "jolly good show", go to work and keep the train on the track no matter what happens,' she slowed her words so that Ana could understand. 'Forget your troubles and try harder. Troubles pass like walking by fire, you have to walk through smoking darkness with a stiff upper lip and no tears, until you see blue sky again. "Keep Right On to the End of the Road" – we sang that song on the long march out of Burma.'

'But there is no blue sky in Grimbleton. It is all fog and grey clouds, smoking gun chimneys and sulphur. Where has the sun gone, Lily?' Ana wept, turning from Su in disgust. 'I no speak to her any more. She is dead. Freddie say she is dead. She tell stories.'

'So you think I am a liar, that Joy is not his girl? You tell her, Lily, you tell her she smell! I am used to sweat and heat and warm sun, the heavy warm rain of the Monsoon weather but this is where we are and we must be grateful, Ma Ana, grateful for a roof over our heads that does not leak, food at the table. Daw Esme does not turn us away. We must give respect to dragon mother. She is sad. She has lost a son and we have our beautiful daughters,' Susan shouted. 'In death we have life, that is what the vicar tell us.'

119

Ana stared down at the face of the tiny woman with delicate cheekbones and flashing eyes. 'How you be so still like boat on a lake, no ripples?' she asked. 'You have no tears. You not honour the dead.'

'Oh, yes, I do! I went on living when all around me were dying. Here is a better life for me. The Japanese bombed our beautiful cities. It was a terrible time. I trekked to India with my family through the jungle. I will not talk about the time of walking bones and skellingtons, when we ate roots and drank water from leaves. I saw terrible things too, many die. What do you know? Better forget what is past. We shall make the best of living here, I know.' She paused and gave a big sigh. 'When it is cold and dark I think of blossom on trees, orchids and perfume of jasmine flowers. I think of spices and making *balachan* pickle with my mother. Her spirit looks down on me with kindness. She expects me to behave like a good Anglo-Burmese so I will. I have Joy and she is my sunshine. I will make sure she walks in sunlight always. We have a friend in Lily, who looks after us all. Then it is not so bad.'

'This is bad! I wanna go home but how can I go home with no husband and a girl child? I have no dowry. Who will wed me now? There is nothing but war amongst my country and ruined towns. There is nothing for me there but starvation.'

'Then we make our own sunshine, Ma Ana,' Su said, passing Dina back into her arms. 'Come, the bath water will be cold and the snake woman will shout at us again.'

'I don't want bath. I want fresh tomatoes

120

warmed by the midday sun, the golden oil of olives ripe in the heat of the afternoon. I want to sit with a glass of retsina, watching the oleanders swaying in the evening breeze. How can I have any of that here?' she replied.

'The Bible says, ask and you shall receive, seek and ye shall find...' said Su.

'You believe that if I pray to holy St Aristaeus my dream will come?' Ana looked up in amazement. How could a Greek saint perform miracles so far away?

'It is written in the Holy Word. Everything comes to him who waits,' added Susan.

'How long I wait?'

'As long as it takes.'

'You talk riddles to me,' Ana snapped.

'I am trying to help you lift up your socks,' Su replied with flashing eyes. 'There you go again, moan, moan. What shall we do with this miserable bag of bones with baggy bosoms?'

'You are a selfish pig. You think you are better than me with your fat baby,' Ana snapped back. 'I not speak to you again, ever...'

'My baby is beautiful. Tell her, Miss Lily.' Su looked for support but Lily had beat a hasty retreat downstairs.

'What on earth is that racket going on upstairs?' said Esme as they tidied away the remnants of the funeral tea: soiled napkins and crumbs, a forgotten umbrella and gloves. 'Go and see to it, Lil, I'm done in.'

'I've been up once. Better to just let them sort it out like squabbling children,' she replied, too weary to want more conflict.

'And what would you know about that?' Esme snapped.

'A pack of noisy seven-year-old Brownies teaches you enough. If I chased after all their fallings-in and -out, we'd never get a badge done. Better to let them sort themselves out.'

'But they're mothers, not children…'

'Then you go and sort them out,' Lily replied. It was all so tiresome.

'I don't like your attitude these days. We never had this before—'

'We never had to deal with Freddie's girlfriends and babies either. Everything's changing.'

'They can't stay here for ever. It's like Manchester Piccadilly, all comings and goings, and you'll want them on their way if there's a wedding to plan.'

'You won't send them away, will you?' The thought of her mother chucking them out was real now.

'Oh, it can wait a while longer,' Esme replied, not wanting another argument. 'Family first and foremost, after all.'

'Ana is crying 'cos she's cold and the food is strange. She wants olive oil and a taste of home, just a bit of comfort.'

'Well, she'll have to want. This is Grimbleton. What's the olive oil for? Is she sick?'

'They cook with it in Greece and in the Bible lands too.'

'What's wrong with lard?'

'Don't ask me. She's homesick.'

'Then she can go home on the next boat and

solve one of our problems.'

'But little Dina, your own granddaughter – why must she suffer?'

'I can't think about that now,' came Esme's reply. 'My head is throbbing with all that talking. At least they've shut up now.'

'I expect they're not talking to each other. The silence is deafening.'

'So what would a Brown Owl do about that?'

Lily smiled. 'Sit them down side by side and see what it's all about, I suppose.'

'What's stopping you? Go to it!'

'Not tonight, Mother. I've had enough for one day. Walt and me have hardly passed the time of day. I miss Freddie too, but the man they talk about isn't the brother I remember. How many more girls did he make promises to? How many more seeds did he scatter?'

'Don't talk ill of the dead, lass. They can't answer back.'

'I'm not so sure about that. I think our Freddie has left us quite a few messages one way and another...'

For two days Ana and Su stomped about in silent protest, speaking politely only when spoken to. For two days everyone tiptoed around them as they glared at each other, hissing like angry snakes. When Su went right, Ana went left, in and out of the house like weather girls in a cuckoo clock, coxing and boxing.

Then there was Ivy and Levi, dodging the flak, and Esme trying to ignore them. Lily was at her wits' end. Should she intervene or stay silent, bang their heads together or go out and get on with her busy life and leave them to come to? Waverley House, big as it was, couldn't contain all the warring factions, or keep the nosy neighbours from prying.

A house divided falls apart, Lily mused. It was time to stand in the firing line and say her piece, but why did it have to be her?

Don't be a marshmallow, be a nut cracknel, she decided, gathering her courage. Let them all chew on that!

7

The Olive Oil Hunt

It was the children who brought the feud to an end. Placid little Joy began clambering to be picked up and fussed while Su was busy tidying the bedroom clutter.

'Lazy slut, she never helps me,' Su muttered loudly whilst picking up scattered clothing. 'How Freddie made a baby with her...'

'I not listen. She think she is Queen of England. I not listen.'

Joy began to cry and that set Dina howling.

'Now look what you've done!'

Lily knew it was now or never. 'Girls, girls, this has to stop right now,' she barked in her sharpest Brown Owl voice. 'What is the matter with you? If I can help I will, but this must stop. The business with my brother nothing can change, but sit down like ladies and let us clear the air.' She pointed to the bed and the basket chair.

'All she talks about is olive oil. What is so important about olive oil? She cries and beats her breast and upsets my Joy,' said Su.

'I think Ana is sad, yes?' Lily turned to the Cretan girl. 'You want to go home? Yes?'

'Yes ... óchi ... I not know.' Ana looked up with tears in her eyes.

'No one is stopping her going to her island. I am sick of this beautiful island with olive trees, oranges and melons. It makes me hungry,' Su responded.

'No go back. Village is bombed. No one there.' Ana shook her head, and Lily wondered what it must be like to have no family at all. Whatever she thought of her own, she couldn't imagine not having anyone left at all.

'I lose family too. There is just Auntie Betty but I will not go back, never. Here is the best place for my Joy.'

'A girl with baby and no man not go back to Crete. All the men are dead. I bring shame on family name,' Ana sobbed.

'Don't be so sorry for yourself.' Su was losing patience again. 'You have made it safely to England. You are lucky.'

'But my sister... How I say it ... soldiers come from sky like falling umbrellas to fight Tommies in the fields. We shoot them down like birds. My brother Stelios hide in the hills and Eleni takes food and guns strapped to her legs. Many Tommies are hit and we hide them in houses. The doctor at Red Cross show me how to tie up

125

bleeding and keep them safe. Then the Germans march into village and search all the houses, smash our door, push us outside. We line up in square and they take the men away. They turn to see if women hide guns. They tear our shirts and shame us. Eleni have big mark on her shoulder from shooting gun, the pressing make a mark. They take her too. I have no mark on my shoulder, I am not taken.

'My mama is screaming and we follow to where they take them. They tie their hands and shoot them and leave them in the sun. My beautiful sister is lying there. The flies buzz over her. How I go back now?'

Lily felt sick just picturing the scene. 'You did your best. No one blames you, Ana.'

The girl shook her head. 'I feel bad inside. Everyday I feel bad. When I run in the hills and down into the town, I think of her. I help in the hospital. I see terrible things...'

Lily sat beside her trying to comfort her.

'Terrible things happened in the jungle too,' said Su. 'My cousin stayed to help wounded soldiers and bring them to the border crossing. They caught him and tied him to a tree and stuck bayonets in his belly. I heard cries over and over in my head, ashamed that I am alive and he is dying and ashamed how much I want to live. A girl must flee the Japanese. They like fair-skinned girls to send to whorehouses. I have to run away but it is over now. We have to look forward.'

Ana nodded and wiped her eyes.

'Soon Dina will walk like Joy and talk proper English like the lady on the wireless,' Su offered.

126

'No, she will talk Greek,' Ana replied.

'What for?'

'So she knows who she is: Konstandina Eleni.'

'That name makes her foreign. Dina is better, like the film star Dina Durbin.'

'Who is Dina Durbin?' said Ana, turning to Lily.

'I think she means Deanna Durbin, the Hollywood star.'

'Huh! Deanna, Diana, Dina – all the same pretty name,' sniffed Su. 'An English name. She must be a proper English girl. You are in England now so why do you need olive oil?'

Ana looked up and smiled. 'Oh, no. You cannot live without the olive tree. We crush the fruit into golden oil. I just want to smell it and touch it one more time before I die. It is the oil of life, oil of the Gods...'

'There she goes again! There is plenty of time before you die,' Su snapped.

Here we go again indeed, Lily sighed, just when things were calming down. 'I've got some Palmolive soap.'

'Tommy soldiers use the oil for piles on bottom,' Ana grimaced. 'All they want is chips, chips, chips.'

'If it's piles troubling you ... we can try the chemist, love, the pharmacy? Timothy White's or Boots will do. It's too cold to grow olives in this country. We did have some little bottles on our stall before the war,' Lily chipped in.

'How can you cook without olive oil? We have big pot in the corner of kitchen. Creta oil is best in world. Does pharmacopia have some for me?'

127

'We could go and find out,' Lily offered with a twinkle in her eye.

'Will you come with us?' Ana asked with shyness in her voice.

'If you wish, we will all go together in search of this golden oil and stockings. I will buy you a new pair to put a smile on your face,' said Su.

'If it's stockings you are after, try the Market Hall. Levi knows someone who sells them without coupons ... but don't say I told you or Ivy will have my guts for garters,' Lily added.

'Guts and garters – where can we buy these things?' giggled Su.

Ana shrugged her shoulders. It was going to take a long time for them to learn the subtleties of the local lingo, and they'd need a referee for all their fallings-out, but at least the pair of them were agreeing on something. Perhaps a joint expedition into town would be a good place to start.

It snowed all night, to Lily's dismay. The morning after, Susan was in the back garden screaming with delight.

'Look! Look, Ana, Christmas card snow!' she screamed, scattering the powdery white with her shoes like a child.

The girls were going into town for the first time. Perhaps the trip would be better postponed for another day, but they were already kitted out for the weather.

The sky was heavy with more snow to come and everyone was out in the back field, jumping, making tracks in the snow and throwing snowballs while the babies toddled and Neville shrieked in delight.

'This is not proper snow,' Ana declared. 'In Germany it was as high as a house.' But even she was racing around, helping to roll snow into a huge scrunching ball.

Lily fell backwards, flat out with her arms outstretched. 'I'm making a snow angel.' Soon Su and Ana joined her, lying in a line like paper cutouts, holding hands.

'Get up at once!' screamed Ivy from the back gate. 'Don't make an exhibition of yourselves. What will the neighbours think?'

'That we're having a jolly good time,' Lily yelled back. 'Don't be stuffy. Neville's fine.'

Ivy clomped through the snow in her gumboots and snatched her child away. He kicked her and struggled so she fell onto the freezing ground in a heap.

'Now look what you've done!'

Serves you right, thought Lily, but she bit her lip. They needed Ivy's big pram for the outing to town.

Lily was accompanying them, to keep the truce and make sure they could navigate the streets into town. The little ones were muffled against the chill and topped and tailed in the large bucket pram, a blue Silver Cross and Ivy's pride and joy. It had taken Lily hours to get this concession from her. Time to go inside and sweeten her up again.

Esme lent Ana a pair of galoshes but Su's feet were so tiny that she wore overshoes that fitted over her bootees.

They picked their way down the pavements, sometimes walking in the road where the kerb was piled high with black slush, over cobbles that rattled the pram springs, making a jiggling ride for the children. It was a slippery downhill slide towards the town centre from the better end of Division Street, past the tannery and Magellan's Foundry, the railway station and over a slippery wooden footbridge. The cold wind stung their cheeks and Lily was glad of thick knitted mittens over her chilblained fingers.

In her pocket was a list from Esme and instructions for Levi from Ivy. Could she risk leaving the two girls alone while she covered for Levi on the stall? They had the price of a cup of tea and a bun each, and were told not to dawdle on the way home for it would get dark early and there might be more snow.

'It's madness letting those two out by themselves,' said Ivy. 'I don't want them hanging around the market, making an exhibition of themselves... You'll have to keep an eye on them, Lil. I don't trust them.'

'We can't keep them cooped up out of sight like prisoners of war,' Lily argued. 'Have a heart. Don't you think that two women who've faced jungle and mountains, prison and interrogation, lived by their wits, scavenging for food and shelter in makeshift tents and first-aid posts, can find their way around Grimbleton without us sending out a search party?'

'I don't know why you're getting so pally with them all of a sudden. I'm sure Walt's not enamoured with all the fuss you make of them,'

Ivy sneered. There was a mean glint in her eye. Whatever Levi saw in this woman was a mystery. Why did she have to rub the sore spot on Lily's conscience that since Freddie's wives arrived there was no time to run round after him like before? If she could split herself in two it would help – no, make it three counting the market stall.

Before Freddie's memorial service, the last time she had made the effort to call into Bowker's Row, Walt was down the pub and she sat all evening listening to the rumblings of poor Elsie Platt's stomach and fending off all her questions about the new arrivals. That thought reminded her to make up a peppermint tisane for Elsie's indigestion.

It was not as if she was deliberately avoiding her future husband and mother-in-law, but it seemed important to keep Freddie's affairs strictly within the family and Walt wasn't family, not yet. Elsie could fish all night but Lily wasn't rising to the bait.

The pavements were clearer in the town but the pram was splashed by trams and buses and children throwing snowballs on their way home from school. They sauntered through the shopping parade, looking in all the windows, but there was nothing to see but cardboard pictures of stock and notices for coupons. How many they would need. They found their way to the outdoor market stalls where the men shouted across the aisles and Ana smiled.

'It is like *agora* in Canea where village people sell eggs and fruit, honey and chickens.'

131

Here there were only potatoes and roots, and not many of them. No fruit, no eggs, no honey, but further on there were stalls selling cotton material, stripes and spots and plain colours by the yard.

'I make pretty dress for Joy,' said Su, shoving through the crowd, picking over the fabric remnants in a basket and barging into the fray. 'And Dina.'

'I make lace for them,' Ana added, not wanting to be outdone, digging into the basket too.

'Here, you lot ... wait your bleedin' turn!' shouted one irate shopper in a woolly checked headscarf.

Su looked up, surprised. 'There is no queue,' she smiled sweetly.

'And which jungle did you come out of?' the woman retorted. 'Go back to where you came from! We don't want your sort in our country!'

'But I am British, like you,' Su said, puzzled by her outburst.

'Pull the other one! I don't see many your colour in my street,' the woman laughed. She turned to Ana, seeing her all muffled up. 'And you don't want to be hanging about with darkies, young lady, not if you want to get on in this town.'

'*Parakaló?* Please, no understand.' Ana stared at the stranger.

'Hell's bells! Two of them as bad as each other... You'd better learn some proper English. We don't want you sort round here!'

Lily rushed over, red in the face. 'Take no notice of her, she's just a rude old biddy!'

''Ere, who are you calling old?' came the reply, but Lily was already guiding the girls quickly out of earshot. Perhaps they weren't so safe in town as she had thought.

There was a wet fish stall, which was closed, and a butcher selling scrag end bits. Finally Ana found a bag of pot herbs, green, red and white bits of herbs, and sniffed it. The stall woman looked at them with suspicion.

'Nowt wrong with my stuff,' she called out.

Ana nodded politely. 'I just like smell,' she said, and they walked away.

They were fingering everything and then putting it back, making Lily pink with embarrassment. Everyone was staring at them. 'We don't touch before we buy,' she suggested.

'How do you find a good chicken if you do not smell it?' said Susan.

'Chicken is for Christmas, if you're lucky. We've not had one for years, just scraggy potboilers from the allotment. You have to get what you're given here.' Lily tried to explain how food shortages were hitting both shops and customers.

'War is over. Why no chickens, no eggs, no fruit?' Ana shook her head. 'England is poor country now. Poor Lily. At home we have chickens and eggs and fruit – oranges, lemons, cherries in our yard – but Jerry steal all food on the island though we hid oil in caves and bury food in hills. They bring dogs to find it.'

'You have sun and so things grow quickly.' Lily tried to explain how damp and cold and long the winters were. 'We have to eat food that keeps us warm: potatoes and stew and hot soup.'

133

'I don't like that,' Susan said, looking at the stalls. 'It makes plenty ladies fat, but not you, Lily. You are a bamboo pole.'

Lily was not sure if that was a compliment or not.

The search for olive oil took them to three chemists, all to no avail. 'No call for that here,' an assistant said, pointing to castor oil and ointments. 'What's yer trouble?'

'She wants to cook with it,' Su said, and the assistant stared at Lily as if they were mad.

'We cook with lard and dripping,' the lady explained, shouting as if they were all deaf. 'Oil is for engines and rusty iron.'

'But we cook meat with olive oil, and make soap.' Ana was puzzled.

'This is England, not the Continent. I've got a bar of Palmolive,' smiled the chemist. 'Will that do?'

They dawdled down to the indoor Market Hall, a huge vaulted building with wrought-iron rafters and a glass roof. The stalls were dotted around the floor in ovals divided into four, with canvas curtains they could pull round at night. There was that oh-so-familiar smell to welcome them.

'We will find oil in here,' said Ana determinedly. 'It smells of market.'

There were clothing stalls and delicatessens, grocery stalls and millinery, sweet stalls and pastry makers, and tucked in the middle was Winstanleys, with a big poster on the back advertising: 'BLISS. NATIVE HERBS. The great purifying kidney and liver regulator. Herbal medicine vendors for 100 years.' Levi was standing in

134

a white coat as if he were directing traffic, while a little woman in a striped overall darted hither and thither at his command.

'Now then, Enid, come and meet the two Mrs Winstanleys,' he winked.

Lily was getting tired of his insinuations but smiled politely at the little woman with iron curls clipped around her head so tight she looked like a pinwheel. Enid Greenalgh helped out when Lil wasn't around, and knew the contents of each box of remedies better than anyone.

'Pleased to meet you... Dreadful news about Fred,' she whispered to Lil. 'Which one is the widow? He was allus one for a lark. It were a right good turnout for the memorial. It was the best that could be done with such a sad do...' She paused, looking at both the girls with sympathy. 'And them so young to be widows. I do know what it's like. My Harry went west at Passchendaele ... sad job all round,' she sighed. 'Are you staying long?'

Levi was quick to jump in with a, 'Just till they get settled ... bit of a shock all round. Can I help you ladies or are you on a sightseeing trip to view the natives at work?' he quipped.

'Ana is looking for olive oil,' Lily replied, searching the shelves.

Levi looked as if they had asked for diamonds. 'Ooh ... no, no. Not had any in for months. Can't get that sort of stuff yet, not since before the war. I can give you Macassar oil or beechnut oil, but that tastes like engine cleaner. There's castor oil to clear your system but no olive oil. Sorry, there's no call for it. Some of our lads saw a bit

135

too much of that stuff in Italy ... you know how it is. They want fish and chips and lard. You could try Szymanski's, the stall the Poles go to. They sell foreign stuff or you could ask the Eyeties at Santini's. I bet they use it on their hair.'

Lily hadn't thought about Santini's. That might be just the place to try.

'You'll find them by the King's Theatre,' she offered. 'Out of the door, turn left and up towards the church. I'll come and join you later.'

'Don't you go telling Mother and Ivy you're into fancy cooking. They like stuff plain and NO garlic. It smells the place out.' Levi tapped his nose in mock conspiracy and Lil felt like hitting him. If ever someone needed taking down a peg or two it was him. Brother and sister they might be, but they had no common ground, not since he came home and took over the management as if he was cock of the midden. It was sad he wasn't the big brother she'd had as a kid. And she didn't like the way he was eyeing Su as if she was a piece of pork tenderloin.

By now Joy was fighting over 'Precious Teddy' and wanting to get out of the pram for a toddle, being nearly a year older than Dina.

'They've got their hands full,' smiled Enid. 'As it is their first outing, you should go with them and I'll hold the fort. I've got my sandwiches in my tin box.'

'But it's your break, love,' Lily replied, knowing how desperate she herself got to get off the stall on quiet mornings.

'I'm fine here, honest.'

Enid was one of life's givers, Lil thought. If only

136

there were more of them in the world. Meanwhile Susan had found the stocking bar and was negotiating for a pair of lisle stockings. She was gathering an audience of onlookers, transfixed by her golden skin and exotic looks. They stood staring at her silk scarf with tassels, the colour of peacocks' tails.

'My friend here is a refugee, a relative of the Winstanleys. She has no stockings without holes. We have money. We can buy some from you, yes?' she ordered like a pukka memsahib.

Shirley, the stall owner, was all fluffed up in an angora jumper in traffic light stripes. She shook her head until Lily sidled up to her and whispered in her ear. Then she ferreted underneath the counter and shoved something into a paper bag.

'You tell Levi that is one book he owes me now. I can't keep doing him favours.' She shot a glance in his direction, patting her hair.

Susan paid for the goods and shoved them under the pram top.

'Thanks, Shirley, love. We owe you,' Lily whispered. It was embarrassing to find out just how many coupons Levi was squandering at that stall. Ivy was behind it, she must be.

'Come on, we'll find Santini's, one last try and then home before dark,' she smiled, guiding the big blue baby barge out of the hall as they launched forth once more on their quest. Everyone was tired and thirsty and ready for a sit-down. Santini's ice-cream parlour was sandwiched between the theatre and the cinema in Kirkgate, with an alley on the other side.

Just to say the word 'Santini's' was to conjure up a world all of its own, snug and warm, buzzing with chattering shoppers, an oasis where the weary of Grimbleton could rest aching legs, smoke, sipping steaming mugs of Bovril, tea or dip a spoon into an ice-cream soda.

There was no room for a pram so they lifted out the infants and put it outside the window. They stood waiting for a corner seat until someone got up to leave. There was a smell of cigar smoke and chicory, the clink of the sugar spoon chained to the table. The tables were wiped clean by a waitress with satiny black hair tied with a scarf, gypsy fashion, around her curls, who darted in and round the bar like a black beetle, while the owner, with a black moustache and greased-back hair, kept the orders coming. It was going to be a long wait for service. Perhaps, Lily thought, she should leave them here and go back to relieve Enid on the stall?

There was always a buzz and a certain smell. She could hear the rattle of Italian being shouted in the back kitchen and the operatic voice of someone singing while they worked. The ice cream came in coloured glasses with fruit syrup on the top and golden wafers stuck at an angle. Ana ordered a scoop in a glass of fizzy pop to share with Dina, but the others ordered hot cocoa to warm themselves through.

'Isn't it cold enough outside?' Su laughed.

'I want to shut my eyes and dream of hot summers. There was bar on Canea harbour. Italians made the best ice-cream sundae in Crete, all the colours of the rainbow. I see "*la volta*" – the evening parade – when everybody walk and show off their clothes ... before the war come and spoil it. You try it?' Ana sighed, waving her spoon in the air like a sword.

Lily dipped her spoon in the ice to savour the moment. It tasted of cornflour and tinned milk, not much else, but it was sweet and gritty and there were ice particles clinging to her tongue. It would do. 'Very nice but very cold.'

Joy was in raptures at the taste.

Ana's breasts were beginning to leak. She needed to nurse and opened her blouse, but Susan gasped, 'You can't do that in here! It is not done in a public place to open your titties to view. Is it, Miss Lily?'

'I have no choice or I leak all over blouse. No one can see. I tuck her into my coat, look. She is happy. I am dry. Everybody happy,' Ana said.

'You are so Greek,' Su replied, trying to distract Joy with the spoon, but Joy was watching, alert, and began to tug her own shirt open. 'Now look what you've done. Dina is too old for the breast milk. She is a big girl. I used a bottle, more hygienic and polite. We do like the British ladies in Burma.'

'British have no time for baby,' Ana snapped. 'They wrap them up and put them out of sight. They do not take them out at night. They like only quiet babies. Here it is like home,' Ana argued. 'I like it here.'

'I thought you were enemies, Italy and Greece?' Lily asked, knowing a little about the conflict between the two countries.

'I hate Mussolini and his men but I have friends

in Canea. Many Italians were my friends. The war is over now. We are all far from home,' Ana sighed, sucking the dregs of the soda, trying not to slurp.

'I hate Japanese, all of them,' said Su, rising quickly.

The truce was over. It was time to pay their bill and gather up the hats and mittens. It was going to be a long journey uphill before nightfall.

When they got outside, it was snowing lightly and the pram was nowhere to be seen. They all looked at each other with horror.

'Oh no!'

Only the tracks of its wheels, disappearing down the dark alley to the side of the theatre, were visible, tracks fast covering over with snow.

8

Maria

There was a kerfuffle in the doorway as they tripped back through the entrance of Santini's shouting, 'The pram's gone! Our shopping is gone!'

'Anyone see pram go walking?' pleaded Susan, her English collapsing with emotion. Lil was trying to hold on to both children, while feeling sick.

There was much staring out of the steamed-up windows, and shaking of heads, but little action.

After the sympathies no one was showing much interest except the waitress, who came running at once.

'Can I help?' she asked, seeing the panic on their faces.

'While we came in for a drink, our pram was stolen,' Lily explained.

'Now Daw Esme will shout,' Susan butted in, all of a tremble, her eyes wide like jet coat buttons, full of fear.

'And stockings. I have no stockings,' sobbed Ana.

'A cup of tea is what you need ... on the house,' said the young waitress.

'What is on the house?' Susan asked.

One of the regulars, who was blowing cigarette smoke into their faces, winked, 'Free, *gratis*, cost you nowt, love. A good 'un is Maria, allus on top of the job.'

'Shutta that flannel, Percy, 'snot for you... *Capisci?* He can buy his own cuppa,' came the reply from the counter. 'That man sit all afternoon with his teacake until pub opens. If I seen you with pram, I warn you. Leave nothing with four wheels outside shop in centre of town unless it is chained with lock. You stay warm in here, Maria will sort you out.' She scurried to the boiler and made a cup of tea for each of them.

'All my shopping and Ivy's pram, oh dear, oh dear!' Susan shook her head, trembling.

'Far away in back street, long gone,' shouted the waitress from over the bar. 'No good people, pickpockets, nick spoons off table till we chain them down, toilet paper from washroom and

141

soap, ashtrays ... all disappear. Anything not stuck down, it walk.' She shrugged her shoulders. 'Now war is over, it is all cheating. No one care. It is all looking after number one.'

'It's just the pram's not ours. We borrowed it for the day,' Lily sighed, knowing it was gone for good and it was all her fault. They were not used to taking it into town. Neville was pushed only to the local shops and the park.

'How can we go back with nothing? It is getting dark and so cold. I am Susan,' said Su, holding out her hand. 'Susan Winstanley, and she is Ana Winstanley. This is kind sister, Lily Winstanley.'

'*Bene*... All you Winstanley girls no worry. I find my brother-in-law, Angelo. He bring taxi and take you home, *pronto*. I am Maria, Maria Santini,' she smiled back with a warmth that made Lily feel slightly better.

'We've no money left for a taxi, I'm afraid,' Lily explained, embarrassed to be caught short. With shopping and paying for the drinks, she had just a few coppers left.

'You pay me later. My fault I am not warning you. You must always keep pram in sight. So many *bambini* since war and not many prams. Are you visiting?' Maria asked.

'We came to find our husbands but he is killed. We bring our girls to see Winstanley,' Susan lied. 'I am the widow of a cousin down south, come for funeral, didn't I?' She looked to Lily for support.

Lily flushed. The poor girl was doing her best to sound convincing but her heart wasn't in it.

'I'm sure Mrs Santini doesn't want to know all

142

our sad business, Susan. I'd better go and get the van from Levi and collect you later.'

She rose as if to leave but Maria darted forward, almost pushing her down. 'You sit. You all have shock. Sit and drink tea.'

It was not that Maria Santini didn't love a drama to break up a long afternoon serving sodas and sundaes, cups of tea and hot Bovril, but her husband was home from hospital and it was not one of his better days, and now there were these three women to sort out.

'Maria! What are you doing?' She could hear a plaintive cry from the top of the stairs.

'Marco! Don't you strain yourself! I'm coming soon,' she yelled back. Leaving him to play with little Rosaria for a few minutes until Nonna Valentina took over in the flat was too exhausting.

Enzo was a lazy boy in the kitchen and she didn't trust him at the till. Not all the Santinis were as honest and hardworking as she was, or feared the wrath of her mother-in-law. They were Nonna Valentina's sons and grandsons, and could get away with anything. Maria was only an in-law.

There was something familiar in the faces of the foreign girls, something she recognised so well: that wide-eyed look of strangers in a foreign land, cold, conspicuous, unsure of the lingo, straining to understand. It was cruel to give them tea but the coffee was not much better, milky and weak.

It was only a few years ago that it had been Maria's own fate; brought over from Palermo by

Nonna Valentina to marry Marco, a distant cousin, the youngest of the Santini brothers. She was soon put to work behind the counter, in the kitchen; one of a succession of brides and cousins expected to cook, clean, have many *bambini* and keep the ice-cream parlour up to scratch while the men expanded their growing empire. The war had changed everything when they were interned for being aliens but the good people of Grimbleton missed their ice creams and made a fuss, bringing them all home.

Marco went to war and now he was upstairs wheezing, not fit to be out of the sanatorium. Rosaria spent her waking hours with Nonna Valentina, or sometimes in the kitchen. She sat in her high chair supervising the preparations with an eagle eye, but it was good for her to see something of her daddy.

'Come and meet my Marco while you wait,' Maria said, taking the tray out to the three women. 'You meet my Rosaria.'

'Thank you,' said the English girl with slumped shoulders, who towered above her. 'We don't want to be a bother.'

'You no bother. Come up the stairs and meet my Marco. It is good for him to have company...'

'Marco, I have a surprise. Poor ladies lost their pram – no-good thieving scum again. You talk to them while I finish orders,' she smiled, ushering them up the wooden stairs to the rooms above, which looked out across at the King's Theatre. 'Susan, Ana and Lily Winstanley ... meet my husband.'

He shuffled forward like an old man. The

144

trousers hung off his buttocks, once firm and strong. His face was ashen but his eyes were still black as coal and his hair smooth as jet.

'I ring Angelo for taxi,' Maria smiled. 'Find *bambini* biscuits in the tin.' It was time to leave them and clatter downstairs. 'You tell them all about us. How your papa and mama come to England for better life. That will keep them entertained.'

After the mix-up all their sons were proud to be called up, for they were British citizens. Now Valentina, the Widow Santini, hovered over them all like an avenging angel. Antonio was running the local billiard hall and American bar. Angelo owned two taxis and a private charabanc coach. Marco ran the ice-cream parlour and the horse and cart selling cones around the parks.

Angelo had failed his medical. Toni did his duty and Marco got a direct hit in his chest on D-Day, coming home a physical wreck. He now spent his time out on the moors in the Moses Heights sanatorium, trying to breathe and gather strength.

There were plenty of grandsons helping run the place but none of them was Maria's son. Rosaria was born prematurely when everyone despaired of the two of them ever producing a child to satisfy Santini honour. Marco was proud and everyone was happy.

Now Maria had to work all hours to keep body and soul together and give Marco the comforts he craved.

During the war the making of real ice cream was forbidden, but the Santinis devised ices made from condensed milk and sweeteners, flavoured with fruit syrups that passed regulations. There were four other rival establishments in the town, all touting for business on the streets, but everyone knew Santini's ices were the best. Thank goodness Lancashire folk liked their ice cream in cornets and wafers, sundaes and floating on fizzy pop.

'I scream, you scream, we all scream for Santini ice cream' was painted on the side of many a horse-drawn cart.

Santini's had the finest site in town, a café squashed between the Regal Cinema and the King's Theatre, with some of the better shops and the parish church close by. It was handy for the theatre queues, audiences nipping in for cones between shows, parades, afternoon shopping. It was a good place for an evening rendezvous, to wait for buses and within easy reach of several pubs.

Children came for knickerbocker glories when they came to see the pantomime, and theatricals called in for snacks between shows. Maria made it her business to know who was in town in Grimbleton, and Angelo got business from her customers. She was training up Enzo, one of Antonio's sons, in the back kitchen but he needed watching. Without a son of her own, Enzo would be expected to take over the parlour when he was a man.

'*Ragazza* for the kitchen, *ragazzo* for the business – girls for the kitchen, boys for the business' Pepe's old rule held in the family and Maria was not proper family until she produced a son. Nonna Valentina Santini had made that clear enough.

Maria and Marco lived above the shop in the flat on the top floor. It was just two rooms and a kitchen where she grabbed a few precious hours with little Rosa before finishing the shift as a cleaner in the King's Theatre to earn some extra money. It was lucky that she didn't need much sleep. Being busy kept her from thinking about the past and Marco's deteriorating condition.

Every Saturday she lit a candle in the Catholic chapel of Our Lady of Sorrows, pleading on her knees for an angel to wake Padre Pio of Pietrelcina from his dreaming so that the blessed healer of the sick would work a miracle on Marco's smashed lungs.

She was young and fit and lonely. Marco was tired and weak, without hope, and she felt more like a widow than a wife. It was not his fault that he could no longer make love to her. They still tried but it was hopeless, and Marco cried in her arms every time. Rosaria was a miracle, a gift from God that neither had ever dreamed would happen.

Their marriage was so brief, separated by war and now sickness. At the weekend he came home if he was well enough but his weeks were spent up on Moses Heights in the sanatorium with glass windows and doors flung open to the four winds.

She would take the bus after work and wave little Rosa to him through the window, leaving her to sleep on a bench while they spent a few minutes chatting about all the goings-on, trying not to let him know how she was coping without him, trying not to worry him. He was growing weaker, his eyes were often misted over with sadness.

147

She felt so guilty to be relieved when the visiting bell rang and she could escape back to the bustle of the town away from his sickness.

On Saturday Angelo fetched him home for the night and they cooked a special meal to celebrate.

Sunday nights, after Angelo picked him up, were the worst. There was no café, no theatre crowds, no cinema queues. The town fell silent and she was so alone. Sometimes then she felt like a bird trapped in a cage, a silent canary whose heart was bursting with song yet whose throat was choked so not a note could come. That was when the loneliness stalked up her stairs and rattled at her door. Only being busy took her mind from such fears.

It was not as if she didn't love the ice-cream parlour. It was her own living opera, in which all the dramas of life unfolded before her. It was a cosmopolitan haven in this northern cotton town. The walls were plastered with autographed photos of stars of the music halls, theatre, ballet companies, all the stars who had trod the boards of the King's over the years: Charlie Chaplin in Fred Karno's Circus, the Lupinos, George Formby, Ben Lyon and Bebe Daniels, Nosmo King, Izzy Bonn and Richard Tauber; all the greats had stepped inside their parlour for a snack.

She loved to creep up into the sixpenny gods, the topmost balcony of the theatre, to see the finales of musicals and operas.

Sometimes she stared at those stars on her walls with faraway eyes. If only she had had her

148

chance to dance and sing, to make music in costumes in the limelight, shine in the footlights. She loved the sad ballets and operas, the dying maidens, the star-crossed lovers; all that drama of life and death unfolding before her into a climax of passion, the soaring orchestra, the tears and the silence. Then the National Anthem was played and everyone rushed out, leaving her to the empty theatre, the smell of stale ale and cigarettes, all passion spent.

It was better than any cinema screen to see actors in the flesh. Some stars would chat to her at the stage door. They looked so ordinary without their face paint, muffled in headscarves and trilby hats, creeping back to their digs for the night. Some went straight next door to the Bear and Staff to drink away their wages, then stagger out, waking her in the small hours. She knew their secret admirers, their secret peccadillos, and she loved them all for they brought the world to her door.

It was easy to transfer these daydreams on to her customers, who crowded her bench seats each day. There were the regulars, shoppers, Charlie Lunn, the uniformed booking attendant who worked the queues in the foyer of the King's and let her know if anyone special was performing. There were visitors and strangers who intrigued her.

In the quieter moments, when she was busy cleaning the chrome coffee maker and the glass domes of the soda fountain, polishing the marble counter top, she would look again and see Romeo and Juliet in the eyes of the couple holding hands

149

over table five in the corner. She was sure the couple who came each Thursday afternoon, who gazed into each other's eyes before leaving separately, were lovers from *Brief Encounter* with 'Guilty' written across their foreheads. Then there were the tearful eyes of the soldier and his girlfriend, saying their fond farewells. Would the girl betray him, like Carmen? Some of the local women behaved like pantomime dames, gossiping and mouthing their secrets like Norman Evans in *Over the Garden Wall*.

There were the poor old souls full of tales of woe, faded actors in shabby tweeds, Svengali illusionists, who paused over their drinks, holding court and signing autographs recalling better days. There were the boasters who scattered famous names into their conversations like sugar cubes into their tea.

There were also some of Angelo's army compatriots from Manchester, who hung around for free drinks, the worst of her countrymen, with greased, slick hair and thin moustaches and lecherous eyes, who would feel up her legs given half a chance: Iagos and Malvolios the lot of them! She loved the Shakespeare plays even if she could not always understand the words, but the coming of the D'Oyly Carte Opera Company with Gilbert and Sullivan operettas she loved the best, and she managed to make it to every performance.

One day she was going to take little Rosa up into the gods to see the ballet. It was never too soon to give a child a taste of the theatre. Angelo's wife, Tina, said there was a new dancing class starting in the top of Church Street Buildings, with a baby class. She could not wait to sign Rosa up for it when she was out of nappies.

Classes and ballet shoes cost money, and she must keep the family happy, keep a roof over their heads in the hope that one day Marco would come home for good, but there was a look in his eye that reminded her of Camille, of Mimi in *La Bohème*, a faraway look in his dark eyes she dreaded. It was as if he had already gone.

The family tried to help. His mother was on her knees in Our Lady of Sorrows every day pleading for his recovery. His brothers visited him when they could, but they were always very busy so it was up to her to visit every moment she was off duty. Sometimes she resented his illness so much.

When she walked into the ward he was grateful, pleased to see her, and yet exhausted by her visit so that there was never a right moment to ask his forgiveness. She had not been to confession for months and it had not gone unnoticed by Nonna Valentina.

Maria was so tired of being the strong one, the breadwinner, the tough little sparrow with not an inch of flesh on her, with cheekbones pointed like ice-cream cones. Always she must smile at the customers, see to Enzo, and keep Nonna Valentina off her back.

Now there was a lull, so she dashed upstairs again.

'I've phoned Angelo. He not be long for you. Where you come from? How long do you stay in Grimbleton?' she asked, curious about the two

151

foreign ladies.

'I am from Greece. She from Burma,' said Ana.

'Soldiers bring you back home,' Maria smiled. There were two Italian war brides who popped in to chat just to hear their own language and moan about the English weather.

'We come alone. We are widows,' said Su, as if she must speak for the both of them.

'My Marco make you welcome? You like this town?' Maria asked, sensing tensions. Ana burst into tears. 'Is all my fault... I come to find olive oil and there is none, no tomatoes, no orange and lemons, nothing but fish and chips and white bread,' she cried. 'We come here to ask you to help us and now we lose Ivy's pram. I no want to go back there.'

'There is not a drop of olive oil in this town. Perhaps little bottles in chemist that taste like cat pee,' she smiled and tapped her nose. 'But not impossible for Santinis to find some for you. Everything you can get at the right price if you know who to ask and you ask right. I can find you a little now, if you wish.' She pointed to a cupboard door.

'No, no ... not from your rations. We can wait,' said Lily, embarrassed. 'You've been kind enough.'

'I have a list too,' piped Su. 'Where can I get chilli peppers, garlic, mangoes, green tea?'

'Hey, one at a time! *Mamma mia*... I can spare you a little oil, real thing from Italy. The rest I don't know. Garlic we grow in garden and tomatoes in shed but it is too cold now. The oil here is no good, rubbish, best for engine in car or suncream. I find something for you next time you come,' she added, knowing they were honest and would return with their taxi fare.

'*Efaristo*,' whispered the Greek girl with the sad green eyes. She looked as if she was carrying the troubles of the world on her shoulders, homesick, cold and pinched in the face. 'You are kind.'

Not bad coming from the lips of a Greek to an Italian. It was hard not to hug her right there, to reach out to her and tell her it would be 'OK' but Maria knew better than to make false promises.

She still yearned for the bustling streets and the heat and dust of Palermo, for all she had left behind, battered by war. Instead she patted the *bambina's* golden curls. 'She looks like an angel. What's her name?'

'Konstandina Eleni, and this is Joy,' said Ana. 'Rosaria is a pretty name too.'

'Will you stay in Grimbleton?' Maria asked, knowing there was not much work for widows now the men were coming back into the mills and factories.

The two girls looked at each other with anxious eyes.

'We will go back to Division Street with no shopping, no pram and no money for the taxi, and so we must find jobs, I think,' said Susan. 'But we will pay you back,' she added hurriedly.

'We'll come back to pay you, I promise,' Lily smiled shyly.

'If you come on a Sunday I make you tea and the *bambini* can play together and I find you some oil,' Maria said.

There was a hooting from the pavement and a battered Austin saloon car was parked, with

Angelo leaning over for his passengers.

'Angelo is here for you. You come next week, yes?' Maria ushered them out of the door, waving, and they nodded and waved back.

I have made new friends, she thought: girls who are not related to Santini men through work and marriage with their myriad ties to the Italian community; lonely hearts, two young mothers with little girls for Rosa to play with.

It was an answer to her prayers. They would keep her out of mischief, give her someone to cook for. It would make her hospital visits bearable and keep her loneliness under control.

How many times had Lily rested her puffy ankles in this café, never knowing what a little firebrand lived only a staircase away, she thought as they made their way home. They might have lost a pram but they'd all found a friend.

Marco had done his best to entertain them but he was a spent fuse. He must have been so handsome before his injury. 'You make self at home,' he had smiled.

Lily had reached out to grasp his handshake but it was limp like an old man's hand. His eyes were sunk deep in their sockets and his hands shook when he dragged on his cigarette. How sad to see someone so young look so broken and infirm. A puff of wind would blow him over; yet another casualty of war.

Here she was thinking herself hard done by in Waverley House, when poor Maria was trying to run a business, care for a sick husband and little girl in this tiny flat. It made her feel ashamed of all her recent bad temper and frustration. Time to count her blessings.

'You will come on Sunday,' Maria shouted as they were leaving, 'all of you and Lily?'

Why not? Suddenly Grimbleton seemed full of possibilities. One visit to Santini's wouldn't rock any boats. There'd be time to see Walter later.

'It is good you make friends, *mia cara*, but Greek and foreign all together, Mamma might not like it,' Marco said with a look of concern on his tired face after the three women had left.

'It is good for me to make friends of my own. I am lonely. They need friends, I think.'

'I understand. I am no good husband, *finito...*' he sighed.

'You get better every day. I can see it in your cheeks,' she lied.

'You think so? I feel so tired. I'm letting my family down.'

'No silly talk,' Maria smiled, kneeling by his chair, leaning her head on his knees. They felt so sharp and bony. 'You are my big hero, my *sposo*, and Rosa's *papà*. We need you to get better soon.'

'But I can't work for you,' he said, slumping back into the cushion. 'This is no life.'

'But I'll work for both of us until you are strong again. I will make you better. All you need is time and rest. And NO SMOKES!'

'You are a hard woman, Maria. The best of all the Santinis.'

Then there was an almighty crash of broken crockery coming from downstairs and some fine Italian swearing in the kitchen. They looked at each other in horror.

'Enzo!' Maria screamed, and made for the stairs.

The following Sunday, Lily and the girls took the bus down to town to collect the Santini pram. They were in disgrace and all hell had broken loose when they'd returned without the Silver Cross.

Lily rapped on the café door and Maria shot down the stairs to greet them.

'You came! Welcome! Come in but first I give you this.' She pointed to a shiny metal go-chair. 'It has a seat front and back. You like? This is for your *bambini*. Keep it as long as you like.'

What could they say, thought Lily. It was a bit battered but serviceable. 'You're very kind,' she said. 'But there's no need–'

'No! It is nothing. It will fold up for the bus. I am sorry, but these people around here... I not understand.' Maria waved her hands in the air as if gathering all of the town. 'In the war they steal and they smoke. They smoke and drink in our café, very cheery, and then they smash all windows. Just because we are Italian. They come one night. I was woken by a terrible noise. They take Papà, Marco's father, to the police station and ask, "Where are your sons?" He tells them, "All my sons are in the British Army in the Lancashire Fusiliers." It is crazy so they arrest him and send him to Bury. It is a terrible place, a camp in a mill with no water and no beds. He is an old man. But the priest make a big fuss and he comes home.

'We had to paint, "We are British Citizens with sons serving in the Forces" on our windows. So I think now that foreigners must stick together.' She finally drew breath.

Lily felt ashamed. She'd seen the graffiti and had read about the riots when Mussolini came to power in 1940. A bunch of local hotheads began daubing paint on the Italian ice-cream shops, barber's and other premises. No better than the Nazis in their ignorance. Even citizens who'd been living here since before the Great War were marched out as aliens but everyone was very jumpy then, expecting invasion any day.

They climbed the narrow stairs up to the flat and there was a wonderful smell wafting down to greet them, spicy, tomatoey, unfamiliar but exciting.

Lily sat upright on the sofa, draped with lacy antimacassars. There were holy pictures on the mantelpiece, a bowl of waxed flowers in the window and lace doilies everywhere. Pride of place pinned to the wall were postcards from Sicily, showing a sea as blue as sapphires.

'Beautiful, yes?' Maria said, following Lily's gaze. 'My country was pretty, not like this mucky town. We have dust and poor people, but not smoking chimneys and black soot. But you get used to anything.' Maria sighed, looking towards the picture of Marco in his army uniform. 'He is handsome, yes?' she smiled.

'Definitely,' Lily offered. 'And Rosa...' Rosa looked up from her toys as the children were plonked down beside her, grabbing at her bricks, bowls and wooden spoons. She was the image of her mother, with black ringlets and dark eyes. She was wearing a little smocked overall on top of her dress. How sensible, Lily mused, to save on washing.

Ana and Su sat upright in their chairs while Maria fussed around them. It was awkward at first. 'You'll have a drink?'

They all nodded. 'Tea will be fine,' said Lily.

'You not want to try my beautiful wine? A present from Italia!'

Lily wasn't sure. It was Sunday but she'd not signed the pledge or anything like that and she didn't want to give offence. 'Go on then. I'll be daring for once!'

The wine was sweet and unusual. Ana knocked hers back with relish, and sighed. Su sipped hers politely while Maria bustled around in the kitchen.

'Won't be long. I hope you like spaghetti. My own special sauce.'

Lily had only seen spaghetti in tins like a can of little worms in pale orange juice. They'd just eaten a good Sunday lunch with apple pie and custard to follow. It was only five o'clock. Crumpets and tea would have been fine but Maria had gone to so much trouble. How to face another heavy meal?

'That'll be lovely,' she shouted.

Maria opened up the table, put on a beautiful lace tablecloth that looked handmade, and some candlesticks. She produced an enormous bowl of wriggling pasta, hot and steaming, doused in a rich tomato sauce that smelled of herbs and salt, and something Lily couldn't quite describe. How on earth would they eat the twirls and snakes of spaghetti without a spoon? All there was on the table was a fork.

Everyone sat politely waiting for Maria, not sure how to tackle the dish. She sat down and stared at them. 'You no like?'

'It looks lovely but how do we eat it?' Lily asked.

Maria burst out laughing. 'Like this!' She twisted the pasta round and round her fork and scooped it up into her mouth.

Su tried first but the dancing swirls just jumped off her fork and back onto her plate. Ana stabbed hers and beat it into submission while Lily tried to suck hers through her lips, dripping sauce everywhere.

'Oh, I forgot the cheese!' Maria jumped up. 'You must have some Parmigiano.'

She brought a slab of hard, crusty cheese and grated it over the bowl, the flakes falling like snow.

Wasn't this the cheese in *Robinson Crusoe,* or was it *Treasure Island?* Lily mused. It tasted like nothing she'd tried before, sharp and pungent. She wasn't quite sure about it but swallowed. This was the strangest Sunday tea: warming, comforting, filling and oh so different.

'I bring ice cream if you like.'

'No, no, please. This is so good and I'm full to the brim. You have taken so much trouble,' Lily insisted, feeling her waistband tightening by the minute.

'It is nothing. I am glad of your company.'

'But you've shared all your rations with us. It

wasn't your fault about the pram.'

'Your mamma was very cross when you got home?' Maria pierced them with her dark eyes.

Lily blushed at the memory of the row they'd received. Ivy had been hysterical with rage. But she lied now. 'They understood how these things can happen.'

'We are in big disgrace.' Su butted in. 'No one is speaking to us.'

'It's not that bad,' Lily countered. 'Oh, I see, you have a gramophone,' she pointed out, hoping to distract Maria. 'What music do you like?'

'Gilbert and Sullivan, and opera. You'd like to hear some?' Maria jumped up and found a record from a case, winding up her handset.

It was something dramatic, played loud and so sad that as they listened, tears streamed down Maria's face.

'When I hear this I fill buckets with my tears. You like it? Poor Madame Butterfly is deserted by Mr Pinkerton. I think of Marco and all the lost boys. I think of so many sad things. War is terrible.'

Su was sniffling into her hanky. 'Poor Mr Stan. We all lose our men in the war.' Now they were all weeping. It must be the wine and the music.

'Have you anything to gladden us up a bit before we go home?' Lily asked, seeing gloom descending like a fog.

Maria found some ballet music, much more cheerful, from the *Nutcracker Suite*.

'I watch the ballets when they come to the King's. I clean the stalls and watch the rehearsals. As soon as she is clean, I take Rosaria to the danc-

160

ing class. It's never too soon to learn to dance. Thank you for coming. Will you come again?'

'Only if you will come to us,' said Su. 'It's only fair, isn't it, Lily? Titty for tat!'

Lily sighed. What was Mother going to say to *that?*

9

Balancing Books and Entertaining Angels

'What did I tell you? I knew they couldn't be trusted out alone.' The righteous wrath of Ivy on the war path was a sight to behold. The bedraggled bunch had arrived back full of apologies and explanations. A week later she was still going on about the pram theft.

'It wasn't their fault,' said Lily, doing her best to smooth the situation to no avail. 'I should have known not to leave it outside. I'm sorry. Maria Santini's given you a pushchair in its place.'

'It's just a greasy hunk of tin. I bet she sold the Silver Cross on the black market before the night was out. They're worth a fortune. How am I going to take Neville to the park?'

'Oh, give it a rest, Ivy. Let him walk and build up his legs. You coddle that bairn. It's not as if you're going to be needing the pram again after what the doctor said about your insides.' Esme couldn't resist a snipe.

'Mother! That's private business,' Ivy sniffed.

161

'I'm sick of this lot cluttering up the place. Listen to that Joy making so much fuss in the playpen. It's like bedlam.'

'If you hadn't shouted at her mother and sent her upstairs in tears perhaps it would be a bit quieter,' snapped Lily.

'I'm not giving into her,' said Esme, turning her back and plugging her ears from the din. Joy was howling in protest at being caged into the wooden frame. Dina was yelling now too. 'It's for her own good. Truby King says all children must learn to be obedient and I've got tea to see to. Polly's gone home. Shush! Your mother won't be long.' Ana had offered to help out on the stall to make up for taking board and lodging. Dina was missing her.

Esme couldn't think for the noise of the screaming infants. Lily was hovering, wanting to give in to her, but Esme waved her back. 'You'll only spoil them.'

Dina's cheeks were puce with rage as she rattled the bars, refusing to be pacified by a line of Neville's wooden cars laid out for her amusement.

'That's right, you tell her,' yelled Ivy from the door. 'It's good for them to scream. They have to learn who's the boss of the playpen. Neville was never any bother.'

'How did you get on at the clinic? What did the doctor say?' Esme asked.

'Just a tickle in his throat,' said Ivy, who never took any chances with Neville's health. 'You can never be too careful, and what with a house full of foreigners you don't know *what* germs they are

162

breeding. He told me to get his hair cut. But it might rob him of his strength.'

Lily bent down to lift Dina out of the pen. 'Come on there, it's not natural to cage them up like puppies.' She smiled sweetly.

Ivy was scowling down at her with a withering 'What do you know about it?' sort of look. 'You don't have to clear up after their trail of havoc or wipe sticky fingers up the stairs. Nothing is safe from wandering fingers. They're into cupboards and through doors in a flash. Those two could roam around unchecked and teach our Neville bad habits.' She paused to nail her mother-in-law with a sharp look. 'How long do we have to put up with these women in our house? It's been weeks now. Time they were finding themselves rooms of their own.'

'You know they won't get rooms to let with small children in tow,' Lily answered, jiggling Dina on her knee. She was getting far too fond of those youngsters, in Ivy's opinion.

'I don't see why they should be living at our expense,' Ivy snapped. 'You don't know the half of it, trailing in and out as they please.'

Esme stood back and let them bicker. It was not an unreasonable request for Levi and Ivy to want things to go back as they were. At first they were too shocked to turn the visitors out of the door. Now the Christmas season was upon them, such as it was, with meagre rations to share and snow up to their back door. How could she send them packing in the snow?

Every night she struggled with her conscience over how to deal with the tissue of lies they were

163

building around these girls. Every night she knelt on the linoleum and did her eternal accounts before the One who knew the secrets of all hearts.

On the one hand, Ivy was right. Esme had gone beyond the call of duty in taking them in the first place. To her credit she had fed them and protected them from public shame, sorted out their paperwork with the authorities and perjured herself in the process. To her credit she had taken in foreigners and it sometimes sounded like the Tower of Babel with them jabbering away to their babies in Greek and Burmese and pidgin English. She made them part of the family, even helped them out financially to start with. Lily was befriending them and now they were all pally with the Santini woman, another foreigner, and a Catholic too, from the ice-cream parlour.

Every Sunday they all took themselves off to her flat for tea so the girls could play with their new friend. They came back scented with garlic, wine and other funny smells. It was not right on the Lord's Sabbath.

'All this gallivanting on the Lord's Day, these spaghetti Sundays ... you needn't go with them. You ought to be with your young man,' Esme argued.

'I've only been twice and Walt doesn't mind. I've never missed church yet. Marco is now permanently in Moses Heights. Maria is glad of company.'

'I should think she's got enough company in that family. They say Santinis breed like rabbits.'

It was Lily who argued that it was no different

from them all going to visit other Winstanleys for Sunday tea or entertaining company themselves after church. Esme didn't hold with going on buses into town in the evening after dark. Lily kept borrowing the van to give them lifts. They were not a taxi service.

That was another thing. The Greek wanted to take a bus to Manchester to light candles in some church on Bury New Road – Greek Orthodox, would you believe, a church full of golden idols – while the Burmese took herself off to St Matthew's parish church with the parishioners from Green Lane. She was driven back in a fancy car and that got Ivy all het up about nothing. Zion Chapel, it appeared, was not good enough for them now. Esme blamed the Eyetie for putting fancy ideas in their heads.

Part of her struggle each night with the internal workings of this spiritual book-keeping was to weigh up the debits, as well as the pluses.

First, there was the bad grace with which she did all the creditable stuff. It was hard to smile and look relaxed when you were harbouring your son's secret lovers.

Ivy was always on guard duty, reminding her of any infringements to their rules, any liberties taken with Neville's toys, and the loss of the big pram was hard to explain away. She watched to see if they used the wrong rations, or left lights on, or the paraffin heater.

Esme had to admit they hardly put a foot wrong. They crept around the house in carpet slippers, made no noise, were very polite and deferential when there was company. They were eager to find work. They saw to their own washing when everyone else used the electric agitator in the outhouse. They kept their rations in a separate cupboard and didn't eat much, shared any shopping and delivering and mending duties. They paid their way as best they could.

To her credit, she bought the little ones warm clothing with her coupons and Lily was knitting jumpers for them. They were doing their Christian duty to 'suffer the little children...' It wasn't easy.

There was an atmosphere growing that she didn't know how to deal with. Ivy was rude and Levi let her go unchecked. The foreigners were pretty girls, full of life, and that reminded her she was getting old and fat and not as fit as she once was.

'Freddie would be proud of you, Mother, but enough's enough,' Ivy would scold, that shrill voice bending her ear.

What if they were entertaining angels unaware? What if this was some spiritual scholarship test the family had to pass? What if she had to make up in life for all of Freddie's failings?

Yet there was something about having a house full of toddlers and young people, the rush of feet on the stairs and laughter of children, that gave her heart a lift better than Wincarnis and feet up by the fire. It was a sign her life wasn't over yet and she was still needed.

The girls lived up in the attic room and sometimes when they were out she crept upstairs to peek at the sleeping infants and gave herself a pat on the back that she had done right by them all.

They were her grandchildren, illegitimate or not. Only the four Winstanleys knew that secret. If some of her neighbours were curious and wondered why the widows were staying on it was easy to talk about room shortages and bombed-out houses down south, and how families must help each other out. It felt right as she was saying it, but was it another debit?

Telling lies was not in her nature; white lies told to protect the good Winstanley name were a burden she must bear to preserve their respectability. Surely that wasn't a debit on her Eternal account? They were honourable lies, she argued.

'Oh Lord!' she prayed. 'You'd better balance my books yourself. It's not easy. Show me the way to righteousness.'

Lily handed over the child into Esme's arms, the Concertina child who bore the name she had always hated but hadn't the heart to confess. She plonked her down in the playpen again to a wail of protests just as Ana came in from the hall with Levi, back from the stall.

'What is Dina doing in the cage? I told you, no cages. I see too many cages in war. Cages no good for children.' Ana pulled her out again and the child, hot and bothered, looked pleased.

Suddenly Esme caught a glimpse of Freddie, defiant and naughty, with those blue eyes looking up at her. It was like seeing a ghost.

'I have to keep her under control for her own good. She might put something in her mouth,' she argued, but Ana was angry, her eyes flashing.

'She is my baby. Dina is too big for a cage.'

'Don't you talk to Mother like that,' said Ivy.

167

'Does she argue with customers like this? They won't understand a word she says.'

Levi shrugged and left the room, not wanting to get involved in the bickering of women. Ana was jabbering away to the child in Greek.

Esme's heart lurched to see Freddie in the girl. How could she let this bit of him go, perhaps never to see her again? How could this bit of her son grow up never knowing her granny? There would only be Neville left, and he looked just like Ivy with curls.

'I wish you would speak English so we can all join in,' Esme said with a sniff. 'Speaking two languages must confuse the child. We don't want her in the backward school.'

Susan had taken her teaching certificate to the Education Department Office to find work with a nursery unit. She was no trouble. Susan had British manners and a politeness that charmed people, and she knew her place.

'We speak home tongue to them and you speak your tongue and they know which is which,' said Ana with defiance. This one didn't know her place yet. There was something rock-like in those green eyes that could not be moved. 'Konstandina is forward girl, not backward girl. You see.'

All this argy-bargy was making her head spin. Perhaps the kiddie was too old for a playpen after all. It was too strange and she was frightened. The bairn had had so many changes in her life.

'I am trying to make Concertina safe from fire, and from Neville when he's got a mood on him,' Esme mouthed slowly. 'I have to get on with my jobs. I am not a nursemaid,' she said, and hoped it would be the end of the matter.

'I know. You good woman but my Dina must be free to explore. Susan says it is good for children to explore. In my country they had white sand and green hills and fields to play in, plenty of aunties and uncles to watch over them,' Ana sighed.

'Well, this is Grimbleton and my house, and I don't want any more ornaments being shovelled into the bin. You need eyes in the back of your head, Anastasia, with that one.' There it was said. 'She will have to go into a nursery if this carries on.'

'I take her to watch dancing class soon,' Ana smiled, and went to make herself a cup of tea with no milk.

'Never, she's nobbut a baby still,' Esme said. Where did this girl get these notions from?

'Maria is taking Rosa, and Susan think good to let girls dance to music. What Joy has, Dina must have,' she said, looking pleased with herself.

That'll be a waste of money, lass, the kiddy can't even walk yet, she thought, but for once she bit her tongue. It was a struggle but it would look good in her Eternal account book. Joy was a pudding, a lump of lard. How a tiny bird like Susan could produce such a round thing was way beyond her but the Winstanleys were big-boned and hefty.

'Whatever you like,' she managed. 'But you'll have to pay for it yourself.' It was a struggle to keep her gob buttoned up when Ivy was hovering, looking daggers.

'I do extra on Saturday for Levi. I find another

169

job but it not easy,' Ana added.

'As long as you're trying, that's all we ask,' Esme said, knowing she could not ask when they were leaving now.

Ivy was sitting with a face like thunder and when Ana left the room she was waiting to pounce.

'You'll never get rid of them now! Dancing classes, would you credit it? Where do they get their fancy ideas from? "Lemody Liptrot School of Dance" indeed. I remember when she was plain Lizzie Liptrot, the fishmonger's daughter, who went on the stage and came back full of airs and graces and a plum in her mouth. I saw her advert in the *Mercury:* Greek dancing, tap dancing and ballet. It'll give them ideas,' she argued.

'I thought you were the one for big ideas.' Esme couldn't resist the jibe, seeing Ivy so put out. 'It'll keep them out of mischief. I expect it teaches girls to hold themselves proper and understand rhythm.'

'Little show-offs is what you'll get,' snapped Ivy. 'Prancing about like Shirley Temple, and you don't hold with all them theatricals.'

'I don't know. Perhaps Neville could go and be the next Fred Astaire. Now *he* had a good sense of rhythm. I don't hold with all that lovey-dovey stuff, but him and Ginger Rogers could fair move across the floor. That's healthy and wholesome, gets your lungs working and heart pumping,' she argued. She wasn't too old to recall the thrill of a bit of romance.

Ivy was looking up with raised eyebrows. 'I'm going to send our Neville for elocution lessons when he's older so he can better himself.'

Esme could see that she had sown a seed of interest. There was nothing Ivy would not do to make Neville stand out from the crowd.

It was after tea was cleared away that the two girls hovered behind Esme and followed her into the sitting room where she liked to listen to the wireless and knit without interruption. It was her time of day for a bit of peace and quiet with a good book on her lap. They closed the door behind them and she wondered what was coming next. They always hunted in pairs, waiting until Ivy and Levi had gone to the pictures so she would be on her own, vulnerable to their pleas with no Ivy to bat off their suggestions. They sat down opposite and smiled. She tried to keep her Eternal account book in mind.

'Daw Winstanley,' said Susan, using her most polite term of address. 'We want to ask your advice.'

Esme sighed with relief, relaxing into the chair. Giving advice was what she was good at. 'Oh, yes? How can I help?' she smiled.

'It is our new friend, Maria. She is having a very bad time. Her husband is very sick in the sanatorium. She has been very kind to us. She has made us dinner many times.'

'So she should do. She cost you our pram *and* a taxi fare.'

'But she found us a new pushchair from her sister-in-law,' Susan was quick to defend her friend.

'And we had to scrub it with Lysol it was so

greasy. It must have been dipped in the fish fryer,' she replied. Ivy had scoured it for nits and other nasties, and refused to let Neville near it for fear of germs but it was not a bad go-chair. It collapsed and took up less room in the hall, and they could squash the two kids in at a pinch.

'Every Sunday she cooks pasta for us – spaghetti – and we have ice cream and tinned fruit. How do we say thank you?' Ana asked, her eyelashes blinking as she leaned forward hanging on the coming words. 'It is polite to return gift with gift, yes?'

Esme was trapped if she said no. It would look as if she was condoning bad manners. If she said yes ... oh heck, they'd caught her in their net but not without a struggle.

'You can repay the dinners by taking her out for another meal in a café as a thank you,' she said, hoping that would satisfy.

'Yes ... but it would be as you say, busman's vacation?' said Susan, so sweetly that Esme hardly felt the hook turning as she wriggled.

'So what are you suggesting?' she said, knowing their request was better laid flat on the table.

'Can we cook a meal for Maria here, one Saturday evening after work? She can find someone to finish off her shift and she can catch the bus to visit Marco and come for her tea. It would be a big thank you,' Susan said hurriedly.

'You want to use my kitchen and my dining room and cook ... foreign stuff for her?' Esme gasped, knowing they had hooked her good and proper.

'We cook for everyone, big thank you meal for

all of you too,' Susan added, glancing up as Lily appeared.

'What a lovely idea,' Lily smiled, looking hopefully in her direction. 'A sort of thanksgiving-cum-Christmas meal all rolled into one.'

It was time to give her daughter one of those withering 'you're letting the family down' looks.

'We like our dinner cooked at lunchtime. Tea time is tea time and nothing fancy in the evening to talk back to me in the night.'

They must know the strict rotation of meals by now. Roast after church on Sunday, leftovers cold on Monday, rissoles on Tuesday, mince on Wednesday, fish on Thursday when the fish van called. Potato pie on Friday and pasties from town on Saturday. It didn't do to change routine.

Then she saw the blessed Eternal audit hovering high in the corner of the room. It would be good to score up another credit. Be generous and accommodating for once, she mused.

Let them try entertaining company on rations. It was not as easy as they thought.

'You'd have to use your own rations. I don't hold with fancy food but you can have my kitchen if you give plenty of advance notice. I don't know what Ivy will say. It's her kitchen too.'

'But you all come to our meal, Ivy and Lily, all are invited,' said Ana.

'Then you'll need everyone's meat ration but I don't want any funny smells wafting down the street,' Esme said, knowing there would be hell to pay when Ivy got home.

'Thank you, thank you,' the widows shouted in unison, and jumped up and down as if they had been given the Crown Jewels. 'We make special dinner for everyone and we have singing and dancing. You will like Maria.'

'I'm sure for a Catholic and Eyetie, she'll do,' was all Esme could manage. I've let the side down again and given into my better nature, she sighed, but she would square it all up on her knees with the Almighty later.

10

Invitations to a Feast

'You will come, Walt, to the thank you do? The family has to give them support.' Lily was telling him all about the prospective supper as they sat in the café on her lunch break the next day.

'So I'm family when it suits you. Pity I wasn't in on them coming in the first place,' he said with his mouth full of barm cake.

'None of us knew they were going to turn up out of the blue. I thought you understood that.' She patted his hand. Sometimes he could look so peevish.

'It's none of my business, Lily, what your family does, but Mam thinks you should never have had them girls in the house.'

'I'm surprised at her, being a widow and taking that attitude. It's the middle of winter and freezing cold and nearly Christmas. Have a heart!'

'I wish you'd give me a bit of your heart. A

man's only flesh and blood, and talking of flesh and blood, come here and give us a kiss.' Walt lunged forward to smack a sloppy kiss but it misfired as her cheek turned from him and his lips sucked in only air.

'None of that now!' she blushed. 'Not in public. I've got Brownie costumes to sew, buttons to find. Not enough hours in the day as it is.'

'What's it this time?' He peeked at the flimsy material in the brown paper bag. 'I was hoping this was summat for your wedding dress. When are we going to name the day? What about next July or August, the mill holidays? It's quiet in the town. It gives us a chance to find a place to rent, just like we promised, and it'll take your mind off all these foreigners.' He smiled a toothy grin, turning to his *News Chronicle*.

He had a point, Lily thought. It was time they set a date and planned ahead. Mother would just have to get used to the idea of her leaving Waverley House but now was not the time to daydream about dresses and bouquets when there were ten soldiers' and sailors' outfits to cobble up for the Guide and Brownie Review dress rehearsal at St Matthew's church hall next week.

It was her big idea for the Brownies to stage the story of Daisy Darling and the little tin soldier. So far she'd ordered military hats and let the mums loose on tricky jackets. The results had been disastrous.

'I can count on you for next Saturday night then?' she said, standing up to pay the bill.

'I'm not sure, Lil. Eating foreign is not my cup of tea. It'll play havoc with my digestion. Let's go

175

to the pictures and have a fish-and-chip supper instead. You know we've a Cup tie on Saturday afternoon. Has Levi got the tickets?'

'Don't ask me. I've promised to help the girls out. It's their way of being sociable and it's not polite to refuse.'

Walt shook his head and shrugged his shoulders. 'Suit yerself, but count me out this time, love. Perhaps it's better if it's just ladies.'

'Could you lend us some coupons then to eke out the rations? I'll pay them back.'

He shook his head. 'Sorry, no can do. Mam is the guardian of the ration books and she's saving up for Christmas. We don't want her to do without treats then, do we?'

'I suppose not,' Lily replied bitterly. Elsie Platt loved her son and puddings far too much to deprive them both of any luxuries on the Christmas black market.

Was this a glimpse of what life might be like in the future, him stumped by the fireside, stuffing her baking into his mouth and no conversation, stuck out in their cottage on the moor, miles from any of the excitement going on down town?

Where was that fluttering tummy, pounding heart, the passion of being together? She got more of that watching Pete Walsh dribbling down the centre of Grimbleton Park to Barry Wagstaff when the Grasshoppers played at home. Something wasn't right but there was too much to do to worry about it now.

Whose big idea was it to give a thanksgiving dinner for Maria and the Winstanleys? sighed

176

Ana. Where would they start? She chewed over the menu like a dog with a bone as she stood sentinel at her new post in the Market Hall, trying to look busy, straining to understand the customers speaking while Levi slept off his beery lunch in the cubbyhole that served as his office. Here were kept all the more expensive items and spare stock. It was awkward brushing past him to reach up for boxes. He was not to be trusted.

Ever since that first meeting his lecherous intentions towards Su were plain for all to see, but now he gawped at her with interest too. She tried to ignore his suggestive tone. The jokes she didn't understand but sometimes Enid looked at her with pity when it was time for her to leave. 'Take no notice, love, it's the beer talking.'

When Enid was around it was easier to dodge his hands, but once she'd gone it was better just to stay close to the side of the stall. Thursday, Friday and Saturday mornings they were busy. That was when workers got their wages and came to buy their supplies.

The beginning of the week was worst. Levi would prowl behind her when she was stock-taking and dusting, far too close for comfort. He had not laid a finger on her yet but she sensed the time was coming and she desperately needed to distract him. She was not used to working alone with a man. In Crete before the war, women in villages were treated with respect and were never left alone in a room, even with their own father or brother, for fear of losing their reputation. An un-married girl wore a headscarf to cover her beauty from display, and public appearances were kept to festivals and church. In towns it was different, and the war had changed everything. She'd even taken to wearing trousers while tending wounded soldiers, living in hill camps with partisans who honoured their womenfolk by ignoring them. When they were captured and transported over to the mainland, she was imprisoned in a women's labour camp, cooped up like cattle, working the land in terrible weather. All hope left her of ever surviving the hardship and starvation, but somehow she had done.

No use looking in a mirror to see the fairness of her youth. Her features had long shrunk to sharp bones on a craggy frame – starvation and the wind had seen to that. Yet Freddie and his soldiers had taken pity on her friends in Athens, picked her out, given her enough food and shelter to restore some bloom. There was never any danger of assault when Freddie was her escort with his Military Police red cap.

Levi was no gentleman, though, and she was not going to stand for any nonsense. There had been too many shameful incidents with guards in the camp. She knew how to defend herself now.

'Can I go look round stalls? I need to find food for the big dinner,' she shouted. 'It is very quiet. No customers to bother you.' She didn't wait for an answer as she sped out of sight to the safety of the vegetable stall. There were plenty of stalls but little to buy that interested her, and she was not speaking to Su since last night.

'What shall we cook?' she had asked, but Su had shrugged her shoulders. 'You said you cook for Tommy soldiers in canteen?' Ana pressed.

'Ah yes, with Chindhe ladies of the Women's Auxiliary Service when we march back into Burma. I follow them. I wash and serve and tidy but no cook. I had to do servant jobs. We all muck in for poor boys who worship us from afar. That is where I met Mister Stan.'

'I don't want to know where you met your blessed Mister Stan this and Mister Stan that...'

'And you go on like a record on a gramophone, Freddie this and Freddie that. He only had you because he thought me dead. I am number one wife whatever Daw Esme say.'

'We're nobody's wife,' Ana screamed in frustration. 'But we keep tongues under hat. That is what Kiría Esme say or we'll be sent home. I no make big dinner all alone.'

'I am not a good cook. Auntie Betty had a boy to do all that, but I can make *lepet*, nice juicy pickle and pretty flowers for table. I will be your helper.'

That was when Ana realised she'd be on her own. Susan had found a post in a nursery school so she must pay for the extra food and help in the kitchen. The meal must be cheap and simple and not use up too many coupons.

Grimbleton seemed to live on a diet of flour-and-water soups, stodgy pastry, soulless bread and sausages that tasted of sawdust. No wonder the herbal stall was so popular. Customers queued for liver pills, indigestion tablets, laxatives and flatulence potions. There were packets of dehydrated vegetables and eggs in a powder. There were shelves of canned meat and tinned fruit, jars of pickles. Where was the life in the

179

food? These provisions were tasteless to her, cooked without love.

In Crete they could live on mountain greens, *horta* and wild spinach, pick living fruits and nuts from their own trees. They did not pour yellow custard over green shoots and call it salad.

The Tommies had turned their noses up at olive oil, at first saying it was fit only for lamp oil but some of them grew to love the delicate flavours of vegetables grilled with oil and lemon juice. Oh, just to pick a lemon from a tree!

Before the war came the Cretan market stalls were full of raisins and fresh fish, the scent of roasting coffee, sacks of beans and rice, barrels of feta cheese and rounds of hard cheese from their sheep, thyme honey, kegs of raki, blocks of chocolate, Turkish delights, halva and fruit syrups and every colour of olive oil; before the tanks came and flattened the olive groves and there was not a walnut or raisin to be had.

If only there were *chios* here, shaped like eggs with their soft flesh, *kalimata*, black and purple bittersweet, earthy old Cretan wine, olives marinated in oil and vinegar dressing.

The taste of the olive was a taste as old as the world itself, a taste of life and love and home. How she missed the silkiness of its texture on her tongue.

How quickly you could learn to exist on boiled porridge dotted with snails and mountain greens, rough corn breads and goat's-milk yoghurt thinned out with stream water. The enemy stole everything from their cellars, their sheep and goats, chickens, their fruit and olive harvest and

180

their honeycombs. They were left destitute. Hunger was a terrible thing. It changed people into animals, scavenging, stealing.

In the labour camps it was worse: in the harsh winters living off soup made from stolen greens and roots and the bones of anything they might snare for the pot. Sometimes Ana lay on her bunk, dreaming of the day when her belly would be full of oil and wine and cheese, *dakos* and sharp spicy sausages.

Cretan food was full of colour and guts and strong smells. There were always garlands of garlic and mountain tea, onions and dried herbs hanging from the kitchen rafters. The family had lived from their garden, the mountains, from hives and orchards. There was kid and lamb for festivals and a harvest from the shore.

The Papadakis were just village folk, her father worked leather. They were proud and wanted for nothing in the stone white house close to the church. She had gone to Canea to help in the Red Cross station until it was overrun, then escaped into the high hills above the port. She was lucky to be alive when so many of her school friends were dead. Sometimes she dreamed that Eleni was chasing after her into the fields. When she turned to wait for her, she vanished and Ana woke with tears down her face.

Ana didn't know whether any of her relatives survived when the village was razed to the ground in reprisal after an ambush in the hills on that terrible day when Eleni died. They were scattered like seeds into the wild wind.

There was no point going back. The country

was at war with itself now. She dare not write for fear of more bad news. Here she could pretend all was well now the war was over. This was where Dina must grow up, in this strange town in this foreign country amongst the people who had taken them in. It was the honourable thing to do.

All this daydreaming would not put a meal on the table, she sighed, knowing she must go back to the stall. Maria would help her out with food if stuck, but she was already beholden to their new friend. Why should a guest provide her own dinner?

Getting out of Division Street each Sunday afternoon was the treat they most looked forward to. Maria was always so full of life and energy, scurrying round the tiny flat that she kept like a palace. She hardly stopped to draw breath, with her two jobs and her husband, Marco, making such slow progress. Ana sensed that if Maria stopped for a second she'd collapse and sink down with exhaustion. Keeping busy was how she dealt with her pain.

Everyone was keeping busy after this war, queuing, cleaning, tidying up the bomb sites, making the best of very little. The Winstanley women never stopped, and if she was married to Levi she'd not stop until she'd run a mile from him.

For a moment she could feel just a flicker of sympathy for the sharp little wife who must share his bed. There was a bitter taste to the two of them and Levi's eyes were hungry for something sweeter.

Ana's own sadness made her feel lethargic. It

was an effort to eat, to sleep in the middle of the night, to get up in the morning, and now she had a big meal to prepare so Su must help with the shopping. Su had the money for extras but how to manage a meat ration for eight people?

As she scoured the butchers' stalls for inspiration she thought of pig for *souvláki* chunks skewered on knitting needles and marinated in lemon, herbs and oils. That was out, for a start, and they could only get meat from the counter where they were all registered. Perhaps some beef or lamb for *stifado*, cooked slowly and eked out with vegetables, but beef for eight? Impossible.

Lily said Walt couldn't spare any coupons because his mother was old. Ivy refused to give a single coupon because Neville needed extra rations, and Levi thought the idea of a meal made from 'foreign muck' a big joke. When she'd asked him to order some olive oil he refused, saying she must use dripping like everyone else. Then he'd laughed and said he might get hold of some if she made it worth his while.

'I will pay good price,' she smiled, but he just winked.

'What I'm after don't cost money, love, just a little time,' he said, pointing to the cubbyhole and she fled, blushing. If his mother found out that his wandering hands were also in the till perhaps *that* would cool his passion.

With a heavy heart, Lily watched Levi ogling Ana from the cubbyhole that served as an office. Business was quiet and they didn't need three staff on duty.

183

Taking the Greek girl down to Winstanley Health and Herbs to work was not such a good idea. It was nearly Christmas and shoppers were too busy trying to eke out their ration coupons to want to bother with pills and potions. Their rush time would come after New Year, when the winter gloom set in proper: a time for tonics and pick-up remedies to prepare, stocktaking and weighing those who wanted to lose their winter excess baggage.

They kept all the more expensive items and spare stock in the back cubbyhole, and when Ana brushed past Levi to reach up for the boxes he would lean back on his stool to feel the brush of her skirt. There was often the smell of liquor on his breath in the afternoons these days, but should she say anything to him?

She sighed. If Ivy got even a sniff of his inclinations, never mind his breath, she'd banish the girls from the house, Christmas or not.

Levi was becoming a worry. Ever since Ana and Susan arrived he seemed to think Freddie's lady friends were his personal harem. When she was on guard there was no bother, but out of eyeshot she guessed he was up to his old tricks. A pass was a pass in any language. It was up to her to put a stop to it and sharp.

'If Levi is bothering you, I'll have a word,' Lily offered.

Ana shook her head and shrugged her shoulders. 'It is nothing. Men are worse during the war. In my country a woman not work with a man alone,' she said. 'A single girl might be a slave to the kitchen and the fields but she has

184

respect. All we have is a good name and I have bad name now. We keep headscarf over our face. War has changed everything. Now there is flesh everywhere and men are tempted.'

Sometimes when Ana talked a shutter came over her eyes like a veil, her eyes would flutter and the subject was changed. Ana was suffering in ways Lily could only imagine. She was learning to respect this withdrawal into silence. 'Look at me, just skin and bone. Who would want to look at such a face?'

There might be silver threads in her hair but her eyes still burned brightly and Lily could see how Freddie would have been attracted to her fierce spirit, her courage and kindness.

'Lily, what shall I cook with no meat ration? This is big worry now.' They had scoured the food stalls for ideas for that special supper, something that might remind them of warmer climates and better times.

It was the knitting patterns on the wool stall that did the trick: a picture of a matinée coat with a fluffy bunny embroidered on it. Lily suddenly remembered Allotment Billy, who'd kept them in rabbit meat all through the war. Rabbits were cheap and plentiful. The flesh was sweet and tasted like chicken if cooked slowly, and he might have an onion or two to spare if they explained their dilemma. Allotment Billy was an old pal of her father's: another survivor of the Grimbleton Pals Brigade.

'There's always fresh rabbit,' she offered in desperation.

'You are angel from heaven, you save bacon. I

185

can do plenty with rabbit and herbs.' Ana flung her arms around her in gratitude.

No one had mentioned anything about herbs. Herbs were going to be a different challenge altogether, but she'd not be defeated now. If Winstanleys couldn't rustle up a spice or two it'd be a poor do!

Mother was a plain cook and didn't bother to flavour food with anything other than white pepper and salt and sometimes stalks of parsley. There was Oxo cubes, of course, but Lily preferred to drink them like tea. The drink was harsh and salty, and warmed her through on cold days.

No one touched garlic except as a medicine, but if she threw in enough garlic salt and pearls from the stall perhaps no one would notice. It was the nearest they could offer in the way of exotic.

There were bay trees growing like ornaments in the Green Lane gardens. Perhaps Su could beg a few leaves when she came home with Dr Unsworth's daughter and family from the parish church. Her being Church and not Chapel was causing quite a stir.

If the worst came to the worst they could scour the local park gardens for the last stalks of thyme, but the ground was under a foot of snow.

'How can we serve a fresh salad when there's nothing green?'

'It's not the season for cold stuff,' Lily advised. 'We can have tinned peas.'

The Winstanleys didn't eat much salad. Levi called it rabbit food. There was not a tin of tomatoes or dried herbs in the house, but sardines or pilchards in oil would flavour the vinegar.

The first course was to be a *mezéthakia*, little plates of olives or cheese, little tastes to whet the appetite. Ana said Greeks never drank without a little food.

'We're a teetotal family, although we haven't signed the pledge and I suppose we've sort of slipped a bit. There's brandy in the medicine cupboard and tonic wine. How about starting with tripe and onions from the U.C.P.? Cows innards are very healthy.'

'No, I do cheese and spinach pie then,' Ana smiled.

'Cheese is rationed. And it's not the season for spinach,' Lily replied, trying to veer her away from big ideas. It would be impossible to find an olive in Grimbleton. 'The only thing in the pantry I can think of is a tin of anchovy fillets in oil but you won't be wanting that, will you?'

Ana snatched the idea with glee. 'We fry potatoes and boil eggs. It is perfect meze.'

Lily hadn't the heart to mention that fresh eggs took some negotiating. There was also the pudding problem. Her mouth was watering from all the tempting desserts that rolled off Ana's tongue: honeyed pasties with walnuts and sweet raisins, fruits poached in wine. All there might be on Billy's allotment were precious sticks of forced pink rhubarb, grown in his secret way especially for Christmas. It would take the promise of a knitted jumper to get some of those off him.

'We've got plenty of bottled fruit in the larder and Bird's custard to go with it.'

'But that is not feast food, that is Wednesday food. I will make yoghurt. I know how from pan of warm milk and flask. You watch. It is delicious with honey...'

Where on earth would she get honey? 'We've got some golden syrup.'

'No. Honey from hills in Grimtown!'

'You mean Grimbleton – oh, I don't know, love.'

'Yes, Grimtown. We will find it for our feast. You will help?'

I will help, though Lord knows how, Lily smiled to herself. Planning this feast was a mad idea and taking so much time. But it was yet another distraction from her thoughts about Walter – not that she had much time to spare him a minute. The poor lad had slipped down the pecking order of her 'must dos'. Days would go by with only a cheery wave across the Market Hall for contact. She was so pushed for time, he never volunteered to help her out and she was too proud to ask. It wasn't right but if she could just get Christmas over with then she'd make up for her neglect. Now they were late from their tea break.

'What time of night do you call this? I don't pay you to go sightseeing.' Levi puffed out his chest in indignation, then ordered them to dust all the stock down. Within minutes he was off meandering round the market himself, doing deals and coming back with booty for Ivy and Neville's Christmas stockings.

On the Friday morning before the dinner party

there was still no honey, but Ana's yoghurt, after two disasters, had set perfectly. Lily now needed to make a trip up to the Jubilee Allotment to see Billy Eckersley and collect the rabbits.

The doorbell rang and there was Pete Walsh, grinning, and Lily in her curlers looking like a rat bag.

'I brought you these,' he smiled, 'for you and your mother.'

In his hand was a pair of precious tickets for the Cup tie against Everton. People had been queuing for hours to get these. Lily felt herself blushing.

'That's very kind of you,' she smiled, wishing her face was washed and her turban wasn't full of curlers. 'Mother's been under the weather. I'm not sure she'll be able to brave the chill. I would love to go only–'

Levi sprang down the stairs, two at a time. 'Now then, mate, did I hear the mention of tickets? You should be on that pitch training, not chatting up my little sister on the doorstep. Where's your manners, Lil? Fetch us a cup of tea for the lad.' He snatched the envelope from her hand without a by-your-leave.

'They're for Mother, not you,' she snapped back.

'She's in bed with a cold. It's your turn on the stall then. Walt can have the spare. Thanks, Pete. I owe you one,' he winked.

Lily was so furious she could hardly speak.

'Peter gave them to me, thank you very much.' She snatched them back. 'You made sure you got yourself a ticket ages ago.'

'Quite a spitfire, when she's riled up,' Levi replied as he climbed the stairs in a huff. Pete stood there saying nothing.

'I'd ask you in only we've got a flap on,' Lily lied. 'Susan and Ana are cooking us dinner tomorrow so we're having a rehearsal: they're temperamental cooks, I'm afraid, and I'm the referee.'

'You'll make the game, though? It'll be a cracker.'

'I'll try,' she offered, knowing there wasn't a cat in hell's chance of her being let off duty. 'It's so kind of you to think of us.'

'It's just that I know what a strain you've all been under lately. A seat at a Cup tie match sort of passes the time, takes your mind off things. Your mother said...' he stuttered.

'Mother said what?' Lily looked at him, his cheeks were bright pink as he leaned forward, smelling of Lifebuoy and Brylcreem. 'You see, Freddie did write to me about Susan. I know it's all a bit awkward for you.'

She was looking up into his grey-green eyes dotted with amber flecks like tweed. 'I see,' she snapped. 'You can say that again. She'd no right to go blabbing our private business.'

'No, it wasn't like that.'

'I'm sure it wasn't, but just right now I'd better see to the girls. There's a lot to do. I'll make sure Mother gets her tickets. Thank you for your concern but we're coping as well as can be expected.' Lily ushered him quickly back into the vestibule and out on to the street. How dare he come in here with his charity when all he was doing was fishing for information? Who did he

190

think he was?

She was all flustered. Pete must know that Susan and Joy were Freddie's girls, not anything to do with the imaginary cousin down south. What if he let slip? She raced up the stairs to Esme's bedroom and banged open the door, throwing the tickets on the bed. Mother had her head under a towel, bent into a steaming bowl of friar's balsam, feeling sorry for herself.

'What's all this about Pete Walsh knowing our business?'

'Don't fuss, Lil. I said nothing he didn't already know.'

'I thought we had to keep it in the family as usual.'

'That young man is as sound as a pound. He won't tell anyone.'

'He'd better not or he'll have me to answer to for offering us Cup tie tickets to salve his conscience...'

Suddenly the towel was off Esme's head. 'That's very generous of him. Happen I ought to make the effort and oblige,' she replied. 'The air will do me good.'

'Levi wants them,' Lily snapped. 'You'll have to join the queue.'

'Give them here. Levi can find other tickets to tout round his cronies. These are *ours*.'

Lily suddenly felt like Cinderella, banned from the ball with the sweeping brush at the hearth. 'You're not having mine. I'll decide who uses this,' she whined, feeling peevish and silly. How rude she'd been to Pete, and for no reason, how prickly, and him only trying to be kind. She

191

hadn't even wished him good luck.

Then she heard a rumpus in the kitchen and made for the stairs.

Ivy was busy preparing lunch before her shopping trip to town and refused to yield an inch of space at the sink for the preparations.

The yoghurt bowl was across the table next to a bottle of Neville's Welfare orange juice. They were going to sweeten it with a little juice; the nearest they had got to an orange for months. Lily hoped by adding it to the yoghurt it would soften the bitter taste, strange to her palate.

Ana was just tipping in the juice when Ivy caught her in the act, screaming, 'What are you doing, stealing Neville's juice? How dare you steal a baby's rations. Pour it back...' Ivy snatched up the bottle as if it was the best sherry.

'It's actually Dina's bottle, not Neville's, so keep your hair on!' Lily yelled from the door, but no apology was forthcoming.

'We can't leave you alone five minutes before you ruin perfectly good food. Look at this curdled milk. It's gone sour with all your meddling. If you think we're going to sit down and eat your messes, you've another think coming,' she shouted so the whole house could hear. 'My child is not touching your foreign muck with all that grease in it. We are going to the King's to see the Repertory Company tomorrow. Mother will be in bed and Lily and Walt will stay at his mother's and listen to *Saturday Playhouse* if they've any sense.'

Ana looked crestfallen.

Ivy was in full flight of indignation. 'You're not

192

welcome, you know; you and your crony, creeping around Mother. I know what you're after ... getting your slippers under the table, but it doesn't wash with me. If you think Esme Winstanley will leave you or your bastards a penny ha'penny...You don't fool me with your greasy stews and fancy dishes,' she hissed like a poisonous snake.

'Please, I no understand, Lily. I have no slippers under table. You will not eat my dinner?' Ana appealed to Lily, but Ivy was halfway out of the door.

Lily flushed with shame in that cold kitchen with the green and white tiled walls. Their grey Jackson gas cooker stood foursquare as the milk pan began to boil over and the pot of vegetables hissed on the flame.

'Ivy, you've said enough. All the more for us if you don't turn up. You're that sour you'd turn the milk,' Lily snapped back

Tears were pouring down Ana's cheeks when Su came in with the two girls.

'No one is coming to the feast,' Ana howled. 'We have big meal for you, me and Maria. No one will eat our food,' she sobbed, as Susan sat her down at the kitchen table to calm her.

'Don't worry. I have found a bottle of wine and paper lanterns for the decorations. Don't ask me how. Shall we open it now and drink all of it? Then we will not care who comes,' Su laughed. 'We will not worry about the dinner pot. It will be a jolly good show! If the dragon mother and snake man and wife do not come to eat then we will do as in the Bible and find good people to share the table. That is right, Miss Lily? We will ask Maria. She will know plenty of hungry people. We will feast and we will sing. We will talk of old times and show those silly buggers how to have good time. It will be a beautiful *stifado*. The dinner smells good. I will set a table fit for the King with folded lily napkins,' she said with a look of mischief in her eyes.

'Wipe those tears, Ana. Don't let Poison Ivy see she's upset you.' Did I just say that out loud? Lily thought. Poison Ivy – it just about summed up her sister-in-law.

Nothing and no one must spoil their feast but all the fun of the preparation was slipping away fast. They would not disappoint Maria. No way. Whatever happened, the show must go on and Lily was determined as never before that that would be the case.

They wrapped up Dina against the cold wind and put galoshes on their feet, making for the top of the road and Green Lane. Lily promised them a walk to show the child Billy's fields where the rabbit hutches were.

Ana was still smarting from Ivy's insult and the injustice of being accused of stealing. Everything was going wrong and now there were no guests for Maria. What was wrong with this English family, not to gather round the table and talk, laugh, drink and feast until they were sleepy? Why must their girls always be tucked up in bed out of the way? How she wished she had not asked Maria for tea.

There had been a thaw, the snow was melting and she could just see the earth peeping up from the dark ground. There was mist swirling through the trees and a smell of bonfire in the air. It was good to be out of the stuffy kitchen away from Ivy's withering looks.

Lily opened the gate into the field where there were strips of ground, little huts and old men bent over the ground, ferreting for vegetables, men in thick trousers and caps, with moustaches just like the old men of home. There were beans withering on canes, patches of fruit bushes and the smell of rotting leaves. It smelled like home.

'What is this place?' Ana asked.

'This is the allotment where people with no garden can grow their own food, keep chickens and ducks, feed up a pig.'

'You have one of these?'

'We did when Dad was alive, but now there's no time. We buy our stuff where we can,' Lily replied, scanning the field, looking for Billy. 'There he is, over in the far corner. Come on.'

'Don't worry, I got them hung for you,' Billy smiled, walking towards them. 'And who's this then?' The man, who had a scar slashed across his face, smiled at the baby and stared at Ana with interest.

'This is Ana from Greece. She's Freddie's...' Lily always gulped when she told a lie.

'Aye, the lass from Crete, I've heard. We were that sorry about young Fred, but let me shake your hand.' He grasped her hand tightly, shaking both her and the hand. 'If it weren't for you lot my Kenneth would be dead and buried years ago. He were in the Battle for Crete, a gunner. He were marched over them mountains down to the beach, three weeks in that heat, but they got him out to fight again. Brave men in the mountains kept him alive. I won't have a word said against them. You are very welcome.'

She was taken by surprise at the warmth of his embrace.

'Thank you,' she replied.

The rabbits looked skinny and she was glad there were two of them for the pot. She looked round the hut with interest. There was a battered leather chair, a little stove and kettle, the smell of pipe smoke and compost.

'Did you force some rhubarb?' Lily asked.

'Sorry, love, too early. Try me again after Christmas. I got you some fresh eggs.'

'Where is your ground?' Ana asked Lily.

'Just over there,' she replied, pointing into the far corner of the field. 'But someone else is using it now.'

'And a right pig's ear he's making of it. The committee is all for giving him his notice.'

'I can work the land. I can grow my tomatoes, garlic, herbs here,' Ana smiled, seeing it all in her mind's eye.

'Oh, no, lass, no ladies here. This is men's turf.'

'Why?'

'We come here to get away from the missus. It would only upset things,' said Billy, looking puzzled at her suggestion.

'In Crete women work in the fields and men go the *kafenio* to play games and chat.'

'This is Grimbleton, we do things our way but I dare say there's merit in your suggestion,' he winked.

Lily looked at them both and then ferreted into her handbag. 'I have something here that might change your mind,' she whispered. Billy looked at the precious tickets. 'Now that is what I call temptation, lass. But it's not up to me to decide. There has to be a committee meeting first. Get thee behind me, Satan!'

Lily put the tickets back and smiled at him. 'Pity. You've got an interesting hut.'

'That's my little palace, the lion's den. This is where I can close the door on the world, have a game of cards and a brew, champion.'

'What's a brew?' Ana asked.

'I'll show you a brew to put hairs on your chest. Come inside and mind the babby on them sharp slate edges.'

They sat sipping something out of a brown bottle that was thick and tasty, and made Ana's legs wobble when she stood up. Lily was feeling at peace with the world. Putting her hand on the shelf to steady herself, Ana felt a dusty jam jar with a sticky web around it. It was golden.

'Honey! You have honey! Look Lily, honey from the bees. How much?'

'Take it, lass. I can't stand the stuff. This owd geyser keeps giving me jars.'

'I buy it from you,' she offered.

'No, you won't. It's a gift from one grateful dad to a Greek, for services rendered to his son. I'll be telling him all about you.'

His eyes were twinkling. 'But if the Winstanley lassie here were to swop yon jar for one of them tickets, I won't say no!'

11

Susan to the Rescue

Su climbed the stairs with a heavy heart. They'd still no guests for the feast. Miss Lily wore such a worried face. Ana was skinning the fur off the rabbits in the kitchen. Too much cooking and not enough people didn't make a good party. It was a pity.

She kneeled by her little shrine; a bedside table filled with photos, pressed flowers and pretty berries she'd collected from the park. What would Auntie Betty think? Was her kindly spirit watching over her with a favourable smile? She was trying to do her best to be a good Christian woman, but at times like this perhaps it was better to place offerings of rice and petals to the shrine of the holy Buddha to watch over proceedings too. This was her first dinner party and it *must* be a success.

Now she had a proper job, thanks to a kind lady at church, Diana, daughter of Dr Unsworth in Green Lane. It was right to keep tradition and go to the biggest church with a high ceiling and dusty banners suspended way above her head. It was lonely at first, sitting in the back row. People stared at her, even in the House of the Lord. Sometimes Joy wriggled and made a noise, and they scurried out into the porch so as not to be a nuisance.

On her second visit it was raining hard and it was a wet walk home, but Diana stopped her car. 'You must be one of the Winstanley girls,' she yelled. 'Collapse the go-chair and hop in. You must be soaked.'

She spoke just like the Chindhe ladies who'd run the Burma canteen, very pukka, but nothing was too much trouble for them in the jungle.

'My cousin was in Burma. He said it was a beautiful country. I never got that far,' Diana added. 'Pity, I think they could have done with a few more Fanys out there. Must be terribly strange for you here.'

Miss Diana Unsworth wore a military-style felt hat and a thick tweed jacket with a cravat in her shirt collar. She had a warm smile and English-rose complexion. Su told her the well-rehearsed story of how she'd landed to some terrible news about Cedric and how the Winstanleys had taken her in. Diana nodded and sighed, and said she would make sure she got a lift each Sunday but they'd have to go early as it was church parade. Su smiled as she told her about the military parades in the church in Rangoon and how she had been a teacher there.

It was Diana who suggested she went to the Education Office with her certificate and try for a post. Now Su could escape to Moorlands School each day, out on the bus up into the high moors above the town, where she could look down over the forest of smoking chimneys in the valley and breathe fresh air, away from the blanket of belching smoke that settled above the mills and factories. No wonder everyone coughed and sneezed.

She loved to sit upstairs on the bus, climbing high past the grander avenues and roads; Victoria Drive and Albert Circus, Regent Rise where the mill owners lived in old houses hidden behind tall trees. She counted roof tops and chimney-pots, especially the tall, sculptured, layered-up ones with golden crowns on top, like pagodas. The richer the house, the more chimneys with crowns on, she thought.

One day, she mused, Joy will live in a grand house like that and she would drive through the iron gates in a big saloon car and Auntie Betty would be glad she had sold her bangles to give her niece the chance to be a true English girl.

Moorlands was a special school and not the sort of teaching she had hoped for. But she must try to help simple minds, poor children cast out from their families to live out on the hillside in this stone school. There were children of all ages in there, handicapped toddlers, some lying in cots or sitting in wheelchairs, others sitting like dummies, motionless, with wandering eyes and flickering hands fanning their faces, rocking back and forth. Moorlands was not a happy place.

She was nervous for Joy in their infant nursery, but the little girl paddled around oblivious to the handicapped children, playing with the few toys while the others rattled their cots and shouted. Not the best of jobs but she was doing her best, for she felt so sorry for the abandoned ones.

The staff tried to make the place cheerful with posters and bright colours, stencils of Donald Duck and Mickey Mouse on the walls, but the corridors were dark and they smelled of Lysol mops and soiled nappies. The ceilings were high so it was always chilly.

On dry crisp days they were allowed to let the children out into the grounds in basket chairs and on crutches, a line of them tied by the wrist to each other so they didn't run off. There were some swings and a slide, but it was too cold and icy to let them play properly.

Su's teaching certificate had not equipped her to deal with these children. She was used to lines of eager faces, chanting words from the board in singsong voices. These poor kids should be in the heart of their families, not out of sight in an institution.

She guessed no one wanted this sort of work and so that's why they'd been quick to take her on. She didn't like to dwell on the fact that perhaps she was taken on because she too was different.

It didn't count that she had an English father and name and education, or that she was well-spoken and well travelled. She was different and it hurt. Thank goodness Joy was lighter-skinned, plump and rosy-cheeked. She must be protected from such hurtful comments and her English would be perfect, so it was worth doing anything to see that her baby got the best out of their new life.

There was no cruelty to the children here. They were well fed and watered, exercised and contained, but days were ruled by the bell and they had a strict routine that the principal said gave their charges a sense of time and normality. But something was missing; something that would make every day different and exciting and stimulating, to distract them from some very bad habits.

The staff sat around the staff room, smoking, knitting, eyeing her with interest. One guy had his feet on the table in defiance when she entered. 'It's come to a poor do when we've got to employ foreigners,' he sneered, loud enough for everyone to hear.

'Come off it, Alf. We were quite happy to let the Poles and French and Czechs come to our aid when it mattered in the Battle of Britain. Give the lass a chance,' said another, coming to Su's defence.

'I'm a qualified teacher. I know Shakespeare and Wordsworth. I was taught by fine English ladies in a Christian girls' school. It is true I have no experience with,' Su hesitated to find the right word, 'such special children, but if you will help me I will try,' she replied.

'I'm sure you have qualifications, Mrs Winstanley ... such as they are. You should be grateful for work at all, considering your status, and once our men are retrained and come back to claim their rightful places in our schools...' the bald man with the ugly sneer snapped back. 'But if you're not happy here... If it's not good enough for you...' he threatened.

It was better to ignore him and the embarrassed looks on the faces of the other staff members and sit as far away as she could.

She needed this job and the nursery place, but it was sapping her spirit to feel so out of her depth and helpless. If only someone would show her what to do!

It was a relief at weekends not to have to travel through town away from the noisy normality of Division Street. It was hard to pretend her job was anything other than a miserable chore. Ana was jealous. If truth were told she'd much prefer to swap places with her any day, such was her frustration.

She opened her Bible at random for inspiration and guidance. There had to be a way to make the Winstanleys come to their dinner. She didn't want Maria to be disappointed by the poor turn-out after all she'd done for them.

She closed her eyes and prayed again, then read the text and burst into a beam of pure delight.

Susan came bounding down the stairs at the double, waving her little leather Bible. 'I have the answer to our prayers.' The boycotting of their feast had lain heavy on everyone's heart. Now she had a grin on her face from ear to ear.

'This morning I am reading a passage from St Luke in my Bible Notes: the parable tells how rich guests refuse to come to the feast and the servant is told to, "go out quickly into the streets and lanes of the city and bring hither the poor, the maimed, the halt and the blind." Suddenly it comes in a flash. That is what we do now, Lily. Trust me, but hurry!'

There was no need to whisk the go-chair down the cobbled streets back into Grimbleton when Gertie was already parked ready and willing. There were no beggars by the bus stops on the way to Santini's as they rattled through the football traffic, afire with a mission to find replacements.

The café was crowded out, and Lily slipped into the back kitchen in search of Maria. There was a cheery large woman with a head full of curlers wrapped in a headscarf serving customers as Maria came bounding down the stairs, took one look at their faces and stopped in her tracks. 'Tonight, it's not off, is it?'

'No, no.' Susan swallowed, seeing that Maria was so eager to come. 'It's just we have a few spare places due to Daw Esme being indisposed with a bad cold, and the honourable brother-in-law having a prior engagement,' she lied.

'Yes, poor Mother is full of germs,' Lily said, backing her up. 'If you want, you can bring a friend or one of your sisters-in-law,' she suggested, but Maria threw up her hands in horror.

'No more Santinis! I have enough of them. They drive me crazy, and Enzo no show up so my friend, Queenie here, leave her cuppa to help me out. Queenie, come and meet Burma Su. I've told you about Su, and Ana from Greece, and this is Lily... Queenie Quigley, shampooer to the stars, come for a rest from old man Lavaroni's hairdressers. Help me out until that lazy son of Toni turn up. She is very good friend, like you,' said Maria, rushing off with a tray to see to her customers.

It was time to seize the moment. 'A friend of Maria's is very welcome to join us. We're making dinner and there is plenty to go round. We don't want any empty seats. You're welcome to join us.'

Queenie mopped her brow and smiled. 'That's

the nicest thing that's happened all week. I'd be delighted. My hubby works shifts. I go in one door and he goes out the next. Having a meal cooked for me will be a real treat, thanks, ducks.'

So that was how Queenie Quigley came to be sitting opposite them at the table, in a paisley print blouse with smocking across the shoulders and all her brown curls pinned neatly into a pompadour film-star style, smoking a cigarette from a holder, next to the other guests they had managed to rake up at the last minute.

The Almighty worked in mysterious ways his wonders to perform. His cohorts must have been hard at work on their behalf this afternoon. He had provided some hand-picked 'uns here and no mistake. How else could they have found such wonderful guests at such short notice, Lily mused with satisfaction much later. It was all a matter of heavenly timing.

On the way out of Santini's, who should be rushing in the opposite direction but the lovely Diana Unsworth from Green Lane, daughter of Dr Unsworth, the girl who gave Susan regular lifts back from the parish church in her smart Morris 8 Tourer? Lily recognised her from the Girl Guides' Association. She was Captain of the Parish Church Troop and a nursing sister in the hospital. Soon they would all be collaborating together in the Guide and Brownie Review. Her reputation for being a stickler for detail went before her, and Lily was a little in awe of this striking girl in her riding jodhpurs and headscarf. They stopped to greet each other.

'I am so glad to meet you,' said Susan, turning

to Lily for approval. 'This is Miss Diana who gives me a lift to church. You are the answer to my prayer.'

'Oh, I say,' said the young lady, smiling at Lily, 'how intriguing!'

'We are having a last-minute supper, Ana and me, a thank you for the kindness of Grimbleton friends.'

Lily hovered, holding out her hand. 'We're so pleased to see you. We'd be honoured if you would join us tonight, if you are free. I am sorry it's so last minute,' she added, hoping the Lord would understand the necessity of a white lie.

'I always think that the best suppers are usually impromptu, Susan. I would be delighted but I've a guest of my own from the hospital staying tonight. You know Eva Matin, the coloured girl from South Africa training to be a midwife? She comes to church whenever she can, but living in the Nurses' Home is not much fun, so I was just looking to see what was on at the King's Theatre.'

'Then bring her along too. The more the merrier at our table, I say. It's good to meet new people,' Lily found herself saying, much to her surprise. This was no time for shilly-shallying. Seize the moment, she smiled. Her resolve was stiffening against any opposition now. That would make six guests and that was enough to make the party go with a swing.

'Eva sits in front of me in church. She always looks so tall and elegant in her navy-blue nurse's uniform and cap; an interesting woman, I think,' said Susan, her eyes bright with excitement.

Once the missing Winstanley place settings

were accounted for, they spluttered back to Division Street in Gertie to tell Ana the good news.

It was true that the newly acquired guests might not be poor or maimed or blind, but two of them were nurses and Maria and Queenie ministered comforts to the hungry and weary, and deserved a treat. That would have to do.

'I was obedient to the spirit of the text. This is the Lord's work,' Susan muttered as she searched for napkins to fold into cloth lilies.

The afternoon was spent trying to keep little fingers out of mischief. Ana was putting the finishing touches to her special rabbit stew and the meze. Everyone had gone to the match. The streets were deserted. Esme had left wrapped up like a fur parcel, determined to sit out the match in style.

Lily did her stint on the stall with bad grace. There were a hundred and one little finishing touches she would like to do to the dining room. The Market Hall was like a ghost town. She stood in the entrance, listening for the roars that meant a goal had been scored. It echoed right around the streets but the silence was deafening.

Nil, nil at half-time. A goalless draw was the worst of results. And then one of the butcher's boys ran in: 'They've scored. Walshie has scored! We're winning...'

How Lily wished she was side by side with Walt, cheering the lads on to victory. She hoped Billy was enjoying his ticket. He had sent them a bunch of late chrysanthemums as a thank you.

One of these days she'd make Levi do the Saturday shift. Someone had to keep the Winstanley till ringing, but why was it always her? She arrived home tired and jaded among the crush of exuberant football fans chattering on the bus. Mother had already disappeared up to bed with hot milk and brandy.

'I shouldn't have stayed for full time but it was that exciting.'

'It was silly to go,' Lily replied, having little sympathy.

'Someone had to represent the family. Yer dad wouldn't have wanted us to miss the match. I'll give tonight a miss, though.'

'Please yourself, but you're going to miss a good evening. Why don't you get up and come down later to meet our guests? It's not like you to give in to a cold.'

'I don't know what's come over you, Lil. Not an ounce of sympathy for a mother with flu...' Esme turned her face into the pillow, looking rather washed out.

'It's just a cold, not flu. It'll pass,' Lily snapped. This was Esme's way of opting out, an excuse not to take sides, and Lily had no sympathy. The whole bunch of them, Walter included, had let her down with their feeble excuses.

Ivy kept out of the way at first, and the toddlers were bathed and put to bed early after Neville. Nothing must ever spoil his routine. The dining room had a display of fresh flowers in the crystal vase and an embroidered tablecloth with lace edging. There were pretty tablemats with ladies in crinolines, which came out when company was entertained. The fire was stoked up when Ivy's

208

back was turned so she didn't see how much coal they were sneaking from the ration. This was not a night for skimping.

By now, Ivy was huffing and puffing in the kitchen, sneering at everyone's efforts but curious to know why there were still seven place settings on show. No one was going to enlighten her.

'I wish I could beat her out of here like my Auntie Betty would shoo the servant boys off the veranda with a switch brush,' Susan smiled while making up a little bowl of leaves and shavings of petals and chopped apple, and placing them by the door. 'This is what we do for good luck,' she smiled. 'To ward off evil,' she finished, looking pointedly at Ivy.

Ana stared at the jam jar of precious olive oil, green and golden, shining before her. She sniffed the top and smiled. The kitchen table was laden for the feast: potatoes and boiled eggs, sardines and anchovies, chopped dried herbs, the best they could find.

The rabbits were seared in a pan. The pickled onions and shallots was pierced with a few cloves. She had begged a tin of plum tomatoes, bay leaves and some of Maria's rough wine. As it all bubbled away the aromas drifted into her nostrils. She could see Mama's cooking pot on the fire simmering. It was as near as she could get to home and it was enough. Everyone kept coming in to sniff the air and taste the juices.

The yoghurt wasn't quite set. In desperation they had added rennet to make a sort of junket, with orange juice and bottled raspberries, and it had turned out quite delicious. Lily contributed butter to make some pastry balls, dipped in fat with honey topping. They kept disappearing as fast as she made them until she shooed everyone out of her domain.

It was funny that she didn't mind doing all the work while Susan did the fancy bits. Su had found them special guests but she would get all the praise for her food. Lily held everything together like sticking plaster. They were a good team.

Yet in her mind's eye was the field where the rabbits were kept and the overgrown lines of rotting vegetables lying neglected. She wanted to dig and grow things again, feel the earth between her fingers. The back garden was too small, but Billy's field was the place. Somehow she would make herself a garden and grow all the things her heart yearned for, and no one was going to stop her just because she was a woman.

12

The Olive Oil Club

They waited nervously for the first guests to arrive and everyone was introduced with a small glass of Christmas sherry that Mother had been hoarding, a peace offering for her cowardice. Maria's gift of a bottle of Italian wine, alongside

Susan's bottle, soon loosened the shyness and conversation flowed so that the room was filled with noisy chatter and no one noticed how late it was getting.

Lily dressed with care in her winter woollen dress with cross-over lapels. It was in a saxe blue that complimented her eyes. It was sad that her family chose to miss a rare treat. There was even a scoop each of best vanilla ice cream, which Maria had carried here on the bus, wrapped up in thick newspaper.

Lily wondered if Walt would change his mind and join them, but in truth she was quite relieved when he didn't arrive. All girls together was turning out to be much more fun.

Diana Unsworth arrived with a hunk of best Lancashire Tasty, which must have used up all her rations for weeks to come.

'One of the advantages of being a good doctor's daughter is we're always getting gifts left on our doorsteps and no questions asked,' she offered.

Queenie Quigley brought a large box of pre-war chocolates in a heart-shaped box, and everyone stared at them in amazement.

'Where did you get those?' sighed Diana, rolling her eyes and licking her lips in anticipation. For a proper English lady she was turning out to be good fun.

'Ask me no questions and I tell you no lies, me ducks,' winked Queenie. 'Let's just say I relieved old man Lavaroni, him being a diabetic, of an embarrassing gift from a grateful client for services rendered.' She nodded and winked again. 'I may only wash the heads and sweep the

211

cuttings, but let's put it this way: a certain star treading the boards of the King's Theatre, even as I speak, is not quite the gentleman he appears, and not quite as young as his black hair would suggest. My lips are sealed but the proof is here.' There was dye still clinging to her fingertips. 'We had to open the shop at midnight so his secret might not be revealed.'

Queenie and her husband, Arthur, came north after being blitzed out of their house in Kent, evacuated with their children for the duration and somehow they had never got round to going back. She'd taken to Grimbleton, finding her niche doing even more jobs than Maria.

Gianni Lavaroni's Hair Salon was the classy establishment favoured by the theatricals, and the old man was taking on a new barber. 'He's got one of them POWs from Macaroni Camp starting soon, now they're being released from prison. This chap jumps off a lorry, walks in and asks for a job. Old Lavaroni can't resist cheap labour – I should know,' she laughed. 'He takes the lad on there and then. I shall send him down to you for his lunches, Maria,' she winked.

'You will do no such thing,' Maria snapped. 'My brothers no like prisoners of war. No like mixing with lazy Italian scum.'

'The war's over now,' Ana said gently.

'You tell that to Angelo and Toni, with poor Marco still in bed,' Maria replied bitterly. If only he would grow stronger, but the least effort tired him out. He was shrinking before her eyes.

They were all used to seeing lorries full of prisoners, in their funny uniforms with circles on

212

their backs, going out to the farms and working on the road repairs. The Italians were always singing and shouting and whistling after a pretty pair of legs.

Lily looked around and smiled, contented by this rich company, such an unlikely roomful of guests, another motley bunch of liquorice allsorts. It was worthy of a photo line-up if only there was film in the box Brownie camera.

Queenie and Maria were dark and spicy, loud and sharp-edged. Maria's cheeks were flushed with wine. Her delight at being given a feast was worth all their efforts. Then there was quiet Eva, with chocolate-brown-coloured skin and fine cheekbones. How gracefully she sat, observing everyone with interest.

Ana was wearing a bright emerald spotted blouse, made up from remnants from a market stall, which set off her coiled red hair. She was flushed with the success of her dishes.

Diana was wearing a bright coconut-pink knitted jumper with intricate lacy stitches, which set off her rose complexion and blonde curls. She sat like a mannequin, straight-backed.

She and Lily were the same age but had never socialised together because Diana went to Harrogate Ladies' College and then joined the FANY in the war. She was a perfect lady, a good listener who asked questions of them all, interested, but saying very little about herself whilst encouraging Eva to join in as best she could.

Eva was full of her work at Grimbleton General and the shortages, of staff and the new National Health Service to come, and how many of their staff came from overseas as refugees. She was hoping to go back to South Africa once she had completed her training.

Ana was listening intently and told them about her voluntary work with the Red Cross in Crete. She lifted her glass and smiled across the table.

'Yámas! Cheers.'

'Yámas, Billy Eckersley!' Lily replied.

'Thank you, Lily. Without your rabbit friend we are stuck.' They toasted Allotment Billy for his services.

'*Yámas*, thank you, Maria, for many happy Sundays,' added Susan, raising her glass too. She was wearing her best silk striped *longyi* in silver and black as a traditional touch. Her ruby earrings glittered in the light and she looked like the wrapper from a blackcurrant liquorice sweet.

'To Maria, and Marco, may he get well soon,' they toasted. '*Yámas!*'

'Bottoms up! Let's have a singsong,' said Queenie, jumping onto the piano stool. 'I'll have you know I'm going to be playing for the new dancing school if I can fit it round my afternoon shift.'

'Not so loud then, Daw Esme is sick,' Susan whispered with alarm, not wanting to cause any trouble.

'Don't be minding her,' Lily shouted back. 'It'll do her good to hear a bit of fun. She likes a bit of a singsong and if you put some ballet music in it, she'll think it classy. Classy, she can stand. It's marching bands she can't abide since our Freddie went.' There was a pause. 'Well, you know how it is with the war, memories.'

Maria bent her head, thinking of Marco, back on the ward, fighting for breath, and the handsome soldier who was sent to war and came back a cripple. If she had not come here tonight, she would have sat alone in the flat. Nonna was taking Rosa home and to church tomorrow morning.

Diana thought of the lines of shrouds she had ticked off, the nurses caught in the blast of gunfire, the mess parties, the concert shows and the smell of the desert air. How far away all that was now. Why had she come back? Grimbleton was so damp and predictable, but tonight it was turning out to be fun.

Su had never seen the room sparkle as it did tonight, firelight and fresh flowers, pretty things and dresses and smiling faces, rubies, pearls, bangles. The room had come alive and it was all her doing. Thank you, she thought, seeing the little bowl of offerings and the Bible.

They stood around the piano, singing songs from the shows while Queenie rattled the tinny keyboard with gusto: 'If You Were the Only Girl in the World'.

'Let's dance, come, I show you...' shouted Ana, springing to life, gathering them all in a circle, raising her hands in the air, circling around the table in time to the music, laughing, her curls shimmering in the firelight. 'See, this is how we dance in Crete.'

They linked arms and circled and laughed as they kicked their legs and folded them across in a pattern, round and round until Lily was dizzy.

215

Then there was a rattle of the door in the hall and the sound of the other Winstanleys returning home from their evenings out. Was it really that time, already?

Lily scuttled to the door, not wanting any unpleasantness to spoil their fun.

'You decided to stay, then?' said Ivy, taking off her felt hat and sniffing the air. 'You can hear the racket in the street, and the curtains still open for all to see.'

'What a grand do you've missed. Ana and Susan did us proud, a proper feast with cheese and then chocolates. What a treat! Now we're having a bit of a dance.'

At the mention of chocolates, Ivy made for the door. 'Is it still going on? I hope you saved some for us, seeing as it's *our* electric and gas you're using up.' She peered round the door with a look of amazement. 'I hope you didn't wake our Neville with that racket? You were right, Levi, it's a right League of Nations in there, even a darkie sitting at the table... The house reeks of olive oil and garlic ... a right olive oil club they've got here.'

'Come in, Ivy,' shouted Ana, drunk with the excitement of good company. 'Come and join the dancing.'

Ivy was in the room like a shot, looking down at the disarray of plates and glasses. 'They're all drunk, and Lil's made herself right at home with Mother's best china, I see,' she sneered.

'Keep your hair on. Mother said it was the least we could do, seeing how many there would be of them and how few of us,' Lily replied with a hard edge to her voice. That woman had more neck than a giraffe, trying to muscle in on their party food like a vulture at a carcass.

'Let me introduce you to our guests. This is my sister-in-law, Ivy, and my brother, Levi,' she offered, going round the table slowly so that Ivy would catch every name. 'Maria Santini from Italy, Queenie Quigley, late of Kent, Eva Matin from Cape Town, South Africa, and Diana Unsworth from Green Lane. I'm sure you recognise *her* name.' She couldn't resist making the point and the last name hovered in the air with promise.

'Diana Unsworth? What, Dr Unsworth's daughter?' whispered Ivy, all of a quiver. 'How nice to meet you... I did not realise you would be coming.' She turned to Levi who was hovering in the hall, half whispering with embarrassment, 'Mind your P's and Q's, one of the Unsworths is here!' The shine of her saccharine smile fooled no one.

'Of course, we had a prior engagement otherwise we'd have *loved* to join you all,' she minced, sitting down in Susan's empty chair, stretching across for the chocolates, disappointed to see that there were only wrappers left.

Lily smiled. It served her right to miss the treats. It was worth all the washing-up and clearing-away just to see that look of disappointment on her puckered lips. The box was empty and the wine all drunk.

It hit midnight but no one wanted to leave, and when they did, everyone promised to meet up again for another supper. Ivy and Levi soon disappeared, leaving the three women to clear away the debris.

Ana surveyed the table with relish, wine and cigarette smoke, all the pleasures of a feast. Her belly was full and her heart content. It was good to entertain strangers and welcome them into the home. In Crete it was the custom to give the guests the best of all you had, however little.

She fingered the leftovers with a smile. If only Aliki and Stelios, could see how women could entertain as well as men, cook and drink, dress up, gossip and dance. These were not the smells of home but friendship and kindness smelled the same in any country. She thought of that old saying about friendship: we have shared bread and salt together, joy and sorrow.

Joy there had been in abundance, but the sorrow of their secrets lay heavy on her heart. Only when the truth was shared about Freddie would true friendships ever begin.

But it was enough for tonight, she sighed as she crept into the attic.

'It was good tonight,' she whispered to Su as she climbed into her narrow little bed. 'Good to be giving, not always taking charity ... yes?'

There was no reply but Su lay smiling in her sleep. One thing was certain: women may be made for men, but women together could have just as good a time. She was already looking forward to the next gathering.

13

A Dickens of a Christmas

'No more carols on the piano, Lil, they're giving me one of my heads,' shouted Esme, who hated Christmas with a fervour bordering on obsession. But it was no use pretending as the weeks were ticked off to the festivities that the season could be ignored any longer. 'Nothing jolly this year, not after all our sorrows. It wouldn't be right to be giddy.'

'There's never been a giddy Christmas in this house, and certainly not after Dad or Freddie. But we've kiddies to think of now. I know how you feel but we have to do something for their sakes.' Lily was hoping for dinner in the dining room with the fire lit and a few token decorations, a proper Christmas tree on display, a bird and all the trimmings. 'Freddie wouldn't begrudge us cheering up his children, now, would he?'

'You know, it's just a pagan ceremony. All that expense for a few days of indigestion.'

'Oh, Mother, it'll be different this year with Su and Ana. They've never had a proper English Christmas. It'll take your mind off things,' Lily argued.

She loved Christmas: all the smells of spices and cooking, tinsel and lantern lights, carols by candlelight and the excitement of hidden presents. She wanted to see the faces of Dina and Joy on Christmas morning when they unwrapped their knitted dollies and toy cot.

It had taken an advert in the *Gazette* to acquire those items second-hand at extortionate prices. Walt mustn't know that the cash came out of her wedding fund. He thought she spoiled them enough as it was. Perhaps when they had children of their own he'd understand how important it was to give them a good time. Poor old Walt had had so little fun in his life, she sighed. It was hard to ever imagine him young and acting daft.

Why must Christmas Day be a cold quick affair: overcooked chicken pieces, a currantless steamed pudding and no crackers? She wanted Ana and Su to feel the warmth of festive joy in this arctic weather; a Dickens of a Christmas that would sweep away the gloom and chill of this terrible winter freeze.

If they could find olive oil for their first thanksgiving dinner then somewhere they could scrounge spices and dried fruit, extra sugar for treats. Levi would not see Neville and Ivy short. Walt and his mother, Enid Greenalgh and *her* mother too, would come for their dinner, so all their rations would add to the feast. No one would want to be left out of the fun and games.

Since Diana was taking an interest in Susan and Ana, Levi's wife was not so quick to miss out on any social events on offer. They were even going to attend the *Messiah* in the parish church, much to Esme's dismay.

'I hope you're not all going Popish on me,' she

sniffed, but in the end the feast of sacred music was too good to miss. Mother dolled herself in her best camel coat with a fox-fur tippet dangling, and a fierce military felt hat.

What a formidable bunch the Winstanleys were, Lily thought as they walked *en masse* down the tunnelled paths into town by torchlight and gaslamp, dressed up in furs and macs against the chill. Three generations of family in harmony for once, a show of strength, she hoped, for the future.

Next year Walt, by then her husband, would be taking her arm, but choral singing wasn't his forte. Being tone deaf must be a terrible burden. Bless him! Walt was being so patient with all her busyness. The whole town was cockahoop since the Grasshoppers were into the next round of the Cup. This time she would not be missing the game. The paper was full of the team, and Pete Walsh in particular. She'd seen him stop to sign autographs at the end of the last home match. He'd looked up at her and waved, and she'd felt her legs go all wobbly. Feeling guilty, she'd scuttled off before he could catch her up.

If only Freddie and Father were here too. Christmas could be such a lonely time when childhood memories came flooding back.

They all enjoyed a good sing, and stood for the 'Hallelujah' Chorus. This effort to be sociable was Mother's one token to the season, however, and it was Lily who ended up buying gifts for the family on her behalf and overseeing all the food preparations.

If Christmas was ever to happen at Waverley House it would be up to her to organise the troops, but it was getting harder trying to fit in with everyone's plans. Mother thought it disloyal to want any seasonal fun, but the children ought to have a bit of what she'd had as a child: carols and sleigh bells, parties and stockings too. It felt like treading on eggshells trying to please everyone but herself. Freddie wouldn't begrudge a bit of singing and dancing, especially in this cold spell. Her chilblains were red raw.

When Lily was playing with Dina and Joy it was easy to forget there was a dark winter outside. She could almost forget that half the family was missing. Children stopped her looking back to what once was and made the future all there was to cling to now. Her promise to watch over them growing up was precious.

But what would have happened if Fred was still alive and they had both turned up? That would have been a right facer. Now there were only secrets to hide, she sighed, and it wasn't getting any easier. Then there was the Guide and Brownie Christmas Review looming large.

It was funny how you never saw someone for ages and then kept bumping into them all the time, she smiled. Diana kept popping up in shops and round corners. At the first joint rehearsal there she was directing proceedings like an army drill parade.

The Guides were doing sketches and the various Brownie packs individual items. 'Daisy Darling and the Tin Soldiers' was not going very well. It was the costumes that let them down, and

222

the hats hadn't even arrived yet.

'There you are, Lily. Nice to see you again.' Diana sprung down the hall. 'Is this lot yours? Who made the rig-outs?' she sniggered. 'Quite an interesting interpretation of a military theme.'

'They're awful. Susan's tried to re-jig them but they can't stand up like that,' Lily replied, looking at the costumes with dismay.

'Can't you make them sailors, then?'

'Nope, they are meant to be tin soldiers,' she said. 'The hired hats with pompoms will look good.'

'In my book, best to keep it simple. Get them to wear a school shirt and make some epaulettes with tassels for their shoulders. That'll do.'

'We can do that in a jiffy, thanks.'

'Wish everything was so easy,' Diana sighed. 'I have to keep telling myself that if I can open a field hospital in a desert storm, with sand and flies and dust, I can lick a few Guides into shape. I did enjoy the supper. You must all come to me next. Eva was thrilled to be asked too. She wants to cook some South African dish, billy bong, I think she said. Ana and her olive oil did well, not tasted that for years. How's Maria's husband?'

'They settled him down again. He's hoping to be out for Christmas.'

'Frightful shame about his chest wound. It must have done some damage for it not to heal. Still, where there's life there's hope, and he's young.'

'So are we,' Lily sighed.

'Sometimes I feel about fifty in this dreadful Guide uniform. There are plans to change the design. Why do I live my life permanently in uniform? Boarding school, then the FANY, now guides – where will it end? I suppose it saves on clothing coupons. My hunting jacket is so threadbare, Mummy threatens to carve up Great-Grandmama's riding habit. Listen to me, must dash... Jennifer Wolstencroft, I can see you slouching. Stand up straight. You're too young for a dowager's hump!

'Don't forget the dress rehearsal, Lily. I've got a few surprises up my sleeve. You don't fancy being the back end of a cow, do you?'

And that was how Lily came to be slithering across the stage in a dusty old pantomime costume instead of sitting in the pictures with Walt.

She was coughing and blind as a bat, with Diana pushing her forwards. 'One two three, collapse, one, two, three, kick out...' Damn, that was her shin! When would she ever learn to say no?

The following evening, Ana was tearful, watching the faded paper twirls being fixed to the corners of the room, trying to explain to anyone who would listen how different Christmases in Crete used to be.

'We have feast of Agios Vasilios, we sing *kalenda* songs with Christmas pie and special bread, roasted kid, oregano, potatoes. On Christmas Eve we give thick soup and sausages, smoked meats – the nine cooked dishes – and afterwards honey and sweetbreads.'

'Stop! My mouth is watering,' Lily laughed.

'It was before the war. We share our food around

the village,' Ana sighed. 'I know it is not the same here. If only Freddie was here ... but I will do best for Dina's sake,' she whispered, hoping Esme was out of earshot.

There was still the one unspoken rule in Division Street that Freddie's name was never mentioned, especially in front of Esme. The shame of his antics and the sorrow at his untimely death were her daily burden. He was banished to the top right-hand drawer of the cabinet.

Cedric, the mysterious cousin, lived in there too, brought out and dusted down like some best china ornament, put out on display for company if awkward questions were asked. His photograph had been cut out from a magazine and stuck in a frame. He explained Su and Joy's presence in the family home. Everyone was told that her husband had died of some awful wounds somewhere far enough away for no one to enquire further.

Then the phantom husband was put back in the locked drawer full of secrets in the mahogany dresser, which contained strange birth certificates, letters of sponsorship and the one photograph that showed Freddie under a pagoda in Pagan alongside a smiling Susan.

Then Su decided to bring out this snapshot to share in the celebrations.

'Put that away,' said Ana.

'Why should I?' snapped Su. 'He is family, my family. Why does he have to stay out of sight? I want Joy to see her daddy on Christmas morning.'

'You tell her, Lily. Put it away! He is my husband. I am number one wife, not her!'

'That is rubbish. This is me and him, not you. Find your own photograph. I am number one wife. He will stay...'

Everyone knew Ana hated that photo and would have shredded it many times. Now she lurched forward to flatten it down. Su pushed it up again. Up and down the poor snapshot went.

'Miss Lily, I am number one wife.'

'She is big liar!'

'Stop it, you two! No one is number one wife,' Lily snapped, at the end of her tether. 'Stop this quarrelling. I'm tired of everyone snapping and snarling. This is supposed to be the season of goodwill to all men. I'm sick of it. Do your own Christmas!' She fled upstairs to her back bedroom and flung herself down on her blue satin eiderdown.

Let them all go hang. She'd had enough argy-bargy. Even Walt was acting peculiar because she hadn't made their date. Every time she had called at his door he was down the pub, or so his mother said. Let them make Christmas happen without me. See if I care. She stamped her fist on the pillow.

Earlier that week, preparations for the Review had been frantic. Lily had thirty excited Brownies to contain, all wanting to be front of stage. Kathleen Walsh had a sweet singing voice and she was Daisy Darling, the heroine. She was the young sister of Pete, whose mother was 'caught on the change', Esme had whispered once. This unexpected happy event was the talk of the neighbourhood at the time.

The paper hats were dished out on pain of death of tearing them, and the simplified uniform was passable. Diana was trying to organise everyone, despite a hacking cough and an obvious temperature.

'Go home,' Lily suggested.

'Not until I get the girls singing "Nymphs and Shepherds Come Away" in tune,' she croaked.

'I don't think they'll make the Manchester Children's Orpheus Choir, however many times you practise. Go home.'

'I should have chosen "White Christmas".'

'If you don't go home, there'll be you in bed and us without a director. Go home!'

'We need to practise the cow with the pianist.'

'I'll find someone. Go home.'

'Are you sure? You will all be coming on Boxing Day to our gathering? I'd like Mummy and Daddy to meet you all. They are intrigued. Bring the whole family, if you like.'

'We'll see, but if you don't go home, Nurse, it'll be your hospital bed we'll be visiting.' Lily found herself being as bossy as Diana for once.

The Guides soon disbanded in a thunderous rush from the stage and the little ones were put through their paces. Mothers were gathering at the back of the church hall, waiting to collect their offspring, waving and distracting the artistes from their performing.

Muriel, the pianist, wanted to practise the cow dance. Lily didn't see the point.

'I need to get the timing right,' Muriel insisted, turning to the waiting relatives and asking for a volunteer.

'Come on, will anyone give Brown Owl a helping hand?' No one spoke.

'Will a chap do?' yelled a familiar voice as Pete Walsh, who often came to collect his sister, came striding down the hall with a silly grin on his face.

'There's no need.' Lily blushed beetroot. 'We can skip it, Muriel, for tonight.'

'Not so fast. There's a volunteer. Let's be having you, hero of the hour. Oh, it's you, Pete ... saw you on Saturday. Like a stag, you were, leaping across that pitch. They must feed you on Guinness. They said there was an England scout in the stand. Wait till my husband hears about this...' Would Muriel Scott *ever* shut up?

Lily didn't want Pete up so close. She hadn't made it up with the footballer since the morning of the tickets in the hall, even though he always tried to be friendly.

'Do you want me front or back?' He burst out laughing at his words. 'No offence.'

'What's he on about?'

'Don't be saucy, young man. Lily here is far too innocent. She leads and you follow.' His mischievous eyes got Lily all confused.

'She's the gun turret and I'm in the rear?' he asked.

'Now stop your cheek and concentrate,' said Lily. 'We haven't got all night. Kathleen needs to be going to bed. I stand and you grasp my waist and listen to the counting. We'll do it without the costume so you'll get the gist,' she ordered, trying to pretend this was not in front of all her girls.

'I see... like this,' he chuckled, and grabbed her

228

by the waist.

'Not so tight. I can't breathe,' she croaked. 'It's one, two, three, and lift your left leg...'

They fumbled and tried again. It was a disaster and everyone roared as they collapsed in a heap on the stage. His weight was dragging her down. She looked up into his eyes, all hot under the collar.

Muriel banged out the chorus line from a Laurel and Hardy film. 'Doop di doop. Doop di doop, Tiddly pom. Tiddly pom... Doop di doop,' came the voice in the rear.

'Stop it, you're making me laugh,' Lily giggled. If Walt could see her now, he'd have a fit. She was glad she had clean underwear on.

'Synchronise your legs,' yelled Muriel. 'One, two, three, up. One, two, three, down, and change over. Then turn.'

'How do we turn?' Pete called. Then he trod on the back of her heels. 'Sorry, sorry.'

'Not half as sorry as I am,' she snorted back, trying not to laugh and lose her balance.

'What we need is two pints of Wilson's best bitter and then we'll make sweet music together. It's all in the timing, isn't it, Mrs Scott?'

'Now stop that, young man, or I'll tell the *Gazette* just what a naughty boy you are. One more time after two...'

'Play it again, Sam,' he whispered, and this time it worked. In step with the music they ambled across the stage and managed a turn without falling over.

There was a clap from the back of the hall.

Now they had to put on the costume and hope

for the best. Lily was so hot she couldn't breathe. 'Stop, we've done enough.'

'Oh, no, I'm not coming out of here until we're feet perfect,' Pete said, squeezing her in a ticklish spot.

For the first time in years she felt like a girl again, tousled, light of foot, harum-scarum, chasing Freddie's gang. For a few precious minutes she forgot she was Brown Owl and Walt's bride-to-be, and that troubled her. She hadn't felt this fun when she rehearsed with Diana.

'If you need a permanent replacement, you know where to come,' Pete laughed, and Lily felt her neck flushing up.

'Thanks, but Diana will make it on the night. I'm sorry I was short with you the other week, only we were that busy...' It was the best she could think of on the spur of the moment.

'Not another word, love. I know how things are for you with Christmas coming up. It's not a good time when there's folks missing at the table. Your brother thought the world of you, you know. He wrote many a time. He was worried for you...'

'What about?'

'Nothing. I spoke out of turn. He said you were the backbone of the family.'

'The doormat, more like,' she said.

'No, he didn't say that... I'm sorry.'

'It's what he meant – Doormat Lil.'

'I didn't mean to upset you,' Pete said, pulling himself out of the costume.

'Don't worry, you've done your good deed for the day,' she snapped, not looking him in the eye. Why did he have to spoil things by reminding her of Freddie? What had her brother been saying in his letters home?

The moment was over, the magic gone.

Now Lily sat sulking in her room, going over that conversation when there was a knock on the door, a gentle tentative tap of knuckles on wood. 'Miss Lily, we've made a cuppa char for you. We are sorry to upset the applecart. We'll help you make a jolly Christmas do. You tell us what to do...'

Ana and Su were careful not to break their truce. Nothing was too much trouble. Su made a little altar of winter jasmine flowers and holly berries, and Ana brought pictures of the Holy Virgin and saints framed with shells and gold paint from the Greek Orthodox church in Manchester as peace offerings for Lily's bedside table.

'You are number one friend to us. Forgive us, we are silly girls who quarrel over no-good boy.'

'I'm sorry, but the festive season is such hard work and it's bringing back so many memories,' was all there was left to say.

The Review had gone down a treat. The hall was jam-packed with proud parents and Lily's Brownies had not let her down. Diana turned up for their star turn in the cow costume and they got lots of laughs. Even Walt thought she'd done well and that was praise indeed.

Now she must turn her mind to all the last-minute preparations to make their Christmas Day as bearable as it could be under the circumstances. She used to love the hustle and bustle in town, the falling snow and the pretty decorations in the shops, the tinsel trimmings, decorating the tree and making secret purchases, but it was so hard to get in the mood this year. Then she recalled the heart of the Christmas Story, about a babe in a manger, refugees and visitors, and it sort of cheered her up. There must always be room at the inn at Waverley House. Freddie would have wanted it that way.

On Christmas morning Joy was tearing open everyone's parcels and Dina chewed on the paper, not really understanding what it was all about. Neville had a stocking full of toys and wouldn't share them. The house filled up with ancient relatives and friends, and the joint of pork miraculously stretched to fill all the plates.

Enid brought a tin of mincemeat pies, which Su and Ana had never eaten before, and Walter's mother brought an apology for a Christmas cake that cut into crumbs. They sat hugging the fire, waiting to be entertained.

They sang carols and played charades whilst the older ladies dozed in armchairs. Ivy was decked up in a new velvet dress and was as sweet as pie for the day, knowing that Diana Unsworth and her parents had invited the family for a drink at Green Lane on Boxing Day and she was desperate to be included.

Why couldn't every day be like Christmas Day – no back-biting, plenty to eat, surprises round every corner, Lily wondered. Ana and Susan rose to the occasion. Where they found that gift of perfume she daren't guess. No one had ever bought her perfume before. This perfume would be saved for her wedding night.

Walt's gift was a warm football scarf and a diary, such a sensible thought. Thank goodness she had knitted him a new jumper with a Fair Isle border earlier in the year and put it away.

If only Dad was here to give her away, but Levi would expect to do the honours if he stayed sober. It was still hard to believe that her little brother was never coming back. Sometimes she dreamed he'd turn up with a knapsack over his shoulder and smack a kiss on her forehead. 'Hello, Sis.' She kept waiting for one of his funny Christmas cards to pop through the letterbox but it never came.

The gathering at Dr Unsworth's house on Boxing Day was a select one. All the years Lily had walked up and down the lane and never realised what a secret treasure their black-and-white timbered farmhouse was. It was crammed between two Victorian villas with a large garden hidden at the back. It was an ancient house with mullion windows, the original manor house of the district when everywhere was just fields and forests, not cul-de-sacs and avenues.

She had never seen such a huge fireplace, with benches set in the side, oak beams in the ceiling and a fuggy smell of woodsmoke and cigars. It was festive, shabby and welcoming, like Diana herself, who had filled the drawing room with neighbours and nurses, friends and relatives.

The more Lily saw of Diana, the more she liked her, but there was always a sadness in her gaze, the wariness of a private person who carried

233

many burdens. They were kindred spirits despite the difference in their education and social standing.

Maria was visiting Marco with Queenie, but Eva was here, off duty, sipping sherry in the corner. Ivy's eyes were on stalks, taking in the large drawing room, the tasteful arrangement of greenery and berries, the family portraits on the walls. Neville and the girls were banished to the kitchen for treats with other small children.

It was Diana who came up to Ana with a brilliant idea.

'We've got this recruitment going in the New Year, an exhibition for trainee nurses and assistants at the Infirmary. They're looking for domestics and ward helps and auxiliary nurses for the special wings for the elderly. With your wartime experience you'd be ideal. Think about it,' she smiled, drifting away to serve her guests with pinwheels of white bread filled with tinned salmon, leaving Ana agog at such a suggestion.

'Once they know I'm unmarried with child, I won't get work,' she whispered in Lily's ear.

'You don't know that,' she replied. This was too good an opportunity for her to miss. Diana would give a glowing reference. No one was likely to ask for her marriage lines. Surely with her Red Cross experience in Crete it was obvious here was someone already hardened to the realities of death and injury? Diana's influence and name would get her through to the final interview and a chance to work as an auxiliary nurse with a view to further training.

Su was pleased with this news, much to everyone's surprise. She had been given notice the week before Christmas, dismissed from Moorlands School because a soldier returned to take up his old position.

'What'll I do?' she asked now.

'You could take Ana's place on the stall,' Lily offered.

'But beware of the Levi's walking fingers,' Ana warned.

'I've tried to speak to him but he thinks it's all a joke,' Lily blushed. Her brother was being more stupid than ever. Thank goodness Enid was close at hand to keep an eye on things.

'I will spike his ardour,' Su laughed. 'In my country we say an unmarried woman is not honoured even if she has ten brothers. Did I tell you about my great escape on the boat? This sailor comes to my cabin, face as sweet as a choirboy, and asks for a mug of water. I turn my back and in he comes, shutting the door. It wasn't water he was wanting, so I smile and say I must slip into some pretty clothes and he must close his eyes. I pick up sleeping Joy, shut the sailor in the cabin and call the guard. I know all their tricks. Levi will not win and I can help you until I find another position. I will see more of Joy. She is such a bright child. I am going to teach her to dance Burmese *pwe* while her feet and wrists are young and pliable. She will shine for us.'

Susan liked to brag about her daughter's beauty and dancing ability. She was going into the baby ballet class with Rosa in the new term.

'When shall we all meet again?' said Diana as they all dawdled in the hallway to gather coats

235

and cloaks and put on ancient wellington boots and gumshoes. It had started to snow again and the paths home would be treacherous.

'Soon. I think Maria has plans for an evening,' Lily smiled.

'What plans are these?' interrupted Ivy, who had been trying to catch the ends of conversations all afternoon. Lily ignored her as they made their farewells and thank yous at the door and slithered back round the corner to Division Street.

'I hope you're not on with another of them dinners,' muttered Ivy on the way home. 'Walt'll have something to say about that! That man's a saint to put up with all your gallivanting. He should put his foot down. People are beginning to talk.'

'About what?' Lily was curious, despite herself.

'How you prefer the company of foreigners to decent English folk like a...' She was struggling for the word, 'like one of them calculators in the war.'

'You mean a collaborator.' Lily corrected her ignorance with a smile. 'The war's over now and if more nations got together over a meal there'd be a lot less fighting.'

'Don't you get clever with me! It's your fiancé you should be dining with.'

'Oh, don't talk daft! Walt understands. It's only once in a blue moon,' Lily retorted with a lot more conviction than she was feeling.

The big surprise for all the children was a trip to see *Puss in Boots* at the King's Theatre; a treat to tide them through the long winter ahead.

'I do not understand,' said Su. 'This is a nursery rhyme story with music, boys are ladies and girls are boys?'

How can you explain pantomime to foreigners, Lily mused, all those performers and dancing girls getting mixed up, or why men are dressed as women and girls dressed as boys? Then there was the business of everyone shouting from the audience and the actors racing on the stage and being chased by ghosts.

Rosa and Joy hid under their seats, and Neville had a tantrum when it was time to go back to Maria's for ice-cream sodas. A good time was had by all but Lily was glad the festive season was now over.

If only the winter would melt away as easily. They'd not seen anything like it for years. It hadn't stopped snowing since November. There was talk of power cuts and freeze-ups, coal shortages and more rationing. Still, it was all good for business if they could find supplies. Colds, flu, bad chests, sprains and chilblains, catarrh, stiff joints and runny noses are what they liked. Winstanley Health and Herbs was in for a busy time.

In the New Year came the visit to Ana's hospital for the recruitment exhibition. The Infirmary was like a little town on its own, with huge red-brick buildings topped by towers and turrets like a fortress. In the olden days it was a place feared because if people were old and poor they would have to stay there until they died, wearing uniforms and shawls and starched caps to show they lived by the public purse.

Diana warned them of the smells in the long corridors. 'I know it looks like a soldier's barracks on the outside. It was built in a time when charity was cold and calculated, measured out in spoons not buckets. Now we've got new wards and a hospital built in the grounds but it does look grim.'

Esme had thrown her hands up in horror at the thought of Ana working in such a depressing place. 'Once those gates are closed, it is still the workhouse,' she said, shaking her head and sighing. 'I don't suppose you had those back home.'

'No,' Ana replied. 'In Crete, a family looks after its own. Our monks and nuns take care of the sick. There are hospitals in the towns. We look after our own in the village ... but who know what happens now?'

There was sad news from her Manchester church of many brave priests who were shot for harbouring escaped soldiers and partisans, their monasteries burned to the ground. The news brought that film of mist and tears into her eyes when she spoke of her homeland, a far-off place, like heaven, out of reach until she died.

Perhaps one day, Lily mused, their children might be able to visit places where associations with Freddie were strongest: Rangoon, the Mediterranean Sea, Athens and Palestine. One day she hoped they might find where he was buried and take his children to mark the spot. At least it must be warm in Palestine.

'The wards are short of attendants. I will get good training. It is not a prison. Prison is in the mind,' Ana said. 'Diana says they have many plans to brighten up the wards now there is new National Health Service to come.'

Ivy was listening, ready to splash her words with cold water. 'I think it's a disgusting place. I've been sick after visiting there with Zion Chapel. It gives me the creeps, all those cots and barred windows. Why do you want to work with feeble oldies and dribblers anyway? The place must stink of wet beds, and worse. You'll get nothing out of it but a bad back,' she added for good measure. 'And there are tramps going up there to the refuge house every night, a load of dirty men and women hanging around scrounging from bins, full of fleas. How can you even think about it, bringing back germs into this respectable house?'

'Ivy, your words make me sad,' Ana said quietly. 'Praise God that you have no idea what it is like to tramp the roads of Europe, itching, starving, selling your body for some scraps of food, not knowing when you will find your way back home!'

No one had ever heard Ana speak like this and there was a stunned silence.

Ivy shrugged her shoulders. 'I'm only giving my opinion, she said, looking for support, but there was none.

'I have seen bad, bad injuries. You cannot know,' Ana continued. 'I am happy to serve old people. I know what it is to suffer shame.'

'All right, you've made your point.' Ivy was silenced for once.

'I think I will like this work. I like the old people. The staff will show me ropes to pull. They are brightening the wards with curtains and new paint, and Queenie comes to set their hair. She brings sunshine and songs to sing.'

'Do they know you are a refugee?' Ivy asked, her ever-waspish questions ready to sting like needles.

'No one asked to see my papers. I will be just Winstanley. I do what I am told. It is better than sit all day on bum like some,' Ana replied pointedly, knowing full well that Ivy was at home with Neville.

'Well, don't be asking us to rub your back.'

'Diana found me the job. Queenie helps. She works for Lavaroni now. Perhaps you'll all have a job there,' Ana replied.

'Oh, we all know Lavaroni's Hair Salon, where they charge twice as much as anywhere else, just to be fingered by that greasy Eyetie with fancy ideas. It's all right for some,' sniffed Ivy, lowering her eyelids and looking martyred as usual.

No amount of Lavaroni's pin curlers would ever make Ivy look like an elegant mannequin. She was a painted doll, pretty enough, but with a hard face when she was thwarted. Now she made a face, pulling her lips in tight but carried on folding the washing.

'Has no one ever told you, you catch more flies with honey than vinegar?' The words came tumbling out from Ana's mouth before she could stop them.

'Pardon me for breathing! I tell the truth as I see it and if you don't like it, lady, you know what you can do. I don't know how Mother puts up with all that traipsing over her best rugs. If the Greek is in and out at all hours, working shifts, how are we ever to get a decent night's sleep?'

'I work night shift so I can see my child in the day, and she is no burden to any of you. I am doing my best to please everybody–'

'That's enough, Ivy. Turn the record off. You've made your point,' Esme interrupted. 'The girl is only doing her duty as she sees fit. It was in the paper about the shortage of trained nurses, and one day we'll all be in need of a good one. Dr Unsworth's daughter must think highly of her to speak up for the girl. Let's start the New Year as we mean to go on. Think on?'

When Esme laid down the law like that everyone jumped. Ana's face was a picture...

Already 1947. Who'd have thought it! Lily sighed, wondering what the new year would bring; more joy than the last, she hoped. There was a wedding to plan, a new home to find away from all this bickering, but Ana and Su would need sorting out first.

So far, so good, with Ana's new job. Su still needed watching, though, when it came to Levi's tricks.

14

Dancing in the Snow

The highlight of Lily's week, come rain, sleet or snow, was always Wednesday. Not because it was half-day closing, but because it was dancing class day and she got to take Dina to collect Joy from the baby class when their mothers were busy.

The Lemody Liptrot School of Dance took up the top floor of Church Buildings, up a winding wooden staircase, past a photographer's studio and accountant's offices, to a glass-roofed studio with mirrors round the walls, *barres* on two levels, a pile of grey blankets to save bottoms from splinters when exercising and a box of resin for *pointe* shoes.

There was a small anteroom where the mothers sat around the walls, which were lined with notice boards, and peered at the portraits of Miss Liptrot in her heyday with the Carl Rosa Ballet Company.

There was the teacher, balancing precariously on the edge of a fountain in diaphanous Greek costume, which left nothing to the imagination, standing in a line of buxom dancers who looked frozen stiff.

Mothers waited for the end of the rehearsal for the annual charity dancing display in the King's Theatre, the concert in which the new baby class would make its début and which was already a sellout.

They were doing *Babes in the Wood* mime and dance, but who were going to be budding stars: the two babes, and the lead robin who carries in the leaves to bury the sleeping pair and summon all the little birds to guard them from the wicked huntsman?

'Is it dancing in the snow day?' Joy asked each morning. She was quite the chatterbox now. Where had the months gone since her arrival, wide-eyed and silent, on Su's knee?

After Christmas, the three of them had fallen into a routine of sorts. Sunday teas were at Maria's house. Monday was washday, the clothes hanging around the kitchen since nothing could be put out with the freeze-up. Tuesday was work and shopping. Then it was dancing class, sitting looking up at the ridges of snow on the glass rooftop, watching yet more flakes falling. Thursday was on the market stall and Brownies for Lily. Friday Lily helped Esme and Polly with cleaning and shopping. Saturday was the stall again and a football match with Walt if Lily wasn't on duty. Walt was fitted in amongst it all like wadding.

The girls and their new friends had all met together on the first Sunday of the year at Queenie's lodgings, squashed into the living room around the dining table for a game of housey-housey.

Queenie had made her own set of number cards and counters and smart little number boards on the back of Christmas cards to place the markers on. Diana was very impressed. 'Last time we played this was in the field hospital in the desert...We played for ciggies, and then there was a sandstorm and everything blew away, knickers, brassieres hanging up, the lot. Great fun!'

'Why do we shout "House"?' asked Su, not quite getting the hang of it at first, but soon she was roaring with exasperation, waiting for the right numbers to come up to complete a line.

Mother would have a fit to know she was gambling on the Sabbath, thought Lily, but surely dolly mixtures didn't count, and the children were wolfing them down under the table where no one was looking.

Arthur, Queenie's husband, worked shifts at the tannery and her older children slept on the sofa, oblivious to the noise. There was a pile of home baking on the table but her tiffin cake, made from biscuit crumbs and cocoa, was soon scoffed along with Arthur's parsnip wine.

Drinking *and* gambling, it was getting worse by the hour.

'Let's have a singsong!' Queenie shouted, and it was round the piano for the old favourites. Maria always sang her heart out and gave them a turn. Diana told them tales of all the famous people she'd seen in Cairo in the nightclubs.

Lily just sat and listened and soaked up the atmosphere of chatter and laughter. This was such a treat after the squabbling at home.

Queenie was now playing the piano in the studio, standing up to watch and play at the same time. Miss Liptrot would be deciding this afternoon which dancers would get solo parts. Madame had big ideas about her dancing school, attracting the best mummies in the district with promises of national examinations and certificates and a smart uniform of purple crossover cardigans and pleated lilac tunics, a colour that seemed to suit everyone.

Rosaria Santini looked so pretty in purple, with her dark curls and olive complexion. Even Dina's sandy mop of curls would look good when her turn came. Joy's black straight hair was so different. Maria was taking orders for knitting cardigans, working into the small hours for the smartly dressed young mothers in fur coats from the Victoria Drive end of town.

Some of the little girls even had nannies carrying small hatboxes with their pumps in, driven by chauffeurs, but none of them was as good a dancer as little Rosa who excelled at skipping and pointing toes.

'Look at your feet, not the sky, Joy!' shouted Madame Lemody.

Joy was really too young for the class but pestered them silly to be included, a right little diva in the making. Dina watched from the safety of Lily's knee.

Dancing had never been Lily's forte. Hockey, rounders, anything with a bat and ball took her interest, but then she'd always played with brothers. Ballroom dancing was something old folk did, and courting couples. Not that she and Walt ever danced.

Maria and Su were worried about making robin costumes with all those graduated feathers and hoods and beaks. Lily had promised to help them make them up but they needed a sketch to work from. She was still recovering from the shame of those awful soldiers' outfits.

Joy looked like a little pudding in her mock-up outfit, with two left feet and no sense of rhythm, but she was still only a baby.

With the loan of Ivy's Singer sewing machine Lily and her friends had managed to create the costumes from just the teacher's pattern. Susan tacked it all up carefully and Madame was pleased with the result.

I ought not to be here, Lily sighed. If she and Walt didn't make time to find somewhere to live after the wedding, there'd be no dancing daughters or footballing sons to follow on. Somehow there was always something stopping them taking the plunge. Take this awful snow that froze Gertie's tyres to the kerb and made the buses scarce. It was as much as they could do to get to work on time and open their stalls. There were that many colds going round, they'd even run out of Nurse O'Brien's herbal linctus. It was an ill wind...

After all the disruptions of war it felt wimpish to be defeated by a blizzard or three, but it sapped spirits and no mistake. It was not the weather to imagine herself walking down the aisle in some flimsy get-up with an arctic gale blowing up her smalls.

Ana and Su were always frozen to the marrow, no matter how many layers she piled on their backs. The Olive Oil Club had put their coupons together to help buy Ana's new nurse's uniform. She ought be saving hers for a trousseau, Lily frowned to herself, but seeing Joy prancing around like a sack of potatoes made her laugh and forget the cold. Susan thought she was going to be the next Margot Fonteyn. Those kiddies were the only bright rays of sunshine in this wintry world.

All the Santini family were putting the Winstanleys to shame, drummed into buying tickets for the matinée show. Tina, Angelo's wife, Maria, and Toni's wife, Sonia, and all Maria's customers were bombarded with a once-in-a-lifetime chance to see Rosaria Santini's first appearance on stage. They would take pictures to Marco, if he didn't manage to get out of the san for the day. He'd made one home visit but couldn't manage the stairs so was staying with Nonna Valentina, which upset Maria.

Dolores Pickles down the road said Marco was a saint in his suffering. Father Michael of Our Lady of Sorrows took the sacrament to him each week. He was clinging on to life by a thread and they were praying for his recovery, lighting candles to all the saints. It looked as if Maria would have yet another job to add to her collection. That woman didn't know how to sit down, but when she did she fell asleep at her knitting. It was as if she had the troubles of the world on her shoulders. Lily wished there was something she could do to help.

One more row and then I've finished the back, dreamed Maria as she was knitting in her sleep, with the chatter of the dancing school waiting room fading into the background.

She could see Marco striding towards her with

247

Rosa on his shoulders and she leaped up to greet him, only to watch the picture fade. Then another face came into view and she fought herself awake.

Knitting cardigans almost paid for Rosa's lessons and it stopped Maria's hands from shaking. She worked every hour and visited her husband dutifully, but the best nights were spent with her friends, sharing suppers, going to the pictures. Lately, however, something unexpected had crept into the few gaps in her busy life, something that was churning her stomach upside down. Something had happened to shake her world even more.

It started when Queenie gave her and Lily a free hairdressing appointment each as a treat. 'You work so hard and no one gives you anything. You spend loads on the children and never a penny on yourself,' Queenie argued, plonking an appointment card on the counter.

For weeks Maria kept changing the appointment until she hadn't the nerve to look Queenie in the eye. She kept tying up her hair in scarves to keep her locks out of the ice cream and as it got heavier and longer, taking a tin of Kirby grips to hold it up.

Lavaroni's was setting the trend for the soft waved look. Not that she would ever need a permanent, not with yards of heavy curly hair, but a shorter lighter style on her head might suit the new look of the times.

She had seen Diana Unsworth off duty from the hospital sporting the new look. If Diana was going with the times then so could she. Ana was so striking to look at now she was filling out, and Su was always so neat and prim in her tailored suit and blouse, her hair caught up in a tight bun in the nape of her neck. She never changed her style, but something inside Maria was aching for release, something to distract from the sadness of Marco's slow progress, from the drudgery of all her chores. She was a businesswoman, mother, wife, daughter-in-law, cleaner. Where was the old Maria? Who was the *real* Maria?

In her dreams, she floated across the stage like Mimi in *La Bohème,* or strode proudly like Tosca. She was six feet tall like a Valkyrie riding to her doom. There was not a heroine on the stage at the King's Theatre that she didn't weep for and imagine herself acting out the great dramas.

She sat in the gods with her mop and brush at rehearsals, wiping tears from her eyes as they died so bravely in the spotlight. Why couldn't life be so full of drama and colour, with velvet, net and satin?

Her life was drab and she was always tired, but lately she had perked up because of her new friends and their kindness. It was time she took herself in hand.

What would Marco think if she walked into the san wearing new clothes and a new look? He would think she had forgotten about his suffering but she could not ignore the kindness of a friend and she asked him what she should do.

'You go and have your hair done all new and give me big surprise, *mia cara,*' he laughed. 'Make all the other men jealous of my beautiful wife.'

With his blessing it was easier for Maria to go ahead and keep the appointment.

The salon was in the smart arcade with a discreet window with screens, and each cubicle was partitioned off so the client could have privacy. There were large black hoods to dry the hair, attached to wires and plugs, and a smell of bad eggs and chemicals that no perfumed soap could disguise. For a second Maria wanted to flee but then she saw Queenie, who acted as receptionist, cleaner, shampooer and teamaker.

'You're in luck. It's Sylvio's day to take new clients. He's very modern. All the young ones like him.' She winked and Maria half recalled Queenie's story about the prisoner of war who had come touting for work when he was released.

She thought fondly of that first gathering at the Winstanleys' house, the night they formed the supper club. Last Saturday they took themselves off to the first house of the pictures next door to see *It's a Wonderful Life* and she'd cried all through it, great sobs that set Lily off and then Queenie, until the people in the row in front turned round and told them to shut up or go outside. The soulless pigs!

That was the trouble with the English. They had no sense of drama. Poor Jimmy Stewart, doing his best and getting it all wrong. She felt like that sometimes. However she tried to please the family, it was never enough.

They'd all trooped upstairs to sample her new spaghetti Bolognese, sitting in silence as if they'd just been to a funeral not a cinema.

'What is the matter with you all? Where is your

soul? It was a happy film with a happy ending. You don't get many happy endings in the theatre. They all die so bravely: Tosca jump off the castle, Mimi is sick. It is so sad. Giselle goes mad and the poor swan maid and her love jump into the lake. I love a good cry ... you get your money's worth of tears with opera.'

The week before they'd been to dinner at Diana's house, dining off bone china and silver cutlery, and Eva had cooked a strange beef dish that was delicious.

It was a change from Maria's own cooking but she liked it best when they came to her.

There was always some friend of a friend – a Pole, a Ukrainian exile, off-duty nurses from the Infirmary where Ana was now working as an orderly, who joined them. It was getting a crush to fit them all in upstairs so they spilled out into the downstairs and piled the tables and chairs together.

Eva got them knitting squares from leftover wool to make into blankets for the refugee camps. Everyone was clacking away, jabbering and gossiping. Some were thoughtful, like Lily, who brought her sugar ration. Others brought what they could spare. Maria lived for those evenings, especially when news from Moses Heights wasn't good.

When Marco had a bad week, she panicked and prayed. When he'd had a good week she could relax and sing, but she could always forget her troubles when the girls came round.

She could never understand the set-up in Division Street. The women stayed on there, despite

251

the sister-in-law who hated their guts and called their friends 'that Olive Oil Club'. They never talked about their dead husbands in her presence. It was as if they had never existed.

It was a strange family, not falling in and out like the Santinis, but coming and going and never meeting up together. Even dear Lily – she was supposed to be getting married soon and they'd never even met her beloved.

One stolen pram had changed all their lives for the better. Salt and honey they might be, but they were the best mamas in Grimbleton, wanting a better life for their daughters than the hard struggle they were living now.

Su said dancing classes made them stand tall and straight, and Madame said it grew a good ear for music and rhythm. She was impressed that all their instructions were in French: *plié, arabesque, port de bras*. She had cut out the article in the *Mercury*, showing a line of babies from the class all smiling at the camera. 'Babies who know French before English and not yet three years old!' They looked so cute in their uniforms, and Rosa looked the brightest of them all. Maria was picturing Rosa's name in neon lights, shining for all the other mothers to admire, when she became aware of a man standing behind her, fingering her hair with interest, ruffling it up and examining her in the mirror.

'This is good hair, madam, but too heavy. It all need big cut,' he smiled, flashing a pair of shiny jet-black eyes over her head. She suddenly felt protective of all her hair and ashamed of day-dreaming. She launched instinctively into Italian.

He responded in a torrent of his mother tongue with a thick northern accent and the rest of the discussion was a rattle of questions and answers.

Sylvio Bertorelli was from the north, from the industrial heartland, used to chimneys and smoke. He liked Grimbleton and had no desire to go home to a defeated country. He had been the barber in the camp on the moors and decided to make the best of his captivity and train himself to be a ladies' hairdresser, and he was ambitious.

As he was chatting, so great chunks of Maria's hair were floating down onto the tiles.

'Stop!' she cried, wondering if there was any hair left on her head.

'You wait and see. It'll be good. Now it is easy to dress and let the curl come through. You have fine thick hair, the very best, Signora Santini. Make your husband very proud,' he laughed, and suddenly it was easy to tell him all about Marco and his family and his chest not healing properly, and all her worries about the ice-cream parlour.

Queenie shampooed her hair thoroughly in a sink contraption that was very efficient but looked too much like a guillotine to be restful.

'I see you like our Sylvio... Quite the ladies' man,' whispered Queenie. 'Poor old Gianni gets all the old dears, now everyone wants Sylvio. He did Bebe Daniels' hair last week when they were on at the King's. She was *very* pleased and tipped him five bob.'

Maria suddenly realised she had no money for a tip. It was hard not to feel self-conscious swathed in towels and sitting still while he finger-curled and pinned coils of hair around her head with setting lotion.

He was full of plans to go on courses in Manchester and bring the latest styles back to the mill town. 'I do great hair, win competitions so everyone want shampoo from Sylvio's,' he smiled.

His film-star looks were striking. He had one of those faces that must have fallen off a marble pillar: thick straight brows, black eyes fringed with long lashes, a wide smile and even, white teeth. He was slim but not thin, broad-shouldered, and had neat hips like a dancing man. His fingers were long, tapered and artistic. It was worth coming to the hairdresser's just for the floor-show.

Common sense said he would be charming with all his clients so that they would come back time and time again. Yet there was something innocent in his enthusiasm and flamboyance that reminded, Maria of Rosa with a new toy, of Marco listening to the football scores on the wireless when the Grasshoppers were winning at home.

Sylvio was used to silly women flashing their eyes at him but Maria was not going to demean herself. When she saw the results of his efforts in the mirror, however, she gasped with pleasure.

'Is that really me?' she said, staring at the transformation of the old careworn Maria, she of a hundred chores and jobs, into this young girl with soft curls framing her features and high-lighting her own large brown eyes.

'You like?' he said. 'Now we'll see your bright eyes and long neck like swan. We can see the shape of your head, yes?' No wonder he was looking pleased with himself.

Queenie stood back. 'Crikey Moses, Ria. Marco will have a new visitor tonight and all the ward'll be jealous,' she winked, and Maria could not resist giving Queenie a big hug.

'*Grazie*... Thank you. I am a new woman now,' she laughed, wanting to walk around town and savour the moment when heads turned and wondered if that was really Maria Santini.

'It will need cutting every six weeks or it will all drop,' Sylvio warned, and she nodded and promised to come back again.

She'd meant it at the time but the weeks went on and the style was growing out and there was never any money to spend on herself. There were clothes and ballet shoes for Rosa and extra fruit for Marco. The walls needed distempering. Always something.

Weeks later, one afternoon when she was rushed off her feet, Maria saw him sitting in the window table drawing on his cigarette, sipping a cup of cappuccino from their new chrome Gaggia steam coffee machine. He looked up when she went over.

'I come to see how my new look model is doing. It is grown...' he said, and she blushed.

'I'm sorry ... no time and you are expensive,' she added.

'I know but the best is expensive. However, I need plenty of practice and a model gets her hair cut free. I have ideas. Will you sit for me?' he asked, flashing her one of his high-octane smiles. 'I need someone with a good neck, good hair and a strong face...' He was pleading with his eyes and she tried to stay businesslike in her reply.

'That would be a fair arrangement but I work many hours. It would have to fit in. I must bring my little girl,' she whispered in Italian, not wanting her business to be broadcast all around the town. Nonna Valentina would not approve, nor her brothers-in-law. Sylvio was not family and Santinis only worked for family.

Her heart was thumping when she walked away. This was dangerous, this excitement, and she knew where it could lead. Only once had she slipped before D-day, when the town was invaded with Yanks going south. There was this GI from New Jersey, one of a gang who hung out at Santini's. He used to sing and dance and make a fool of himself and he made her laugh and forget the war. He had a roving eye and flattered her loneliness. They had gone dancing and one thing led to another, a brief encounter in Queens Park. She vowed never to betray Marco again. Then Marco came back on embarkation leave and her shame sent her to confession and back into the arms of the Church.

She had promised the Virgin that she would be a good wife and mother, and resist temptation when it walked through the door again.

This is just a business arrangement. She would be chaperoned by Queenie and Rosa. What harm would there be in having her hair done regularly? Customers liked to see a smart woman behind the counter. She planned to tell Marco all about this exciting venture but somehow she never got round to telling him about Sylvio's offer.

Somehow they always had their styling sessions

when Gianni had gone home and Queenie was busy at the dancing class. Nothing improper was ever suggested but it hovered unspoken like smoke above the ceiling.

Every time Maria decided not to go, but every time there was always some reason why she could not let him down. Sylvio was an artist and an artist needed a model.

She felt so exposed when he washed her hair and she was lying backwards in his hands. He always smelled of cologne, and his hands were gentle but firm, massaging her head. How she ached for the touch of a man on her neck, even if it was only his hand with a towel.

He sat so close to her when he styled and trimmed her hair she could feel his warm breath in her ear.

Sometimes she took Rosa along but she only fingered all the trays of curlers and brushes and distracted her from sitting still, fearful of some accident with scissors. This would have to stop.

Yet everybody was commenting on the transformation, especially when she began to treat herself to a few sample lipsticks and pots of foundation cream. She found new earrings to dangle and show off her style. When strangers in the café asked who did her hair she gained solace in advertising Sylvio's skills. The thought of letting someone else be his model was unthinkable. The dates of their sessions were ringed on her calendar with crosses like kisses. The very thought of those meetings set her heart thudding with anticipation. She tried not to think of them as assignations but why did Romeo and Juliet keep coming into her head?

There was no time to think about Sylvio's hands on her neck, his burning eyes and the stirrings so deep in her groin when she thought of kissing him. It was mortal sin, it was madness, but these wicked thoughts warmed her cold bed better than any hot-water bottle.

I must be strong, she thought, knitting in the waiting room. Just one more row, she thought.

'Wake up, Maria,' whispered Ana as she picked up the knitting off the floor. She was here to collect Joy from the rehearsal. 'You were far away.'

'Eh?' She jumped up. 'I fall asleep over my knitting. I am getting old,' she sighed, gathering the wool into her shopping bag.

'You are too much on your feet. When you sit you sleep,' Ana replied as the girls came spilling out of the studio, closely followed by their teacher, who beckoned the two of them into the studio, away from the other mothers.

'I have decided to make Rosaria one of my Babes in the Wood. She'll need a long dress,' she smiled, pushing paper sketches into their hands. 'They all do their mime well and are reliable. I don't think they will freeze in the spotlight. We will do extra rehearsal for them,' she added, and as they went back into the waiting room there was a *frisson* of jealousy as the little dancers were wrapped up against the winter cold.

It is a sign if I am good then my child will do well, Maria smiled. This is my reward. Rosa's talent was already showing and she would have the brightest, prettiest dress she could find.

Ana beamed with pride. 'I knew Rosa was a good dancer,' she said, and then, looking at Joy, they both paused. 'What will I tell Su? She will have to help make clothes.'

'You could ask Lily to help you. Poor Joy, she will be disappointed.'

Joy skipped ahead down the stairs, unawares until she stopped on the bottom step, turned round and gave them all a beckoning call with her hand, very exaggerated but the meaning was clear.

'Look at me, this is how you do it. Miss Lip-rot says I am number one robin. I go first and when you lie down I cover you with leaves, very slowly, and then I bring in all the baby robins. Miss Lip-rot says I'm a star. I have note for my mummy.' She looked at them, producing a piece of paper from her pocket.

'Is this true?' said Maria to Rosa, who was jumping down the steps as fast as she could.

'Yes. Joy is first robin because she's fat and robins have round tummies,' said Rosa with a sneer.

'Shush. That is not kind,' Maria said, trying not to smile at the truth of her words.

Ana looked at her with raised eyebrows.

Later that week Maria sat with Marco in the wings of the theatre, watching the dress rehearsal as the lights flashed around the stage and her child tiptoed through the make-believe forest in a flurry of bright pink satin edged with cream lace. It was Rosa's Cousin Angelika's first communion

259

dress, cut down, dyed and trimmed with lace stained in tea. Rosa looked a little angel.

It had taken all of Marco's strength to climb the stairs to watch the rehearsals. They held hands as tears rolled down their cheeks, tears of pride. Rosa was so young and yet so confident on stage. They saw no other child but her.

'One day she will be a star,' Marco whispered. 'Santini girls can be as good as boys, you'll see. I'll give Rosaria what she needs: sequins, bouquets and encores. Then everyone will be proud, yes?' he said, smiling.

Maria nodded and kissed his cheek. 'You are so right,' she replied, knowing it would take all of her hard work to make this dream come true.

15

The Miracle Cure

If Levi patted her bottom one more time she would whack him like Auntie Betty used to beat the *mali* from the veranda. Ana had warned about his wandering hands but Su was never quick enough to swerve away.

'Oops,' he mocked. 'You are such a tiny lass but in proportion. No wonder our Freddie took a fancy to you.' His eyes were sludgy grey, nothing like Mister Stan's blue sapphires.

How silly and naïve she felt, so gullible like some stupid loose woman. Why did she stay on in this cold country and take these insults? She realised now that Stan had never intended them to marry. He was like all the other *thakin* who kept their mistresses happy with false promises, lengths of silk, but now it was as if he had never existed and in his place was this fool.

I am the daughter of a British man with a proper English name, she thought. No one can take my passport from me, but still she was treated as some foreigner. Customers gaped at her but she would never give them the satisfaction of seeing her discomfort.

She liked the stall and the bustle of the market, the smell of the potions and herbs, and the foreign-sounding names on the boxes of herbs reminded her a little of the great markets of Burma with spices all the colours of the rainbow. In a town of soot and engine oil, fish-and-chip fat and fog, their stall smelled of sunshine and faraway places.

She had a good eye and ear, and was quick to improve her knowledge; what to give to whom and how much and when to ask for help. Levi knew his herbs from his roots and spices, but he was cheating Daw Esme and that worried Su.

There was a box of dried leaves on the top of the store cupboard that they were not allowed to bring down for dusting or to serve. It was a box regularly emptied and refilled but no accounts of its sales were ever kept in the books. Levi insisted that he alone must dispense this remedy and she wondered what sort of powerful medicine it was. They were allowed to portion it out into tiny packets so it must be very efficacious.

'What's this for?' she had asked Lily one Saturday.

'It must be one of Winstanley's cure-alls, a secret recipe handed down from father to son, I expect.' Lily sniffed at it, turning up her nose at the smell. 'Something soothing and cooling, I expect, or something to loosen the joints. We get a lot of call for rheumatics round here...' she added.

'It may be a special potion for floppy dicks,' Su whispered. 'That is why only a man serves it. Business is good for it.'

'Susan!' Lily was blushing and giggling. 'It's the cold that's bringing in customers.'

'So why doesn't the sale go down in the book?' She was curious how much Lily knew.

'Levi has his own system with special customers and his regulars, and is very particular about serving them. You'll soon recognise them,' Lily smiled, and turned back to her packaging.

His regulars were a strange bunch, not the sort of customers who usually came to the herbal store: smart ladies in large brimmed hats, wanting remedies for headaches, constipation, skin complaints and neuralgia, 'old biddies', as Levi called them, with swollen ankles and bunions, who needed tonics and remedies for flatulence and bladder control. Then there came vegetarians, who bought special tins of nut cutlets and vitamin drops, and old men in mufflers wanting tonics for chests and aching joints.

Levi's specials were younger men in long mackintoshes and no hats, sometimes wearing berets and bicycle clips, ex-soldiers with war wounds and scars, the coloured man who played drums in Toni Santini's billiard hall and American bar off Mealhouse Lane. There were toughies with cold fish eyes, who undressed her with their stares.

They came only when Levi was on shift. Money was exchanged and packets were handed over and not a penny of it went in the till. Her curiosity was aroused until one day she asked him outright, 'What is this stuff?'

'A special tobacco to ease the joints,' he answered, not looking at her for once when he spoke.

'Shouldn't it go in the book?' she continued, trying to catch his eye.

'No need for you to bother your pretty little head with any of this. I'll deal with it in my own way. I like to deal with these customers direct. It is strictly my business so no more questions,' he said, dismissing her curiosity.

One afternoon when Levi was out at one of his endless meetings and she was alone on the stall, she found the wooden steps that folded into a chair and climbed up to examine the shoebox more closely. She sniffed the herbs, inhaled and shut her eyes. There was something in the distinctive odour that took her back to that troopship journey to England, to the back streets and music clubs of Rangoon where men chewed roots and grinned, the sort of dens of iniquity that the headmistress of her school warned her girls never to go near but all had risked a peek in, nevertheless.

It didn't look like tobacco but it was dried and

crushed, hidden up there for a reason. Perhaps it was a potent concoction, as Enid had said, highly prized and efficacious, subject to strict rationing. It was not fair that Levi gave it only to his men friends, so she pulled out two packets and stuffed them in her overcoat.

Maria's mother-in-law had a terrible backache. Why should she not have some relief from *her* pain? How could he be so mean as to ration it only to men?

If Daw Esme only knew about his cheating heart it would 'upset the applecart', as she often said. Daw Esme was a fair woman, distant, strict. A mother deserved more respect from her son but as the proverb said: bone in chicken, relatives in man, that one can't avoid.

There were so many secrets in the household. Division House, it should be called, not Waverley. How the two lodgers and their daughters were closer relatives than everyone thought, how Lily's wedding day never came, how she, Susan, had kept her own store of pure gold bangles hidden from prying eyes to buy extra treats for Joy, how they must always lock the bathroom door from Levi's Tom peeping. Nothing was as it seemed but as the proverb said: 'You can stop speaking to someone but you can never stop being related to them.'

Ana was training to be a real nurse, thanks to kind Diana and Eva. Maria spent more time now in Lavaroni's with Queenie, but the gang always met up at dancing class to watch their girls blossoming into star turns. Joy was a little slower than the others but Su was teaching her to dance

Burmese style and one day Miss Liptrot would give her a solo spot in the big display. She would have to wear the full *pwe* costume and that would cost money.

If Auntie Betty, God protect her eternal soul, could see her standing like some common servant here, she would be shocked. But it would do for now until that great day when Joy Liat would make them all proud. She must be educated to marry well and then she would repay her mother for all her sacrifices by producing many grandchildren in the big house with many chimneys. That was what was keeping Susan smiling.

Everything she was doing was for Joy. Only the best school, the best clothes, the best chance for her to shine would justify all her sacrifices.

She did not trust the Winstanleys to help her achieve this goal. Only foreign mothers shared the same dream. Su, Ana and Maria would make a good team if they stuck together.

She smiled to herself, thinking of all the ammunition she had about Levi's devious scams: the false accounting, private prescriptions and the obnoxious attempts he made to seduce her. If only he knew how repulsive he was to her, a mere shadow of his brother's handsome features.

Levi was a big bellied man with a flabby mouth. How had Ivy ever managed to kiss such a horror. He reminded her of one of the gargoyles grinning from the roof of the ancient parish church, lewd-eyed, bold and grotesque. Yet there was something compulsive in looking on such a sight, if only to mock it. This made all his fumblings bearable.

His weaknesses made her feel strong and strangely superior. I am smart biscuit lady, she thought. I will watch you and bide my time.

One day he would go over the top and she would be waiting then to show him up for what he was. She had the family name to think of, she had the ear of his mother and the Olive Oil Club to back her up. He would get what was coming to him in spadefuls for all he had dumped on to her in the past.

When Lily came to collect Joy for her dancing class, Susan slipped the packets in her pocket for Maria.

'Tell her to give this to Nonna Valentina for her bad back. It is a very special herb to give good relief. She must brew in tea or put it in a pipe and smoke it, I think. Let me know how it works. There is more where that came from,' she laughed.

'If it's that good, I'll take some for Walt to try out. His back's been playing him up again.'

It was a week later that Maria rang the house and asked them to stay for supper after dancing rehearsal and babysit while she had another session with Sylvio. 'I can't ask Nonna. She thinks it not right for married woman to go out alone at night.'

'How's her back?' Lily asked.

'I need to talk to you about that,' Maria said. 'But not over the telephone.'

Su made a note to slip some more packets of the potion into her bag and when they arrived at the flat, bringing Rosa back with them, Maria was chopping onions, tears rolling down her face.

'Watch out, your mother-in-law's talking about you,' laughed Ana, who had Greek sayings for every occasion.

'Not me ... not me, but Susan. Nonna Valentina lives in praise of your wonderful remedy. She has had the best night's sleep in years but sadly I told her there was no more. Do you know what that stuff is?' She turned her black eyes, red-rimmed with crying and laughing.

'It is Winstanley's Wonder Weed.' Su winked at Lily. 'You like it? I have some more here,' she smiled, pulling a packet out of her bag.

'Put it away! You want we all go prison and lose our girls?' cried Maria, crossing herself. 'It's hashish!'

'What you mean, hash... How you know?' cried Ana, crossing herself as well.

'I give my mother-in-law the packet to make tea but that greedy woman grabs one of the Santini boy's pipes and mixes with tobacco and smokes it. Suddenly she is not dragon but sweet smiling lady full of joy, and then she falls asleep. Then Toni comes in and shouts. "What's that stink?" and look at me with dagger eyes. "Where you get this?" he screamed, and threw the packet on the fire. I said it was a gift, that you gave it to her in all innocence, but he started laughing and told me that it was not something to give his beloved mamma ever again.'

'So what is so special about it, then?' Su asked.

'Susan, it is marijuana, hemp, dope ... not allowed. If they find I smoke dope I will lose my job, we'll lose café. Where did you get it from? Not your shop? Get rid of it or you and Lily will be in heap of trouble.'

'Not before I try it for size. If it is so special I want to know what the fuss is about,' Lily answered, making to take the bag. 'Let's have some and see for ourselves.'

'Not in my flat you won't. The smell can drift down the stairs and anyone in the parlour might recognise it. I warn you, it's not the stuff to smoke around babies or children. If the police get hold of your source, Winstanley Health and Herbs will be history,' Maria said, wagging her finger.

'We could make herbal tea,' Su offered, but Maria was having none of it.

'Toni and Angelo know you've got it. They think you all make fool of Mamma. I tell them you innocent girls, just trying to help Mamma. Just get rid of all of it, for everyone's sake. You are holding a grenade in your bag. It go off and we are all in trouble.'

'What shall we do, Lily? If Daw Esme finds out what Levi's up to, she will close down the stall and there will be no job and no money for you. She will blame us and I will lose my job too. I am sorry,' Su cried. 'I wish we had never looked, but we wanted to give Nonna Valentina some relief. If she has no pain, she is kind to you and will let you have your own life. I'm sorry.' Su suddenly felt a wave of panic at the piles of hash in the shoebox. 'Levi is a crazy man.'

'No, he is clever man. What better cover for a drug than to put it on a shelf in a herbal shop? Who would ever suspect?' said Maria. 'You'll have to get rid of it.'

'How?'

'We'll think of something.'

All the way home Lily wrestled with this terrible discovery. What should she do? If the police found out what Levi was up to, they'd close down the stall, and with no business there'd be no money. What a disgrace if it all ended in the courts!

'So sorry, all my fault,' wept Su from the back seat of Gertie. 'I want to help everybody and now I bring shame on Daw Esme.'

What on earth were they going to do? The drugs must be got shut of to save the family honour, but how? Freddie would've known what to do, Lily thought. He must have seen plenty of that stuff in the Far East. Oh heck, and now Walt'd got some in his pocket too.

Lily tossed and turned all night. A time bomb was waiting to go off on the cubbyhole shelf and the clock was ticking away. Their good name was at stake. Her brain ached with thinking of schemes to dispose of it all without drawing suspicion. Her dreams were full of leaves, dried tea leaves floating like confetti over the town hall steps.

'Must go early,' she yelled from the door the next morning, grabbing a piece of toast and Marmite and rushing for the first bus into town, to open up the stall before Enid arrived. How could she live with herself if such an innocent was brought before the court as an accomplice? It was all Levi's doing, so it was up to her now to sort the matter out once and for all.

She should just face Levi with it, challenge him

outright, but she felt a coward. Although what the eye doesn't see the heart won't miss, she thought as an idea slowly formed in her mind.

Her hands were shaking as the shoebox came down off the shelf and she opened it. One by one she unwrapped each twist, shook out the contents into a paper bag and replaced each sachet as best she could with a mixture of dried herbs: sarsaparilla, meadow sweet, camomile and lemon balm and a sprinkling of the weed on top so it smelled right. She replaced the twists carefully in the box so it looked undisturbed. The hemp she siphoned into a jam jar for future use and popped it in her shopping basket under the counter.

Only then could she relax and only then were the canvas curtains opened to reveal the stall to the public. She put on her white shop coat and smile.

Enid was surprised to see her in so early but Lily fled to find some sequins for Joy's special *pwe* headdress. The jam jar was burning a hole in the bottom of her basket.

No sign of the tampering was noticed and, anyway, Levi would say nothing. How could he confess to dealing in drugs? No one was supposed to know about this secret hoard or its significance.

Lily was going to watch to see who came for their supplies. She was still too shocked at Levi, still couldn't believe he was capable of such treachery. What had happened to her brother to make him do this?

Over the next few weeks it became clear that he

hadn't a clue what he was selling. She didn't flush the herbs down the pan; something stopped her. No, this was her insurance. It was proof. If Levi ever turned nasty she would confess everything to Mother. Two could play silly games.

When he appeared at the breakfast table the following week with a black eye and bruises, Esme was quick to give him a grilling.

'Son, whose war have you been fighting?' she asked, but he shrugged it off.

'Just an argument with the coalhouse door in the ice,' he replied as he tucked into his fry-up.

Ivy said nothing but she turned to the others and snapped, 'Don't go looking at me! I'd nothing to do with it so you can take that smug look off your face, Susan Brown.'

Later in the morning Levi darted down to the telephone kiosk and returned with a face like thunder.

'Anything the matter?' Lily couldn't resist, her eyes wide and innocent.

'Nothing I can't handle. You can't trust anyone,' he muttered. 'No one's been fiddling in the back, have they?'

Now was her perfect chance to confront him but she flunked it. 'Why should they? But you're right, though, not to trust anyone, not even your own kith and kin.'

'What's that supposed to mean?'

'Think about it,' she said.

None of his special customers ever came when Lily was on duty. She'd eyed him all morning like a hawk. The telltale jar was hidden in her hope chest at the foot of her bed alongside the embroidered tablecloths, pillow slips and nightdress holder.

Curious, she had sniffed the weed. It sort of smelled harmless, like stale Weetabix. It certainly looked harmless.

The box on the shelf stayed empty for weeks, much to Su, Lily and Ma's relief, but there was still the matter of Walter's little package to deal with.

The two of them were sitting in the van overlooking Leaper's View, the beauty spot and lovers' rendezvous above the town. The snow-plough had been through and cleared the lane. It was good to be out in the fresh air, Lily thought. It was the first time they'd been alone for ages.

'Have you thought about our honeymoon yet?' she asked. 'It would be nice to go somewhere romantic.'

'Blackpool or Llandudno?'

'Let's try further afield ... the Continent – Paris or Rome. I've been looking in some magazines for ideas.'

She'd scoured the newspapers for weeks. There was a whole world of travel opening up now the war was well and truly finished, ships turning back into cruise liners and planes to whisk tourists abroad. There were permits to travel to certain resorts. Why should they have to watch it on the silver screen and not try to go there themselves?

'Let's be daring and sell some of Granddad's shares, forego the fancy wedding spree and go to Paris! It would be so exciting, don't you think?'

'I thought you'd prefer hiking in the Lake District,' Walter said, yawning. 'You mustn't go spending your inheritance.'

'We could try Switzerland, in the Alps,' she said, suddenly feeling excitement at the thought of snowcapped mountains and yodelling cowmen.

'I've seen enough snow this winter to last a lifetime,' Walt yawned again.

'Am I that boring?' she snapped. 'We've waited years to wed so let's push the boat out and do it in style, give the *Mercury* something to write about...'

'I thought you didn't want a big do,' he said, staring down at the flickering lights of the town.

'I don't, but I want a proper honeymoon, away from smoke and the grime, just the two of us together, all alone, sightseeing and trying new things.'

'It's a long way to go for just a week, Lil.'

'We could fly. I've been doing some research. They're beginning to expand commercial flights out of Ringway. There's a whole new world for us to explore. We'd be the first in Grimbleton to have a foreign honeymoon, like royalty!'

'I'd rather not think about flying through the air in a tin can, love,' he offered, stifling another yawn.

'Where's your sense of adventure? There are all sorts of new jobs on the go now, jobs for girls on aeroplanes as stewardesses. I read it in the paper. I'd love to have a shot at doing that.'

'No wife of mine'll go out to work. You'll have enough to do looking after us,' Walt yawned

273

loudly this time and she could see the plate of his false teeth.

'A girl can dream, can't she? If only I'd been born a few years later... Still, our children will get those chances. I do want to go abroad.'

'We'd need a passport,' he said as his eyelids closed into a doze.

'Walter Platt, what's got into you tonight?' she shouted, shaking him awake.

'It's them tea leaves Susan give me for my back. I made some up and drank it. It tasted terrible and now I can't keep my eyes open. Don't bring me any more, I'd rather have a sore back.'

Oh, no! thought Lily. How was she going to explain this away? 'You'd better let me throw those leaves on the fire if it's not doing you any good. Shall I get us some passport forms then?' she continued, changing the subject and knowing this was an opportunity not to be missed.

'Do what you like, love, but let me get some kip.'

Lily gazed over the snowy landscape with relief. This was no romantic rendezvous, but in Paris it would be different.

A week later the men in shabby overcoats and trilbies came back to the stall, in dribs and drabs at first, hanging around smoking in the café opposite, waiting for Levi's return from the pub. The box was full again and each sachet was twisted and sealed.

Su wasn't here to help her. It was her sewing and mending afternoon. Enid was taking her mother to the doctor. Lily hung back while Levi totted up the takings. The chance would come when he took the money to the night safe at the bank and she was left alone to lock up.

The dried parsley and mixed herbs were all ready to package up. She would use the same twists and tape, adding just sufficient weed to make them look genuine and make sure the first few were all weed, just in case. Her hands were shaking and her heart thudding. She must not leave a crumb of evidence.

A few days later, Lily closed up as usual, taking the short cut behind the Market Hall to catch the bus home. She always scurried along the dark alley as the lamps were dim and she had some takings to bank.

There seemed to be some kerfuffle ahead, people crowding around a drunk on the cobbles, but it was a bit early for anyone to be drunk yet. The man lay in silhouette, prostrate, in a bad way.

'Lad's bin set upon,' an old man in the flat cap and muffler said. 'They ran off when we turned the corner. I don't know what the world's coming to when a working man can't go about his business. Did we fight a war for this?' He looked down at his wife, who was kneeling, dabbing blood off the man's face. 'Better get the bobbies, Ethel. This lad's going nowhere.'

It was only when Lily bent over to see if she could help that she recognised the battered face of her brother. 'Someone get an ambulance quick! He's unconscious... Oh, do hurry!' she cried, holding his hand.

'Oh, Levi, what've we done?' she whispered in

his ear, trying to rouse him. It seemed like hours before Levi was stretchered off to hospital and Lily gave the policeman all his particulars, trembling with the shock of what had happened. Her cheeks were burning up with shame. This was all her doing.

She rescued the van keys from Levi's pockets and drove home like an automaton. What if he died? How was she going to break the news to her mother? She let herself in through the porch, her hands shaking, calling everyone into the kitchen to tell them the news.

Ivy was hysterical, grabbing her coat and hat, Neville was howling, and Esme was as white as a sheet.

'What's going on? Ivy, I'm not daft. First a black eye and now a beating? What's he been up to? Another woman, is it? Hubby found out?' Esme stopped her at the door, her eyes glassy with tears.

'No, no ... it can't be that... Someone's got it in for him. He wouldn't say,' she croaked.

'Is he in debt? My son's no saint but if it's money... You've allus lived above your means. Word gets about if a debt is not honoured. I should've been told,' Esme continued, barring her exit.

'No... I don't know. He said some supplies had gone missing. Someone was cheating him, I don't know. You know Levi,' she cried, sobbing.

Lily bowed her head. It was time to own up. She took a deep breath.

'There's something you should know. You see, I think this is all my doing...'

'No! Is all my fault, Daw Esme. Don't listen to Lily. Please, I was only trying to help. I have made it worse,' Su confessed later on.

Esme sat down in shock.

'No!' Lily shouted. 'Don't say any more.'

Out it all poured, like sugar from a sack, spilling out in all directions – the guilt, the worries of the past weeks. 'I found these herbs that did not go in the book. I asked and he told me it was for bad backs. I think it would be good to give to poor Mrs Santini and Walter... I try to save you all from prison,' she said. 'It was me. I changed the tobacco for herbs. I switch the packets with Lily. I did it for you, Daw Esme, so no one is harmed,' she cried.

'Whatever are you on about, Susan? What has tobacco got to do with this? We don't sell tobacco,' Esme said.

There was nothing for it but to explain the whole sorry scam.

'Your son, he sells hash from a shoebox. They came to the stall for supplies to smoke in their pipes. I gave some away and we found out it is a bad smoke. Lily and me, we took it away in a jar and put old herbs in its place. He sold them harmless herbs, not dope. Then they were cross with him and he finds out and brings new stuff and we did it again. I don't want us to go to prison. It is wrong to sell mystic smokes. I think they were angry and set on him in the alley and made it look like a robbery.'

There was a deafening silence as her words sunk in.

277

'You have a good business and he was cheating you,' she added, but Ivy lashed out as if to hit her.

'Don't believe a word of it! Levi would never do that. She is making up lies. She is jealous of us because she can never be one of us!'

'I am a good woman. I do not cheat, Daw Esme. Every time he sells a packet and never puts it in the ledger, he cheats you, Daw Esme. Every time he changes prices and pockets the difference, he cheats you. When he buys and sells ration coupons under the counter – and selling hash will ruin a good business – he cheat his mother!'

'What exactly is hash tobacco?' asked Esme, with a weary voice.

'Mother, surely you know about narcotics: laudanum compounds? This is hemp, another narcotic plant. You drink or smoke or breathe it and it gives you nice dreams,' answered Lily. 'I've been reading up in Dad's old books.'

'Lots of herbs can do that. What's so bad about giving people a good night's rest?' said Ivy.

'It's illegal to use these drugs. You go to prison if you deal in drugs for pleasure. Maria told me,' Lily replied. 'It was Maria who recognised what it was and warned us to get rid of the stuff.'

'You mean my son runs an opium den?' croaked Esme, with her head in her hands.

'I might've known the Eyetie woman would be mixed up in this. Kettle calling the pot black, in my opinion,' Ivy hissed. 'You should watch your back with her.'

'What do you mean by that?' Lily asked.

'Far be it from me to spread gossip, but surely

278

you've noticed what a bandbox and fashion plate she has become lately. Don't tell me with a sick husband in Moses Heights she has the spondulicks to go tarting herself up to the nines. Every time she comes round here she's had a shampoo and set, and more besides,' Ivy snorted with satisfaction.

'Maria's a hairdresser's model. That's no secret. If you worked half as hard as she does, perhaps there'd be time for all of us to get glammed up,' Lily answered.

'Trust you to stick up for foreigners. Mark my words, it'll all end in tears. That Romeo at the sink is on the sly. Walls have ears. If her in-laws find out she's being soft-soaped by that ball of grease there'll be slaughter on the streets. I've seen what gangsters do to their molls.' Ivy was wagging her finger in righteous indignation.

'Oh, go and boil yer head! Talking rubbish, as usual. Why do you always see the worst in folks and ignore what's staring you in the face?'

Su had never seen Lily so fired up. Now Ivy would get her overturning.

'Pardon me for breathing, Miss Hoity-Toity. I tell the truth as I see it. If you don't like my words–'

'If you don't believe me, come and see the stuff I've got in the jam jar. I wonder why our Levi had to deal in forbidden drugs. To keep you in all the fancy goods no one else can afford. You've made a criminal of my brother with your pestering! It's not right to use our stall to fund that extravagance so I had to protect everyone.'

Now at last the pennies were dropping. It was

Su's turn to join in the fray.

'Ask Ana why she was so eager to leave the stall. Go on... A man like that is not worth protecting but the good Winstanley name is. My Stan would cry in his grave to see his mother shamed. If you don't believe me, wait a second and we'll bring down some evidence that will speak for itself. Ask your precious husband to explain that to his mother. I shall be pleased to hear what he says then!'

'I'm not taking this from you. Who do you think you are? One of us? Hah, just you wait! You've not heard the last of this, blaming a sick man who can't defend his corner. Just you wait, you lot'll pay for this!' Ivy ran out of the room.

What a to-do! Esme sat in the chair with her head in her hands, not looking at any of them. Ana was crying, slopping tea over the cups. Su feared that the Battle of Division Street was about to begin.

Lily was silent, 'What have we done?' written all over her face. She was going to get all the blame.

Su sighed. Girls were the same the world over. As the proverb said: 'An unmarried girl has no honour even if she has ten brothers.'

It was as if poor Lily was the villain, not the son, in the mother's eyes. Those two rubbed along like shoes on the wrong feet.

16

The Joys of a Family

Esme Winstanley looked down at her son lying in the bed with dismay and relief. He was still out for the count and under sedation but he would live.

'What were you playing at, son?' she sighed. What was happening to her family? First Freddie and now Levi letting her down. What had she done to deserve such disappointment in her children? She sat slumped like an empty sack, sipping hospital tea that young Sister Unsworth had brought for her. What must Diana be thinking about all these antics? The Winstanleys used to be a respectable family and now they had more secrets than the Secret Service.

No one must say a word out of turn. She had laid that on thick with a trowel.

'Family first and only, Lily. No blabbing to anyone, not Polly, Enid or even Walt. Let's just say Levi fell and banged his head and knocked himself out on the ice.'

The nurse had said the ward was full of broken hips, and legs and ankles. If only this winter ice would shift. There had been three power cuts last week, but the hospital had its own generator and was safe. They'd lit candles and storm lamps, huddling by the fire. The coal in the bunker was shrinking and still the blizzards came. No wonder people wanted cheering up.

Was that what these funny tea leaves did? Cheered you up so the world looked sunny and warm and full of good cheer? What was wrong with that, then?

Out came the old white coat from the back of Esme's wardrobe. It had shrunk since she'd last put it on, but she was down at that stall first thing next morning to examine the books and sort out the stock.

There would be no more layabouts and dodgy dealers shuffling up when they saw *her* on the warpath. A hundred years of respectable trading was not going to be jeopardised by the stupidity of her son. She would stand sentry for as long as it took until everyone got the message that families stand firm in a crisis.

Susan was a bright girl, and Enid scuttled around wondering what was up but asking no questions. Lily's mind was not on the job. Esme was worried about that girl. The Lord was certainly sending her her share of trials.

Levi must learn to shoulder his own burdens and not rely on her for handouts. Lily must stop shilly-shallying and name the wedding day. The trouble with children was they all needed kicking with a different foot.

She made up a proper roster for Saturdays so Lily could have time to sort out her wedding plans and Susan had time to spend with Joy. And what were they doing still harbouring these two lodgers? Truth was, Freddie's ladies were the least trouble of all lately.

If only Redvers was here to guide her. What should she do next? Wasn't it enough to have lost one son without now being in danger of losing another to greed and meanness? How could she bring back Levi from the dead? Put that in your Almighty pipe, Dear Lord, and smoke it, she prayed, looking to the ceiling in defiance. It's over to you now!

The terraces were filling up slowly for the last match of the season. Lily was impatient, standing in the dampness on a rare afternoon off. Spring was in the air at last. No more snow but the pitch was waterlogged and the concrete stands were sodden. Walt was late, having stopped off for a pint or two of Wilson's best bitter.

I don't know what I'm doing here, she thought, looking around the familiar faces huddled against the chill. She supposed it was a relief to get out of the house and the bad atmosphere. Since the funny business with the stolen hash Levi was not speaking to anyone. His bruises were healing and no bones were broken, but his temper was that foul. He had a face on him like sore feet. Ivy and the war had a lot to answer for. It was her fancy ideas that pushed them to spend what they hadn't got. Neville was being a pain in the bum, throwing his dinner across the kitchen. He'd got the girls playing up too.

Ivy ignored everyone and the atmosphere in Division Street was like a blocked sewer. Mother went around as if there was a big black cloud above her head. Ana scurried off on hospital duty, out of the way, while Susan spent her time upstairs sewing sequins on a costume for Joy.

Lily was the pig in the middle, as usual, and Walt didn't help matters. Where was he when she needed him? Everything was going wrong.

The supper club wasn't meeting any more. Maria and Queenie were caught up in Sylvio's latest hairdressing competition attempt. Diana and Eva had nursing exams to pass. Soon it would be the summer season and the dancing class would close. It ought not to matter but, to her consternation, it mattered. She missed the gatherings, the gossip round someone's fire, the outings to the pictures. Perhaps she ought to organise something herself.

It was not as if there weren't a hundred other things she ought to be doing. Only last week she and Walt had sat in the vestry of Zion listening to the Reverend Atkinson going through all the paperwork and arrangements for their summer wedding. It had finally been booked for the first Saturday in August. They would be sitting down to a cold meat salad in Zion Sunday school hall with a small square fruit cake covered in a plaster of Paris icing, a gift from Crompton's Biscuits. Dina and Joy would be the little bridesmaids and Neville the pageboy, if Levi and Ivy turned up at all to the do. Susan was going to help Lily make her outfits.

It all ought to be exciting, but here she was, thinking about a day out at the seaside with the Olive Oils when there was the business of applying for passports casting a cloud on the horizon. Her forms were signed and sent off, but Walt had done nothing about his. He said he'd lost his birth certificate! He was still not convinced about going abroad and suggested they went to the Isle of Man instead. Why couldn't they agree on anything?

There was some good news. On one of their jaunts to the edge of the moor they found a small stone-built cottage to rent, a house with thick walls and an outside toilet, a long garden with a wonderful view. It would need bottoming out from top to toe, and distempering in bright colours. They ought to be up there now sorting it all out. As newlyweds they could claim extra coupons to buy furnishings. At last, here was a home of her very own to plan, away from all the feuding. Roll on August!

So what was the point of standing here watching a lacklustre end-of-season game?

Even Pete Walsh was injured and out of the team. Barry was playing like a one-legged blind man. It was wet and windy, and she was not in the mood for cheering and catcalling. They were out of the Cup and second in the league.

Walt was late for the kick-off. They always stood on the same terrace, third row from the back, with the Division Street fans. She waited another ten minutes and then turned back down the stairs and out of the stadium. The two of them seemed to be on parallel tram tracks, side by side but never close enough to touch, these days. She blamed it on all the funny business going on and having to hide things from him. The sooner they were wed and together, the sooner all their misunderstandings would be sorted out.

The thought of all the preparations was making

her nervous. She hoped they didn't end up like Levi or Ivy, bickering and rowing. Nothing was turning out as she hoped.

Perhaps it was this blessed chill. What was needed was a bit of cheering up, a cup of hot Vimto and a seat in Santini's to cheer her flagging spirits. It would be good to see Maria's bright face in the café. She could relax and make a list of all her plans, and pop in the travel agent's on the way back to see what was on offer. She was determined to make their honeymoon special, even if she had to do it herself.

'You look *bellissima*,' Marco smiled, sitting on the open balcony of the sanatorium in his dressing gown. 'You have the big show tonight?'

'I can't stop long but I just wanted to show you.' Maria kissed him, patting his head like a dog. 'How are you feeling?'

'How do you think? I am sick of this vista, snow on hills. Nice on a Christmas card but I'm sick of living in a Christmas card. I wanna come home and see Rosa and Mamma, not sit like a lump of dough in this chair. I am trying to get strong but when I walk too much, I can't breathe. I wanna go home with you... All this costs too much money.'

'Be patient, the *dottore* says not yet. It is too smoky and sooty. Perhaps in the summer.'

'The summer'll never come for me,' he whispered, turning his grey face from her in distress.

'Soon the snow will melt on the hills and the garden will grow flowers. Rosa and I will come to have picnics with you, and she will show you her dancing steps.' It was hard to stop the panic rising in her voice.

'Make it soon, *mia cara...*'

Maria sat on the bus home with a heavy heart. This has got to stop, you mustn't see Sylvio alone again, she ordered herself, repeating it over again, fingering her rosary for the strength to resist temptation.

If only it were that easy to shut off the excitement, the longings and the fantasies. He was everything Marco was not. He was young, fit and full of energy, full of creative dreams. He was talented and eager to succeed. Everything he'd achieved was by his own hard work. His path was not smoothed over by family connections.

Perhaps Marco would have returned from war with such vigour if he'd not been so badly wounded. They would've made plans to change the décor, improve the café and have more babies.

Now his poor body was like a sack of straw, his spirit so fragile and tired, but he clung on to life for her sake, patient in his suffering like a saintly martyr. But I don't want a saint for a lover, I want real flesh and blood, strong arms to hold me, strong thighs to press on me, the warm breath of sucking lips, she cried in shame.

No one could accuse her of neglecting her husband. Every possible visiting hour, she turned up. She should have shares in the bus company, so many tickets she'd purchased to get to the ward on time and back between shifts. Faithful in her presence but not in her body.

This evening she sat on the upstairs deck in the twilight, watching the twinkling lights of the town fading as the road rose higher onto the moor and the dark starlit night. She could do this journey blindfolded: round the bend out of town, up under the arched railway viaduct and past the grammar school with its windows ablaze with light. Onwards and upwards to the terminal stop and the iron gate leading to the long flat single-storey sanatorium, with windows open to the sky and balconies facing the windswept lawns, facing away from the foul air and the dust, catching the west wind over the Pennines.

No one could accuse her of not doing her duty by Marco but duty didn't warm her toes at night, duty put no skip in her step. Duty kept her at her post behind the counter and doing the books at night.

She'd sensed the loss of him the minute he was carried from the troopship on a stretcher. He was as much a victim of war as all the names on the Grimbleton cenotaph; a Tommy with an Italian name, while Sylvio was the enemy, defeated, despised by her family. Marco was a frail shadow of what he might have been and it was not his fault. In the eyes of the Church he was her *marito* and she was dirt, a faithless wife. How could she think of betraying him?

She had done her duty and come from Sicily to marry one of the brothers. That was the arrangement and she was grateful for the chance of a new life. The family had once visited from England and it was an honour to be betrothed to such a successful *famiglia*. By the time she'd arrived the other brothers were spoken for and it was assumed she and Marco would make a fine couple. He was gentle and shy, and she was so naïve and ignorant.

The wedding was lavish, with dancing and music. They had taken the train to London for their honeymoon and saw all the sights. Then came the miscarriages, one after another. Marco joined up and one brief reunion resulted in precious Rosaria. Now when she looked at him all she felt was loving pity.

How could she be honest and tell him she didn't care for him in that way any more? No words would ever come out of her mouth to hurt him. The truth would kill him and she couldn't do that to such a brave man. It was tempting to blurt out all her feelings and dump them on him once and for all, but the price of loving Sylvio was to carry all this guilt like some huge rock on her back.

It was her burden, not Marco's, and yet of all the men she knew she sensed he might understand and forgive.

She was dying too, living a half-life of secrets and lies, trying to stay cheerful and busy for Rosaria's sake. Yet Rosa was not enough. How she yearned for another baby at her breast and the clutter of little ones to distract her from this constant aching.

The ice-cream parlour was not enough. It would never be her business without Marco by her side. Santinis only gave to the sons, so it would be Enzo's café one day, not Rosa's. It wasn't fair. The cleaning jobs kept her so active she slept with exhaustion each night.

The only consolation in her life was those stolen moments with Sylvio when she could forget the dreary world. She loved how he styled her hair this way and that, trying new cuts and lotions. Her head was like a lump of clay from which he created such amusing sculptures for the competitions.

Their next job was to prepare the mannequins for the Fashion Parade in the town hall, the one that Diana's mother was organising for the Hospital Comforts Fund.

Levine's would be showing off their most exclusive range for the smart ladies of town. Rumour had it there would be some of the 'New Look' fashions on display with frilly underskirts and merino wool boleros.

For one evening, perhaps, they could work together and no one would suspect. Time disappeared when she was lying in his arms and there was only the hush of the silent salon and the flicker of neon lights flashing outside as they made love on the floor. This was the time of dreams, when they wished great falling stars full of wishes, silly love talk, the 'what ifs' when the world they knew faded into the distance, with its rationing, coupons and drabness. For these few hours she lost all her 'must dos' and feasted on these precious stolen moments but when they separated she was back in the real world, pacing the floor in the small hours of the morning, seeing the pain on Marco's face.

This life of lies was tearing her apart and it couldn't go on. Marco would want her to have some life of her own but not this treachery. He thought the Olive Oil Club and Rosa's dancing success were enough.

He'd nearly killed himself to see Rosa dance. If only he knew the way things were. Of all men he would understand, but he trusted her and how easy it is to be believed when you are trusted completely. Once that trust was betrayed it could never be repaired. Better to carry the burden alone and not hurt him any more. Better to give up her lover and sleep easy.

'Our Lady of Sorrows, please help me!' she prayed. 'A mamma must put her children first and make sacrifices.' She prayed for the strength to resist Sylvio and walk away. This could not go on.

Now, as the moon rose over the dark purple hills and the stars shone like icicles in the clear sky, she sensed resolve and purpose and a cleansing. It was going to be a fresh start. From now on she'd devote herself only to her husband and child and the success of the business.

She was blessed with good friends in Lily, Ana, Su, Queenie and Diana. They believed in her. They must be enough. Giving into passion, to temptation was a sin. No more fancy hairdos and vanity. From now on her mind and heart must rest only on the blessings she'd been given. There was a roof over her head and they wanted for nothing. Marco need never know about her little lapse, as he'd never known about the GI, all those years ago. A terrible thought stabbed her in the gut. Was Marco being punished for her sins? Surely not? Better to sort it out now.

Tomorrow she would face her first confession for months, do every penance and attend Mass once more to blot out this backlog of sinning and make him better.

There was chaos in the café when Lily arrived. Enzo was struggling to keep up with the afternoon shoppers.

'Is Maria in the back?' she asked.

'She's upstairs, lazy cow!' he snapped.

It was not like Maria to shirk a busy shift. Time to find out what was wrong.

She was curled up on the little sofa, covered in a blanket, sobbing.

'Whatever's the matter?' Lily said, going to put the kettle on the stove.

'I'm bad woman, Lily.' Her sobs shook her whole body.

Maria was not making any sense, but Lily knew a cup in her hand and a chance to talk it over might help. 'You're a good woman. What's brought all this on?'

'I have to tell someone. I am terrible woman in mortal sin. What will I do, Lily?'

'Shove this down you. I've put sugar in it,' Lily replied. 'It's not that bad, surely? No one could do more than you for Marco.'

'It's not how it should be with us. We are married. We should share bed and loving and now I betray *mio marito*. I am lonely. I do my duty for the Santini family but my toes are cold at night and I find warmth in the arms of Sylvio Bertorelli. They will kill me if they find out. I disgrace the family name.'

So Ivy's gossip was true. Lily sighed. Not that it was a surprise when she had seen how those two looked at each other. This confession was way out of her league. What should she say? What did she know of such things? Better just to listen and say nowt but a friend needed support at a time like this.

'It's hard for you on your own. He'd understand. You're only human.'

'No, you do not understand our ways. They will kill me! Sylvio make me feel like a film star but it is wrong what we do but, oh, he loves me.'

'I don't know what to say,' Lily whispered. 'It must be hard.'

'I am dying inside. One child is not enough for me. Rosaria needs brothers and sisters. I do not like this family. It is all making money. Angelo and Toni would kill me and take my child from me. I don't deserve such a husband.'

'You're doing your best to protect him. You're only human, Maria.' What else could be said that was not going to make her feel worse?

'When I am with Sylvio, we lie under the stars, make snow angels, wishing great dreams for the salon. We are like Romeo and Juliet. There are no rations and coupons or icy grass, just moonlight and kisses, but it is all ended now. I have to think of Marco.'

'You were happy together once?' Lily asked as she sat down, a wonky spring digging into her bottom. Better to let Maria get it all out of her system.

'I was glad he was the only one left to marry. The others are ... poof! It is hard to carry secret,

Lily. It is like a big rock on my back that bends me in two. It is better to give up my happiness. Marco doesn't deserve a faithless woman. I have to be strong for both of us.'

Lily nodded, thinking how she had to be strong for Walter. He was like a lost little boy sometimes who needed a shove in the right direction. It wasn't that he didn't love her in his own way but he was not good at showing his affection.

'What are you going to do?'

'I will tell him,' Maria sobbed, 'Sylvio, I can't see you any more. No more competitions. People talk and I can't risk Rosa. I have such a pain in my stomach and my head.' She was sobbing until she was hoarse.

Why did the film *Brief Encounter* come into Lily's mind? She had queued with Enid to see it twice. The heroine had to choose between her doctor sweetheart or her family, and it all ended in tears. It was like going through the mangle watching that film, they were that wrung out. Passion like that was unnerving and it worried her. The film music was ringing in her head at the very thought of all that pent-up emotion.

The only courtship she was experiencing was a very steady away sort of loving. But how did anyone do a day's work after all those shenanigans?

'We have to do Diana's fashion show. I will tell him then,' Maria sobbed. 'The fates brought us together and showed us what might have been. It is cruel but life is cruel, I think. No more Lavaroni's, no more shows. I go to confession,' she sobbed, wiping her eyes. 'Now I must go downstairs. How are things at home?'

'It was as bad as you feared. I destroyed the hash. Levi was beaten up and now Mother is ruling the roost. We are all in disgrace.'

'You are a good family. It will pass...'

'Oh, Ria, if only you knew the half of it, but my lips are sealed. Believe me, all families have secrets.'

'Don't say a word to anyone,' Maria was pleading. 'I'd better go.'

'You wash your face, go down there and I'll fetch Rosa from her nonna's house. I'll make you both some tea and we'll go and see Marco together. You ought not to be on your own tonight,' Lily offered, glad to feel needed.

'You are a good egg, Lily. You will make Walt a fine woman.'

Oh heck! Walt would wonder where she had got to again. There was just time to nip on the bus to leave a message and the shopping with his mother.

But when a friend was in trouble it was company they needed. Walt could wait.

There would be years together in that little house on the hill, years and years of it, not like Sylvio and Maria, the star-crossed lovers. It was so sad: just one moment of stolen passion. Who was it said that all passion ended in the grave? Now she was getting as bad as Maria with her romantic fantasies. Why hadn't she ever felt like that with Walt? When she looked at him lately all she wanted to do was criticise. What was wrong with her? Was she jealous of Maria and Sylvio, jealous of adulterers? It was all so confusing.

17

Cinderellas in Ballgowns

'I'm sorry, girls, but you're going to have to sing for your supper tonight,' said Diana, tapping her pencil on her wine glass in the Unsworths' dining room. She had fed them on grilled trout with game chips and the last of the apples in the loft, made into a crumble with oats and ground nuts and a bottle of Daddy's best wine. Someone had to fly the British flag when it came to cuisine.

'Mummy has asked for the Olive Oils to help with her charity mannequin parade. It's for the hospital so I want some good prizes for the raffle,' she paused for breath and to read off her list.

'Lavaroni's have agreed to do the hairdressing, Battersby's the shoes and Levine's the clothes, but they want some local girls to model the outfits: tall girls who can stride out in the New Look.' She looked straight in the direction of Ana and Lily.

'Su, I want you to help with the raffle. Queenie and Maria are committed to Sylvio so, you two, you are volunteered.'

'I'm no clotheshorse,' Lily protested.

Why did that girl put herself down so? She would look elegant if she just bothered to stand up straight.

'I no walk across stage,' said Ana, who was blossoming by the day. She was another who slouched into her uniform.

'Of course you will. It's for a good cause and it will give Lily some practice for her wedding day. Once Sophie Levine is finished with us, we won't recognise ourselves. Anyway, the audience'll be looking at the fashions, not at you. I hope everyone here will sell at least a dozen tickets or else.'

The faces opposite her looked down at their dirty plates. Was she being bossy again? She couldn't help being enthusiastic.

It was just that over the past few weeks, with exams, Diana had missed their gatherings and gossip. Everyone was going round with glum faces so they all needed something to cheer them up and what better than a late spring fashion show?

Keeping busy was what had kept her sane all these months since her return. Coming back to Grimbleton was not what she had intended, but when Binky upped and left her and found a new playmate, she had crawled back from Cairo with her tail between her legs.

She was too old to be living at home and Mummy was puzzled why there were no boyfriends calling round. How could she explain there never would be and that her heart was still aching for Binky Ballard?

The Olive Oils had saved her sanity. She loved their company and living all their mysterious lives at second-hand. Guiding was fun and her job was important, but being an auntie to all those little girls was like having her own nephews and nieces.

Being an only child was a pain at times: the golden egg that must deliver for all the expensive education she had received. They still treated her as if she was home for the hols, not as an adult, a senior nurse with years of experience in battlefield hospitals. There were things she couldn't tell anyone of what she had seen. Daddy guessed but said little.

Friendship and loyalty to the team was what had seen her through the worst of times and the best.

She had thought that Binky would be ready to settle down and set up home, find work together, but Binky had other ideas. It was hurtful to know she was just a war time fling, not a lifetime's love. It hurt so much she never wanted to feel anything again.

Better to go home and lick her wounds for a while, sob into her pillow and pull herself together, rise to the challenge and all that bosh!

Thank goodness she had found a bevy of lonely, limping women to mother along.

Each one of them was as tough as desert boots but they just didn't realise it yet.

Lily was at the beck and call of her brood. Maria was having some sort of emotional crisis. Su and Ana were mystery guests – definitely a tale to tell there – and poor Queenie didn't know which day of the week it was, she was so busy rushing from job to job.

If you want something doing ask a busy person, went the saying and it was true. No one protested too loudly, no one refused to lend a hand. All they needed was a bit of organising and she had that ability in spades.

'Right,' she ordered. 'This's what we'll do...'

On the afternoon of the parade Lily found herself having her hair lopped and chopped and set into waves. She'd just been to a rehearsal in the town hall, learning to pace down the catwalk while Sophie Levine pointed out all the features of her outfit.

Diana had marched her off to the corsetiere in Silver Street where she'd been shovelled into the tightest boned corselet and brassiere, two sizes too small for her, yielding up precious coupons for the pleasure.

'Foundations are basic, Lily. Like a body without bones, a dress without a corset has no structure,' Diana insisted.

'I thought *buildings* needed structure,' she replied.

'Exactly, my point... You know what happens to a house without foundations?'

What a surprise to discover she'd a bust after all, and the neatest waist.

'I can't breathe,' she protested.

'That's the point! It'll make you stand up and breathe properly, not slouch. Posture, think posture.'

It was all right for Diana – she was slim as a lath, more like a boy than a girl. Everything looked neat on her.

Ana was quaking in her shoes, trying to find an excuse not to turn up, but she was transformed by a good hoisting harness. When Diana was on the march there was no shilly-shallying in the ranks.

Esme had lined up half of Division Street to support the effort by buying tickets. What if I stumble and fall and make a right fool of myself? Lily wondered.

It was funny how, once the clothes were put on, she felt a different person, no longer good old Lil, but more like a Lily or even Joan Crawford, American and glamorous. Until she saw herself full of curlers in the mirror.

Sylvio was stomping around, giving orders with a grim face instead of his usual grin. Had Maria done what she had promised and given him his marching orders? Happen it was for the best.

Maria was keeping out of everyone's way, just shampooing and towelling off. Queenie was playing pig in the middle, pretending there weren't any tensions in the salon.

Ana refused to have her hair cut, so now it was coiled in a sophisticated chignon at the back of her head and covered in a net headscarf.

Susan was sulking because she wasn't modelling and she was the prettiest of the lot of them. Ivy had refused to buy a ticket so they saddled her with the babysitting, for once. Esme had put her foot down and insisted she pull her weight.

Maria couldn't wait for the salon to empty, for the models to rush across to the town hall, for Gianni to disappear upstairs so she could catch Sylvio on his own.

It had been a long afternoon and she should

have taken her half-day visit to Moses Heights but there were so many heads to do.

This time she wanted to face her husband with a clear conscience. She would go for visiting time as usual on the evening bus with Rosa.

Sylvio had been in a bad mood all morning. Gianni was breathing down his neck, saying what styles he must show. The trouble was they were yesterday's hairdos, not suitable for the New Look clothes.

'He won't let me do anything new,' Sylvio complained as he shot into the wash cubicle.

'*Il poverino*,' Maria smiled. 'Just be patient, one day everyone will want your ideas.'

'We have to get out of here ... start a new salon.'

'Now's not the time,' she whispered. He was barely out of the POW camp, without any money to set up on his own. It was too soon for Grimbleton to accept him. 'One day, perhaps ... you will show them all.'

'We will do it together, yes?'

Maria drew in a breath. 'There is no "we". I am married. I have baby and big family. I must work for them.'

'No, I take care of you both. We go away.'

'Stop this!' she cried. 'This is a silly dream. This can't go on. You know it's wrong. We will be punished.'

Sylvio grabbed her tight and shook her. 'What are you saying? We are good for each other. I will wait for you ... until Marco...' He spoke in desperation.

She couldn't believe it. 'What are *you* saying? Jesu Maria, you are one crazy man! It is not our time. It will never be our time. I came to England to marry. You came to fight England. I am from the south and you from the north. We're never meant to marry. Don't say another word.' She crossed herself in horror. 'If the family finds out we are both dead.'

'Fate has brought us together, Maria.'

'And Fate is cruel, showing us what we might have had. I am sorry but I must go.'

'Stay, don't go. I love you. There will be a way.'

'No, Sylvio, no more Lavaroni's for me, no more secrets, no more sneaking, *finito... Capisci?*' She tried to sound cold but her voice was shaking.

'I don't believe you. If you don't come, I'll go. I don't care,' he snapped. 'Please, come back. We can be just friends.'

She stared at him. His eyes were full of tears, pleading with her. It would be so easy to fall into his arms, to forget all her vows just for another second of his loving.

'I have to go. One of us has to be strong. Two wrongs don't make a right.'

'You never loved me...'

'How can you say that? It is love that makes me walk away now. Love for you, love for your safety, love for my child and my husband, but Rosa comes first and always. I must do what is best for her now.'

She slammed the salon door behind her and did not look back.

The catwalk down the centre of the Civic Ballroom was lined with hot-house plants. It smelled like a floral pavilion. There were chairs lined in rows facing each other. The seats were filling up with the great and the good of Grimbleton, all sitting in frocks and hats, waiting to be entertained. It was a full house and the raffle prizes were good. Lily bought five bobs' worth, hoping to secure the main prize of a ticket on a cruise round the Hebrides donated by Bill and Avril Crumblehume, the owners of Longsight Travel who were friends of the Unsworths.

Her hairstyle was a shock. She was expecting something like the concrete set Esme got from Mavis Tatlock each week. Gone was the hosepipe coil round her head and in its place was a sleek bob, more Veronica Lake with a bang over her forehead. Who was this stranger peeking at her through the fringe?

There was no time to be nervous as there were six outfits to fling on, one after the other. Her favourite outfit was a two-piece linen suit in a dusty pink with full skirt and frilly petticoat. You could make three dresses from the material in the skirt alone. After all the shortages it seemed so extravagant to be floating around in such luxury, but she wasn't going to faint now and let the side down.

'Next we have Lee, our English rose...'

'Where's Lee?'

'It's you, get on!' Diana shoved Lily forward. It was now or never to the end of that long, long walk. She fixed her eyes on the clock at the end of the gallery and strode out onto the precipice with her smile plastered firmly onto her face.

'By heck! Is that our Lil? What've they done to

her?' Esme stared in disbelief as her daughter swanned down the catwalk like a professional. 'Who'd've thought it?'

'She's turned out right bonny,' said Doris Pickvance with a sniff. 'Just wait until her wedding day. You're in for a treat there.'

Esme saw the rest of the parade through a veil of tears. Where had all the years gone? Lily Longlegs, with a pair of plaits like ropes, had gone for good, replaced by this swish young lady with a waspy waist and softly turned hair. When did our Lil get to be such a fine-looking lass? she wondered. It was as if the scales were falling off her eyes and she now looked at her daughter for the first time. How could she ever have dismissed her as plain? How come her sons had got all her attention? They had dazzled her with Redvers' charm while all along Lil was blossoming into this lovely young lady.

When it came to the finale, she was floating past in a satin ballgown with a sequined bodice in deep midnight blue. Ana was by her side, looking very sophisticated in sea-green velvet that showed off her full bust and red-gold hair.

Diana Unsworth wore a figure-hugging black number and the bridal outfit was worn by one of Levine's assistants. It was fitted with a long train. Perhaps, Esme thought, she ought to let the moths fly out of her purse in a good cause and buy Lily a wedding dress from this shop. She would stop the traffic in one of their gowns.

Esme was that proud and yet so sad that none of the men was here to see the transformation. Suddenly she felt as if life was passing her by. Her

304

children were grown now and didn't need her. She was getting old and faded, like a waning moon. Lily's moon was waxing full. It was *her* turn now.

In the flurry of the changing room everyone was on a high. Lily slid herself out of the ballgown with a sigh: time for Cinderella to leave the ball and back to plain clothes and porridge. Time for Lee to change back to Doormat Lil.

For a few hours she had been pampered and preened but this wasn't real. Time to be getting back to decorating the cottage and settling down.

Wearing these dresses was dangerous. In outfits like these, it was easy to pretend she was stepping aboard a Dakota and flying off to Paris and Rome, travelling the world like a film star, not a shop assistant, scrubbing floors and counting boxes of sennapods. It made her feel restless and ready for a change.

There was more to life than the stall. Levi and Mother could manage without her. Enid would always help out, and Susan. She was surplus to requirements. Time for a change. Then she remembered there was a wedding to organise and Walter to enthuse. Wasn't that a challenge enough?

Someone was shouting for Maria but the funny thing was she had not appeared to see the display.

'She's wanted at the hospital,' said Enzo Santini, looking as if he had run across town.

Lily buttoned up her coat and grabbed her handbag. There was trouble and Maria needed help. No more daydreaming. This was for real.

18

Moses Heights

In her eagerness to get away from Sylvio, Maria skipped the show and, with Rosaria, jumped on the first bus to the hospital. Rosa liked to sit on the top deck watching out of the window. It was just another outing with Mamma for her, but today it was life or death for Maria. There was so much to make up for. This time she didn't mind the long walk up the driveway, or the chill air. To see her husband and begin again was her goal.

They'd arrived too early and stood in the foyer waiting for permission to go down to his open ward. She was surprised then to see Sister Jarvis scurrying towards her, her starched cap flapping behind her like sailcloth in the wind.

'Thank goodness you've come. Did you not get my message?' the nurse spoke softly.

'No? What's up?' Maria's heart was thumping now. She'd not gone home but rushed from salon to café, grabbed her child and jumped on to the bus.

'I'm afraid Mr Santini has had a relapse. Rosaria must stay outside, of course, but you can come straight down. I think your family will not be far behind,' she continued as they strode down the corridor at speed, shoes squeaking on the tiled floor, limbs pumping with shock and dread.

'He was fine on Sunday... What's gone wrong?' Maria whispered, stopping in the doorway of the side room where her husband lay prostrate, breathing into an oxygen mask, his face the colour of ash and his eyes sunk into their sockets.

'Marco, it's me ... what have you been up to now?' she whispered in their mother tongue. She kissed his limp hand and sat down beside him.

'One minute he was sitting up, his usual self, and then we found him collapsed. His heart isn't strong. Come outside.' Sister Jarvis pointed to the open balcony. 'His heart is struggling after all these years with bad lungs.' The nurse paused, looking into Maria's eyes. 'You may want to call his priest.'

'Oh, no!' she cried, her knees going weak. Surely it'd not come to that, not when she was coming back to him? This was too cruel. There'd been false alarms before but even she was shocked by the change in him in just a few days.

'I want Rosa to be with us,' she asked.

'We don't allow children, as you know. It'll only frighten her and you don't want her to make a fuss and disturb the other patients. Rules are rules for everyone's good, Mrs Santini.' The sister shook her head.

'Please, he must see his child. It will give him hope and fight. He's not been able to touch her for weeks. What harm can it do either of them now? Rosa is too young to understand what's happening.'

'I insist. No child enters a ward for fear of infection but she can watch from the balcony for a few minutes,' Sister Jarvis replied, not looking

Maria in the eye.

Maria made for the hall and took Rosa round the outside walkway whilst trying to explain what was happening.

'Papa is sleeping and he's very, very tired and must rest,' she said, clutching Rosa's mittened hand and willing herself to stay calm. 'We'll play peep-o with him out here. You can wave but not go inside. He'll hear you and know you are there,' she added. 'Father Michael Grady will come and sit with him.'

Rosa stood by the open window, staring at her daddy as if he was a specimen in a jar. 'What is that?' she asked, pointing to the mask and the tubes.

'It helps his heart to tick tock,' Maria replied, torn between wanting to reassure her child and hold her husband, dreading the moment when the Santinis would flood into the sickroom and take over. She would be an onlooker then, the stranger in the midst. Her heart railed at sharing precious moments with anyone else.

Doctors came and went, nurses fiddled with the tubes, but Marco was slipping away, unaware of any of them. It was like sitting in some strange play going on all around her, a slow-motion action unfolding before her.

They watched Father Michael, who now knew the secrets of her heart in confession, administer the last rites, and Marco's brothers lined up, caps in hands, standing silent and awkward. Nonna Valentina was on her knees, wailing as if he were already dead.

Then came the welcome news that Lily was

waiting in the foyer. Trust her friend to be there. Leaving the balcony, Maria ushered Rosa towards her.

'Say night, night to Papa, give him a kiss...'

Rosa stood back. 'No... I can't see him.'

Damn the rules, Maria thought, lifted Rosa up to the bed and let her kiss his forehead. Then she whisked her down the corridor, relieved to see a familiar comforting face even if it was coiffed and made up from the fashion show.

'Thank God you come! This is no place for Rosa now. Marco is dying,' she croaked, tears streaming down her face.

'I'll take her home with me ... you go back. I'm so sorry. We'll take care of her. Come on, Rosie, let's go play with Dina and Joy.'

Nonna dozed on her knees, praying for a miracle. Maria sat wide awake, stupefied by guilt and disbelief at first, but now rigid with shock. She'd come to rededicate herself to her marriage, renew her vows, cleansed by confession only that morning. Now everything was turned upside down and all she wanted was for Marco to beat the odds and live.

'Live, Marco,' she prayed, but he slipped from them as the lemony dawn rose above the hills. His struggles were over.

She must embrace her old life, blameless, give him the honour and respect in death that she'd neglected to show him in life. She was a widow and free to make her own decisions but bound tighter than ever before by her guilt.

It was only when they laid him out and Nonna wept, 'My poor son, he had no life,' that the pain surged into every sinew of her body and a weariness like a cloak of lead made her slump into the chair in despair. She watched a skein of ducks flying in arrow formation silhouetted against the sky and felt a flash of envy for her husband.

'No more pain, Nonna, no more beds and open windows and basket chairs now.'

Soon it would be time to leave but not before she had cleared out the clutter from his locker and bedside table, all the myriad little things that still smelled of him: the green sheets of their local sports paper, sacred pictures, a crucifix, a half-eaten bag of sweets and a little snapshot of the three of them taken on a trip to the seaside. She would leave everything tidy and neat, grief or no grief. It gave her hands something to do.

Scrumpled in the drawer, half hidden among the postcards, was a letter. Curious, she opened up the page and read it.

MR SANTINI,
YOUR WIFE, MARIA, IS A TART. ASK HER WHAT SHE GETS UP TO OF A NIGHT WITH LAVARONI'S NEW HAIRDRESSER. THE REPLY WILL NOT PLEASE YOU BUT IT IS RIGHT YOU KNOW WHAT KIND OF WHORE SHE BE. READ HOSEA CHAPTER ONE.
A WELL WISHER.

Maria scrambled to find the envelope also typed in capital letters. It was addressed, 'MR SANTINI, THE SANATORIUM, MOSES HEIGHTS, NR GRIMBLETON'.

She shoved the letter quickly into her handbag, out of sight but not out of mind. Never out of mind, every word etched into her heart. She felt it thumping through her ribs. Could Nonna Valentina see it throbbing with guilt?

You have killed your husband, came the words bursting through her eardrums. He had read that poisonous letter and the shock of it was too much for his frail body. You might as well have stabbed him in the heart with a knife yourself. What he must have suffered: shock, disbelief, fear and doubt, and all borne alone.

Someone hated them so much as to want to shame her and hurt her husband, but who? Who would do this to them? One of the family? Surely not. If a Santini had suspected anything, she'd have been banished from Marco's deathbed long ago.

With his dying, for one brief moment she'd wondered if she'd escaped the wrath of God but no, she was found out and would be punished. There was now nothing she could ever do to make it right but pray for his forgiveness from across the grave, pray for his soul to be at peace, have Masses said for his release from such a torment and for the salvation of her own soul.

Only three of them knew of this dreadful exposé and one of them was now dead. She must find out who had done this and kill them, pay them back for all they'd done to an innocent man. She wouldn't rest until she was avenged. Marco didn't deserve this cruel end, with only his wife's betrayal for company in his agony.

The Santinis need never know, and Rosa must

never know, but this terrible guilt must live in her heart for ever.

That this was the work of a woman, she'd no doubt. There was something peevish and cruel that smacked of jealousy and malice, but who and why would be her life's work to find out. When she found that devil, oh, how she'd suffer for this. An eye for an eye was too good for her but revenge was a dish best eaten cold.

She kneeled by Marco's body and prayed in silence.

Marco, I will avenge your suffering. I take it upon myself to live like a nun until you are avenged. I will sacrifice any future happiness. I will live only for Rosa's happiness. I will make you proud of me and honour your family name, but please forgive me for my weakness. I didn't mean to hurt you. Forgive me for being weak when you were so strong. Forgive me…

It was almost dark when they parked in Division Street. Lily held the sleeping Rosa over her shoulder.

'Where've you been, Lil? I've been that worried. Not another waif and stray to take in for the night?' Esme was standing in the hallway staring down at the child. 'Walt's in the other room and he's not a happy man. He's been all over Grimbleton looking for you.'

'There's been an emergency.' Lily sat down, suddenly exhausted. She told them the sorry news and then she made some cocoa for Rosa.

Su appeared and whisked the child upstairs. Ana was on shift and the house was quiet for a change. Walter was listening to the wireless and ambled in when his programme had finished.

'I thought we were going to make a start on Well Cottage. I gather you've been all dolled up down the town hall. Mam said you could feed a man for a year on the price of one of the rig-outs.'

'I'm very tired,' Lily replied. 'It's been a rum do at Maria's. They say Marco Santini's not going to last the night so I brought Rosa back here. There was no time to get your shopping in.'

Tears were rolling down her cheeks, tears of sadness, exhaustion. If ever she needed a pair of strong arms around her it was tonight. 'Hold me, Walter, hold me tight.'

'What's brought this on, old girl?' He patted her on the arm.

'Just hold me. I need a big hug. You won't leave me, will you?'

'You daft happorth! What would I be doing that for?' he grinned. 'I'll get you a biscuit. You've had a shock. What on earth have you done to yerself ... all that make-up, and who's been chopping your hair?'

'It's modern. Isn't it?'

'It'll soon grow out. You don't look the same.'

'I don't feel the same, Walt,' she whispered as he made for the kitchen.

The phone rang at seven on the Sunday morning. Marco had slipped away before dawn and Angelo was coming in his taxi to collect Rosa.

Later Maria phoned to thank them for taking her child for the night. 'Oh, Lily, it is terrible. I have to see you. I was going to start all over again, clean slate, new start. Now it's too late.

313

How can I forgive myself? It should be me who is dead. I killed him!'

There was no making sense of her. Grief was controlling her senses. Maria was taking Marco's sudden collapse hard. The Santinis would wrap themselves around her friend, make a big fuss of Rosa, buying her toys and sweets and treats as if to make up for her loss. It was not going to be easy to see her alone. Then there was the matter of Sylvio Bertorelli...

Three days later Kirkgate came to a standstill as the cortège left the café, pulled by black horses with plumes. It was a beautiful morning and all the shops and businesses were shut in respect for Marco's passing. Mourners followed in a dignified procession to the Catholic chapel. Everyone was dressed in black, and the women wore lace mantillas over their heads.

The Italian community turned out in force: the Gambas, Morellis, even their ice-cream rivals, the Falconis, paid their respects and Gianni Lavaroni turned up with his wife in a fur coat. Snow was still covering the moor tops in the distance.

Maria looked so thin and haggard, and little Rosa, in a coat a size too big for her, held on to her hand.

All the Olive Oils turned up to give their support and sat at the back out of sight: Diana, Queenie, Su and Ana, watching the ceremony with tears in their eyes. It was Lily's first visit to the ornate chapel, its walls lined with statues, alcoves with candles burning, the great crucifix hanging from the ceiling. How different from Zion and Freddie's memorial service.

How different the Santinis and Winstanleys dealt with death, she mused. Here was passion and suffering, sacrifice painted on every wall, reminding everyone of their mortality. These age-old rituals were comforting in their familiarity but strange to her ears. Each to his own, she thought, praying that Maria would find consolation in the ceremony.

Lily called into Santini's most days to see how she was coping but she was never alone in the kitchen or upstairs.

'You're worn out. Take a break. Marco wouldn't want you to be so sad,' Lily said the day after Marco's funeral, offering her a brew of herbal concoctions to strengthen her blood.

Susan brought posies of flowers to cheer her table.

Ana looked her over with concern. 'It is time you see a doctor. You can't go on like this. You do your best. It was always going to end this way, surely?' she added.

Now that Ana was training as a nurse she had strong opinions about everybody's health. Out of her bag came her special icon of the Blessed Virgin to comfort Maria, and Lily noticed the soft walnut eyes of the Virgin filled with kindness. 'Dina and me, we light a candle for his soul at our church.'

When Enzo and Nonna had gone, Maria broke down with relief. 'It is me that should be dead. I killed him ... I killed him!' she sobbed, her head banging on the cushions of the sofa.

'Stop this! It is grief talking.' Lily hugged her. 'You kept him alive much longer than his condition would predict. You were a good wife to him. You visited him. On Ana's wards no one visits the old and sick. You did all what was expected.'

'I betray him. I kill him.' Maria continued crying. 'I was too busy loving Sylvio ... only *you* know we were more than friends. I betray Marco's trust and the shock of it killed him. I am a bad woman. How can you say good things to me now?'

They sat on either side of her and held her. 'We all knew about Sylvio. Anyone could see how it was for you... He brought a shining light into your eyes. You were discreet. These things happen,' whispered Susan, taking hold of her hand. 'And I should know.'

'I am not a fit mother but I had sworn never to see him again. It was over and that is my punishment, and I have to live knowing Marco knew everything... I killed him. I broke his heart.'

'You told him the truth?' said Ana, her eyes wide, looking up at Lily with surprise.

'No... I couldn't bear to lose his trust but I find a letter, nasty letter by his bed when I was clearing his things.' She pulled a crumpled note in an envelope from her handbag and shoved it in Lily's hand. 'Read it!'

Lily shared it with the others, each shaking her head in disbelief.

'He gets that letter. The shock is too much for his heart.' Maria bent her head. 'Lily, it broke his will to live. Someone hate us so much they do

316

this to a sick man.'

'Who was it?' Lily asked.

'It can't be family. What if they send them a letter too? There is no name, that is the coward's way, but it is typed proper.' She shoved the envelope into her hand.

'How can anyone do this, Susan? I have to know?'

The two of them looked at the letter long and hard. It was stamped in Grimbleton on white notepaper, much crumpled with rereading, and fingermarked. They looked at each other but said nothing more.

'Forget this filth and get on with your life. That will be your victory over this poisonous snake,' Lily said. 'But we'll all help you find the snake, won't we?'

'No! You must tell no one,' Maria pleaded. 'Nobody knows about this, not even the priest. It is my burden, my punishment. I will seek revenge and you will help me?'

'We'll help you. What are friends for but to help each other through tears, bread and salt, sorrows and joy shared alike? I know what it is to be without hope,' said Ana. 'You came to our rescue and now we come to yours ... if only you knew...'

Lily waited for the truth about the Winstanleys to come tumbling out but Ana stopped just in time.

'You've had some beautiful cards. Let's open these.' Su pointed to a handful of unopened envelopes, shoving them into her hand to distract Maria.

'This is from Queenie... Oh, no!' Maria

screamed pulling out a note.

Miss you at the salon. Sylvio walked out after the fashion show. He has gone AWOL. Look after yourself.
See you soon. Love, Queenie

As Maria read the note she fell on the carpet in a faint, lying flat out.

Ana kneeled over her. 'Sip this,' she whispered, feeling for her pulse. 'You're going to the doctor if I have to drag you there myself, she said.

'Yes, Sister,' Maria croaked 'It's too late for doctors now. I am in big trouble. I have to see Sylvio. There's something he should know.'

What a sorry tale, Lily sighed. Just like Shakespeare, all ending in tears and tragedy. Timing was everything in life. Get it right and everything falls into place, but miss your cue and it's curtains.

It still amazed her that Su and Ana turned up on the same flight, the chance in a million that was. What if only one of them had come? What would have happened then?

Then she recalled the big fight at Waverley House. Was it Ivy who said Maria's romance would end in tears? Was it possible that...? Surely not? Had her own sister-in-law a hand in making sure that it did?

19

Changing the Guard

The racket coming from the kitchen would wake the dead, Esme thought as she hung over the banister rail in the hall, wondering what on earth was going on. This house was getting more like Bedlam and Paddy's Market, with toys and clutter everywhere. Neville, Joy and Dina were squabbling over the Noah's ark toys at the foot of the stairwell.

'Mine!' shouted Joy.

'It's mine!' Neville yelled. 'This is my house!' whacking her on the head with a lead giraffe. Joy kicked him and he started to scream. It was time to step in before there was blood on the Axminster. Neville was yelling for his mum. All hell was breaking loose.

'Get this clutter off these stairs before someone breaks their neck,' Esme ordered.

Everyone could hear Ivy shrieking and Ana shouting back. They were having yet another barney.

'There they go again, Lil. It's like Mount Etna erupting, giving me a splitting headache. This can't go on,' Esme said, as they scurried in the direction of the fracas. A house full of temperamental women was getting on her nerves.

'It was you! You sent letter. *You* killed Marco

Santini!' Ana was waving a kitchen knife in the air. 'You are very wicked woman,' she shouted, jabbing the knife in the direction of Ivy, who was trying to make Levi's sandwiches.

'I don't know what this mad woman's talking about,' Ivy snapped, looking up as an audience gathered in the kitchen. 'I don't know what she is on about, do you, Mother? Foreigners, they're all the same, making accusations. It was her as nearly got our Levi beaten to pulp,' she retorted, stabbing a fork in Susan's direction.

'He get what is coming up,' Ana shouted in her defence. It was funny how her much improved English fell to bits when she was angry.

'Put that knife down, lass,' Esme whispered to Ana. 'There could be an accidents.'

She was weary of all the bad feeling in the house lately. Susan and Ana wouldn't speak to Levi and Ivy. Neville and the babies kept biting each other. She was fed up with the lot of them.

'I just don't know what's got into you all. What sort of example is this to the kiddies? I've just about had enough of you lot going hammer and tongs, and now the kiddies are copying too. I thought we'd got over all that silly business. Levi explained his mistake about the herbs. It was all a misunderstanding. Susan and Lil had no right to interfere,' she added, trying to be fair.

She knew her son was lying, not believing one of his excuses, but he'd made a big mistake and she must give him a second chance. He was her son, after all, and they were all having to live with Freddie's even bigger mistakes.

Levi was shaken by his beating, nervous she

320

might chuck him out of the house or cut off his wages. He would shape up now she was keeping the books herself. It was partly her fault for being lax and letting her involvement slide. Her lazy son always did need a kick up the backside.

You don't choose your offspring, she mused. You get what you're given and make the best of them if you've any sense. He was family and that was what mattered. It was up to them to sort him out but if he slipped up again he was out on his ear, son or no. There was only so much she could take from him.

Susan was leaving the market stall to try for another teaching post and good old Enid was back full time, keeping an eye on Levi.

'I can't have you making accusations like that, Ana. Why should Ivy have anything to do with anything? It's sad about Mr Santini but he's been ill for years. Come on, spit it out, what's brought this on?'

'Maria's husband get nasty letter and it broke his heart with shock. Maria is in terrible state. She is very sick. We think Ivy sent that letter,' Ana accused. 'She was angry about the hash. She said she would pay back Maria. Lily and Daw Winstanley, they hear your bad words. I think you write out of evil heart,' she spat out her accusation at Ivy, and turned back to her chopping, banging on the table. There was no stopping that girl when she got an idea in her head. Poor Freddie never stood a chance once she got her claws in him.

'How dare that woman talk to me like that? Why should I write to a Wop?' Ivy replied, her

321

lips tied in a string purse of righteous anger.

'Because you are bad woman who want to spoil Maria's happiness,' Ana replied.

'We don't approve of adultery in this house. Any woman who goes with another man when her husband is sick deserves everything she gets. It's all round the town that she's no better than she should be, that so-called friend of yours!' Ivy furiously packed the pile of sandwiches in a lunch box, slamming the lid.

'Is this true, Ana?' said Esme, sitting down at the table to face the both of them. Better to be informed of the true facts before she made a judgement.

'What Maria does in her private life is none of our business. Maria's a kind woman and good to all of us. We all make mistakes.' Ana refused to look her in the face but her cheeks were flushed.

'So what proof have you got to blame our Ivy for some poison-pen letter? It's a serious charge, my lady,' Esme countered with a calmness that belied her racing heart.

'I no need proof. I know in here,' Ana shouted, stabbing at her heart with the knife again, thankfully with the handle rather than the blade but still giving them all palpitations. 'That woman hate us. Her never like Maria and wanted to get back at my friend.'

Esme paused, folding her arms. 'I think you should apologise to Ivy right now and it'll go no further. You just can't be making stories out of thin air. Why should Ivy risk her good reputation to write such an evil thing?'

Ivy was sitting with Neville, looking like inno-

322

cence personified, her head bowed like a suffering saint, but Esme was cautious. No one spoke. It was time to talk turkey and get the steam out of this nonsense.

'I can't have all this argy-bargy in my house. It's getting me down, the atmosphere amongst you. It's time you all sorted yourselves out and made your peace. If you can't live together then you'll have to find somewhere else to go. Heaven knows, I've done my duty by you all for long enough. I want no more sniping and backbiting. Is it too much to ask for a bit of peace and quiet at my age?'

She rose and left them to stew in their own juices. For months now she'd done her duty, kept a roof over everyone's head and covered up the family shame, months of lies and half-truths. They all needed a good shaking. Why should she put up with this rumpus any more? Three generations in one house was never going to be easy, even in a big house like this, but all the bickering was getting beyond a joke.

Esme retreated into the front room by the marble mantelpiece, too tired to knit or read or do the mending, sunk back in a chair with shut eyes. She was at a difficult age for women, 'on the change'. All these hot sweats and flushes were playing havoc with her sleep and her concentration, but this accusation buzzed in her head like a demented bee.

The trouble was there was no one here to share her worries with, no one who could see the funny side of things, no one to tease and make them all laugh, no one like Freddie or Redvers. It was hard putting on a brave face in public, and she had cried herself to sleep many a night thinking about them.

What troubled her most was the thought that Ivy *could* be capable of writing such a letter. There was something in her tight-lipped silence and pious gaze that made her shiver. Ivy was all for number one, and precious little Neville was turning into the same. He was being groomed to expect better things without the cash to back them up and it had put temptation into Levi's path.

Ana was on the way to becoming a right starched apron. She'd an answer for everything these days. It was 'Dr Jacob says this,' and 'Sister Diane says that'. Esme's lodgers were getting too big for their boots. Had they forgotten just how much they owed to this family?

Susan was quiet enough, but sharp, and she fussed and overfed little Joy until she was far too bonny for her own good. Their whole lives revolved around the blessed dancing class and supper club.

The novelty of having such exotic grand-children was wearing off fast. Much as she'd grown to care for them, she was glad to see the back of them at the end of the day, but as they grew larger and noisier what would happen then?

Suddenly she wanted to just get shut of the lot of them. Waverley might as well be a boarding house – in and out on shifts, creaking stair rods and pulled lavatory chains, waking the household, trampled carpets and strangers in her kitchen.

I've done my duty, she thought, looking at the

men in her life, at Redvers and little Travis on the piano, and Freddie's military portrait with his cap at such a rakish angle, which only now could she bear to display. The family were well established now. She'd seen them all through difficult months, kept the show on the road. Now it was her turn to retire from the fray.

At least she was lucky enough to have funds to give her some choice. Redvers said it was good for a woman to have a bit of money stashed away, and she was well provided for. It was about time there were a few changes in this house, and soon, before she grew too old to enjoy herself.

With her eyes closed it was pleasant to imagine another way of life. Then she recalled there was Lil's wedding to pay for, and her heart sank. That must be the first priority.

'Are you all right, Mother?' Lily asked, creeping into the room, searching for the *Gazette*. 'I've cleared them all off the stairs. Can I show you something in the paper?'

'Not now, love. I'm done in. I don't know what Redvers would make of this lot,' Esme sighed, fingering his photo. 'I've tried to keep the show on the road, Lil. It's about time there were a few changes in this house, and soon, before I get too old to make them.'

'I'll soon be out of your hair. That'll be one less to worry about,' she offered. Her wedding day was only eight weeks away now.

'I've been thinking about that. You looked that swish in the ballgown. Do you want something from Levine's? You can have all my coupons.'

'It's all in hand, Mother. Can you imagine one of those puffballs going down the aisle in Zion? I'd get stuck on the umbrella stands. No, thank you.'

What had changed Mother's mind? It was not like her to fling out compliments.

'Are you sure you're doing the right thing? I hear Mrs Platt is not well pleased with Walter giving up his housekeeping money to do up that place.'

'It'll be fine,' Lily murmured, picking up the *Gazette* and leaving the room.

It was Diana who had pointed out the advertisement in the Jobs section of the *Gazette*.

LONGSIGHT TRAVEL: require the services of a reliable shorthand typist with telephone skills to help administer busy office, friendly manner essential.

'It's a new business organising bus tours around Britain and they're hoping to branch out into the Continent if they can get petrol concessions. It's got your name written all over it.' Diana had shoved the page in front of her.

Lily had gone into the Crumblehumes' office to collect the raffle prize and liked the set-up. She had a new hairstyle, soon to have a new name, so why not a new job?

But I couldn't leave the stall, could I, she wondered. Why not? Levi ignored her, Enid could do the job standing on her head and needed the extra pay, and now that Su was going, Lily wasn't

326

needed for guard duty.

If truth was told, her heart had not been in the stall for a long while. All those years seeing the business through the war and no thanks for it. Why shouldn't she do something new, something for herself?

Now the war was over people wanted regular holidays. For two weeks every August Grimbleton ground to a halt when factories, mills and schools shut down for the wakes weeks to go to the seaside *en masse*. Austerity and rations, nothing would stop the annual holiday.

Only last week she had read something in the *Manchester Guardian* that suggested that soldiers who travelled across the world would someday want to take their families to see just where they had fought. People might want to go further afield than Blackpool or Morecambe. Honeymooners might choose hotter climes than Scarborough and Rhyl. The prospect of a new challenge at work was irresistible.

A letter replying to the advert was written without a second's hesitation.

The interview, when it came, was a surprise. Avril Crumblehume was heavily pregnant, a neat checked smock over her skirt.

'I must tell you we've had many replies but we're looking for someone who can see a wider picture than just issuing tickets, someone who would be prepared to travel with our customers and see to their comfort, to report back on any hiccups while I'm out of action. Do you have another language?'

Lily muttered something about French Matriculation. 'I'm willing to learn more.'

'So why did you apply for the position?'

Lily was ready for this one. 'The idea of travel excites me. It always has. I'm already planning a trip abroad for my honeymoon. I read in the paper...' she brought out the newspaper cutting, 'there has to be a future in foreign holidays.'

'That's the spirit: enthusiasm, willingness to learn and an eagerness to please! Those are just the qualities we're looking for. As you can see I'm going to be away for quite a time but I'm not quite ready for the kitchen sink yet. We all did our bit in the war so why should we gracefully retire out of sight so the men can have all the fun? I think not. Diana Unsworth recommends you highly. I hear your house is full of women on the move.'

They spent half an hour going through secretarial duties and Lily completed the shorthand test with ease, but had she done enough to convince them of her commitment and efficiency? She had never wanted anything so much for a long time.

'You've done what?' shouted Walter from the landing of Well Cottage when she told him. 'And I wasn't even consulted on the matter, not once?'

They were trying to tackle the peeling wallpaper in the upstairs bedroom. It was a losing battle. Well Cottage was aptly named. Lily discovered a well hidden under the scullery floor. This old house was built over everlasting springs and damp was a major problem.

'Think about it, love. It's a new company and they're eager to try new things. They are wanting staff to try out new venues,' she explained.

'You mean we'd be their guinea pigs,' he retorted, unconvinced.

'It means, my precious, that we can go to Paris and perhaps get paid for part of our honeymoon. I hope you've sorted out that passport,' she shouted from up a ladder while trying to paste the paper back on the ceiling.

Once they got some coal fires going to warm the stone, it might be a little less damp, but that fusty smell would take a bit of shifting. It might help if Walter could do his share, but his back couldn't take any stretching and he had no head for heights. He was good at brewing up the tea and dishing out advice, but not much else.

Lily was not fazed by his infirmity. There was a brilliant osteopath who worked with Grass-hoppers players. Pete Walsh swore by his efficacy. His injury had cost the team dear but now he was fully recovered. Only last week he'd come to collect his sister, Kathleen, from Brownies again. It was getting quite a habit, him hovering around while she cleared up and Kath went out into the playground to do cartwheels and handstands. He helped Lily put the chairs away and the stuff back in the cupboards. They often stood and chatted over the task. It was then she told him about Walter's sufferings in the back department and he was so sympathetic. She also told him about her new job and the chance to travel.

'Don't worry, Terry'll make a new man of him, I promise,' Pete laughed, and she sighed, hoping it was true, for Walter Platt of late was pretty useless in all departments and she was fast losing patience with him.

The next week Pete asked her about her job as if he was really interested. Nobody else in the family had bothered much about the big change in her life. Why couldn't they be enthusiastic for her? This new post in town was something she'd done off her own bat. For too long she'd been dependent on the family business. This was a new start and she decided there would be no more Lil or Lily, but she'd use her mannequin name, Lee, to mark this new beginning. It sounded much more snazzy and professional. Like Lee Miller, the famous war photographer, who took pictures of herself in Hitler's bath!

'What do you mean, you've decided to sell up?' said Levi, choking at the news on his extra breakfast rasher of bacon the next morning. 'What about the business? Have you gone mad, Mother?'

Esme was smiling as she shoved more fried bread on his empty plate. 'I had the best night's sleep for years. I can't think why I didn't think of it sooner. They're building some bungalows up at Sutter's Fold, with grand views and fresh air, a good breeze for the washing to dry and no sooty marks to worry about,' she smiled, eyeing them all. 'Or maybe I'll flit to St Anne's, by the sea. It's about time you lot learned to stand on your own feet but I'll want a bit of my share out of Health and Herbs. You'll have to make yourself a living from it. The business'll still be there for Neville,

330

of course, if you don't drink all the profits out of it, but I've decided to retire to the country and spend my money while I'm still game enough to enjoy it. It was Lil who gave me the notion.'

All the eyes at the breakfast table turned to Lily. What had she done now?

'It was Lil getting that new job that gave me the inclination. If stay-at-home old Lily can shift herself as well as take on that lanky loon, a cottage with water running down the walls and a brand-new job, then I'm not too past it to make some changes here, myself.'

As Esme spoke it was as if the years were rolling off her, her eyes sparkling with mischief.

The look on Levi's face was a picture. 'I think you've had a bad turn. You need your head examining,' he sulked. 'Bungalows cost money.'

'I may sell this house as an investment property and I've still got my Crompton's shares. I won't starve but I'm not scrimping just to leave you a tidy packet to flush down the loo of the Conservative Club. I fancy a change,' she said, just as Ivy popped her head round the door.

'Everything all right?' she smiled.

'No it's not, said Levi, with his mouth full. It was not a pretty sight. 'Mother's decided to sell up and leave us all in the lurch.'

'You can't sell Waverley House? Where will we go?' Ivy replied, looking at her husband in panic.

'Why ever not? You always wanted a place for the three of you across town. You've never liked Division Street.' Lily couldn't resist adding fuel to the flames.

'We can't invest in the business *and* buy a

proper house,' snapped Levi.

'And there's Neville's education to see to. We were hoping you would see your way to helping us send him to the preparatory school one day. He'll need extra coaching to get a place at Grimbleton Grammar School,' Ivy whined in the little-girl voice she used to get round Levi.

'That's the joy of a family, lass: all those decisions to make and sacrifices to ponder over. If you want my opinion I should get yourself a decent roof over your head first and forget about giving Neville airs and graces. If he's not the sharpest knife in the Winstanley drawer, better to let him find his own level. He'll be the happier for it.'

No one spoke and Lily kept her head down, sinking into her seat and trying not to smirk.

'This is all your doing,' Ivy said, pinching Lily's shoulder as she went past. 'How can you deprive our son and not pay his school fees?' she asked Esme.

'I'm not answering that one. I think it's about time you cut your cloth to suit, young lady, as Redvers used to say. I've spoiled you all and it's time for a fresh start. I've made up my mind.' Once that steel glint was in her eye there would be no turning her.

'You're being very cruel, Mother,' said Levi. 'Did you know about this?' He turned to his sister but she shook her head.

'I half wondered if Lily might not like to come and join me, and leave that lazy fiancé of hers to get off his backside and do an honest day's work for a change. She's turned out the best of the bunch. I have to say my sons have been a bit of a disappointment, but I suppose I've only myself to blame.'

'You've taken leave of your senses,' said Ivy. 'But I'd like to be a fly on the wall when you send those two foreign spongers packing with their noisy tribe of showoffs and that Olive Oil Club of theirs. They'll have to fend for themselves at last.'

'Don't worry, I have plans for them too.'

'I hope you don't favour them instead of your own flesh and blood,' Ivy hissed.

'Joy and Dina are family too, like it or not, Ivy. What I'll do for them is only fair. They are the future. I've had my day and you'd better get on with making the best of yours before it's too late,' she added.

'Is this all because of that stupid letter?' Ivy glowered around the kitchen. 'Those two have turned this family upside down. We were happy enough before they barged in and ruined everything. I still think they are both having us on. You're too generous, letting them stink out the house with garlic and oil. They've lowered the tone of the place.'

'All the more reason why you three will be happier out of here in your own home. You never liked my friends much, did you?' Lily replied. She couldn't believe she'd ever been scared of Ivy's tongue-lashings.

'Well, at least we won't be consorting with adulterers' children. I hear that slick hairdresser's done a runner and left that tart in the lurch. I knew she'd have to pay for her sins,' Ivy smiled.

'Mr Santini was a war hero and innocent. He

333

didn't deserve to hear that way. I worry about the twisted soul who wrote to him with such spite. I wouldn't like it on my conscience that an innocent man had a heart attack on receiving such bad news from a stranger, with not even a chance to hear his wife's side of the story. You never know what goes on behind closed doors... Look at all *our* secrets?' Esme whispered.

The silence was deafening so Lily added her own pennyworth. 'Imagine you were lying in bed and someone sent a letter telling you that Levi was playing away. You would want to have it all out with him, wouldn't you?'

'Why are you saying all this to me?' Ivy was going red in the face. 'It's nothing to do with me.'

'Of course not,' Esme chipped in. 'I wouldn't like to think my son was married to the vicious soul who did that to a dying man. I gather the letter was typed and the police can easily check a typewriter to see if it was the source of the typescript. They will soon find the culprit.'

'Has she taken it to the police then?' There was a tremor in Ivy's voice.

'Oh, I expect so. It's a criminal offence, after all, but it doesn't concern us, does it? I think justice will be done in its own good time,' Lily smiled, turning to her mother. 'So you've made an appointment to see the solicitors to sort out your affairs and rejig your will, no doubt, while you're at it?'

The effect of such mischief was electrifying. Suddenly both Levi and Ivy were on guard.

'Mother, you shouldn't do anything rash.' Levi's voice was all squeaky.

'Thanks for your concern, son, but my mind is made up. I'm leaving Division Street for pastures new. This old house'll have to fend for itself from now on. I feel like a breath of fresh air and a bit of a change. Who's for a trip to the seaside?'

20

A Bit of Blackpool Air

Esme's unexpected treat took everyone by surprise but the weather had faired up and she was determined to have a change of sky. First up for attention was the Rover, sitting on bricks in the garage, for an overhaul, some acid to top up its battery and enough petrol to get them there and back. It would be needed for the wedding, so out of mothballs it must come.

It was going to be done in style or not at all, she smiled, recalling the days she and Redvers took trips to the Trough of Bowland before the war, snug with blankets, Thermos and picnic baskets, bats and balls and a change of tyre in case of a puncture.

She didn't feel up to driving herself but Lily would oblige. She was competent enough these days, but fixing the day out around all her daughter's work, meetings and decoration took a bit of doing. She wanted to give the kiddies a treat to remember. Freddie would want his kiddies to have a day out in the sun.

Levi was going to hold the fort at the market under pain of dismissal if there was even a penny out in the till. Esme had to start trusting him again.

Everyone was tiptoeing around her since she'd announced her decision to upsticks and move. It had even shocked her. Nothing could change these last bleak months, but a walk down the Promenade might just lift everyone's spirits. Surely Blackpool had got itself together after all the wartime restrictions?

How she'd stuff them all in the car would take some planning, especially as Lily'd asked if Maria and little Rosa could be included. How could she say no to a poor girl who'd just lost her husband?

She still felt uneasy about that letter... If it was Ivy's doing then they ought to make up for it somehow. Ivy was not invited but Neville would come out with his grandma. The mums would have to squeeze in the back with their babies on their knees.

Esme smiled. It would be like old times, with a car full of excited children watching out of the window. Who'd be the first to see Blackpool Tower?

Punctures permitting, they'd make the Prom by noon, and a fish-and-chip treat in Lyons Corner café, a snooze on a deck chair and some ice cream on the pier.

It was funny how she felt all perked up about moving on. Change was in the air. It was all very strange.

'I want you all ready by nine sharp,' she ordered. 'Family in best bib and tucker, we're on parade.

Don't forget the potty, nappies, a damp cloth for sticky fingers, and we'll tie the pushchair on the luggage rack.'

Maria sat in the back, squashed between Ana and Su, trying not to be sick. Rosa was bouncing on her knee in excitement, dressed in her best church cotton dress with frills, and her usual tidy smocked overall, and all Maria could think of was keeping her meagre breakfast down.

Perhaps it was a mistake to come but the chance to get away was too tempting. She stared out at Preston docks, the long brick walls, the funnels of grey ships reminding her of the harbours of home all those years ago.

Seagulls screeched overhead and through the window flap she smelled the salty air. So many memories came flooding back to her. Her life was in such a mess now. She could hardly breathe.

It was kind of Mamma Winstanley to ask them out. She was a widow too, and must understand why she had to dress head to toe in black, as was the custom, but it drained all the energy out of her. She felt such a wicked woman. If only they knew her shame. What was she going to do? Soon she must go away, leave Santini's, take any job, but where?

Su stood on the edge of the sands looking out at the gunmetal sea shimmering in the afternoon sun. The golden sands seemed to stretch for miles but her mind was worried with news of Daw Esme's move. Soon Lily would be leaving. Ana had her hospital work. How would she and

Joy survive on their own? Perhaps she might find a job in service in a place that would take a widow and child.

The sun went behind the clouds and she was glad of her neat jacket. Perhaps she could take in sewing or try again for a teaching post.

The children were playing on the damp sand, eyeing each other up. Neville was trying to boss them about with his spade. Rosa bashed his sandcastle and there were tears. They were little more than babies. What would the future hold for them?

Esme was snoring in a deck chair, shoes off and stockings rolled down. They owed so much to this kind lady. She'd taken them in like a good Christian woman; now they would have to go.

Ana watched the line of grey donkeys plodding up the shore with children jiggling on their saddles. How different the sea was here, rough and speckled like fish scales, not the turquoise and silver of the Mediterranean. The donkeys were not pack mules or beasts of burden climbing up the mountain tracks, faithful warriors bringing supplies to the *andartes* hidden in the hills, but toys for children to play with. She didn't understand.

The sands were dotted with families playing bat and ball, having fun. Her heart was heavy with longing. How were things back home? Would she ever return? A wave of homesickness rushed over her. What was going to happen to them now?

Lily watched her friends all looking out to sea,

silent and sad, close to tears, each of them lost in her own little world. Mother was having forty winks, oblivious to the storm cloud above their heads.

Blackpool was doing its best to be cheerful but it looked so battered and tired, and there were still signs of war on the beach. She ought to be decorating at Well Cottage, not gallivanting, as Walt would say, but someone had to drive the car. It was quite an extravagance on Mother's part. The moths had flown out of her purse and she'd treated the girls to everything. Was this guilt money for leaving them in the lurch?

Lily had heard said that 'the change' did funny things to ladies of a certain age. What was going to happen to Freddie's children once Division Street was sold? It was all very worrying.

Here they all were, sitting in their own little bubbles of misery, and the sun was shining again, the sky was brightening up. There must be something she could do to cheer them up.

'I'm just going down the Golden Mile to see if anything is open,' she shouted. 'Back in a mo!'

They found ice-cream cones as they strolled down the Central Pier to stand out into the rushing tide, and took a ride in an open-topped landau down the other side of the Prom, past the grand hotels. Then they made for the Golden Mile and the candy-floss stand.

'I'll buy you all some,' Lily offered, laughing as Ana tried to bite into the pink fluff. 'It's nothing.' She looked so disappointed. 'Like cotton wool. You like, Ria?'

Maria shrugged. 'It is big trick, just spun sugar

339

in a machine.'

Esme pointed out the little rock stall. 'We can't go home without a bit of Blackpool Rock, but you'll need your coupons.'

Through the window they saw a man working the toffee into long tubes like broom handles, then working it smaller and smaller, fitting in the colours into letter shapes.

'It'll crack my dentures,' Esme called.

'Come on, over here,' yelled Lily, pointing to a striped booth with a thick velvet curtain. 'Here's a fortuneteller... Come on, my treat.'

Everyone hung back, uncertain. The notice said, 'Gypsy Bolero, Psychic to the Stars. Satisfaction Guaranteed'.

One by one they all trooped in, but Esme held back. 'I don't hold with telling fortunes, Lil.' But even she went in and came out smiling.

'I have to hand it to her, she knew her stuff. She told me after many sorrows I'd be moving on to a higher plane with lovely views and my children's children would travel to the ends of the earth, that I was blessed with many generations to come to make our family proud. What do you think about that?'

'She told me that after my sorrow I will find great happiness and new work, and my little girl will be a big star one day,' Maria smiled.

Ana nodded. 'She tell me I have very clever girl and one day I will see my island again. I am happy.'

'She said I have a very good businesswoman hat on my shoulders, I will sell houses and make lots of money,' Su added. 'But, Lily, you must go in

340

too. Go on, it was your big idea.'

Lily was pushed through the curtain and sat down.

'Did I do all right for you?' smiled the gypsy, smoking her clay pipe. 'In the right order?'

'You did just fine. You've put a smile on their faces.' Lily got up to leave.

'Not so fast, dear ... have one on the house?'

'No!'

'Come on ... only fair you do it too ... hold out your hand,' she ordered, and Lily sat down again reluctantly, opening her palm.

'This is a strong hand with much heart. I see many changes here. I see foreign shores and a long and happy marriage ... not yet, in a year or two. It is a good hand...'

'Well, it can't be mine then. I'm getting wed next month!' snapped Lily, shooting out of the door.

'Well?' Everyone was waiting.

'Come on, time for the paddling pool and a trip round Stanley Park. Might as well make the most of a beautiful day.'

Esme was left in charge of the little ones, wading into the paddling pool to play with them and pick them up when Neville pushed them over. She could see other grannies looking enviously at her brood, so different but appealing with their curls and baby chatter. What will life be like for them in the future? She prayed that there'd be no more wars or depression to spoil their lives.

'I am thrice blessed,' she smiled, knowing she really meant it.

341

They sang all the way home, from nursery rhymes to Maria giving a sporting rendition of the aria from *Madame Butterfly*, 'One Fine Day'.

That girl had a lovely voice and a good heart. Esme hadn't enjoyed herself so much for years. She'd let her hair down and no mistake.

Only Lil was silent. Something was up there and no mistake. How she'd changed in the last few months, grown stronger and more independent, but her eyes were heavy and sad. A mother could tell when her kid was unhappy.

They dropped Maria and the sleeping child back at their digs. Neville had hardly been a spot of bother. One sharp word from his grandmother and he did as he was told. That was the joy of being a grandma: she could hand them back at the end of the day.

Sleeping children always looked adorable but in Esme's eyes those sleepy heads were the finest in all Grimbleton; the future Winstanleys in the making. They must want for nothing.

After a subdued supper Su, Ana and Lily trooped into the big room. The girls were hesitant and fearful, knocking on the door wide-eyed and ready to hear the worst.

'Is it true, Daw Esme? You are moving and we must leave?' asked Su.

'One day soon I'll be too old for these stairs. This is a home for families, not pensioners.' But Esme was smiling.

What's the old rogue up to now? Lily wondered. She's enjoying this, watching everyone jockeying for position. Esme Winstanley was as fit as a butcher's dog. Years yet of chapel flower rotas, welfare clinics, Ladies Guild meetings and missionary fund-raising bazaars.

'We can't buy your house ... we shall be sad to go but your health must come first,' said Ana.

'Look, I've not right decided yet whether to sell outright or rent it. If I do, then you're welcome to stay on and look after the property until such times... Who knows what will happen in the future? You are young still. You have to make your own lives now, but I've had enough of being a referee. Once Levi finds a place of his own to live, there'd be room to take in lodgers or bed and breakfast for commercial travellers. This old villa would soon pay its way.'

'Would you trust us to run a business for you?' asked Su.

'I don't see why not. You girls are honest and hardworking. You keep your own room spick and span. It'd be up to you to make a go of it,' Esme replied.

'You are a good woman, Daw Esme. How can we repay you?' Su asked.

'Just you let your daughters grow up to make us all proud that they carry the name but just let's keep this to yourselves for a while. Don't let on to Ivy or you'll never get shut of them. Time enough to tell them when they've flitted house.' She winked at Lily, seeing the look of relief on her face. 'By the way, did Maria Santini really go to the police with her letter?'

'No,' Lily whispered. 'She told me this afternoon she's too ashamed. I think she'll be looking for rooms to rent soon. If she asked, could she come here?'

'If she can pay the rent and serve up breakfasts perhaps she can have my room when I'm gone. That'll be one in the eye for our Ivy, having the Olive Oil Club under one roof. She'll be out that door faster than a dog with fleas.

'I have to admit I always did like that Italian's spirit. Not afraid of hard work, is Maria, even if she is a bit on the theatrical side. You've made yourself some good friends there, Lily. Your dad used to say you're as rich as your friends but to have a friend, you have to be a friend first. It shows your heart's in the right place. But do you really think it was Ivy who sent the letter?'

'Sadly we do, Daw Esme,' said Su. 'She knew what was in the letter before we told her, but it'll go no further now. Maria has enough to think about.'

'The sooner Levi gets his family on its own, the better. I've been too soft with him. I'll see right by them, for Neville's sake, and then I'm going to get myself up in the hills or by the sea. Squabbling children are like mountains, best viewed from a distance, but my door'll always be open for you, our Lil, if you change your mind. I'm only a bus ride away.'

Why did Mother go on so about Walter? He was doing his best. His mother wanted her slice of him too. The wedding was only weeks away so it was time now to give it some thought.

For all her harsh words Esme had found them two gold sovereigns, the ones Granddad gave her for passing exams. The jeweller in town would beat them into a wedding ring and there'd be enough left over for two tiny crosses for the little girls to wear.

'I'll always keep my eye out for them both; no favourites, mind,' said Esme. 'They're the last link I have to my son.'

21

Here Comes The Bride

There wasn't an ounce of sleep in her that night. Lily, staring up at the bedroom ceiling, felt panic rising in her chest as she waited for the dawn chorus of sparrows chirruping on the slate tiles above.

The contours of each piece of furniture were so familiar: the mahogany tallboy, the little roll-top desk that came from Granny Crompton's house, the oak dressing table. Two watercolours hanging from the picture rail, and the peony-flowered curtains were so much part of her childhood and growing up.

This room was always a quiet refuge at the back of the house away from the thunder of the traffic, away from noisy brothers, or now Neville screaming with colic in the night. Slowly, though, her home was turning into a house of quarrelling women. Nothing was as it once was. How could it be? The war had put a stop to that.

Of course Mother had the right to move on from Division Street some day, but the thought that her childhood home and all its memories were going to be broken up came as a shock to Lily.

It was scary enough to be moving out herself, but not to have Mother in her usual armchair in the front room was unsettling. What if Ana and Su fell out? She couldn't always be there to sort things out.

Well Cottage was so tiny, with low ceilings and twisty stairs. The two of them were both beanpoles and kept banging heads on the rafters. How would they fit in?

And there was another thing. It was going to be quiet up there until she got used to the silence of the hills. It wasn't really their first choice, but so little was on offer. A long way out of town on the bus, too far for visitors to pop in – who would come and see them there? She hadn't even got the use of the van now, since abandoning the shop.

Levi was being so mean she was no longer sure that she even wanted him to give her away. Why did any woman of age need someone else to give them away? She was not a piece of furniture.

Transport for her new job was going to be a problem. The Rover was no longer on stilts in the garage, but that belonged to Mother. Without transport she and Walter would be reliant on buses, on lifts. Whose idea was it to move so far out? It was Walter's dream she was following. It had been easy to be swept along by his schemes and go along with his plans at first but now she felt uneasy.

It all seemed so romantic and old fashioned

when they first discussed moving out into the country, but now it felt impractical.

Bill and Avril Crumblehume, who owned Longsight Travel, lived above their business, but they were looking for somewhere bigger to rent now they were expecting twins in the autumn.

The one good decision she had made was in going to work for them. There was never a dull moment and so much to be done before the local mill holiday week. Not everyone could afford to go away when the mills shut so they were advertising mystery tours and day trips to the Lakes and Southport, to York Minster and Museum by charabanc, and seats on excursion trains to the seaside. Then there was the coach trip to Paris, via the cross-Channel ferry. This was to be Longsight Travel's first continental excursion. Unknown to Walt, she'd reserved seats for their honeymoon on the bus. With so many regulations and details to finalise there was hardly time to think about her own wedding day.

Sometimes, during the tea break in the morning, she found herself staring out over Longsight Square, with its railings and statue of Abraham Longsight, one of the founding fathers of Grimbleton. The lilac bushes were almost over and the first of the municipal rose bushes was coming into flower.

In its own way this square was just as peaceful a setting as the surroundings of Well Cottage. The bustle of the town streets was muffled by trees, with everything ready to hand there: shops, work, the park and picture house.

The challenge of this new job excited her and

she wanted to go to night school to improve her French skills. How would she arrive on time for classes when the wintry nights became snowy and dark and the buses infrequent?

Oh, what's wrong with me? she sighed. It must be wedding nerves. Surely all she ever wanted was to be going down the aisle with the man she loved on her arm, a home of their own? All these wishes were coming true and yet her mind was full of the leaving of Division Street and its number eight bus route. This was crazy when there was so much to look forward to, and yet...

Everything was changing. Maria was free now. Ivy and Levi would soon be out of their hair too. There was so much to do. She ought to be glad for everyone, and most of all for herself. She should be excited about her marriage but so many 'ought tos' and 'should dos' and 'must dos' and 'have tos' were ringing through her head.

Walt had come up trumps with Well Cottage. Mother was going along with the wedding plans and not interfering. Elsie Platt was not complaining, for once. So much to be excited about, grateful for and yet... What was wrong with her?

Was Walt insisting they live out of town just his own way of keeping her close at hand? There was no doubt he was jealous of her friendships within the Olive Oil Club.

'It'll do you good to get away from that rum lot. I don't trust girls in trousers. Ever since the war, you see them gadding about in slacks as if they were fellas. That Diana is a one for wearing pants. It's not natural. Your shape isn't made for trousers,' he added, while she was bent double in

348

a boiler suit, trying to make inroads into the jungle of weeds in the back garden. 'And what's all this about a party in King's Park? We've enough to be doing here.'

This was the annual pageant party that started off the wakes celebrations with an open-air band and dancing, fairground stalls and a theatre display. Lily was taking the Brownie pack for the team sports races and meeting up with the others to go round the fair. It was to be her last outing as a single woman. She suspected the Olive Oils had some plan to dress her up as the mill girls did before a wedding but she didn't mind. It would be good to get together again.

'I have to go if it's going to be my last time as a free woman,' she snapped.

'You've changed, Lil,' he said, eyeing her long legs in the khaki boiler suit.

'Don't call me Lil. I'm Lee at work, now. Don't you think that's modern?'

She'd gone with her flash of inspiration when she started in her new job, introducing herself as Miss Lee Winstanley. 'It sounds so professional, don't you think?'

'Why bother when you'll be Lily Platt in a few weeks?' Walt was not impressed by the initiative. He didn't like change.

'I know ... but I've always hated Lil.'

'You never said.'

'You never asked. A new beginning and a new name.'

'What's wrong with being my sweet Lily of the valley? Look, here's some under this wall. It smells a treat and looks beautiful in my eyes, plain and simple, a no-nonsense sort of flower. That's what you are,' said Walt, as he tugged at the weeds. 'I've let you spend time sorting out that foreign lot but now it's you and me together. That's what we both agreed, wasn't it?'

'You're right. We've waited such a long time. It's a shame to spoil the fun with niggles, but I just wish...' She hesitated, not sure where her argument was heading.

'What's up now? What niggles?'

'We've never got carried away much, have we? I hope it's going to be all right,' she blushed. 'You know, the marital side of things.'

'You don't want to be carrying on like that Santini woman. That's just sex. I hope you know I've more respect for you than to try anything on before we're wed,' he stuttered. It was Walt's turn now to fumble for words.

'What's wrong with a bit of sex? We're engaged. We've got the whole place to ourselves but you've never suggested we have a proper practice...'

'You want us to anticipate our wedding night, Lily? I'm shocked at you. Is this the sort of stuff you talk about with those girls? No wonder they all landed in trouble. It's not like you to be so forward.'

'That's how I feel. Let's be adventurous! Please don't resent me going to King's Park with them all. It's for a good cause and I must support the dancing class and my Brownie pack. I'm their Brown Owl, after all.'

'I'm glad you mentioned that. I assume you'll be giving that up. It's too far to travel after a day's work. We won't be making a habit of gallivanting after we're wed. A man and wife should be just for themselves. It'll be so cosy up here, just the two of us and no one to interrupt us. We want to be together, don't we?' He hugged her with such a broad grin on his face that it unnerved her for a second.

His words gave her a sleepless night. The thought of having no friends to visit, no more Olive Oil gatherings round the fireside, was unsettling. Modern marriage must be a partnership, not one of boss and slave, with the wife always the one having to give in to the husband's decisions, surely? Not that that was the case in Levi's poor marriage. They were both as bad as each other.

'We'll have to have visitors, to show them our house and thank them for their wedding presents. I can't see Elsie wanting to stay away for long. And I do want to see the little girls too,' she said, smiling across at his mud-splattered face.

'Anyone would think they were your real family?'

'But Walt, Dina and Joy are my nieces. Ivy and Levi have more or less cut me out of Neville's life—'

'What do you mean? I know Dina's Freddie's girl, blood but the other one – she's only the London cousin's kiddie, nothing to do with you!'

'Oh, come off it, Walt! Why do you think Mother let them stay so long? There's no Cedric Winstanley. Never was. Freddie met Susan in Burma. I thought you'd have guessed by now...'

'No one tells me anything ... the sly bugger! All the more reason to keep our distance from them

351

now. You Winstanleys certainly know how to stick together. Who'd have thought it?' he smirked, shaking his head. 'I don't know what Mam'll say, us being related to darkies! It just shows you never can tell, even with respectable folk. We'll never hold our heads up in Bowker's Row if they find out. It's a good job we're moving away!'

'Don't be like that. Su and Ana are more like sisters to me than Ivy ever was. That's why the little ones are going to be my attendants – if we can get enough coupons together to finish their outfits. They must feel free to visit us as they please.' This was non-negotiable.

'Not likely! Look what they've done to your family: split it down the middle,' Walter snapped back. 'We don't want them or their bastards coming up here.'

She didn't like this side to Walt, this cold judgemental streak. And all this fussing about wearing trousers – where did that come from? There were echoes of his mother's voice in those words. This mean streak must be sorted out early on. She would humour him into seeing the harshness of his opinions, alter his prejudices. I can't be living with a little Hitler laying the law down, she thought.

He'd have to get used to her wearing slacks around the house. They gave her freedom to work and warmth round the ankles. She could work faster without corsets and stockings. It saved on clothes. Muhammadan women wore trousers all the time in Bible lands, Diana said. Besides, everyone was glad enough of women in trousers during the war, shinning up buses and factories, aeroplanes and batteries. Why did they want them all back in skirts now it was all over? Were they afraid they could do jobs as well as the men? Maybe better?

'You didn't mean all that, did you?' she asked, looking across at him. He was hacking stubborn undergrowth with his knife and a steely eye.

'Not another word on the matter, Lil. Let's just get this garden sorted before it rains.'

Ana was hacking at the undergrowth with a furious satisfaction. The hand scythe sheared down the grass and nettles of the vegetable plot. Whack went Ivy's head! Whoosh went Levi's torso! Here, she could vent all her frustration on the hapless weeds.

It had taken the patience of a diplomat, the cunning of a black marketeer and the persistence of a marathon runner to get the committee to make a decision in her favour. Allotment Billy had proved to be versed in all three.

Just as he began to dig over the neglected soil, wheelbarrow tons of cow dung to enrich the neglected soil, came the news that Mother Winstanley was leaving, and who knew where they would be next year? Just when she had begun to settle in to this strange climate, this rough northern town and understand some of their ways, along came uncertainty again.

She had such plans for her plot. Here she would grow vegetables – beans and peas, salads, thyme and mint, sage and onion sets, soft fruits; fresh food. She loved free afternoons when she could wheel up Dina and busy herself just digging, thinking and dreaming. Here she was closest to the earth, and when the sun shone on her shoulders, it was easy to pretend this was Cretan soil. Here all the sadness of hospital duties, the aching limbs and the memories of her wartime suffering were forgotten once she got down to work.

It had been on May the twenty-first, the name day of St Konstantinos and his mother, Agyia Eleni: the name days of her sister and her daughter, that she'd taken possession of the plot. It was a good omen. At home they would bring cakes and little gifts to Dina; drink sherbet water. No one here understood how special that day was. They were all too busy shouting and fighting.

She brought orange juice and biscuits and a special picnic to the allotment, for her and Dina to celebrate together. 'We must never forget who we are, Konstandina: daughters of Crete. "Freedom or death" is our island cry in times of trial. Your grandmother searched for the body of my *papou*, when the Turks fought him in the hills. She dug up his body with her bare hands from the rocky grave and brought him home. We are strong and proud. Your Aunt Eleni died a hero for our freedom. I named you well.'

Together they had sat sprinkling crumbs and good wishes over the plot and now all her efforts would bear fruit. Dina was toddling, engrossed by the ladybirds. Here they could speak their own language without interruption.

Now Ana didn't notice Su standing behind her until a shadow fell over her patch.

'I always know where to find you. How can you bear to get your hands so dirty? We have to talk.'

354

'What about?' Ana snapped, not wanting to hear what was coming next.

'What we do when Daw Esme leaves.'

'Do we have any choice?'

'I think so. I pray every night for guidance. I think, mango among fruits, pork among meat, tea among leaves are the best, and Waverley amongst houses is the best lodging house.'

'How can we stay?'

'If Daw Esme will let us rent, then we can find plenty of good customers to live in. You have room, I have room and the rest we let. What do you think?'

Ana put down her spade. 'You wanna share with me?'

'Yes, I think we make better friends than enemies. We have enough of them,' Su replied. 'Our daughters are half-sisters. We share the same man who never came back and chose between us. We must make the best of a bad job, I think, and never tell the truth about Freddie. That must be our secret, yes?'

What could she say? 'I am not going to do the cooking. I wanna be a nurse.'

'Then I will learn to make a good English breakfast. The lodgers bring their own ration card and buy their own food. They use the kitchen. I think it's a very good idea, yes?'

It was the best of ideas to stay put, and Ana need not give up the plot. Both would have separate space, and no Ivy sneaking around making trouble.

'I shake your hand,' Ana smiled, reaching out to grasp Su's tiny fingers.

'Ouch! You have the paw of a bear. How will you get a man if you crush him to death?' Su winced.

'I didn't have much trouble in Athens...'

Su gave her a fierce look but said nothing. It would always hang between them, this rivalry, this envy of the time each had shared with Freddie, but somehow it didn't hurt so much now. Better to live together than hang separately, went the proverb. It could work. It *must* work, for it was the only solution on offer.

'Do you like them, Brown Owl?' Ten faces were beaming in the circle as Lily unwrapped their wedding gifts with care. There was a striped tea cosy with a pompom, six knitted dishcloths, and six embroidered coaster mats. 'We got our knitters' badges. We unravelled two jumpers to make them. You do like the colours?'

'They're lovely.' She beamed at the black and yellow football colours of the Grasshoppers.

Everywhere she went people kept shoving gifts into her hands: a tray cloth with tatted lace edges from Dolores Pickles, a lovely glass vase from Mrs Pickvance across the road, and now this. She suspected her little pack would be forming a guard of honour when she and Walter came out of Zion Chapel. All this kindness was making her weepy.

Esme had given her a hundred pounds.

'Don't spend it on the house. Buy something for you. It'll go towards a second-hand car. I don't want you stuck out in the wilds for the want of some wheels.'

Speechless, shocked by such generosity, Lily had burst into tears again.

'It's not like you, Lily. You do look a bit peaky. Have you collected your dress yet?'

Now was not the time to tell Mother that the idea of a long white gown had never appealed. It would drain what little colour she had from her cheeks. Anyway, what an extravagant waste of coupons to wear a dress only once. It smacked more of Victorian custom than the modern ways of doing things. All the extra coupons had been spent on beautiful material for the little bridesmaids and Neville's pageboy suit in cornflower-blue satin and velveteen – if Ivy could be persuaded to let him come.

It felt mean to have kept everything a secret from Mother but it was Lily's day and she was determined to do what she wanted for a change. After all that had happened this year, it was only a minor rebellion. Elsie Platt would take one look at the colourful suit and think she had something to hide. Sadly she was still 'virgo intacta'. There was no shifting Walt once, he got an idea in his head. She just trusted he was worth the wait.

Su was helping her put together a two-piece linen suit in a deep rose pink that warmed her complexion and lightened her hair. Ana was spending hours embroidering blue flowers on the pockets and collar. All that was needed was the borrowed hat to arrive in a hat box from Diana Unsworth; a hat that had once graced Royal Ascot before the war; an extravagant straw affair straight out of a Gainsborough portrait. She felt

357

like Anna Neagle in it.

'Something old, something new, something borrowed something blue.' Everyone was making quite sure that she would look the picture on the big day.

'You must have a rehearsal so you feel comfortable and I can adjust those sleeves,' Su ordered.

Since Ivy and Levi's sudden departure into rooms near Albert Avenue across town, and Mother's impending move, Su was planning to open the spare rooms to commercial travellers. Waverley House was going to have to earn its keep now.

'I have a gift for you,' she whispered, ushering Lily upstairs on the night of the party in King's Park. 'But first you must try on your outfit.'

Lily stood in front of the mirror, not recognising the reflection staring back at her. Who was this willowy blonde in the stylish dress, her hair softly curling around her face? Since the fashion parade she had gone the whole hog and had one of Lavaroni's permanent waves. No more curlers and rags and wave clips torturing her scalp. She was a modern woman now.

'Here, you like it?' grinned Su, handing her a shoebox tied with ribbon. 'It is for your wedding night.'

Inside the tissue paper was a film of soft silk, a whisper of coffee-coloured gauze, a nightdress that would add the finishing touch to her trousseau. Lily gasped and held it against her body in disbelief. 'It's gorgeous. Where did you get such stuff?' She was blushing at the thought of wearing such an exotic extravagance in front of Walt on her wedding night.

'It is from Auntie Betty. She sent it in parcel for you for all your kindness to me and Joy. You like?'

The tears came gushing again. 'I don't deserve such a lovely gift. Thank you.'

'It is nothing. Come downstairs now. All is ready,' Su ordered.

What was going on? There was the sound of voices in the hallway and the dinner gong was ringing a summons. She hung the wedding suit back in the wardrobe out of sight and put on her best summer cotton dress with bolero cardigan. It could be chilly in King's Park after dusk.

They were all standing at the foot of the stairs, chanting, 'Here comes the bride, sixty inches wide!' Queenie and Maria, Rosa, Joy and Dina, Diana and Eva, Stefania, a new Polish recruit to the club who was training at the technical college, Ana and Mother, smiling from the doorway. Everyone was dressed up and raring to go.

'Not so fast, Miss Winstanley. We have a little something from us to you,' said Diana, producing a parcel from behind her back.

'It needs a bit of explanation,' said Queenie.

They pushed forward a large box wrapped in brown paper and string. Lily tore it open. Inside was a leather suitcase with safety straps and brass buckles. It was a work of great craftsmanship. She fingered it with astonishment. 'It's beautiful. How thoughtful.'

'Well, not exactly... We know how you want to travel abroad. It's not exactly modern, but prewar. My hubby knows someone in the tannery who buys up bits of leather and sews up bags.

This is one he had made up out of pre-war hide. I got him to have it embossed with your initials but the daft happorth forgot you were getting wed and put L.W. on it. I hope Walt won't mind it's not L.P.'

'It's perfect,' Lily sniffed. 'You shouldn't have...'

'Hey, none of that! We've got a supper to eat, come and see.'

It was all too much, the table groaning with pies and salad greens. There was a bowl of home-grown strawberries, trifle and a homemade sponge cake.

'We thought we'd do English this time, in honour of the bride,' Maria laughed. 'No olive oil or garlic when we're off dancing. Ana got eggs from Billy to make a proper sponge.'

Queenie sat down at the piano, playing a selection from 'Bless the Bride', and they all sang while Lily smiled through a veil of tears. She was too churned up to eat much.

What was going on? It felt like standing at the top of a huge cliff and the time to jump was nigh. But why must she jump off? This was where she belonged, right here, right now, not stuck on a moor miles from her friends.

For one brief second she wanted to stop the clock, unwind the hours, forget all the plans for the future. Why get wed, when everything she wanted was right here? Oh, heck. She was going crazy. Nothing was making any sense.

Ana produced a handkerchief made of lace, and wild poppies from her allotment were pinned into Lily's hair. 'In Greece we dress up the bride-to-be like this,' she laughed.

Tonight she would be paraded around the town. There was nothing to be done but to grin and bear it. It was only a bit of tradition, after all. No one begrudged a bride-to-be a little fun and games before her big day. You do this only once, she sighed, so make the most of it!

22

Dancing in the Park

The arboretum in King's Park was strung with fairy lights. There was an avenue of plane trees lining the walkway festooned with banners left over from VE Day. Crowds thronged up towards the entrance to the sports field where the last remnants of Zion Chapel Brownie pack, those not away on holiday, were scampering towards the racing tracks to compete in the fun sports. In the distance a brass band was playing a Souza march. It was going to be a hectic evening.

There was no escaping from Lily's gang of giddy minders as they marched her up to the gate. Someone pinned a card to the back of her cardigan saying: 'Here comes the blushing bride.'

'I've got to see to the races and cheer the girls on first,' she insisted. This was her ploy to get rid of all the dressing up, but the others were sticking to her like limpets. Diana was searching the crowds, hoping to gather in all the stray Olive Oils. Maria wanted to watch her Santini nephews racing for Our Lady of Sorrows School, before she dashed off with Su to dress Joy and Rosa for the fancy dress tableaux when Joy's dancing costume would be on show; hoping for first prize, after all those months of work, for her Burmese headdress. Ana pushed Dina along to watch the show in the very pushchair that had started their friendship all those months ago. Soon she would be old enough to join in the class.

No one could miss the fact that since Sylvio had left Grimbleton, all the sparkle had gone out of Maria's eyes, and the fire from her face. Her skin was drawn over her cheeks and her black shirt and skirt hung loosely over her frame. Her hair was scraped back in a widow's bun. They were all worried about their friend, whispering their concern behind her back.

Rosa sensed the atmosphere and whined for attention but Maria was lost in her own thoughts, pushing the go-chair grimly on.

Su looked like an oriental princess in her festive *longyi* skirt of printed flowered cotton edged with a rich emerald border and neat boxed jacket. Diana was in her Guide uniform, busy rounding everyone up like a sheep dog, pushing Lily ever forward into the crowds. It was going to be a long evening.

The sports races were duly run, the Brownies dispatched to their parents, and then it was time for the dancing display. Queenie was standing thumping out the tunes on the piano as turn after turn of Liptrot tinies cartwheeled and somersaulted over the grass in an exhibition of formation acrobatics and solo turns.

The fancy dress parade, on a British Empire theme, drew admiring crowds as the Union Jacks fluttered and each country of the Empire was represented by a little girl in costume – Britannia with her shield, South Sea island girls in grass skirts, an Indian wrapped in a sari and many other gaily dressed children in kilts and Welsh hats paraded past them. They cheered loudest when little Joy shuffled across the stage and struck her *pwe* pose in her sequins and silk, a tiny figure dwarfed by the other contestants, smiling and waving from the podium.

'Already she is bright star,' Su sighed.

'Why is no Greek girls? We have nice costume,' sniffed Ana.

'You are not Empire. I am a British Empire citizen,' snapped Su.

'If they have countries of Europe then Ria and me, we dress the girls, and you can watch for a change.'

'No squabbling in the back there, you two. We're all citizens of the world now,' Lily said.

Was it possible those two could ever be friends? They'd always be rivals after what her brother did to them. Yet in a funny way that's what united them against the world. Who else understood just what they'd been through? Not even Maria, who was treading her own lonely path, could imagine their plight or the secrets that bound them together.

Ana and Su were chained together by memories and promises betrayed, but also by their golden girls, Dina and Joy, who'd never know they shared the same father.

No Winstanley must ever tell them. Esme insisted on that. What would become of them in the future? That's why she had to live close by, to help them through. They were family no matter what Walt said. He could like it or lump it. Hark at me: a right Bolshie these days, Lily smiled to herself. A far cry from Doormat Lil.

After the fancy-dress parade, the judges walked around with their clipboards deliberating. This was holiday time and no one must be disappointed so all the children were given sixpences in little brown envelopes. Su was not impressed.

'They are all winners,' Lily tried to explain. 'It's the taking part that counts.'

'Someone must get the cup. It should be my Joy. She is beautiful,' Su insisted.

What was it with every mother that she thought only her child was the best, the most deserving? If ever she had kiddies, Lily decided, she would not want to brag about them all the time.

The cup was given to Britannia and her retinue, and everyone cheered.

'That's not fair!' Su grumbled.

Lily walked away in frustration to listen to the madrigal singers who were fal, lah, lahing and trilling to everyone's enjoyment in the evening sunshine.

It was almost like a pre-war summer fair, but Merry England on the green was now shabby and full of make-do-and-mend clothes. Candy floss and ice cream, hot pies and peas, crisps and pop were in short supply. The summer frocks on display were darned and tired, faded with washing, but who cared when the sun shone?

Lily kept thinking about the Winstanley outings of the past and memories of happier times: Freddie and Levi in the wheelbarrow race and the three-legged run, Mother and Dad strolling together, arm in arm, admiring the bedding plants made into a clock with plant dials. It was the little details long forgotten that tinged this event with sadness.

No amount of persuasion would make Esme come and join them. In the past they brought Neville to displays, but he was banned from contact with Lily until the wedding. She was still not sure if Levi's family would turn up, having moved out of Division Street in a huff and a puff, but already the atmosphere was lighter.

Walt said he and his mother were expecting company bringing wedding gifts. He ought to be by her side too, sharing the jollifications, but since the last clearing-up session at Well Cottage, the night of her failed seduction effort, there was coolness between them that was troubling.

No wonder you did this wedding malarkey only once, Lily reflected. What an expense and palaver for just one day. So many decisions to make about catering and flowers and hymns, what to pack for the honeymoon and whether they'd scrape together enough coupons to furnish the cottage with curtains and bedding.

Feeding the five thousand at the wedding breakfast in the church hall was going to be a nightmare. Princess Elizabeth in her palace wouldn't be going through this rigmarole when it came to her nuptials. There'd be no counting slices of ham for her.

Tonight was to be a night off, so why was it feeling like an endurance test: how to get through it without making an utter fool of herself and weeping into her sleeve?

It was as if the whole of Grimbleton was strolling through the park: young and old, old schoolfriends, now married and pushing prams, brothers in army uniforms on leave, members of Zion Chapel, linking arms and giving their children piggyback rides. The world and his wife was out that night, but how lonely it could be in a crowd.

Even the gang around her were distracted by their own troubles, whispering them in her ear as if she didn't have enough of her own.

'What do we do if Daw Esme decides to sell Waverley House, Lily?' whispered Su.

'I'm that worried about Maria,' whispered Queenie.

'Should I write letter to Sylvio? I not know what to do, Lily,' whispered Maria.

Sometimes it felt as if everyone wanted a piece of her, pulling her loyalties in one direction and then the opposite. Walter wanted his old Lily back. Mother wanted sensible Lil. These women all wanted a listening ear.

The only bit of her life not complicated was the new job with the Crumblehumes. In the office she was just Lee, the new assistant. There was so much to learn about the travel business but she was enjoying every minute.

She never knew who was coming through the door or where they wanted to go. The other day an old man had thrown a bagful of five-pound notes down in front of her. 'I want to go to China to walk the Great Wall and I want to go by train!'

The thought of giving up work to raise a family was now a serious headache, not a joy. She wanted time to enjoy being wed before being tied down by nappy buckets, but at the ripe old age of twenty-nine she must just buckle down quickly and have a go.

Reverend Atkinson had given them both such a talking to about how there was no better calling for the modern woman, now the war was over, than to bring up a family and support a husband in his work. Lily's heart hadn't stopped fluttering since.

What's wrong with you, Lily Winstanley? Get a grip. This is your night out with the girls, one last night of freedom before ... what? When the cage door shuts, what then?

She dawdled behind the others, trying to lose them and slip off home but, turning down a path through the bushes, Queenie was quick to halt her.

'Where're you sneaking off to now? There's the big band from the Astoria doing some numbers. It's dancing time for you.'

'Oh, no, not for me. It's been a long day...'

'The night's still young. Come on, where's your spirit of adventure?' Queenie insisted. 'If an old married codger like me is up for it, then the bride-to-be must polish the floor with her slippers and let her hair down.'

'No, I'm not much of a dancer, really. I ought to be on my way. Walt wouldn't like me to–'

'What Walt don't know won't hurt him, duckie. Enjoy yourself. Don't be a spoilsport. Time enough for sitting down with the old man when the wedding cake's gone mouldy.'

There wasn't much choice but to tag along and try not to yawn. Dancing was not their forte. Between the two of them, they had four left feet when dancing at the church socials, tripping over each other, apologising and laughing. Walt had no sense of rhythm, and with his backache they were both nervous in case sudden jerks might set it all off again. He was such a martyr to his back.

It wasn't that swing music wasn't exciting, but the church didn't play that sort of stuff and Esme didn't like it on the wireless. It was common and too lively for chapel tastes, but Maria was always playing music in the café and it always got Lily's toes tapping. Just because your parent didn't like something didn't mean you had to go along with it too.

It was so easy to slip into old habits, she thought. Doormat Lil might be stuck with the Home Service on the wireless but Lee Winstanley would be up for the Light Programme and the big band beat.

The Joe Crombie Orchestra was letting rip on the makeshift dance floor, which looked more like a boxing ring than a cabaret. There were fairy lights hanging down from the trees and the moon was lighting up the purple orange sunset. There was still heat in the evening sun.

'Very continental,' said Maria, looking up wistfully as dancers were drifting across to a slow foxtrot. They were playing Glenn Miller and it brought back such vivid memories of the GI and that shameful episode in the park. Everything was conspiring against her at the moment.

'You look tired out,' said Lily, touching her elbow. Rosa was fast asleep. 'Go and sit down. I'll watch her.'

'*Grazie...*' What would she have done without her friends? But if they knew the truth... Since Marco's death she had not stopped for one minute, cleaning, cooking, visiting Nonna, sewing – anything to take her mind off what was going to happen.

At first she thought it was all the strain that had stopped her period. It had happened before but she couldn't recall when she had last had to buy sanitary pads. In the aftermath of her grief her body seemed to be floating six inches from her head. The sick feeling and tiredness was only to be expected, but suddenly her breasts were so tender and full, and she couldn't bear the smell of the tea urn. It made her want to throw up so it wouldn't take a soothsayer to tell her what she already knew deep in her heart.

'Can you keep a secret, Lily?' she whispered. 'I have to tell someone. I am in big trouble. I can tell only you. I think there's a *bambino* on the way. What shall I do?' she gulped, sinking down onto the grass, not waiting for the reply.

'So that's why you've been fainting in the café? Ana was worried,' Lily said, sitting down beside her.

'If the Santinis find out, I will be banished for bringing them a bad name. What shall I do? I was making a fresh start and now this, and no man...'

'You'll survive. Believe me, you'll not be the first to be let down.'

'How can I tell everyone? I'll have to leave. They will not want to eat with me...'

'Of course they will. We're your friends, and friends stick with each other no matter what. Believe me, we *all* have secrets. If I was free to tell you, I'd tell you one of my own but I made a promise.'

'I know, you are good woman and good friend. I can trust you.'

'Don't worry, there'll be a way through, Ria. We'll think of something.'

Things just couldn't get any worse for Maria, could they? She was going to need all the friends she could get, Lily mused. A baby on the way should be a moment of joy, not an event full of shame and dread. Maria had been longing for another child, but now... How could she explain it away? What a mess. Why was life so complicated? This news took the last ounce of pleasure from the outing, knowing that her friend was carrying such a burden. Sylvio ought to be told the news and do the decent thing, but it wasn't her business to interfere and yet ... how easy it was to solve other people's problems from afar.

She watched the dancers gliding across the floor and a flood of envy flushed her cheeks. Why wasn't she here with Walt, canoodling in the twilight? How could he prefer his mother's company, the 'Battleaxe of Bowker's Row' as Esme called Elsie Platt? Perhaps he was trying to keep her sweet.

There was no love lost between the two mothers-in-law. The newlyweds were going to have to play fair with both sides or there'd be trouble. Married life was already losing its appeal.

Anxiety was spreading right through her body, making her twitchy and irritated by the soft music. Diana was waving to a group of young men in smart blazers with badges on their pockets. The crowd parted in admiration as some of the Grasshoppers began to circulate around the dance floor, choosing partners. That was all she needed, seeing a bunch of Freddie's friends enjoying themselves. They were the usual suspects: Barry, Clive and their gang making their way in her direction. Freddie would have loved the party.

Ana waltzed around with Clive, laughing at one of his feeble jokes. How she had changed in appearance and confidence from the frightened girl who arrived at Ringway on that wet afternoon so many months ago. Now she wore her nurse's uniform with pride and her limbs were fleshing out at last.

It was strange to think that this time last year Freddie was alive, far away but alive and full of mischief. Lily still couldn't believe he wasn't coming home. One day she would pack that new suitcase, find where he was buried, and go and pay her respects there, however much it cost.

Someone tapped her on the shoulder and she spun round to see the broad face of Pete Walsh, smiling at her.

'Fancy a turn, front half or back half?' he joked,

recalling their frenetic pantomime dance.

'I don't know, I'm watching Rosa here,' Lily spluttered.

'Get her on that floor,' snapped Queenie. 'I'll see to the kiddie.'

There was no time to protest as Pete led her out onto the wooden planks. Now she was going to make a complete fool of herself. Her heart was racing as he lifted his hand into her own.

'Young Kathleen tells me celebrations are in order,' he whispered. 'When's the big day?'

'Two weeks on Saturday,' her voice squeaked.

There was silence as he led her across the floor in a waltz. It was like cruising down the dual carriageway in third gear, no double de-clutching, no stalling, no spluttering, just a smooth gliding waltz as if her legs took instructions from his. They were floating, swirling around like a top, dizzy.

'You're a good dancer,' he said, holding her hand when the music stopped suddenly.

'I'm not. I've two left feet. It's you that's the expert.'

'Let's do it again,' he laughed. 'I might as well make the most of you before you get snaffled up by old Plattie, lucky chap.'

There was no time to say no or remove her hand from his. For the first time in weeks she was enjoying herself. Someone else was making the decisions and sweeping her around. It was a revelation how a good dancer could change steps and direction, follow the music and take care of his partner at the same time!

Dancing with Pete Walsh – who'd've thought it? He was still unspoiled by his popularity in the town, still scoring goals but this was the off season when the footballers were on half-pay, going back to their old jobs part time. He was helping out at his uncle's brewery.

She had been his biggest fan. Now dumbstruck by the scent of his breath on her cheeks and the flash of his bright eyes grinning at her, her heart was thumping.

'What you staring at?' he teased.

Thank goodness it was dark and he couldn't see her blushes. 'I was just thinking about Miss Sampson's class seven and you being the ball monitor. I never thought you'd make such a good job of football.' It was the best excuse she could muster.

How could she tell him what a warm smile he had or how she wanted to finger the dimple in the middle of his chin?

'You've been going out with Walter Platt for years. I always hoped you'd get him out of your system and look in my direction,' Pete whispered in her ear.

Was this some sort of joke? 'I beg your pardon?' she snapped, suddenly feeling hot. 'I don't understand.'

'Forget it, Lily. It's the Wilson's brown ale talking. I always did have a soft spot for you, even in class seven,' he coughed, and she could see he was in earnest.

Well, now's a fine time to tell me, she sighed. What a turn-up: Pete Walsh fancying me! Yet now she thought about it he was always popping in on his way through the Market Hall, and made a point of meeting his little sister from Brownies.

'I think it's marvellous the way you've championed Freddie's friends. I always knew you had a good heart. I only wish I'd...' He stopped, embarrassed.

'Go on,' Lily smiled. 'It's nice hearing compliments instead of curses.'

'Walt must have told you a hundred times what a good-looking woman you are. Our Kathleen worships the ground you walk on. The trouble with me is I'm backward in coming forward.'

'Not when you're scoring goals you're not. That last one against Arsenal in the Cup was a gem.'

'You saw it?'

'Heard it on the wireless when I was on duty in the market.'

'How're you enjoying your new job?'

'You know a lot about me all of a sudden,' she replied coyly, flattered by this interest.

'I know you're at Longsight Travel now. My uncle Ernie and auntie Glad are going on their tour to France. He was in the Great War. He wants to show Glad where her brother fell.'

The tune came to an end and Lily stopped. 'You're a good man, Peter Walsh, but I'd better stop you before the tongues start wagging. We've danced four dances on the trot.'

'Who's counting? Come on, one last one and then I'll let you go.'

It was a boogie-woogie, another Glen Miller number. Everyone was jiving and jitterbugging. Lily felt all fingers and thumbs but suddenly she didn't care. Dancing was fun when the man knew what he was doing. She would go along with it just this once. She was in the mood for a bit of frivolity. They twirled and she danced around him, not caring if she was showing next week's washing. He spun her round and caught her and she raised her hands, waving to the others, who were watching her amazed. Then it was over and he caught her in his arms.

'Just one kiss for old times' sake,' he laughed, then plonked a soft kiss on her lips and pulled her tight.

She felt a ripple of excitement from her toes to her suspenders. All her elastic was pinging, her head was swimming and her knees just crumpled. If only you could bottle that sensation up like a good piccalilli, sharp and sweet, tangy with a zing, she thought. You'd be a millionaire.

'No, no more, please!' She fled his embrace, covered in confusion, down the steps right into the path of Levi and Ivy.

'Well! Who's a sly horse then? Just wait until Walt finds out you've been setting your cap at Pete Walsh, kissing and canoodlin'. He was all over you like a rash,' Levi smiled and winked.

The two of them must have been lurking down the side of the dance floor and seen the whole episode.

'That's no way for a bride to be behaving, Lil, and in front of the whole of Grimbleton. It'll be all round the park that Brown Owl was making an exhibition of herself.' Ivy was enjoying every moment of her triumph. 'Not so much the pure little Lily of Laguna, are we, two-timing your fiancé on the sly?'

'Oh, give over, Ivy. I was doing nothing of the sort. You're only jealous. It's none of your business what I get up to on my last night out. I expect my brother will drag my fiancé around all the pubs to make a right fool of himself and no one will say a word because he's a bloke.' No one was going to spoil this moment. 'Why shouldn't a woman have fun too before she's chained to the kitchen sink?'

'You've got very cocky since you joined that club of yours. You wouldn't catch me with that greasy lot...' Ivy added, seeing Queenie, Ana and Su eyeing her with suspicion.

'And none of us would want a mealy-mouthed, jumped-up little hypocrite who sends poison-pen letters, as our friend,' screeched Queenie. 'We know about you.'

'Say that again, you old bitch,' Ivy spat out, unaware that Maria was coming up right behind her.

Face to face with the poisonous witch, Maria had heard all the jibes and she saw the worried look on Lily's face.

'You shutta yer mouth. You bring trouble wherever you go,' she yelled, lunging forward to push Ivy out of her path.

'And you're no better than you should be. Get out of my hair!' Ivy sprang back, lashing out with her hand to punch her. She ducked just in time.

'You insult my friend! You kill my Marco. I kill you now.' Maria was beside herself, spitting fury and grabbing at Ivy's hair, tugging until lumps came off in her hand.

A crowd was gathering.

'Get off me, you trollop! You're all the same... rubbish, foreign scum, the lot of you. You're not welcome here.'

Lily was trying to push in between them, pleading with Levi, 'Get your wife out of here. She's not welcome, can't you see?'

He pulled Ivy away, but she turned on Lily. 'You call these trollops your friends?' Ivy spat the words in her face.

'Just how many close friends do you have, my lady?' yelled Susan, red in the face. 'We've never seen anyone come calling for you, all the time we live with you. Poor Neville will be one lonely boy if you think you're above everyone else. No wonder Levi has walking hands,' she screamed back, not caring who overheard the row.

'Who does she think she is, talking to me like that? Do something, Levi. Do her precious friends not know that she's no more Mrs Winstanley than Madame Butterfly? Go on, Lily, you tell them who these two *really* are; a couple of foreign whores with bastards on the make, stealing your brother's name, telling lies, worming their way into this town like grubs.'

'Shut up, you've said enough!' Levi was trying to push Ivy in front of him and out of the way. 'Let's get out of here.'

'Just get her out of my sight,' said Lily. 'Will you tell Mother or shall I that your darling wife has just spilled the sack of sacred beans all over the park? Are you a man or a mouse? Sort her out or else I will!'

He was standing there staring as if he'd never seen her before. 'Hell's bells! You're more Winstanley than I thought, our Lil. Never thought you had it in you. Poor old Walt doesn't know what he's letting himself in for. Wait till I tell him what a spitfire he's wedding,' Levi replied, shaking his head.

'Shut up and leave me alone, and never call me Lil again!'

'I'm going to tell Walt what you've been up to tonight.' Ivy straightened her skirt, pouting, red in the face.

'I don't care,' Lily snapped, but her hands were shaking.

Maria took a swipe, a fine right hook that floored Ivy, sending her staggering across the floor while the band played on. 'That is for my Marco, God rest his soul, and for my friends, *capisci?*' She sucked up her mouth and spat an arc of spittle over the prostrate woman. 'If you go to *polizia* and make big fuss, I bring letter for them to read.'

It was like the gunfight at the OK Corral, on-lookers gawping and all those accusations shooting out like bullets from a gun. All Lily wanted to do was creep away alone to relive Pete Walsh's kisses, hear his compliments soothing her ears and the touch of his strong hands on her waist. It felt so disloyal, so confusing, but so right.

Time to creep away and hide somewhere far away to sort it all out once she had given her friends an explanation. The vow of silence must be broken. She took a deep breath and began...

'So now you know the truth about the Win-stanley tribe,' she said, relieved that the secret of Su and Ana's relationship was now out in the open.

The Olive Oils were all sitting round in a circle on the grass with a tray of hot tea, too stunned by the fracas to dance on. The children were fast asleep in their pushchairs and the midges were beginning to bite.

'Don't bring that tea near me ... it makes me sick,' whispered Maria with a sigh. 'I am up the spout, as you say, up river and no paddle. That is my secret. Now you know my secret too. Any more to share?'

Diana smiled. 'None of us is Persil white, but golly, what an evening! Better than a night at the pictures. That Ivy got more than she bargained for.'

'Mother'll disembowel them when she finds out. The honour of the Winstanley good name is now in jeopardy and it's all my fault,' Lily said, dreading the scene to come.

'Why? Because you were flirting with that handsome young footballer?' laughed Diana. 'What was wrong with that?'

'Nothing but when Walt hears about it, there'll be trouble.'

'We're not going to tell him, are we?' Queenie asked.

'We're not going to tell anyone else any of our business,' said Diana. 'Mum's the word, right, girls?'

'All for one and one for all,' Lily smiled. 'Let's have a powwow.'

They sat in a circle as darkness fell, each with their arms around the next one's shoulders, huddled, whispering in the dark, telling secrets no one else would ever hear. They would have stayed out all night but for the park keeper.

'Now, ladies, the party's over. Hurry along.'

Next morning Lily rose early, not wanting to face her mother. She had not slept a wink, pacing the floor, going over yesterday's excitement; trying to push the unexpected thrills of dancing with Pete, the embarrassing public row with Ivy and the secrets that they all confided in the park out of her mind. *Something* must be done about that and soon. But the jungle drums had been beating and Walt was round at the travel agent's first thing, demanding an explanation.

'I can't leave you five minutes with that lot before you make an exhibition of yourself. I'm surprised at you,' he said, pink with indignation and puff.

'It didn't take long for Poison Ivy to lash her venomous tongue in your direction,' Lily replied. 'It was only a bit of fun. She's making a mountain out of a molehill as usual.'

'But you were seen canoodling with Pete Walsh like a brazen hussy. Is that a proper way for a fiancée to behave?' Walt's lips were pursed into a peevish line just like his mother when she had a strop on her, a thin line of disapproval that did his face no favours.

'It was one farewell kiss, for old times' sake, nothing at all. Why didn't you come along to the dance and join us and then none of this would've happened?'

'Because I trusted you to behave yourself and not show me up like some giddy bitch on heat,' he snapped, loud enough for Avril Crumblehume to hear and back out of the door blushing.

'And what's all this about Ivy being savaged by the Eyetie? Honestly, you can never trust foreigners with drink in them.'

'Oh, Walt! Don't show your ignorance. Sometimes you can be such a prude. My friends wanted me to have a good time and came to the rescue when Ivy was insulting me. Maria had her own score to settle.'

'Fancy fighting like fishwives!'

'It was Ivy who provoked them.'

'So you say.'

'You don't believe me?'

'I don't know any more. You're not the girl you used to be, Lil.'

'Don't call me Lil. I'm Lee here.'

'I'll call you what I like. You're my wife.'

'Not yet I'm not!' she turned on him.

'What's that's supposed to mean?' he snapped back, towering over her.

'I'm not sure,' she replied, storming back to her desk. 'By the way, did your passport arrive in the post?' It was time to change the subject.

'Why should I want a passport?' He cocked his head, puzzled.

'For Paris, the trip and our honeymoon,' she sighed. 'For the ferryboat across the Channel.'

'The only channel we'll be crossing is the Irish Sea. The Isle of Man will suit us just fine. What would I want with snails and frog's legs and all that foreign muck? Honestly, Lil, I don't know where you get these big ideas,' he said, searching the papers on her desk, shuffling them out of order. 'Of course, I might have guessed. It's that

Olive Oil Club of yours, putting such fancy notions in yer head. The sooner I get you up to Well Cottage the sooner you'll come down to earth. We'll have to choose your friends more carefully next time but I'll be on hand to guide you.'

'But I thought we agreed. Avril is counting on us to help on the charabanc. It's their first trip. Ernie and Gladys Walsh are going on it.'

'So I suppose Pete Walsh will be going along for the ride too. If you think I'm spending my honeymoon with him in tow, you've another think coming,' Walt snapped.

'What's Pete Walsh got to do with the price of beans? This is our honeymoon, our first advent-ure as a married couple. It's what we planned.'

'It's not what I planned. The honeymoon is the groom's decision.'

'That's so old-fashioned. Modern couples decide things together.'

'Not in my book, they don't. A man must be master of his household. Start as you mean to go on, I say. That's why your Levi has trouble with his wife.'

'I want our marriage to be a partnership. We each work and earn a wage. We've waited so long... Any road, what my brother does is his own affair.' She carried on at her desk, pink with fury.

'Perhaps we've waited too long, Lil...'

'Oh? How come?' she sighed, weary of all his arguing.

'It's all the strain of waiting to fulfil our love that's getting to you, the strain of not having a man to guide you on the right path, too many women giving you the wrong advice and big ideas. Girls are the weaker sex. They aren't meant to make big decisions and go their own road. Look what happens when they do: bringing up bastards, working all hours, straining their brains studying for jobs beyond their capabilities. A woman's place is in the home, by the hearth, tending to the needs of her hubby, not gallivanting here and there with opinions all her own.

'Look how happy you were when you ran Waverley House, before the invasion of foreigners spoiling everything. Who was it we could count on to see to the household chores and Neville, keep Levi and Ivy happy and your mother settled and content? Who was it who manned the stall yet had time to give my mam a helping hand and never a cross word? You were so reliable and easy to please. Once I get you all to myself, the old happy Lil will return to the hearth and be content.'

'Is that how you see our future?' she asked.

'Of course, don't you? Think of these past months as a bit of a blot on the landscape. Together we'll put it all behind us, love, forgive and forget. I forgive you this time.'

She nodded and tried to smile but her lips stuck together. 'I must get on with my work. There's so much to do.'

'Don't you worry your head, love, about this,' he replied, dismissing the whole office in one swipe of his hand. 'As soon as we're settled you can stay at home. Once you're a married woman, this sort of work'll be too much for you. Whatever the sacrifices, the doing without, no wife of mine will shame me by having to earn a living. So don't be fretting. It won't be long now until you can leave all this behind for good. Won't that be exciting?'

He plonked a kiss on her forehead and squeezed her arm with affection. Lily felt dizzy with fear.

'Is everything all right?' Avril waited until the coast was clear. 'You look as if you've seen a ghost... Let's have a brew.'

'I'm fine. Sorry about the floor show ... it's all been a bit of a shock,' she replied, still feeling weak. What on earth was she going to do now?

23

The Mission

Lily went round to Lavaroni's Hair Salon the moment it opened at ten o'clock, knowing Queenie would be in early before Gianni began his morning appointments.

'We have to find Sylvio Bertorelli and fast. Do you know where he went?' There was no point in shilly-shallying with Queenie, who had her ear to the ground when it came to gossip. Surely someone must know his whereabouts?

'I wish I did, ducks, but he just disappeared and old man Lavaroni won't have his name mentioned in here. He might be trying his luck in London but I can't believe he'd just walk out on

Maria. Perhaps he blames himself for Marco's death. I'm not sure he even knows about it. He's a good lad. Wherever he's gone he'll be a success. Do you want me to ask Gianni? He'll bite my head off but it's worth a try. I'm worried about Ria and little Rosa too.'

She eyed Lily up and down and winked. 'It was a right humdinger in the park with that sister-in-law of yours. She deserved all she got. You just stood there and sorted her out without a flinch. That perm really suits you, by the way. If you're not careful you'll be turning into a right glamourpuss. Are you having it shampooed and set on the morning of the wedding?'

'I haven't booked anything yet. We need to sort this out before I go away,' Lily replied. Hair-styling was the least of her worries. 'Can we meet up at Division Street later in the week? You'll have to excuse the mess. Mother's on the move soon and she's having a fit of packing. There's china in boxes, and books and watercolours stacked up. She wants a right sort-out before she leaves. We haven't dared tell her what happened last night.'

The Olive Oil Club was in session behind closed doors. Diana was in the chair. There was nothing better than sitting at the head of a table giving orders, getting things done in her view.

'We've got to find Sylvio,' Lily started. 'Don't ask me why but I think he'll not be far away. Between us all we can do it, but Ria mustn't suspect. She's too proud to seek our help. Did you find anything out, Queenie?'

'Not much, but there is one clue. Gianni muttered he's had a call from some hairdresser in Manchester wanting a reference for Sylvio. Needless to say he sent him off with a flea in his ear.'

'Did he remember the name?' asked Diana, hoping for a quick breakthrough.

'Nope, or if he did he wasn't going to tell me. I think he's glad Sylvio's gone. Now he's got all his old clients back and no competition.'

'That's not much help,' said Su. 'Finding a guy in a city is like finding a hairpin on the pavement.'

'I can ask at my church in Manchester. I can find out about hairdressers,' offered Ana.

'Brilliant!' Diana smiled. This was a team effort. Then she remembered the Chamber of Trade. There were lists of shops in Grimbleton. There was bound to be one in Manchester. 'If we can find out all the names of the hairdressing establishments in the city, we can visit and ask around for Sylvio Bertorelli. Someone will know of him. We'll give them this number and get them to ring us.'

'There's all the Italian community to go at as well; café owners and ice-cream vendors, that sort of thing,' Queenie added.

'No,' Diana interrupted. 'The community is small and family links are long tentacles. Toni and Angelo might get to hear. There might be trouble for Maria. We don't want her to guess what we're up to. Who else knows the city well?'

Manchester was somewhere Diana avoided for shopping. Mummy liked Kendal Milne and St

Ann's Square. She found it quite depressing every time she passed the Salford hospital where all those nurses had been killed in a direct hit. Everything was bombed and gutted after the blitz. The cathedral was being rebuilt. Sometimes she ventured in by train to the Free Trade Hall to hear the Hallé Orchestra. The rest of the city was a mystery to her. She preferred London.

'Bill and Avril at the travel agency might help us,' Lily offered.

'What about Pete Walsh and the Grasshoppers? They play United and City. What if young Sylvio's joined a men's barber, not a ladies' hairdresser? Perhaps Pete could help us. This is going to take ages otherwise,' said Queenie, not wanting to depress them.

'What's the big rush?' asked Su.

'Maria told us her secret. Where were you?' snapped Ana.

'And I want this sorted before my wedding,' Lily said, still being the peacemaker.

She felt guilty that she had not confided her own precious secret to them all but it was not the right time or place, and she couldn't be sure how they would react. Her head was buzzing with plans and ideas, half formed and too fuzzy yet to be put into words. Maria needed their help and that was enough to be going on with now.

Every time Lily thought about the coming wedding day her mind froze with panic.

Apart from the wonderful nightdress and the new suit, she'd not enough coupons to go rash with a trousseau, but she must buy some holiday

387

slacks just to prove a point. But who could be bothered about clothes when a friend was in danger?

What'd happen if the Santinis found out Maria was carrying another man's child? What if there was violence and shame, and she got thrown out of the flat? She needed Sylvio and her friends for protection. There had to be a way to find him but she was running out of time.

Walter's demand that she cut down her circle of friends after their marriage was gnawing away inside. He was being unreasonable, but he was jealous and that showed how much he loved her. This mission gave her something better to think about other than all his insecurities. Meanwhile she must get on with her tasks, the first of which she would rather enjoy.

'I know this sounds daft but we need your help as a detective,' Lily stuttered, standing pink-faced on the whitened doorstep of number ten Eccleston Place, the small terraced house where Pete Walsh lived at home with his family.

'Come in, come in... It's Lily Winstanley, Mam,' he shouted from the vestibule.

'Put the kettle on, Kath, it's Brown Owl. Come and sit down.' Pete's mother ushered her in, ripping off her pinny in honour of the visitor.

'It's very kind of you but–'

'No buts, Miss Winstanley, pleasure to meet you. I've heard so much about you. I hope our Pete's not been up to any trouble.'

Lily was ushered into the neat front room with its three-piece suite, draped with lace antimacassars. The piano in the alcove was covered in Pete's trophies and team photographs. They were treating her like a guest of honour. Her cheeks were pink with blushes at such a warm welcome.

I hope he doesn't think I'm chasing him, turning up at his doorstep, she thought. Who'm I fooling? I just wanted to see that grin on his face and the dimple on his chin. No one had arm-wrestled her to come and ask him to help. She was a more than willing volunteer.

'I'm on a sort of secret mission to help a friend,' she explained. 'But it's rather private. We were hoping you'd be able to help us – and the other boys, if they can.'

It was important to use the royal we, to distance herself from choosing to be the eager messenger on this quest. It was important to sit primly, straight-backed and not get distracted from her task by looking at his lips and recalling his impulsive kisses.

His mother closed the door discreetly with a, 'Do you take sugar in your tea?' This was going to be a best china occasion.

'How can I help?' he smiled.

She told him the gist of their investigation and explained that he might have some contacts in the city. His eyes never left her face as she covered the angles where he might prove useful.

'You say Bertorelli was an ex-prisoner of war? He might have gone back to Italy under the repatriation order. There's a lot going back home now.'

'We never thought of that, but somehow I don't

think so. He was very friendly with a friend of ours here. I'm sure he'd want to stay but perhaps not in Grimbleton. It's hopeless, isn't it? A needle in a haystack,' she sighed.

'Not necessarily, but I'll have a word round and see who goes where to have their hair cut. From what you've said, though, I guess he's a ladies' man, an artist with ambition. Short back and sides are not very inspiring, are they?' Pete tapped his own crop. 'Still it keeps you cool in the sun.'

'What sun?' There had been mixed weather for days, sunny then showers.

'Just you wait, after a winter like last we'll get a corker of a summer. You'll have a sunny wedding day.' He smiled and she felt herself blushing again.

'I wasn't thinking of my wedding day but of all those folks forking out for a week in Morecambe and it pours down.'

'Trust you to think of someone else,' he replied, staring so hard she dropped her eyes from his gaze. 'Is there anything else, I can do? I can help you look, if you like?'

'No, thank you, you've done enough,' she squeaked. It was time to leave before she embarrassed herself.

'Enough of what?' said his mother, edging a tray of tea and scones around the door. 'Sit down, lass. You need feeding up before your big day. Come on tell us all about your plans.'

There was no escape from their fussing and kindness. If only Elsie Platt would give her a welcome like this every time she turned up, things would not feel so desperate right now.

As Pete predicted, the weather turned just as the holidays were over. Out came the sun, streaming down on the sooty black buildings, the bomb sites decorated with rosebay willowherb springing up everywhere. The tarmac was melting and the pavements hot as Lily, Diana and Ana gathered in the shade under the cathedral with a map to carve up possible sightings and venues. The search for Sylvio was underway.

Susan was minding the children. Diana had brought her car, with Ana. It was the best they could muster on a Saturday afternoon. Queenie was working in the café after the salon closed at lunchtime, keeping an eye on Maria.

Ana had a list of good hairdressers around Deansgate and King Street. These were to be their first ports of call. Diana had the trade list, pages long; a daunting prospect. Queenie found them the trade newsletter in the salon, advertising local warehouse suppliers. Perhaps someone might recognise Sylvio's name there on an order, but none of them would be open on a Saturday afternoon.

It was hopeless, and so tiring with not a single lead to show in this sticky heat. Heads were shaken politely and hands pointed to another salon up the road, round the corner, in the back street, down the lane. All their contacts yielded not one jot of hope of ever finding him.

Pete had sent a list of city barbers and the names of some footballer ex-prisoners of war.

As the afternoon wore on Lily sank into a weary slump, hot and thirsty, jaded and bad-tempered by the heat. Her toes were rubbing in her ancient sandals, unused to going barelegged. They met up by Lewis's Arcade ready to go home. It was almost five o'clock.

'I'm not going anywhere without a drink, an ice-cream soda, anything to slake this dry throat,' said Diana, who was for once looking dishevelled and perspiring in the heat in an aertex shirt and smart khaki slacks. It was good of her to give up her day off duty but she seemed to enjoy ordering them about.

Diana was a bit of a mystery, bossy and kind, polite and yet distant, all at the same time. She had not spilled out any secrets, no handsome pilots or wild parties to confess. She was part of the club but not really at the heart of it as if she was holding something back.

Perhaps it was because of her public school education. She was local and yet not a Grimbletonian. She was their officer, not rank and file. She was leading her foot soldiers from the front, brave but distant.

They picked their way through milling crowds. 'You'd think they were giving stuff away,' Lily said, looking round in amazement. She loved the bustle of Saturday streets, the heat of the chase for bargains. Pavements trampled with the weary feet of shoppers carrying baskets and bags, window shoppers browsing to see if there was something they could afford. Manchester was abuzz, but even Grimbleton had its moments. How would the silence of Well Cottage suit after all this excitement? Was she really a gumboots and gabardine sort of girl?

In two weeks' time she would be floating down the aisle and onto a coach bound for Dover, if she could persuade Walt to change his mind. It was not too late.

If it was as hot as this she would need some pleated shorts and a swimming costume in her new suitcase. It was sitting at the foot of her bed, waiting to be packed.

Finding seats in a café was a struggle, but eventually they sat round a table, ticking off all the places they had on their list.

Ana shook her head. 'He gone to London. It is no good, Lily. We never find him.'

'No, we've only just skimmed the surface. Perhaps he's gone to Bolton or Oldham or Wilmslow. There has to be a way. I know he's here. I just feel it in my water.' It was hard to convince them of her instinct that the man was hovering just out of sight.

'Time's running out for you, old girl,' Diana said. 'Sylvio'll have to wait. You've got a big day ahead. Down the aisle for you soon.'

As Diana was speaking, Lily's eyes meandered out through the dusty window onto the street and the building opposite, to a tall red brick church rising above the other roof tops. 'Aisle, Altar, Hymn,' went the old joke about a bride's personal vows. That was just what she was hoping would happen with Walt.

Aisle, Altar, Hymn and a church... Why ever hadn't she thought of that before? She leaped up out of her seat, that stuck to her bottom in the heat.

'Where're you off to now?' Diana shouted. 'We

393

ought to be heading home.'

'Stay here. Give me two minutes, I've got an idea.'

Lily shot across the cobbled street, holding her breath as she walked into the church. It was dark and cool inside, silent with just the flickering of candles and women bent over in prayer.

It was late Saturday afternoon and she knew enough about the Catholic faith to know it was a good time to hear confessions. There was a cubicle with a curtain drawn that was doing good business. One by one the penitents rose and entered the box, coming out and walking down the aisle out into the daylight. She had time to think just what to say. When it was her turn she sidled into the seat, her heart thumping.

'Before you start, I'm not a Catholic but I'm trying to help somebody who is...' It was time to confess the whole sorry tale to the unseen priest. '...So you see, if you can find Sylvio Bertorelli for us... We've searched the soles off our shoes down your pavements but we're strangers here. But I thought who would know his flock better than a priest, and priests know other priests... Sylvio is a good man. I'm not asking for confidences to be broken but for him to get in touch with us. You have to help us, please,' she begged. 'It's for the best of causes. It will give the chance for two good people to find each other again.'

There was silence. Then the priest spoke with an Irish lilt. 'How will I be making contact if I find such a man – and I'm not promising that I will?'

'Give me a ring at Longsight Travel.' Lily

scribbled the number on a scrap of paper and shoved it through the grille. 'Ask for Lee Winstanley, and if I'm on my honeymoon, ask for Queenie Quigley at Lavaroni's Hair Salon, Grimbleton. Sylvio used to work there. Or Sister Diana Unsworth at Grimbleton General Hospital. He has to come back to Grimbleton, and soon. That's the message. Thank you, I've taken up enough of your time.' She made to leave.

The priest peered through the grille. 'If everyone had friends like you, the world would not get into such a mess, now would it? God bless you. I'll do what I can.'

The others were waiting outside the café, furious at her desertion. 'Where've you been, Lily? We are so worried.' Ana was pointing at the time on the clock tower.

'I've sorted it. With the Roman Catholic Church on board now, we might just have a chance,' she laughed. 'Why didn't we think of it before?'

'You crazy woman, this is just a little church in back street here.' Ana was not impressed.

'The arm of the Church is long, Ana. Anything's worth a try but come on, time to go home and paint my toenails.'

'Lily, that's not like you,' Diana laughed.

'I know. Isn't it fun?'

Each morning at work when the telephone rang, Lily jumped just in case it was for her. On the Sunday night before the wedding, the girls were going to meet after church, as they'd recently resumed doing, for one last supper in Maria's flat. If no one had heard anything from Manchester by then there was going to be such dis-appointment.

The following Monday Pete called in to the travel agency in Lily's lunch hour to find out how things were going but the look on her face told its own story.

'It'll be all right,' he said. 'Just be patient. Come and bring your sandwiches out into the fresh air. We can keep an eye on the shop from the square.'

It was a beautiful afternoon, baking hot, and they sat on the nearest bench in Longsight Square Gardens. He asked her about her wedding plans and Walter's back, and about her plans to chaperone the cross-Channel trip.

Lily would miss meeting up with him at Brownies. Watching him play football wasn't the same as sitting next to him and seeing those eyes flash and those lips... Had he really kissed her? Had she dreamed all those lovely things he'd told her? Why was it when they were together she wanted the minutes to go so slowly and for the sun to stand still in the sky?

It wasn't right to be fancying Pete Walsh like this, was it? It wasn't natural. She jumped off the bench. 'I'd better be off,' she said. This was temp-tation. What if someone saw them together? Walt wouldn't understand and he'd be hurt. It must be last-minute nerves or something.

She was about to take the biggest step of her life. The great steam train of wedding prepara-tions was rolling into the station. It was time to jump aboard. Why did she wish she could stay on the platform?

'I never knew I had this much stuff. Take what you want for the cottage, Lil. Where did we get so much clutter?' Esme sighed, looking over her bare cupboards with grim satisfaction. She was going over each room, one by one.

She had her eye on a bungalow at Sutter's Fold, halfway up the hillside. The building was coming on a treat, with its neat sitting room, two bedrooms and modern bathroom. It was small but she wanted it that way so no uninvited guest would come muscling in on her territory. She'd had more than enough of that in the past.

It had one of the best views over the town, and a garden that would be no trouble, but the best bit was that it had central heating from a coke boiler-cum-cooker in the kitchen, heating the radiators. No more coal fires to make every day. All mod cons, and far away enough for neighbours not to see your smalls on the line.

Now all that was left was to see the girl wed and settled, sort out the rental with the others and let them get on with it. But first there was the royal visit to attend to.

Walter and his mother had invited Esme and Lily for tea to discuss all the final arrangements for the wedding day. Sitting across from Elsie Platt was not one of life's joys and Esme admired Lil for taking on that harridan.

If ever there was a home without warmth and welcome this was it, Esme thought, sitting perched at the end of horsehair with a smoking fire and that sour smell of boiled vegetables up her nostrils. She grimaced. All the corners of this front parlour could do with bottoming out.

'This time next week, Lil, it'll be your big day. I wish our husbands could be here to share your joy,' said Elsie. 'Only a widow knows what it's like to be unwanted, alone without that someone special to care for your needs.'

'I've done my best, Mother,' Walt smiled.

'I know, son but a son's a son till he gets a wife, a daughter's a daughter all your life. Isn't that so, Esme?'

'I hadn't quite thought of it like that,' Esme said, looking to Lily with raised eyebrows. 'Think of it more that you've gained a grand lass in Lily rather than lost a son.'

'But when he's gone, who will see to me?'

'Happen you'll have to see for yourself as I have all these years since Redvers went to his rest.' Esme's hackles were rising now.

'With respect, Esme Winstanley, your circumstances are different from mine. I hear you've bought a brand-new bungalow, out of town. You don't have to make ends meet like I have, all these years.'

'Mother...' warned Walt.

'No, you listen to me,' Elsie continued. 'This wedding is an expense, with all those guests we don't know to cater for. You two've got your little cottage out of earshot. One day it'll be me as is found at the foot of the stairs and no one will know I've gone to my Maker,' she sobbed. 'I'm too old to be left to fend for myself.'

'Elsie Platt, you're younger than me by a long chalk. None of this self-pitying talk. Young couples need a fresh start and no interference from us until they ask for it. These two have waited long enough – years they've waited – so don't go spoiling their day. It's not fair!'

'What's not fair is my son being wed to a house full of foreigners with babbies. It didn't take him three guesses to know who their father was... You Winstanleys are no better than the rest of us. My poor son'll have a wife who wants to work outside the house and gad about with her friends, day and night till all hours. I hear they can't cook a square meal between them and they were all fighting in the street. I don't know how you put up with it.' Elsie folded her arms across her ample bosom. The first salvo had been fired across the bows.

Esme was not going to take these insults sitting down. She rose up and stared out of the window. The nets were a disgrace and the aspidistra was covered in dust.

'What I put up with is my business! I'll have you know my girls are capable and kind-hearted, like Lily here. You should be grateful she's taking your spoiled son on. It wasn't my wish to see her throwing herself away on a lazy loon who's never done a decent day's work in his life!' She hoped this blast would meet its target.

'Don't you, call my Walter lazy. It's not his fault he has no bones in his back.' Elsie was wagging her finger and spitting feathers of fury.

'I rest my case,' Esme replied. 'Spineless, and you've only yourself to blame, Elsie Platt.' Gloves were off now.

'Don't you go calling my poor fatherless son names! At least he's never given me a minute's worth of trouble, not like *some* sons I could

399

mention! At least he's not fathered a pair of bastards!'

'Don't you dare mention my sons in the same breath as him.' Esme pointed a gloved finger at Walt. 'They fought for King and Country. One died in His Majesty's service. What did he do in the war but get under everyone's feet?'

'Stop this, both of you!' Lily screamed. 'I can't stand any more of your sniping, Elsie Platt. It's not you I'm marrying but him. I know what I'm taking on. You've made him what he is and I don't want any interference from either of you!'

'Well, that's told us then, hasn't it?' Esme sighed, but she had to hand it to the girl for once. She was sticking up for her own. Pity he wasn't much of a trophy.

There he was, sitting hunched up, miserable, his ears sticking out like jug handles, his body sagged down with embarrassment. What did the lass see in him, Esme thought. It was going to need some firm handling to lick him into shape.

'I think we've all said enough,' Esme said, plonking her cup of weak tea on the table and wrapping her cardigan around her shoulders, feeling a shiver go down her spine.

So it was out then: all their dirty linen was hanging on the line for everyone to see. Who'd spilled the beans?

'Lily, I want a word with you. What's been going on?'

'It wasn't me, Guide's honour, Mother,' Lil stuttered as they were driving home in comfort for once. The black Rover saloon was now in regular service, warming up for the big day.

'Ask Levi what happened. Ivy insulted my friends and she spilled the beans in the park. She let rip as only she can. The rest just happened. Maria had a score to settle and settled it. Don't worry, none of my friends will say anything.'

The more Esme heard the worse it was getting.

'I don't know what the world's coming to. The sooner I'm on way out the better.'

'Now you sound just like Ma Platt,' snapped her daughter. 'I'm sick of all these secrets in the family. Better out and dealt with. Now you've made things bad for Walt and me.'

'You can't mean to marry that drink of water in there. You can do better than the Platts. It's not too late to call it off.'

'Will you give over, harping on about Walt? Yes, I'm going to have to rescue him from all this mollycoddling, find him an osteopath to sort his back, get him some nice clothes to wear, but he's *my* mission now, a full-time job. I can't nurse everyone's wounds when I've got him to sort out. Underneath he's a nice chap – weak, I admit – but as the saying goes, "Aisle, Altar, Hymn".'

'If you really believe that, young lady, you're a bigger fool than I thought.'

They drove the rest of the way home in silence.

The spaghetti was bubbling and the sauce ready to serve. There was the usual crush in her flat but Maria was glad of company. Diana was looking at her watch, Queenie kept peering out of the curtains and Lily was falling asleep, *la povera*. She should be at home getting ready for the big day.

When she had married Marco she had not slept

for a week with excitement, sewing her lace dress and veil. She looked wistfully on the wall at their portrait. It was another lifetime ago. Now there was new life in her belly, life she didn't deserve, a gift that would take a lifetime of penances to give thanks for.

Everyone was jumpy and chattering when she was just out of earshot. Were they talking behind her back? Had they changed their minds about her? Without the Olive Oils she was lost.

This meal she was preparing with love and gratitude. Ana had brought broad beans from her allotment and handfuls of mint to make a paste. She had found chopped nuts and fresh berries to add to the fruit sundae. Food had brought them all together and soothed their anxious times. How could she ever thank them? But they were ignoring her now, smiling to each other. What was going on?

'Lily? Wake up! Last-minute nerves?' Maria was bending over her. 'Don't worry, we'll all be there to see you off.'

'I don't want–'

There was a loud rapping downstairs, a thundering on the café door.

'Wadda you want now, Enzo? Forget his head if weren't stuck on,' Maria yelled. 'Shutta that noise, you wake Rosa. I'm coming.'

'You stay here, I'll go,' said Queenie, waddling from the door down the narrow staircase. 'I can see to it.'

'Who is it?' she yelled. 'Tell them I'm out.'

Queenie puffed up the stairs with a strange look on her face. 'There's someone to see you, Maria.'

'Bring them up then,' came her reply.

'No, I think it's someone you might like to see on your own, ducks.' Queenie was winking and smiling. 'Go on down.'

'I go but why they can't come uppa the stairs?'

What was all the fuss about? She turned for the stairs and looked down.

'Santa Maria!' From inside her came a scream, an animal howl as she clattered down the wooden stairs. 'Sylvio!' She galloped down into his arms.

The rest was a rattle of Italian, hugging, kissing with a passion.

The girls were all grinning, peering from the top of the stairs. 'Thank you, thank you, everybody! How you find my Sylvio? You bring him back to me!'

She wrapped herself round his body with delight, kissing him as he clung to her.

'I didn't know, I'm so sorry. What has happened?' Sylvio wept. 'It is a miracle. I go to confession. I tell him everything and he say, are you Sylvio Bertorelli?' He turned to the tearful faces. 'How can I thank you?'

But they had already found their coats and hats, making their way down the stairs, leaving the couple to a private reunion.

The Olive Oils had triumphed so why was their passionate coming together making Lily feel so sick, so envious, so emptied of hope for herself?

'We did it then,' she sighed.

'*You* did it, Lily. That trip to the church must have done the trick. I think the Italian Mafia is alive and well, praise the Lord! Time to be on our way. We're not needed here.' Queenie winked and skipped on the linoleum.

'Your turn for joy next, Lily,' said Su.

'No, I don't think so, not like that,' Lily sighed wistfully.

The sight of those lovers clinging together like limpets clawed at her insides making her feel queasy. They were like two halves of a whole, separated and now back as one. Together they'd sort things out, find a way through the coming tunnel of disgrace into a place of their own in the sunlight, safe from the gathering storm. Lily wished she hadn't seen them.

I should be glad for them, rejoice in their coming together, in them finding each other, she raged. What was wrong with her then? Why was she so put out? Her own wedding day was at the end of this very week, a new beginning to look forward to. These feelings were ridiculous.

Pull yourself together, Lily Winstanley. What are you thinking of?

There was no need to answer that question. She made her excuses and left.

24

A *Brief Encounter* Moment

After making a quick exit, the leftovers of the Olive Oil Club found themselves outside Santini's in the deserted street. It was a warm Sunday night, hardly dark yet, only the screech of the swifts overhead broke the silence of the Sabbath. Nowhere to go and nothing to do, and no one wanted to play gooseberry on the young couple in the flat upstairs. They needed to be alone.

'We can go window shopping,' suggested Su.

'What we would have, if we could have but we can't... What's there to see that we haven't seen a hundred times? Windows full of cardboard cut-outs, posters promising stuff we can't get hold of – what's the point?' snapped Lily.

'Who trod on *your* toes?' said Queenie. 'I thought you'd be chuffed the two of them have found each other again and it's all your doing?'

'I am, I am...'

'So?'

'Nothing, nothing you'd understand. I'm fed up, tired out, but I don't want to go home yet.'

'It's late, Lily. You need your beauty sleep,' Su offered. 'We must catch the bus.'

'You go on. I think I'll walk for a bit, clear my head.'

They walked on ahead, leaving her dawdling behind with Queenie and Diana. Soon Ana and Su and the others were out of sight.

'Do you really not want to go home yet?' said Queenie, her warm brown eyes scanning her friend's with concern.

'No.'

'So what's this about? Tell Auntie Queenie. Last-minute nerves?'

'I need a drink, a large one.'

'But you don't drink,' said Diana. 'I've never seen you touch a drop, except a bit of wine when we have supper.'

'I need something to get me on my way and cocoa won't hit the spot.'

'Are you sure? Everything's shut now but I know a little club we can go to, down a back street,' Queenie said. 'I'm not sure it's your sort of place but women go in there and don't get bothered. Arthur's taken me in there once or twice.'

'Lead on, Macduff! Are you coming, Diana?'

'Trust a Londoner to know the dives of Grimbleton better than a native! I'm intrigued. Lead me into temptation,' she laughed.

They slipped down Cheapside, past warehouses and office blocks, turning into a side street, hidden from view until they came upon a scratched sign which said 'The Coal Hole' on a painted door. A surly man nodded them through, down into a cellar with steep stairs.

It was like going into the underworld, a secret tunnel under Grimbleton, a subterranean world Lily never knew existed. She felt a flicker of nervousness but it was too late to turn back now.

Women didn't go into public houses – not respectable Winstanley women – but she was curious to see who was in the smoky twilight world, sipping beer, listening to a man tinkling tunes on the piano, a man she recognised as one of Levi's infamous customers from the market stall. She could smell the perfume of the wonder weed in the air but said nothing.

'I'm not sure this is quite what I wanted, Queenie.'

'Don't worry, you can get a cup of tea if you like. I know Paddy's wife, Sadie. We do her hair. She'll see you all right. You've led a sheltered life, girl. If you're going into the travel business then you should know that every town and city has its secret dens, dives and boltholes. Grimbleton's no different from London, just on a smaller scale, that's all. You can get anything here if you know who to ask.'

'Yes, I can smell it,' giggled Diana.

'You mean black market stuff from spivs, favours from ladies of the night, gambling?' Lily whispered, her grey eyes wide with alarm. What if she was taken for a loose woman? At least there was safety in numbers.

'We've no need to worry on that score.' Diana grabbed her arm. 'I think your honour is quite safe. Think of it as part of your education.' They were peering round at the couples huddled in the corners.

Her eyes were getting used to the darkness, the only light candles flickering in old wine bottles. The smell of ale, cigarettes and spirits assaulted her nostrils. There were familiar faces from the market, customers of the Santinis, who looked up at her in surprise.

Levi and Freddie would know about this sort of place, but down The Coal Hole she felt like a visitor from Mars. Mother would have kittens if she found out about this den of iniquity in their midst.

The women sat huddled in a corner table. Lily ordered half a pint of Wilson's mild, trying to look sophisticated; the only brand of beer that came to mind. It was Pete's tipple from his uncle's brewery. Queenie wanted a port and lemonade and Diana had a pint of bitter. It felt daring to be out so late but that chapel voice in her head kept whispering: 'This no place for you, in Satan's den, drinking Beelzebub's brew. No good can ever come of defiling the Lord's Day. Go home now and repent. Why are you exposing yourself to temptation, sister?'

Her first taste of beer was a bit of a shock. It was warm and nutty, comforting as it slid down the throat. No wonder men liked a pint at the end of the day to slake their thirst and warm their innards. The second slipped down even easier. The third just gave her a warm glow. Her spare budget was blown in the space of half an hour.

'I'd go easy if you're not used to it, duckie,' warned Queenie.

'Let me try yours,' Lily smiled, tasting the port and lemon on the table. This was fun. 'I'll have one of those next.'

'I think we should be on our way now, Lily,' Diana interrupted. 'We've work in the morning. I shall have to drive you home. They'll be worried about you. Home James for you, before we have to carry you out.'

It was as she was turning for her cardigan on the back of the chair that she noticed a couple in the corner canoodling. It was Shirley, the bottle blonde from behind the stocking bar in the Market Hall, holding hands with an oh so familiar figure – her brother. Levi looked up and held Lily's eye, frozen like a rabbit caught in a headlight.

'Lil,' he croaked, 'what are you doing here?'

'I could ask the same of you,' she snapped, staring at him with glassy eyes, trying not to stumble with the shock.

'What's up?' asked Queenie. 'Oh...' she added, seeing who it was.

'Just get me out of here.' Lily turned, but the ceiling was swirling above her head.

'Hold on to my arm,' ordered Diana. 'This was not a good idea. Come on, fresh air for you.'

'Don't fuss. I can manage on my own. I'm not an invalid.' Her voice sounded as if it was coming from her toes, and each leg stumbled up the stairs as if it didn't understand orders, her mind befuddled by the sight of Levi and that floozie making eyes at each other. Queenie grabbed her other arm.

'Look at the state of you. We can't send you home like that. You're going to have to come down my place and sober up. You're going to have a head on you like a helter-skelter in the morning. Let's get her out of here.'

Linking arms, they staggered towards Queenie's

house, passing the foot of Bowker's Row where Walt was, no doubt already tucked up in the land of Nod. The sight of his street name stirred something inside Lily and a smile erupted over her face. It was suddenly important to tell him what she had just seen. Did he know about Levi's little secret?

'Let's give Walt a surprise visit, see if he gives me a welcome like Sylvio did Ria. Let's wake my intended up for a little chat.'

'I don't think that's a good idea,' Diana suggested. 'We mustn't disturb the peace. Come on, not long now. You can ring home from the telephone kiosk at the bottom of Featherstone Road or, better still, I'll give them a tinkle and explain you're unwell and I've taken you home with me. You can go on to work from my place in the morning.'

'No! I have to speak to Walt first. It's important.'

'It can wait till the morning, ducks. Believe me, things said in drink don't come out right. Let's be having you!' Queenie was pushing her out the way.

'No! I'm just going to ring his bell.' The idea was in her head and it was not going to be shifted. It wasn't that late. It was funny how the cobbles kept sloping away from her but she was soon at number four and rapped the door knocker hard. No one answered.

'Open sesame!' she yelled. 'It's Lily of Laguna, with a sweet serenade.' There was no movement but curtains twitched across the road and lights went on.

'Lily! Come away now, you've made your call. That's enough.' Queenie was coming to drag her back again.

'No! I know you're in there, Walter Platt. What's the matter with you? Shall I come up and wake you with a kiss...? I've got something to tell you, something you should know.'

The sash window was raised and a sleepy head popped out. 'What's going on? Is that you, Lil? What's up? Who's died?'

'Come and give your fiancée a big kiss!' she yelled with her arms flung open, looking up to see him in his blue striped pyjamas.

'Lily, come away,' Diana whispered, pulling the arms of her cardigan.

'Not before I get a proper kiss from him. I want to know what it tastes like.'

'She's drunk,' said another head, wrapped in steel curlers and a pink hairnet. 'Go home, Lily Winstanley, and don't show yourself up. Walter, shut the window! What'll the neighbours say?'

'Walter! Don't take any notice of her, the old battleaxe. Come down here and give me a kiss! You're marrying me, not her,' she argued, seeing him looking down at her, his hair tufted up like a Roman helmet.

'Lil, I'm not talking to you until you're sober.' With that the window was shut and the light went out.

'I told you it wasn't a good idea,' Diana said. 'Come on, time to go home. You'll feel better in the morning.'

'But I only wanted a kiss,' Lily squeaked, feeling as if all the air was sucked out of her body.

411

She woke a little later in Queenie's parlour on a hard sofa covered in a grey army blanket. Her tongue felt like cork matting and she had only the vaguest recollection of the jaunt to The Coal Hole. Then she recalled Levi's guilty face, a little boy's look caught stealing jam tarts from the cake tin.

In turn, they filled in the rest of the gory details and she turned hot and cold with embarrassment.

'You weren't yourself earlier,' Diana explained softly as if to a patient. 'There was no shifting you. You kept going on about kissing Walter. But he didn't want to play at that time of night.'

'He never wants to play,' Lily muttered. 'But my brother was playing away for both of us. Didn't you see him?'

'What's new about that, ducks? Given half a chance most men play away, and if I was married to that Ivy...' Queenie was shoving yet another cup of Camp coffee into Lily's hand. 'Drink up.'

'I'm sorry to put on both of you. It's not like me. This wedding is getting on my nerves. I'll be glad when it's all over.'

It was almost dawn when they drove up through the town. Diana had phoned Waverley House with excuses for Lily, but she was puzzled. Lily was acting out of character.

'What did you mean earlier about being glad when it's all over? It's only just beginning for you two. The wedding is just for a day, marriage is a life sentence, so be sure it's what you want,' she said, staring at the road ahead.

412

'What's that supposed to mean?' Lily replied, wrapping her crumpled cardigan around herself for warmth.

'You heard me. I'm your friend and I'm worried. Think about it. Last night's little episode was quite an eye-opener on all fronts. It's just not like you.'

'Put this down to nerves. Walt and me've waited that long, I'm bound to get jumpy.'

'If that's all it is, then fine. It's your life, not mine, but think on.'

'What are you saying?'

Diana pulled up by the pavement. 'Listen, I've been watching you and you've been so edgy since that episode in the park. I'm concerned, that's all. Not every woman has to be married to have a good time and be fulfilled. There are other ways ... look at me.'

'Oh, don't tell me you've not got some bloke on the sly? That's why we never see you hitting the town with some handsome doctor on your arm.'

Diana felt herself boiling up. 'It's not like that for me.'

'Don't tell me you've never been in love. I won't believe you. All those pilots and officers you nursed in the war – I bet they were all round you like flies to the honeypot.'

It was time to put her straight. 'Yes, I've been in love,' Diana sighed.

'Who was that then?'

'Binky Ballard, an officer serving in the same hospital. We made plans just like you, but people can change and it didn't work out. Not every romance ends with a wedding ring.'

413

'I'm sorry. Why did it end? Was he killed or did he find someone else?'

Diana took a deep breath. It was now or never. '*She* found someone else, Lily. Binky was my best pal but one day she just packed her bags and left me. Not every love is straightforward.' She was glad of the covering darkness so she couldn't see Lily's face as the penny dropped. 'Don't tell me you hadn't wondered why there were no men in my life?'

'To be honest, I've been that wrapped up in myself and the Winstanley dramas, I hadn't noticed that you were unhappy too.' Lily paused and turned to face her. 'Is this your big secret? I'd never've guessed. You don't act like a...'

'Like a lesbian? That's the proper word, a lonely word in a town like this. "The love that dares not speak its name" is all around if you know where to find it. You don't choose who you fall in love with. It just happens and kept on happening to me at school, in the army. It's difficult to explain...' There were tears in her eyes and she bent her head.

Lily grasped her hand and patted it. 'That's why you came back to Grimbleton, is it?'

'I suppose so. I thought it would be safe and predictable – which it was until I met you lot. One dead soldier and his two women, one drug-pushing brother and his snake of a wife. Romeo and Juliet at the hair salon, and you struggling to keep every plate spinning in the air, pouring oil on troubled waters. Each of us is searching for happiness, one way or another. It's no different for me. Love, betrayal and rejection are the same feeling in any language.'

'I'm sorry,' Lily smiled. 'You must have felt so alone.'

'No more, I think, than any other soldier returning from the war. One minute there's danger and excitement, then its boredom and humdrum. You live as if every moment is your last. You dream of coming home and when you do... A war like that comes once in a lifetime and it's hard to settle in civvy street after all that. Ask Levi or any of the men in drab demob suits, confused, disorientated, unable to settle to anything much. Their buddies are scattered, far flung, and some memories will fade, but the heat, dust and danger will never be forgotten, nor the blood brothers who shared danger together. Don't be too harsh on him. You can never know what he went through that changed him so much.'

'I'm just so sorry you felt you had to hide it from us. We're on your side.'

'Not everyone like me dresses like a man and smokes a pipe. There must be many sad souls out there, in this town, hiding who they really are for the sake of their families and their jobs.'

'I've decided to study psychiatry, perhaps retrain, move away for a while. If I stay here, I'll only brood. But enough of my worries, it's you we need to sort out.'

They were both crying now.

'I didn't share all this to make you feel sad or guilty,' Diana continued. 'Meeting up with the Olive Oils has made life here bearable and given me the oomph to make new plans. I can't sit sulking at my misfortune and living like a child in her parents' house. Time, I think, for us all to go and make our lives happen, doing the one thing that will give us the greatest satisfaction and fulfilment. If marriage is what you want, above all else, go to it! If you're not sure... What is that saying to you? I trust you won't tell anyone else about all my little quirks... One day when I'm not so sore, I'll come clean, perhaps, or maybe not.'

Suddenly Diana was feeling lighter, hopeful and relieved. Better out than in, went the saying. It really was time for her to move on.

'Thank you for trusting me,' Lily replied. 'I'll not let you down.'

'And don't sell yourself cheap, Brown Owl. Go home and be prepared!'

Diana's revelation was spinning round Lily's fuzzy head all morning. How lonely she must have felt among them. How generous and trusting she was in confiding such a secret. If ever this came out, she would be ruined and her position at work compromised.

Minds were prejudiced against such loving. It had taken her aback for all of five minutes until she thought, why shouldn't a caring woman like Diana be allowed to love whom she pleased?

Her suffering made the petty quarrel with Walt fade away but what was she going to do about Levi? If Ivy found out she'd skin him alive. Somehow she knew he'd be making contact. No surprise, then, when he was round at the travel agent's first thing, cap in hand, looking washed out.

'It's not what you think, Lil. Shirley's just a

friend. We have a bit of fun,' he whispered. She bent her throbbing head down, trying to keep a straight face.

'Pull the other one. What's got into you lately? I don't know you any more. I used to look up to you. I would have done anything for you once. I ran the blooming business straight as a dye and who goes and cooks the books? Then there was that box of dope. Dad would turn in his grave to have a son into such stuff. You need sorting out good and proper. Tell me why I shouldn't go and tell Mother some more good news about you?'

'So you haven't told her yet?' His eyes were glassy, like a dead fish on a slab.

'Who do you take me for, Levi? It's as it always was. All for one and one for all. I don't tell on you if you don't tell on me, not like *some* I could mention. Right?' she smiled, too exhausted to crow over his humbling.

'Thanks. I owe you one, sis.'

'You've got to sort this out for Neville's sake. Ivy's no paragon and she had no right to do what she did to Maria, but cheating on her doesn't help,' she added.

'You're right, as usual, Miss Goody Two-Shoes. I know about that stuff with Marco Santini... I know it was her and I feel bad about it. She gets these ideas in her head. I can't keep up with her expectations of me.' He sat down on the bentwood chair, his head in his hands. 'Nothing's turned out as I expected. I can't seem to let go of things, memories, stuff from the war. I saw so many pals go west. Why should I be the one to survive, and now my brother's dead? I can't

417

believe we'll never see him again. I just want to blot things out. Shirley's good fun, she takes my mind off things. Ivy just makes things worse.'

Lily recalled Diana's words and suddenly felt for him. 'Then put your foot down and say no to her wants, once in awhile. Time to put up or shut up, Levi. Where's your backbone? You're a Winstanley and we're made of granite. You've a good business to run, a little son to follow you, a future to build. That's more chances than many of your pals got. I'll not say a word if you buck up.'

'Thanks,' he croaked with relief.

'You and I haven't seen eye to eye for months but we can try and do better if you'll keep your hands off skirts. It's not the answer. Besides, you're the only brother I've got now.' She touched his arm in a gesture of friendship.

He looked up sheepishly. 'You're a good lass. Walt should be proud to be getting you down the aisle and I'll be proud to escort you there.'

'We'll see about that when the time comes. I want you to make sure Mother is looked after. You're head of the household now. Winstanleys expect. Go on, better open up shop and let me get on or I'll be getting the sack. Think on, Levi. No second chances at this life, I reckon.'

The funny thing was he didn't say a word about her own little jaunt to The Coal Hole; not a flicker of curiosity or disapproval.

Suddenly all she felt was pity for the man who'd been the bane of her life for months. He was family, after all, and they must stick together now. Family First into the next generation. Whatever was happening, she hoped that they'd seen the last of Doormat Lil.

Her second visitor came in his lunch break as she was sorting out the itinerary for the coach trip to France.

'I hope you've got a good explanation about last night. I can't leave you five minutes with that lot and you make an exhibition of yourself in front of the street. Mother hasn't put her foot out of the door all morning because of you! I'm surprised at you in that state,' he said, pink with indignation.

'It was only a bit of fun.' Where had she heard that excuse before?

'That's not what I'd call it, and on a Sunday night of all nights. What will your mother say? Honestly, Lily, I'm beginning to wonder about you. It's not the first time this has happened, is it? What about the other week in the park?'

She hung her head. 'We were just having a bit of a do, a celebration. My head's paying for it now. Never again.'

'Serves you right, but it's beginning to be a habit. I thought we'd agreed to cut down on all those gallivantings with those wild friends? They only lead you astray. We don't need people in our lives like that, do we?'

'We need a bit of fun in our lives, a bit of adventure to compensate. If I give up the Olive Oils, I'm trusting that you've done right by me and sorted out that passport at long last. Avril's banking on us to turn up and chaperone the old folks. That way we get a free trip. There has to be give and take in a marriage. I do this for you and

419

you do that for me, even stevens. Start as we mean to go on, you told me. Humour me in this one thing and I'll compromise on my friends.'

She watched him struggling with her words, trying to wriggle them one way and the other to his advantage.

'They've been a bad influence on you. You never used to argue with me or get drunk,' he answered, fiddling with his trilby hat.

'I got drunk because you never show me any affection or kiss me like you meant it, not like Maria and Sylvio,' she pleaded, knowing they must have this out once and for all.

'Are they at it, again?'

'"At it"? Is that all it means? I want us to desire each other so passionately that we don't mind who sees us *at it.*' There, her disappointment was nailed to the door.

'That's behaving like two dogs in the street. Sex has its place in the bedroom but it's not the be-all and end-all of love. It's there to control natural urges.'

'Sometimes, Walt, I feel you've no urges towards me at all.'

'It isn't all it's cracked up to be, this sex malarkey,' he argued.

'How would you know? We've never tried it.'

'Men just know these things. Besides, you and I are too old for all that steamy stuff. You've been watching too many pictures.'

'How can you say we're too old for passion? My mother missed my father something rotten. She worshipped him and he always had a twinkle in his eye for her.'

'That's not very ladylike. Mother says that nightly occurrences have to be endured, not enjoyed. Ladies do it to beget children.'

'So that was why there was only one of you? I did wonder,' she quipped.

'You can be so coarse, Lil. Dad died for his country...'

'Sorry, but I want more out of marriage than a quick fumble in the dark once every blue moon.'

'And I want a lady for a wife, not a good-time girl cavorting round the streets at all hours, only after one thing.' Walt was red in the face now.

'I'm sorry,' Lily said automatically.

'That's better. I'm glad you realise you're speaking out of turn. We'll be fine once we're on our own; in heaven with the door closed,' he smiled, patting her on the arm.

'So you keep saying, but I want to be sure that you love me.'

'Of course, I love you. I must do to put up with all of this nonsense.'

She leaped forward. 'Then show me.'

He was backing off. 'Not in your office. You never know who'll come in. We save all that for the big day. It'll be worth waiting for.'

'OK,' she sighed. Walter made a hasty exit, leaving her confused and disgruntled once more. Are you a stick of rock or a marshmallow? She sat down at her desk, all of a wobble.

Diana was right. The impulse of her heart was urging, Go to it, girl. It's now or never, and it was Lee Winstanley's voice she was hearing, not Doormat Lil's. What was she going to do about that?

25

Gretna Green Temptations

It was dawn on her wedding day when Lily poked her head out of the eiderdown. She must have dozed off for a few hours, dreaming of how it had all come to this.

Everything was in place, ready and waiting. At the end of her single bed was the half-packed suitcase on the floor, the suit hung on its coat hanger. The hat was cradled in its leather hat box. She sniffed the leather of her unworn shoes – two-toned peep-toes in white calfskin with brown trim – and felt empty. The initials on her case blazed out in the sunshine from a crack in the curtains.

It was going to be a golden day, speedwell-blue sky, dry pavements and no muddy splashes on their outfits. Just the day she'd always dreamed of, and yet... Something wasn't right. Perhaps a few more minutes under the covers again, snuggled down, and this panic would disappear.

What was it about those initials, the wrong initials embossed on that case? How unsettling was it to see L.W. not L.P.? Those letters had been haunting her all week; a reminder of the day she must change her name for ever, lose an identity and perhaps independence, along with the freedom to come and go as she pleased. Now everything was so muddled up in her mind.

Walt's threats were ringing warning bells in her head, a noise she could no longer ignore. Why blame two gold letters on a suitcase for all this unease? It was too late for second thoughts.

It was all Pete Walsh's fault for dancing with her and for kissing her and making her doubt. Perhaps it was Maria and Sylvio's fault for showing her what real passion was about, showing up the lack of it in her own romance. Perhaps it was Ana and Su's fault for showing her how to upsticks and follow a dream, however crazy, or Diana's courage in facing her own loss.

Jumping from the bed, pulling open the curtains, staring out into the early morning with heart thumping, she sat down at her bureau and searched for her Conway Stewart pen among the pile of thank you letters waiting to be posted after the wedding.

Suddenly she knew what she must do. Eureka! All the fuzziness of the last frenetic days was rinsed clean away in her head by an ice-cold splash of clarity.

Her romance with Walt was one of those arrangements that had seemed so splendid at the time but felt a mystery to her now. When she conjured up Walt in her mind's eye there was no spark of desire, no flicker of lust, nothing but an urge to mother him and sort his problems out. Doing that for the rest of her life was no basis for a marriage, surely?

When Pete Walsh danced into her dreams in his football shorts, she felt jumping jacks and Catherine wheels spinning inside, and rockets going off in all directions. He was like her favourite liquorice blackcurrants in the purple wrappers, fruity smooth on the outside but inside something to get your teeth into, rich and spicy, a sweet that lasted on the tongue.

Beside him Walt's pecks of affection tasted of candyfloss, fluffy and sweet but all air and no substance when you tried to bite into it. It looked good until you tried it. You'd never get sweet satisfaction for your precious coupons. He wasn't good value for money.

Her eyes were once blinkered by duty but not any longer.

The two of them were not suited and never had been. Better to call it a day now. What she was about to do was for the both of them before they made a big mistake.

How could she marry a man she didn't fancy, and try to live a lie? Better to find it out now before the vows were promised. Now or never, that was the challenge, but how was she going to live this down?

Her hand was shaking as she rummaged in the drawer for fresh paper. The drawers were almost bare. Everything had been transferred to Well Cottage in boxes.

There was no easy way to let him down gently with this one. But start as you mean to go on was Walt's motto.

They had hardly exchanged words since Monday, both being busy with arrangements, chasing trestle tables and linen cloths, enough chairs to sit fifty guests, ordering ham off the bone from the butcher's, wine glasses for the toast in Vimto cordial as the church would have no liquor on the premises.

Being busy kept doubt at bay for a while. Avoiding him put back the moment of truth a bit longer.

As the week dragged on the cage door was looming ahead, getting larger and larger. No wonder she'd been like a bear with a sore head, and the new Lee kept bobbing up with words of wisdom in her head, unsettling things even further.

Now it was crunch time. Could she salvage the day? There was still time to hold back the tide of events. It was early in the morning, chance to slip out and put the note in his letterbox and seek refuge with the Crumblehumes. They would know what to do, but first she must concentrate and put her thoughts on paper.

I've eloped with myself, Walter. I can't go through with our wedding. I know I've left it a bit late but not too late for all the catering to be cancelled. No precious rations will be wasted. The cake can be divided up between the families.

Apologise to your mother for all this upset but her heart was never in our union and neither is mine. I'm doing this for both of us.

You said yourself I wasn't your old Lil any more. I hardly recognise myself sometimes. I'm not who I was, but then no one should stay the same for ever, I suppose. You have to keep growing on and changing or you get stuck in a rut. And you know what they say about ruts being more like graves than springboards to life? I don't want to be buried alive.

425

You don't love the woman I've become and I won't be put down any more. I'm not ready to settle down just for the sake of it. There's more to life than getting wed. There's a whole world outside of Grimbleton I want to explore, and with my new job I can begin to see some of it for myself without having to rush home and make your tea.

I'll be taking the coach to France with Longsight Travel, a working holiday just to get myself out of everyone's hair. You'll cope without me to worry about.

We'll be a nine-day wonder in Division Street but that's nothing new since Ana and Su arrived. You and your mother'll happen be glad to distance yourself from my disgraceful family, but I love them all, and my friends.

You shouldn't have asked me to choose. Either-or is never a good idea. Why not both-and? Compromise is part of a good marriage. The parson told us that in his talk.

I hope you find the happiness you deserve. Forgive me for the upset but I know it's the right decision for both of us. Don't be bitter. Think of it as a lucky escape.

Sorry and all that.
Lee Winstanley

She foraged for an envelope and shoved in the letter, making sure it was labelled as 'Urgent'.

Now she must write a note to her family before slipping away quietly. Mother would see that the minister was told. He would inform the registrar and so forth.

Dismantling a wedding was like knitting waiting to be unravelled, stitch by stitch, loop by loop, layer by layer. The wool could be rolled up and used for something else, given time and a bit of understanding.

Everyone's disappointment was another matter, she sighed, closing the lid of the suitcase tight.

No one was stirring. By the time she reached Avril's, all hell would be let loose in Division Street. Let them get on with it for a change.

Esme had tossed and turned all night, trying to remember everything on her list.

It was no good, the sweats had got her and she needed a brew to cool her down, so she waddled downstairs, hoping not to give the milk man a fright in her faded candlewick dressing gown and hairnet; no point in wasting a good shampoo and set.

She could hear movements on the landing and the creak of the third step on the stairs. She stood by the kitchen door, mesmerised as her daughter struggled with a suitcase, trying not to make a noise.

'So where are you off to at this time of morn, and with a suitcase packed?'

Lily froze, caught like a child with her hand in the biscuit tin. 'I'm leaving Grimbleton. I can't go through with it.'

'And not a word to your mother?' Esme shook her head in mock reproof. 'I know mams and lasses aren't always the best of friends but I think I'm owed an explanation, seeing as it looks as if it'll be *me* clearing up your mess. The kettle's on the hob, by the way. No use going on an empty stomach.'

'You'll not make me change my mind,' said her daughter, looking relieved, ashamed and confused all at the same time.

'Who said anything about changing your mind? Why is everything between us always such a battle? I'm on your side. If nothing else, Lily, remember that.'

There was such relief in her daughter's face on hearing those words as she sat at the kitchen table, clutching a cup of tea in her trembling hands.

'I feel awful, and I know it's late in the day but I have to go.'

'I've seen it coming for months,' Esme answered. 'I do worry about you. I've only wanted your happiness above my own, whatever you might think. Every time I tried to open the subject you jumped down my throat. I may be old-fashioned but I do know a thing or two, and you and Walt were never suited.'

'I know, I know now, but this mess's not what I wanted. All week doubt's been crawling through my head, chewing up all my good intentions. It comes down to three choices. If only I can ignore his pompous attitudes and make it work. If only I can shut my eyes to his views and his mother and not let them get to me. I just hoped my fears would go away but they got worse, not better. I've been as jumpy as a dog with fleas.' Lily looked across to the familiar lined face, her mother sitting in all her morning glory, as if she was seeing her for the first time.

'We had noticed but thought it was wedding nerves. So you realised you couldn't lump it. Did you try to change it then?'

'It's silly but it was when he wouldn't even get his passport that it dawned on me that Walt was one of life's stay-at-homes, a steady sort of chap with no ambition but solid as cement when it came to how his wife should behave. If he can't listen to me now what hope is there after we're wed? That's when I knew I'd have to leave.' Lily searched for her hanky up her cardigan sleeve. 'Like it, lump it or leave – that about sums it up, don't you think? I'm sorry I'm like a leaking tap,' she wept. 'I was daft to think I could change him. If he won't budge before we were wed, he sure as hell won't after he's put the ring on my finger.'

'I knew something was up. I just wish you could have talked it over with me. I've let you down in so many ways, putting on you.'

'It's not you that's let me down. All the arrangements, the church, all your outfits... That's what's worrying me: all the expense, the disappointed children and embarrassment.'

'Outfits can be worn any time, lass. Churches are usually empty on Saturdays. Nothing's been baked that can't be shared out. Money is only money, but this is your life and your future, and that's far more important. You're a champion, Lily. Your dad would've been proud of you and he was as good a man as ever put a shirt over his head. I miss him that much. You never get over the loss of a man like that. He was my strong wall in a time of crisis. I wanted a man like that for you but Walt's weak and you can't lean on a broken fence.'

'Oh, Mam, what a mess I've made of it all.'

'Better to be strong now than suffer a lifetime of regrets, I'm thinking. What're your plans?'

'I'll catch the coach tomorrow. Today I'll just disappear. The Crumblehumes have been wonderful. I might ask to rent their flat when they find somewhere bigger for their new family. It's time I stood on my own feet. My friends will understand, I hope.'

'You'll do fine as long as you follow your heart this time. It sees clearer than your brain,' she said, feeling her own tears welling up. 'What a pickle we get ourselves into when we don't talk things over.'

Lily got up and hugged her. 'Thanks. I'm sorry.'

'Now none of that, just get yourself back upstairs. You've done nothing to be ashamed of. There's nothing here that can't be undone in time; I'm not having you wandering the streets on your wedding day.'

'What about the wedding presents?' There were boxes piled up in Well Cottage.

'I'll get Levi to deliver them all back after work.'

'Ivy will be crowing with glee,' sighed Lily.

'Levi will understand. Believe me, if he could turn the clock back and do a runner before his wedding, he would. He's got a life sentence there. Now upstairs out of the road.'

'I've got a letter for Walt. He's got to know first.' Lily pulled the letter out of her handbag in a fluster.

'Give it here. I'll make sure he gets it, if I have to deliver it myself. Now upstairs. We won't say anything till I've rung Reverend Atkinson. He'll know what to do. This won't be the first time this has happened. Just stay calm and say nowt. Upstairs, and I'll bring you some breakfast, just as we planned.'

'I couldn't eat a thing,' Lily sobbed.

'Upstairs, my girl, and I'll bring you a brandy.'

'Just some hot water in a cup,' Lily said, climbing the stairs. 'What I need is a herbal tea and there's something in my hope chest that might settle my nerves. Drastic times deserve drastic measures. I've got just the cure. Are you sure you can manage?'

'I'm not in my dotage yet. Leave everything to your mother; she knows best.'

'Thanks, Mam.'

When Lily had crept back upstairs, Esme was about to phone Levi when she looked up and saw him creeping through the back gate with an attaché case. What a relief!

'Now, son, I want you to stay calm and give me a lift. This morning I want you to be chauffeur, postman and brother to your little sister for once.'

'But I've left Ivy,' he squeaked like a lost boy. 'I didn't go home last night. I've been wandering all over town. It's a right mess... I've brought my suit.'

'Be that as it may, *your* marital problems are the least of my worries now. It's your sister who needs sorting out. Yours will blow over, hers won't.'

'What's happened?'

Esme shoved the envelope in his hand. 'We're going to deliver this to Bowker's Row. It's her letter of resignation. Our Lil is declining the post of resident dogsbody to Elsie Platt and her gormless son, that's what.'

'Hell's bells! Ivy'll play pot. She's cut up one of her best velvet frocks to make Neville's pageboy suit.'

'This is not about her or your son, it's your sister's big day and it's going to be ruined if we don't do something, and fast.' She was in no mood to pander to Ivy Southall as was. 'Family first, Levi, and it's an emergency. We must look after our own.'

'I don't fancy facing the wrath of Elsie with a strop on her by myself,' he replied.

'That's why we go together, to deliver the glad tidings like one of those sheriff's posses. I never took you to be a coward.'

'I never thought of myself as one either, until I came back to Blighty and found myself with an albatross of a wife round my neck. She's making a right sissy out of my son.'

'Then do something about it ... but not today. Today is Lily's big day, or was, and we've got to salvage something out of it for her. Redvers would expect, Freddie would expect. Give me five minutes to pin my face on. I don't want to miss Elsie's face when we present this summons at her door.'

'I'll put on another brew then.'

'I think we'll be needing something stronger before this day is out but first I must ring the Minister. We don't want anyone turning up at Zion. He can put a notice on the door and tell them they've got a boiler burst, for now.'

'But it's high summer, Mother.'

'He'll think of something. I don't want the world knowing our business. Won't be long.'

This was going to be the biggest challenge for years but the Winstanley honour was at stake. She would wake the two in the attic to see if they had any ideas.

It sounded like bedlam downstairs, muffled sounds past her room, the phone ringing, the doorbell jangling as the bouquet and posies arrived from the florist and telegrams of congratulations arrived in the post. Someone was on overdrive down there, shouting instructions and giving out lists.

Lily lay smiling under the bedclothes, content to let them get on with it after a long hazy sleep and wonderful dreams. This was the life, being waited on hand and foot. All her quandaries had vanished in a fug of swirling dreams, floating over a lake in her midnight-blue ball-gown, waltzing and laughing with not a care in the world. Levi's herbal tealeaves had come in useful after all these months and hit the spot.

The deed was done. No going back or dithering. This was her decision and it was time to face the worried features peering round her door to see if she was still sleeping. Time to put on a brave front of courage and resolve.

You're not a child, she sighed. Tomorrow it'll all be past history, but how would poor Walt take this desertion? Perhaps he was already taking his comfort down The Coal Hole with his best man, Sydney Beswick, drowning his sorrows in Wilson's best bitter? No one would blame him.

He didn't deserve such humiliation but Grimbleton life would roll on whatever they did or didn't do today. Families would be catching trains for Blackpool, visiting relatives, catching charabancs for mystery tours, mowing their lawns and going down town to the market, unaware that she was turning her life upside down.

She opened the door to see Levi's best Masonic outfit, black jacket with pinstriped trousers, complete with a buttonhole white carnation in his lapel, hanging over the banister. He won't be needing that today, she sighed, fleeing back into her room.

Reality was striking home at long last.

'Are you all right?' Su put her head round the door.

'I will be when I know Walt's got that letter. Have I done the right thing?' she cried.

More tears and wet handkerchiefs followed when Ana and Su brought more cups of tea and sympathy. The phone was ringing and hushed voices in the hall muttered.

Lily sat on the bed, surrounded by Dina and Joy bouncing up and down, already dressed in their petticoats and puffy blue satin dresses with velvet sashes.

At least they had something new to show for the day and the little crosses made from the sovereigns were waiting in their boxes. They were still here. She'd forgotten to give them to the best man for safekeeping.

'Everyone sends love.' Ana tried to smile, but her eyes were sad.

Only last night she had brought in some

crocheted gloves with a sugar lump squeezed into the palm. 'You wear the sugar in the glove to make sure your life together is sweet,' she explained. 'It is Greek custom.'

'I'm so sorry to spoil everything.' Yet Lily was feeling as if a blanket of concern and love was being wrapped around her shoulders. 'And it's such a lovely day.'

They parked the Rover out of view of Bowker's Row. Esme didn't want prying fingers all over their polished bonnet. No use telling the world their business on this bright morning. The doorsteps were all donkey-stoned white for the weekend, the windows were open to let in fresh sooty air. Children were already playing hopscotch on the pavement and the paraffin man's horse had just done a dollop outside Walt's front door. Serve 'em right!

They marched up the street to number 4. This was not a back gate occasion. There was no reply so Levi thumped harder on the knocker. Esme peered through the valance curtains that could do with some starch and dolly-blueing.

'Shall I shove it through the letterbox?' Levi asked.

'No. This is a face-to-facer. Bang again.'

A neighbour from across the road came to join them. 'They're not in, love.'

'When're they back?' Esme asked, thinking the Platts'd gone to meet someone off the bus.

'Dunno, love, not for a bit. They've gone on holiday. Cancelled the milk yesterday. I saw them off with their suitcases to the bus stop. That's right, isn't it, Hilda?' Another woman, in wrap-around pinny and turban, stood with a cigarette hanging out of her mouth, watching them all. 'The Platts've gone on their holiday?'

'Caught the boat train to Heysham last night, Isle of Man; nice for Elsie to get a bit of sea air. She's not a well woman. I thought Walter was getting wed soon, someone said so, but it all fell through. There was some girl making a racket at all hours last weekend. Happen he's best out of it. Who are you?' She looked them up and down as if they were tallymen come to collect the rent.

'Just visiting,' Esme replied, going hot and cold, stuffing the letter back in her pocket.

They walked back to the car in silence. She turned to her son. 'Who's going to break the good news, you or me?'

It seemed like only minutes before Levi and Esme appeared through the vestibule, looking hot and flustered. Lily was sitting at the top of the stairs and shouted down.

'You've done it then?' she sighed.

'Not exactly,' her brother stuttered, not looking her in the face.

'You didn't go and put it through the wrong door?'

'There was no one answering the door.'

'So what've you done with my letter then?' Lily cried, suddenly panicking. 'He's got to know.'

'Calm down, lass. A neighbour came out to see who was making the racket. You know how nosy they are round there.' Esme looked up. 'She said they'd gone on holiday to the Isle of Man.'

'There's no easy way to tell you this, Sis, but Walt and his mother have eloped to Douglas without so much as a word to any of us. Done a moonlight flit!'

Esme was sitting on the hall chair, puffed with indignation. 'He got in first, Lil!'

Everyone looked up the stairs to the bride-not-to-be. The tears were rolling down her face.

'Blood and sand!' she roared. 'I never knew he had it in him, the bugger, leaving me in the lurch.' She didn't know whether to laugh or cry. What a wedding day! In fact it was better than any romance from the library, and no mistake. What a relief! Walt's own bid for freedom had let her off the hook. They'd done the dirty on each other. Even stevens and all that, but it was still a shock.

'Don't look so worried,' she said, seeing the concern on their upturned faces. 'I'll survive. Give me that letter back. No one need know. I bet the jungle drums'll be beating all over Grimbleton soon but it's me that'll get the sympathy vote, I hope. Let's just keep it that way. We'll just keep this under our hats, another Winstanley secret to add to our collection, right?'

Now they could relax for the first time that morning. 'So what are we going to do with the rest of my big day? I suppose I'd better get changed. There's still all the catering to sort out.'

'Leave that to us,' smiled Su, nodding to Ana. 'You have friends to do that. You have enough to do. Your day is not over yet.'

'You reckon? From where I'm standing, it looks pretty bleak.'

'Wait and see, Miss Lily, you wait and see. A day not over until the sun goes down.'

The emergency breakfast meeting of the Olive Oil Club was held in Diana's dining room in Green Lane at eight o'clock. There were Force flakes and milk, toast and crumpets, rhubarb and marrow jam and milky coffee to fortify the troops. Those present were looking to their commanding officer to chair the meeting and do something to salvage the day.

Diana was hoping for some kip before the wedding began. She had been on night duty and was hit with the news by a distress phone call from Su. There was no time to delay.

'Let's take this in order of priority. No chance of a change of mind?'

'The groom put the Irish Sea between him and his bride last night.'

'Righty ho... Vicar and church?'

'Being done as we speak. Mother of the bride is seeing to all of that official stuff and making sure the Brownie guard of honour is disbanded,' said Queenie, who had come straightaway on the bus.

'Catering?' Diana consulted her list.

'Sandwich production at the church hall halted. Cake can't be returned but the plaster of Paris decoration and silver tray have gone back. Maria will organise.'

'Photographer?' Diana queried.

'Friend of Levi. He's dealing with that,' Su offered.

'Transport?'

'That depends on what we decide. Mrs W.

438

would like things to look as normal. She wants Lily to have some sort of do.'

'I see. And location of said "do"?' A semblance of a vague idea was forming in Diana's mind. Thank goodness she was used to thinking on her feet, improvising at the last minute.

'I don't think she's got that far.'

'And poor Lily, how is she coping?'

'Sylvio's going to set her hair. Ana is taking her out to the allotment to pick strawberries. We have a few hours to change plans but that is all,' Su replied, looking anxious.

All eyes were fixed on Diana to pull a rabbit out of the hat. She shut her eyes for inspiration but nothing would come. All she kept seeing was a river, or was it a lake, with swans gliding across. Where was it? Of course, suddenly everything was clear and she knew just what they might do.

'Right, folks, Operation Top Hat is what we'll call it. And keep it under your hat until the appointed hour.' She outlined her idea and how they might organise it. No one thought it was a crazy scheme. In fact they were all full of suggestions.

'Queenie and Maria will be the quartermasters and forage for suitable supplies. I shall be in charge of relocation, logistics and overall command. I leave diversionary tactics to Su and Ana. Transport and communications will be left to Esme Winstanley and son. We will reconvene at noon, ready for departure at appointed time, thirteen hundred hours, when bridal party should be leaving for the church. Any questions?'

'What if the bride wants to vamoose?' asked Queenie.

'You keep her, by force if necessary. Just keep her busy and get her and yourselves ready. Meeting is closed. If we're to pull this off, everyone will need a phone, some foot soldiers and helpers. Find whoever you can to help and bring them along. Good luck, and thanks for coming at such an ungodly hour.'

'You are a miracle worker,' whispered Su.

'No, if we pull this off, we'll all be magicians,' Diana replied, crossing her fingers under the table.

26

A Mystery Tour

She had come with Ana to the allotment just to get out of the house, away from the phone calls and reminders that this should have been a day of celebration not a funeral.

'Come and see how my garden grows. We pick strawberries and Billy says we pick fruit for him too,' Ana said as she marched ahead, pushing Dina, who was now back in her little leggings and jumper.

Ana's patch had filled out since Lily's last visit, with lettuces, saladings, onions, and garlic she had grown from Maria's cloves. There were clumps of mint in pots and thyme, sage and other pungent herbs. Their plot had never looked so good.

They bent over the strawberries that peeped like rubies out of the green leaves. Dina was trying to help but treading on more than she was picking.

Lily could smell the setting lotion on her hair. Sylvio had washed it in the bathroom basin, trimmed it again and set it on soft curlers. He brought a black-hooded hair dryer, which Queenie had borrowed from Gianni.

'I wanna thank you many times for finding me in Manchester. I heard about Marco from nurse in hospital who have her hair done. I felt so bad. I just ran. I was crazy man but I go back to Gianni and beg him to take me back. He call me no good, say no ... so I tell him I will stay in town and join Pickering's hairdressers. He change his mind pronto.

'I will make Maria plenty proud but I ask one favour. She must leave the Santinis soon when they find out about us. It will be big trouble. She need to find house to stay. Is possible ... she come here?'

With her head stuck under the hood and the racket from the whirring air, all Lily could do was nod. There was no way she could stay on in Division Street herself.

Maria could have her room and keep the peace between Freddie's ladies. When Mother moved out there could be a whole League of Nations lodging in the house. Why not? That would give Doris Pickvance a bone to chew on.

Now she felt the sun on her face as they turned to Billy's raspberry cage. Ana was picking bowls and bowls, as if she was feeding the five thou-

441

sand. Was she going to make jam?

'That's enough, surely?' Lily said, feeling hot and sticky.

'Oh, no, plenty more. Come on.'

This was not how she planned to spend her wedding morning but beggars can't be choosers. 'You like it here?'

Ana smiled. 'When I am here, I am honorary man. Billy has nice son, called Ken, see over there.' She was pointing in the direction of a young man hoeing his patch, who waved at them. 'If I am stuck, he help me. He was Tommy soldier in battle of Kriti. He knows my island. We talk many times.'

'Oh, *do* you?' Lily smiled. 'And is this Ken married then?'

The look on Ana's face was a picture. 'I don't talk to married men. He lives at home.'

'I bet he works very hard on the allotment for his father then?'

'Yes, he is very diligent. He makes *krasi* ... wine from his berries like we make with grapes.'

'Just you watch yourself, Anastasia. He thinks you are a widow.'

'Oh, I will tell him truth one day, but not Dina here. She must never know.'

'She'll have to know sometime, but not today. Look at the time, we've been up here hours.'

'You are right. Time to go back and get dressed up. Dina!' she smiled and raced after her daughter.

Dressed up? What was there to get dressed up for now?

There was no point in packing again. Lily looked at her wristwatch and sighed. In another half-hour she should have been on her way to the church. Only Zion's doors would be locked, and the waiting Brownies would be wondering what was happening. It was going to be a long day, skulking in the back garden out of sight. It was too good an afternoon to waste indoors.

It was all very quiet downstairs. Everyone seemed to have vanished, probably busy taking stuff back to the shops from the church hall kitchen. What a waste of coupons.

The effects of Levi's herbal tea were wearing off but it still felt as if all this was happening to someone else. Perhaps it was a dream and she would wake up to the ticking of her Mickey Mouse alarm clock and the day would begin all over again.

She felt a bit peculiar, a bit shaky. It must be too much sun on the allotment.

Not that her mind was changed. No matter what happened next, the relief was genuine enough. What to do to fill the rest of this day, though? Her mind was like a blank sheet. All she did know was it was better not to be on her own. The house had gone quiet. Where was everybody?

As if answering her prayer, Esme appeared with Su and Ana. They were dressed up in their best clothes; Mother in a gunmetal slub silk dress and jacket with a straw hat covered in dark cherries and dyed feathers. Ana was wearing a smart navy-blue dress with inverted pleats in the front and Su was in a bright orange silky concoction.

There were marigolds pinned to her bun.

'What's going on?' said Lily. Had she been dreaming after all?

'You're to get dressed, and sharpish. The car's coming at one.'

'What car? The wedding's off, isn't it?' she croaked.

'That's for us to know and others to find out. The Daimler's coming for you as planned. I don't want the whole of Division Street knowing our business so put your glad rags on and a bit of lipstick.'

'I don't understand...'

'You will. Trust us, we know what we're doing. Here, put a comb through your hair. It's a good job you had it done this morning.' Mother disappeared round the door.

'What's going on? Has she gone mad? Everyone must know I've been stood up!'

It was hard to talk with clothes being shoved at her in all directions, her new corselet, petticoat, stockings and shoes. Then it was time to slip on the dress and jacket.

'It is all about saving face, Lily,' said Su. 'In my country it is the custom. You not show the enemy your fear. "Wise man's anger never come out.' You smile when you are sad and put on very best clothes. You fly the flag. We are flying the Winstanley flag today. You will see. It will all be right, but first we must go through a special play. No one has to know our business, where we go or what we do.'

Sitting down in front of the mirror with Ana teasing her set hair into shape and clipping it

444

back, there was little room for Lily to manoeuvre. The hat came out of its box while she powdered her nose and applied a little Max Factor rosy lipstick. Her eyes were still puffy from tears and sleep, but once the hat was in place and pinned firmly on, Lily felt quite the glamour puss. Shame there was no wedding to go to now.

'You look like a film star, Lily,' Su said as they opened the bedroom door and she glided down the stairs in a dream.

Levi was waiting at the foot of the stairs with the two little girls and Neville in his velvet trousers and cream silk smocked shirt. His curls were plastered down in a parting like Little Lord Fauntleroy.

'You scrub up well, Sis,' winked Levi.

Esme handed her the bouquet of pink roses and ivy that sprayed out in front of her. She put on Ana's lace gloves and felt the sugar lump in the finger. Perhaps life could be just as sweet without a man by your side.

'I think you're all mad,' she whispered.

'Knock 'em dead, Sis,' whispered a voice in her head. Freddie was behind all this madness. Dad would be roaring with laughter at their antics.

'The show must go on. Time enough later when everyone'll see the funny side of it.' Esme was eyeing her up and down with satisfaction. 'You look champion. I'm not sure that picture hat's going to get through the door. Whoever made that was on top of the job. Your dad'll be proud of you today, and Freddie too. Come on, no time for tears. Let's get the show on the road. Smile everybody, and look as if you mean it.'

Lily floated out of Waverley House like a Rose Queen with her procession of attendants, waving as the unsuspecting neighbours gathered to wish her well.

I deserve an Oscar for this performance, she thought. Vivien Leigh has nothing on me. She kept wondering if this was still a dream from the funny baccy, but the Daimler was real enough with the white ribbons on its bonnet.

The Winstanleys were on top form, not a flicker of embarrassment. Redvers would have been proud of his family, united for once. No one suspected a thing. Esme, Levi and the bride were all squashed in the back of the limousine, with the attendants on their knees. No one could say they were extravagant on transport, though. She turned to see if Ana and Su were following behind. What was going on?

They drove round the block, down Green Lane and out away from the town towards the moors, away from Zion and the puzzled onlookers, waiting for a show that would never happen. Eventually the Daimler glided to a halt.

'What now?' whispered the bride-not-to-be.

'This is as far as we go by taxi. There's the Rover parked up, and Levi will chauffeur us the rest of the way. No point in overdoing it on petrol coupons. We've made our point,' Mother explained, ushering them all out onto the pavement.

'Just tell me where we're going?'

'All will be revealed in good time. Be patient, lass. I'm not quite sure, myself.'

It was hard to be patient with Neville jumping

on her knee as they piled into the Rover, still with its white ribbons too. All dressed up and nowhere to go. This was ridiculous.

Lily thought of Walt sunning himself in a deck chair on the beach. She hoped he had been violently sick on the ferry across. I'm never going to speak to him again, she whispered to herself. How dare he beat me to it!

Tonight they should have lain together on the new mattress at Well Cottage. She'd moved heaven and earth to get enough coupons for that. Then he had the cheek to suggest they postpone their nuptial bliss until they were settled. 'Best not to rush things,' was his excuse.

What would they have been like together, a couple of fumbling halfwits? It would have been a disaster from the start. What a wonderful feeling of release.

They were driving north now, away from the red brick of dye mills and factories, out towards the white stone villages of North Lancashire. The sun was shining as they turned into a long drive, through wrought-iron gates with rampant lions sitting on the top. On and on they cruised, winding through shrubbery and oak trees, the tyres scrunching on the gravel as they turned into a circular driveway.

'I don't understand. This is private land. We don't know anyone round here, do we? What's all this in aid of? Someone please enlighten me.' Lily's heart was thumping with excitement now. The mystery tour was turning into an adventure right enough.

Then she saw the white stone of the castle

447

turrets. She'd seen it once on a postcard. It was Cardwell Towers. What on earth were they doing here?

There were blackout curtains still at the windows, and smoke coming from a chimney. Her hands were shaking. There were cars parked under some trees and one of them was Diana Unsworth's blue sports car.

'Well, I'll be blowed! Trust her to be up to something. Come on, spill the beans before I burst my elastic,' Lily smiled, pointing at the assembly of friends.

Esme turned from the front seat and smiled. 'I take my hat off to you in your choice of friends, Lily. They've come up trumps and no mistake. Just wait and see what they've sorted out for you.'

The children spilled out of the car, crumpled, confused, blinking into the sunshine. Queenie Quigley's black van was following slowly behind. Out poured Ana, Su, Maria and Rosa from the back, all dolled up in their wedding attire. Avril and Bill from the travel agency were waiting smiling, holding a basket of bread buns.

'I don't believe this!' Lily smiled shyly. 'What's going on?'

'The wedding may be off but the party's still on. We've just jiggled things around, made a few phone calls, and Bob's your uncle: a picnic in a private park, no prying eyes, no confetti, no awkward customers, just friends together. It's too lovely a day to sit indoors and mope.' Diana rushed forward to give Lily a hug. 'I hope you don't mind us taking over.'

'Mind? It's the kindest, nicest thing that has

ever happened to me. I don't know what to say.'

'Then get your gloves off and help us unpack the picnic. We've got the run of the place until dusk. There's a lake down there. I thought we could take the rugs and chairs down under the shade of the willows and set up our picnic. I expect everyone is starving. I know I am.' Diana was already lifting boxes from the trunk of her car.

'Did you know about this, Mother, and you, Levi? How did they manage this at such short notice?'

'Co-operation, delegation and lists, the secret of any good enterprise,' laughed Queenie, staggering with a basket of covered tins. 'Diana's not a hospital sister for nothing. As soon as she heard the news, she was on the blower, giving us orders right left and centre. Quite the tornado in full flight. We're just carrying out orders.'

Levi was making himself useful carrying chairs down from a summerhouse with Bill Crumble-hume, and a gardener who was looking askance at this motley party dressed up to the nines, making divots in his lawn.

The children raced ahead, excited, like figures in some Victorian portrait – Rosa wearing her Babes in the Wood lace dress with the sash, Neville in his knickerbockers. What they would look like at the end of the day was anyone's guess.

Lily was speechless and shaking with excitement. This was ten times better than any stuffy wedding breakfast in the church hall. She didn't want to sound ungrateful but it was worth all the drama just to be standing there, dressed like a toff in the midst of a set worthy of *Gone With the Wind*, amongst the people dearest to her in all the world. How on earth they fixed all this in a few hours, she would never know, but it was wonderful.

Levi made to go but she stopped him. 'Have a picnic with us,' she smiled, but he shook his head.

'I've things to do, Sis, while Neville's here, out of earshot. Ivy's been ringing round. I'd better sort things out between us.' He hugged her and promised to pick them all up later.

Poor man would get an earful from Ivy when she found out what she'd missed. The Olive Oils were giving their bride a blow-out to remember. If only her brother would stand up to his bossy wife and tell her straight that if she'd played fair with Lily's friends she would have been invited too.

Well, what you sow you reap: wheat and weeds together sometimes. Now there was all this joy just because she picked up two strays and lost a pram. What a tale to tell her grandchildren one day – if she ever got round to having any children of her own, that was. There was a full contingent: Eva, Stefania, Polly Isherwood and even Enid Greenalgh. Lily was glad they'd brought Enid along for she didn't get out much and would be company for Esme: ten of them, and children carting picnic baskets like sherpas in their high heels and finery. What a sight.

The shadows of branches flickering on the lawn was a scene from an old Master painting. The noise was of children racing, wood pigeons cooing from the rooftops. Was this really happening? She must find out more.

'Why here?'

'Let's say you were bringing the hat back to its rightful owner. Cardwell Towers belongs to the Marsdens. Hilly's a friend of Mummy. She's District Commissioner. We sometimes take guides camping out here.

'As soon as I heard the news, we had an impromptu meeting at HQ, by the way. Everyone wanted to do their bit. I got this vision and I just knew Hilly would come up trumps: Guider to Guider, Be Prepared sort of thing, you know how the rule goes. It's her Ascot hat you're wearing and it's very becoming on you.

'We're just lucky that there were no events today in the park and they've gone to some sailing regatta at the Reservoir. Hilary and Monty are keen yachtsmen. She was delighted to loan us the grounds. I expect we'll meet them later on. Oh, and she said to tell you she once did a runner before the war, bolted from some dreadful army type, lucky escape and all that. Only happy to oblige with the hat and the venue.'

'I don't know how to thank you,' Lily replied.

'That's Guiders for you: always ready to fill the breach, so just sit down and eat up. We're not going until it's all finished. You've paid for most of it, after all!'

People kept coming up and patting her on the shoulder, touching her hand and giving their condolences as if she'd suffered a bereavement but it didn't feel like that at all. How could she explain that a heavy lead cloak had disappeared

451

from her shoulders or that there were coiled springs in her peep-toes? Even her head was fizzing like pop for the first time in months.

Chairs were brought out and a table laid in the shade with a fine linen cloth. A tray full of glasses sparkled on a wooden trolley with soda siphons and mysterious bottles coloured like jewels: emerald, ruby and rich topaz, and a jug of homemade elderflower lemonade. A picnic basket was groaning with fresh buttered rolls and slices of cooked meats under a net cloche – ham, pork, beef. A bowl of lettuce and tomato, cucumber and celery bulged by a huge raised pie with a golden crust. A pair of silver salad servers sparkled in the sunlight.

'This is not the ham salad we ordered,' Lily cried. 'This is a feast.'

'Allotment Billy gave us the tomatoes and the rest. We traded in some of the ham for the cooked meats, the piccalilli is last year's from my pantry and Maria has made you a special salad dressing,' Diana announced.

'It is olive oil vinaigrette, Mamma's recipe with summer herbs. You will like.'

She looked young again, with black curls, freshly cut by her lover, framing her face. Her dress was a silky mourning lilac with white polka dots and on her head she wore a peekaboo sun hat with a scarf wrapped round it.

'I don't know what to say,' Lily croaked.

'Just eat up and we'll be happy,' laughed Esme, who had a napkin tucked under her chin like a bib. 'Try and not get grease on your outfit. SOS, everybody.'

'Yes, Mother. Stretch or Starve, folks,' Lily said,

452

watching everyone tucking in.

There was silence in the group, just the chink of glasses and forks on someone's best china plates, the rustle of the breeze in the willows and the sound of ducks hovering for titbits by the lake edge. It was perfect. So much trouble taken to make this impromptu wonderful picnic happen.

From out of Queenie's van came an ice tub of Santini's best vanilla, a bowl of freshly picked bilberries and the strawberries and raspberries she had picked with Ana. So that was what the visit was for! There were also shortbread biscuits shaped like hearts.

'The baker gave me those for you. He said to tell you he was sorry and that if he didn't have a missus he'd marry you himself. You're a good customer and he hopes things will buck up,' Queenie said with lips stained purple with fruit.

'So everyone knows then?' Lily asked, fearing the worst.

'Only the caterers when we took the cake decorations back and swapped them for these cream sponges. We've filled them with strawberries. Try some,' ordered Diana, who was looking cool in the heat, and despite her organising, wearing a linen oatmeal dress with a printed silk scarf draped around her shoulders.

'I'm stuffed to the gills,' Lily smiled, eyeing the cheese with relish. 'But I'll try some of the Lancashire. Where did that come from?'

'Ask me no questions and I'll tell you no lies. Let's just say a little bird owed me a favour,' piped Enid with a giggle. 'This is the grandest do I've ever been honoured to attend. I was not going to come empty-handed.'

Soon there was the drowsy murmur of gurgling bellies, belts being loosened and stockings rolled down or taken off, bodies slumped in chairs as the sun rose high. No one could eat another morsel.

They lay content on rugs, in the shade, watching Neville and Rosa making daisy chains and Dina and Joy struggling to keep up. There was space for everyone to stretch out and snooze, but Lily was suddenly awake watching a dragonfly on the lakeside, its iridescent wings shimmering like mother-of-pearl. The setting was so beautiful, so peaceful and so unreal, and soon the sun would slide down behind the copse and her big day would be over.

'I want to make a toast,' she declared, stirring them all from their reveries.

'I want to thank you all, Mother, family, friends, for your kindness and the honour you've done me in saving the day. There are no words to describe how I'm feeling now. I think you could go a lifetime and never have a day like this one, or friends like you lot. I'm that choked up. Thank you, one and all, and to the Olive Oils for saving my day!'

They raised their glasses and sipped the warm white wine.

'Fill them up again,' said Diana. 'Here's to our dear friend, Lee, the Lily as was. May she find true happiness one day soon.'

'To Lee Winstanley!'

'Bottoms up!'

'To absent friends.'

454

'And here's to the one who got away. May his piles be many. Bottoms up!'

'One last toast.' Lily stood up. 'To the friendships of our Olive Oil Club, long may they continue. Our name started out as someone's snide remark but now I'm rather proud to be an Olive Oil ... the first but not the last, I hope, of the Olive Oil brides... Pouring oil on troubled waters is what we've been doing these past months. Something magical has happened today and each one of you has played your part.' She lifted up the salad dressing jar, watching the oil glinting in the sun.

Ana stood up then. 'In my country we have saying for good friends. We have eaten bread and salt together, joy and sorrow. Today we, true friends, have tasted both. *Yámas!*'

'And thank you, Ana, for first setting us the task of searching for liquid gold. We may not be the United Nations but every time we sit down and talk, share a meal, talk about home, we learn something new. Together you and Susan – all of you – have changed my life and broadened my horizons. Cheers! There ought to be more clubs like ours.'

'Hear, hear!' They clinked glasses in unison.

'Who wants a cup of tea?' shouted Esme, reaching for the Thermos flasks in the last basket. Everyone groaned but no one refused.

Rosa was cartwheeling in a line and the others tried to follow, collapsing in a heap. It was time to stroll around the grounds inspecting the roses and the long border, admiring the view and pretending for just another hour that they were

455

queens of all they surveyed.

Soon Dina wanted a piggyback and their linen skirts and finery were crumpled. Time to collect the plates and pack the baskets, shoo off the wasps and fold up the napkins. The gardener hovered, eager to see them off his lawn and into their cars.

Lily put the picture hat in its box with a sigh.

'Let me take another photograph,' yelled Diana, but Lily shook her head.

There was no need to record this day. It would be etched into her mind to that last dying breath; the day she discovered she was loved, valued and respected.

You're a millionaire in friendships, she thought, but it doesn't half take it out of you. Now she was bushwhacked, drunk on emotion. She'd take no rocking to sleep tonight. Tomorrow it was off to France, all on her own.

And Afterwards...

It was pouring down next morning, typical Grimbleton summer weather. The sky was as grey as it had been blue the day before. It was time for Lily to put the final touches to her packing, put on her trews and windjammer, sturdy shoes and headscarf. No point wearing fancy clobber if she was sitting in a coach for hours on end.

'Have you got sandwiches for the journey, something to read, liver salts in case of any

456

tummy bother? You are going abroad. Watch out for strange men. I hear they're a bit free with their fingers out there.' Esme was hovering.

'Don't fuss, Mother. I'm all sorted, passport, money, emergency money. I'm only going for a week,' she sighed. 'More's the pity.'

'I know that, but the sea can be rough. Shall I come and see you off?'

'No. I'll slip out quietly. Diana said she'd run me to the bus station. It's wet and chilly to be standing around, but thanks all the same.' She gave Esme a hug.

'What's that for?' The Winstanleys weren't huggers as a rule.

'You know very well. For being so understanding, and for yesterday.'

'Wasn't it a grand do? Who'd have thought it, us living it up like the gentry, and what a blow-out! I've had to loosen my stays. No one will believe it.'

'Let them think what they like when I've gone. I'll be up at Well Cottage, clearing up, after that, and out of earshot,' Lily said, gathering all her stuff together. 'Then I'm going to rent above Longsight Travel. I'm a townie, not a country bumpkin.'

Just for today she would sneak out of the back door into the garden and out into the back lane. Diana would be waiting for her at the lane end. No one suspected she was still in Division Street.

Right on cue, Diana was revving up the car, waiting. She looked as if she hadn't slept for a week.

'How can I ever thank you for yesterday? It was

better than any wedding day,' Lily said.

'Don't say that. One day you'll find the right chap and it'll be music, sweet music,' she replied.

'I'm not going through that charade. Next time it'll be Gretna Green, but not for a long time. I'm finished with men.'

'That's a pity. I did rather hope now that Walter's history you might look in another direction. In fact I took the liberty–'

'Don't say another word on the subject. My ears are closed. Just get me and this suitcase onto that bus on time and I'll send you a postcard.'

The bus station was deserted at first light on a typical Sunday morning. Diana dropped Lily off close by, shouting, 'Have a wonderful time and don't forget the Olive Oil!'

They were making an early start to catch the evening boat from Dover. The maroon coach, with gold lettering, had its hatch up for the luggage. Avril was counting the customers, checking they all had the right documents and coupons. The driver was having a smoke, watching the line-up of cars delivering his charges.

Glad and Ernie Walsh were fussing over their cases, and looked up and smiled. 'Now then, hope it's better weather over the channel, Miss Winstanley.'

Someone in a gabardine mac was lifting a case into the bowels of the bus. He turned and Lily blushed at the sight of Pete Walsh, no doubt helping his uncle and aunt with their luggage.

'Sorry to hear about yesterday. I gather there was a bit of a mix-up,' he said.

458

'That's one way of putting it,' Lily murmured, wanting to bluff it out.

'You're seeing Uncle Ernie off then?' she asked, trying to look composed and casual.

'Not exactly. There was this spare seat, a last-minute cancellation, so Mrs Crumblehume said. They gave me a call so I'm here to keep the numbers up,' he said, glancing up to see her reaction. He had the cheek to wink. 'All very last minute, of course. I was going camping in the Lakes but it seemed a waste of a passport not to fill the seat. I got one when I was chosen for the Reserves for the friendly International match against Belgium last March but of course everything was snowed off. Miss Unsworth said–'

'I might have known she'd be behind the choice of replacements.' Lily's voice was squeaking as she looked down at her suitcase with renewed interest. Just wait till she saw her again!

Perhaps those letters knew more than she did. All was not lost, after all. If ever she might need the case for another honeymoon, well... Miss Winstanley might become Mrs Walsh – another L.W. Now that was a thought to chew on, she smiled.

Don't be so daft! Lee was in charge again. After all she'd been through in these last twenty-four hours, how could she even think of such romantic nonsense?

But for now, the *'Fair Stood the Wind for France Useful French Vocabulary List'* was in her bag to mug up the lingo on the coach. The big adventure was about to begin.

459

This Large Print Book for the partially sighted, who cannot read normal print, is published under the auspices of

THE ULVERSCROFT FOUNDATION